PENGUIN BOOKS

Josephine Moon was born and raised in Brisbane, and had a false start in Environmental Science before completing a Bachelor of Arts in Communication and then a postgraduate degree in education. Twelve years and ten manuscripts later, her first novel, *The Tea Chest*, was picked up for publication and then shortlisted for an Australian Book Industry Award. Her bestselling contemporary fiction is published internationally. Her books include *The Chocolate Promise*, *The Beekeeper's Secret*, *Three Gold Coins* and *The Gift of Life*.

In 2018, Josephine organised the 'Authors for Farmers' appeal, raising money to assist drought-affected farming communities. She is passionate about literacy, and is a proud sponsor of Story Dogs, which brings dogs into schools as reading companions for children learning to read, and The Smith Family, which supports underprivileged Australian children during their school life.

She now lives on acreage in the beautiful Noosa hinterland with her husband and son, and a tribe of animals that, despite her best efforts, seems to increase in size each year. There is always at least one dog or cat by her side while she writes, and frequently a horse staring at her through the window. She wouldn't have it any other way.

Josephine Moon

the gift of life

PENGUIN BOOKS

PENGUIN BOOKS

UK | USA | Canada | Ireland | Australia
India | New Zealand | South Africa | China

Penguin Books is part of the Penguin Random House group of companies
whose addresses can be found at global.penguinrandomhouse.com.

Penguin
Random House
Australia

First published by Michael Joseph in 2019
This edition published by Penguin Books in 2020

Cover design by Louisa Maggio © Penguin Random House Australia Pty Ltd
Cover photography by bernashafo/Shutterstock, Cheryl Zibisky
Author photograph by Anastasia Kariofyllidis
Typeset in Minion Pro by Midland Typesetters, Australia
Printed and bound in Australia by Griffin Press, part of Ovato, an accredited
ISO AS/NZS 14001 Environmental Management Systems printer

A catalogue record for this
book is available from the
National Library of Australia

ISBN 978 1 76089 361 3

penguin.com.au

For Daisy –
fur baby, pancake thief, destroyer of socks,
guardian of babies and toast crusts,
comedian, angel and endless joy

1

'So, it's been a year since The Tin Man opened?' the journalist asked, checking her notes. She was young and shiny and chirpy, which gave Gabby hope the article would be a correspondingly positive one.

'That's right,' Gabby said. She nodded to the glass wall that separated the front of house from the back of house, through to the roasting machine that was currently in action, her new coffee roaster Luciano efficiently pouring a big bucket of green beans into the hopper right at that moment. 'Now we've launched our own specialty roasting service, with three signature blends.'

The young woman flicked her long black hair off her shoulder, nodded and wrote down more notes.

Gabby handed her the signature blend card, with the name and description of each creation. 'Would you like to try one? I can get Ed to make you one now.'

'No, thanks, I don't drink coffee. It sends me cray cray,' the journalist said, her laughter tinkling.

'Ah, fair enough.' Gabby's optimism for this story nosedived, which was a shame. One year in, the business was doing well – any business that made it through its first year was on a good footing – but if she was going to pay back her business loan in any kind of timely manner, or start making enough profit to consider one day buying her own home again, rather than living with her dad, then she really needed to be speeding up its growth. Investing in the roasting machine had been risky and involved significant additional debt, so she needed as much publicity as possible.

'It's beautiful in here,' the young woman said, gazing around admiringly. 'Did you do the interior design yourself?'

'A lot of it. My sister Pippa is a graphic designer and she has a real eye for these things, so she had input as well.'

In the middle of The Tin Man was an aged twelve-foot wooden ladder, worn smooth and dried hard as amber, suspended from the ceiling and entwined with crimson flowers and fairy lights. On the whitewashed wooden floor, overstuffed chocolate-brown leather chairs were adorned with sheepskin throws, and the tables held posies of flowers. A long glass cabinet displayed coffee cream macarons and latte cupcakes. Sounding through the space was the constant whir, clack and froth of the coffee machine, the chatter of businesswomen and men, bursts of laughter and the bells and buzzes of mobile phones. Gabby liked the bustle and the noise. It was evidence of *life* all around her, a life she desperately wanted to be a part of for many more years yet.

'I pulled out the article we did on you last year,' the journalist said. Gabby wished she could remember the woman's name. It was one of the side effects she lived with these days – poor short-term memory. People's names in particular were often just out of reach. 'I love that you named this place The Tin Man because he was

2

looking for a heart, and you needed a heart and had a heart transplant! That is so cool.'

'Mmm. I was one of the lucky ones.' In truth, this line of promotion made Gabby slightly uncomfortable. She'd used it as a publicity angle when she opened the cafe and the media had lapped it up. Organ transplant stories were always a welcome happy news item for them and Pippa had helped her get as much traction out of it as possible. They'd even had a morning television crew come and broadcast from the cafe, and she was certain it had helped lift business. She was happy to talk about organ donation and encourage people to discuss it with their families, and certainly the hospital and medical staff loved positive media coverage too. Still, she felt vaguely reluctant to use it again this time. It was the ever-present, gnawing guilt that she was alive because someone else had died.

The journalist, perhaps sensing her hesitation, closed her notebook and put it into her bright pink silk bag. 'I think I have everything I need. I better get back to the office and type this up. It should be in tomorrow's paper.'

Gabby stood and shook her hand. 'So quickly? That's fabulous. Thank you so much for coming.'

'You've done really well here. And your heart is all good? Everything's okay?' She looked nervously at Gabby's chest.

Gabby plastered a smile on her face. 'Everything's going great.' It was imperative that she appear strong and capable. She couldn't be the weak link in the cafe's success. She walked the journalist to the front door, where they paused momentarily to admire the rainbows cast from water splashing in the fountain. 'It's my two-year anniversary this Saturday. I might even have a drink to celebrate,' she said – jovial, reassuring.

'You should totally do that!' Then the journalist was gone, leaving Gabby to stand for a moment and reflect on what this place had grown into in the past year.

The Tin Man was nestled in a small sandstone complex, in a square set back from Chapel Street in Melbourne's South Yarra, alongside a clothes shop and a hairdresser, with a dazzling fountain in front. Mid mornings, sunlight reflected off the fountain and created a spray of whirling golden sparkles on the floor-to-ceiling windows of the cafe.

Each morning the person who'd opened the cafe wheeled out a small coffee cart to the street and stayed there till 9 am, catching those who were too busy to come inside as they darted for buses and trams or hurried on foot to work or school. Gabby was proud of this place – she wanted it to one day be the legacy she left for her children. Hopefully the newspaper article would be one more piece of effective publicity to continue building this dream.

Pippa arrived at eleven o'clock the next morning, carrying the newspaper. She was looking fabulous as always, in a charcoal-grey apron dress over a long-sleeved black tee, with black tights and boots, and her long hair in two plaits. A chunky black-and-white necklace and flawless matt make-up completed the outfit. She looked younger than her years, trendy and so artsy. Gabby sat next to her at a table in the corner, away from the noisy coffee machine, and they put their red heads together to read the article. Pippa had become something of an unofficial marketing and publicity manager for Gabby and would scrutinise every piece of media about The Tin Man.

'Oh, I see what you mean about the chirpiness,' Pippa said as she read.

'It's a bit over the top, but that's better than underwhelming.'

It was a half-page colour spread, with lovely photos they had provided of Gabby, Ed making coffee, the glass cabinet and its gorgeous cream-filled contents, and artfully placed coffee cups on a wooden table.

Pippa tapped the page. 'Listen to this: *The Tin Man's delectable range of signature blends are guaranteed to please any coffee enthusiast.* Well, that's a bit fabulous.'

Gabby read aloud next. '*In-house coffee roaster Luciano Colombera brings his Italian heritage to the trade, imbuing every roast with stunning authenticity.*'

'He'll love that,' Pippa said, grinning.

Luciano was a tricky man, one Gabby hadn't quite worked out yet. He blew hot and cold, happy to chat some days, distracted and moody on others.

Then Pippa frowned.

'What is it?' Gabby angled the paper to read. 'Where are you up to?'

Pippa pointed to a paragraph lower down the page.

Gabriella McPhee named her cafe The Tin Man because she is a heart transplant recipient and wanted to honour her journey while building her dream business. She says she is one of the lucky ones. The two-year anniversary of her heart transplant is this weekend, October 5.

'Oh, no,' Gabby groaned. 'We're not supposed to give out the date. I just mentioned it at the end, after the interview was finished. I didn't think she'd put it in.'

Pippa rested her chin in her hand. 'Maybe it will be okay.'

'Maybe.' There was nothing she could do about it now; she'd just have to wait and see what happened. 'Anyway, tell me what's going on with you.'

Pippa sighed and closed the paper, handing it to Gabby. 'I don't know.'

'What do you mean you don't know?'

'Harvey and I aren't in a good place. We haven't been for a long time.'

Gabby waited for more information. She'd known things weren't great, but she'd expected they'd bounce back okay.

Pippa shrugged and looked out over the customers in the cafe. Gabby followed her gaze. Nearly all the tables were filled and there was a hum of chatter throughout. 'We've been trying date nights for a while in an effort to reconnect. Things are awkward, all the time. We snap. We fight. There's no joy any more.'

'That's tough,' Gabby said, genuinely sympathetic. She and Cam had divorced five years ago and she remembered the feeling of hopelessness the final years had brought. She knew Pippa and Harvey fought. She could feel the tension in their house but simply thought they were suffering the exhaustion that everyone in the modern world seemed to be feeling.

'Did something happen, in particular?' she asked cautiously.

'Not an affair or anything, if that's what you mean.' Pippa stiffened. 'Well, not that I know of.' Her jaw was set grimly.

'Harvey doesn't seem like the affair type,' Gabby agreed. Harvey was one of those straight and boring types, in her opinion. She wouldn't have thought he had enough imagination to have an affair. Then again, the quiet ones could surprise you.

The idea that Pippa and Harvey might be on the verge of a split was unsettling in its own right, but for Gabby it created a whole other level of angst. Pippa and Harvey were a solid contingency plan to care for Gabby's three children if – more likely *when* – she died. But Pippa already had four children of her own. Raising seven children would be a stretch even for two working parents, let alone a single mother.

Of course, Cam was the logical choice to look after their three children, but lately he seemed to be barely coping with the shared custody they had agreed on.

Just ten more years, she silently pleaded. In ten years her youngest would be twenty, which was still awfully young to lose your mother, but at least she would be an adult.

Pippa sipped her tea in silence and Gabby kept her fears to herself. This moment wasn't about her; it was about Pippa. Marriages fell apart for all sorts of reasons. Pippa and Harvey had met when they were young, when she was studying graphic design at college and he technology. Statistically, they were prime candidates for relationship breakdown.

'Have you thought about counselling?' Gabby ventured.

Pippa flinched. 'I have. And I know this sounds pathetic, but the idea of it just fills me with dread and . . . humiliation.'

'You're far from alone in this situation.'

'I know.' Pippa rallied some energy. 'Maybe we just need a bit more time, you know? Both of us really putting in the effort. A cleaner wouldn't go astray, either. The daily grind of domesticity is killing me.'

'That sounds like a good, practical place to start,' Gabby said, allowing a gossamer thread of hope to hover between them for a moment.

They chatted about lighter subjects for a while, until Pippa said she had to go home to get some work done on a brochure for a client who owned a beauty salon. The lunchtime rush was in full swing, the line at the counter stretching towards the door. Gabby gave Pippa a large, big-sister hug and waved goodbye, sad to see her so unhappy. Life was just too short to be miserable.

She turned to see how she could help out in the cafe. She didn't need to work the floor; she'd set up the business that way from the start because, as a heart transplant recipient, she couldn't always be relied upon to be fit and able to work. Still, she loved it here and needed to feel useful and engaged.

As she neared the counter, someone caught her eye. There was a woman in a pink shawl sitting against the green wall of living plants. Gabby had seen her earlier on when she was talking to Pippa. Now she realised the woman had been nursing the same cup of coffee for some time. She didn't mind that – customers often sat on a lone cuppa. Looking at her properly now, though, the back of Gabby's neck prickled.

As she watched, the woman looked up and their eyes met. Gabby started, then offered a smile, but the woman flushed and turned away, pulling her shawl tighter around her thin body.

Gabby took a step towards her, planning to ask her if she could help her out with another drink, not because she felt the need to sell another cup but simply as a way to start a conversation. If there was one thing she knew only too well, it was that people had all sorts of drama going on in their lives and sometimes they just needed a stranger's listening ear to help them through.

She didn't get the chance. The woman got to her feet, slung her tote over her shoulder and scurried to the front door, pausing infinitesimally before the life-sized Tin Man at the entrance before disappearing down Chapel Street.

'Everything okay?' Ed asked from behind the counter.

Gabby smiled but felt uneasy. 'Yes, I just thought I saw someone . . .' She shook her head. 'It doesn't matter. Can I help you here?'

The young barista *bang-bang*ed her filter basket over the knock box and turned a dial on the machine to rinse it with water, ready to start on the next order. Ed peered over her shoulder, searching for Lin, their kitchenhand and general all-rounder. Through the glass wall they could both see her stacking the dishwasher with the efficiency of a sword fighter.

'Order for Tony!' The second barista, Kyle, still wearing a black and yellow Richmond scarf after the previous weekend's AFL grand final, dusted cappuccinos with chocolate powder, clicked on two plastic lids and positioned the drinks in a cardboard takeaway tray next to a long black and a flat white.

'I think we're running low on whipped cream,' Ed told Gabby, her perfect blonde brows knitting together.

'I'll get it.' Gabby pushed through the wooden swing doors into the kitchen. 'You're doing a great job, Lin,' she said as she passed the kitchenhand on her way to the fridge.

'Thanks,' Lin said, flashing her beautiful little dimples. To support herself while studying at university, the young woman split her working hours between The Tin Man and her family's restaurant in Chinatown.

Gabby retrieved the cream and glanced across the room at her new coffee director. On the day of the interviews Gabby had been sick and in hospital – nothing serious, just a common cold turned nasty and her doctors had wanted her on an antibiotic drip for a couple of days. Pippa had stepped in to conduct the interviews and had chosen Luciano Colombera for the job.

The first time Gabby had met him, he'd been in the roasting area, crouched down near some hessian bags of green beans, testing their moisture levels the old-fashioned way – by cracking them between his teeth. If they hadn't been dried properly they wouldn't roast properly, and from the way he was frowning he was either seriously unimpressed or concentrating to the point of pain. He wore Blundstone boots with jeans and his sleeves were rolled up to his elbows, and he sported a dense whiskery growth of dark hair on his jaw, which matched his dark eyes. By anyone's standards, the man was hot.

'Hi,' Gabby had said, striding to him with her hand outstretched. 'I'm Gabriella McPhee, owner of The Tin Man, and Pippa's older sister – you met her at the interview.'

He craned his neck to look up at her from his squatting position near the beans and held out his hand.

'Luciano,' he said, giving her an appraising look that wasn't unfriendly, but wasn't warm either. She couldn't get a read on him. She took his hand, feeling her heart tapping nervously. He squeezed her hand just right – not too hard or slack, but confident. They hadn't talked long. Or, more precisely, *she* hadn't talked long, because he was evidently not a big talker, and this dark and broody mood was something she'd come to know as one that could descend suddenly and then vanish just as quickly.

Now, she still knew little about him. He'd had an animated discussion with Kyle about football – he also supported Richmond – and he was always particularly polite to Lin, which Gabby really appreciated. You could tell a lot about someone by the way they treated the lowest ranking staff in a business. She'd heard him have many long phone conversations in Italian with Marco, their coffee trader. And the man sure knew how to roast a bean. Yet often when she spoke to him it was as though he stared through her for a second before pulling his mind back from far away.

She watched him now as he scooped gorgeous chocolate-coloured beans from a bucket and onto the scales to weigh them. She considered calling out to him, determined to keep trying to build some sort of connection with him, but decided to wait until he was less busy. Instead, she turned back towards the front of house with the cream in her hand. She pushed open the swing door. Her eyes darted to the table by the wall, where the woman with the pink shawl had been sitting just moments ago. Her chest squeezed tight, almost to the point of pain.

Running.

She was running down a dark alley.

A streetlight cast a sickly pool of orange.

The Gift of Life

Her breath rasped noisily in her ears as cold air scraped down her throat.

Fear spiked her blood.

Bright lights.

She was trapped.

2

Krystal bundled the four boys onto the tram for the short ride to Richmond Library, where they were heading for a free nature talk. This was her gift to Roxy for her thirty-third birthday: one whole day free to do whatever she liked. Roxy had had a difficult time choosing between staying in bed eating cream buns and watching Netflix all day, or doing something a bit wild like riding a motorbike or jetskiing.

In the end Krystal had made the decision for her, paying for her to ride the Colonial Tramcar Restaurant, where she would enjoy a decadent four-course lunch and plenty of drinks as the plush tram trundled through the city. Her bestie was the kind of person who loved alone time and had no qualms about eating on her own.

Roxy had thrown her arms around Krystal's neck and almost cried with delight. 'I won't have to share my food with anyone,' she'd whimpered. 'I can drink all I like and get a cab home. I won't have to talk to a single soul!'

Krystal was still glowing with the gratifying feeling of getting a special gift *just* right. These days, aside from her own two boys, Roxy was the most important person in her life.

She sorted the boys into two-person seats on each side of the aisle. Roxy's eldest, Kyan, sat at the window, Krystal beside him with her youngest, Olly, on her lap, and Roxy's youngest, Austin, sat with Jasper on the other side of the tram. They were best friends, both in the same prep class, which was how she and Roxy had first met.

The tram left the station. Olly swung his little feet, bumping his heels first against Krystal's jeans-clad legs, then tapping the seat in front of them.

'Don't kick the seat, sweetheart,' she said, putting her hand on his thigh.

'Why?'

'Because it will annoy the person sitting in front of you.' The woman in the seat ahead adjusted her peach-coloured hijab and turned slightly to smile at Krystal, the kind of smile mothers gave each other to say they knew only too well what little kids were like. Krystal smiled back, grateful.

The tram clattered along the road while, beside her, Kyan played a handheld plastic game that was filled with water, jabbing at buttons to shoot rings up through the liquid and try to hook them over plastic spikes. Across the aisle, five-year-old Jasper and Austin were chattering and laughing about monster trucks with laser guns and lava tanks. Olly reached his hands up behind him and looped them around Krystal's neck, and she rubbed her face against his light brown hair and soft cheek, breathing in the scent of Vegemite.

She closed her eyes, trying to focus on the feel of Olly in her arms, trying to stop the endless cycle of ruminations that had kept her awake most of the night after seeing Gabriella McPhee in the flesh yesterday.

The tram lurched to a stop and she guided the boys out the door, Kyan continuing to play his game, making squawks of excitement as he neared completion. Jasper wore a bright yellow and black long-sleeved tee with an image of Thor on the front, while Austin had a T-shirt with Ant-Man. The boys shared a love of Marvel comics and all superheroes, though both Krystal and Roxy cringed at the extreme violence in them.

She paused for a moment and gathered the four boys together, waiting until the yellow and green tram had departed before they started moving. She held Olly's hand in one hand and Jasper's in the other. Jasper had Evan's floppy dark hair and treacle-coloured eyes. She simultaneously couldn't wait for him to grow up so she could see how much he looked like his father, and wanted him never to grow up at all, never leave the safety of her nest. What had happened to Evan had forever altered her, made her nervous of her boys ever leaving her sight.

'Austin, take Jasper's hand while we cross the road,' she said. Austin did as she asked and the two boys grinned at each other, her heart swelling at their precious friendship. 'Kyan, just give your game a break for a moment while we cross the road, okay?'

'Okay,' he grumbled, clearly thinking that at eight years of age he was too old for this mollycoddling.

They crossed the road for the short walk to the library in the brisk spring weather, the kind that fooled you with deep blue skies and bright sun but had a sneaky cold breeze that would shoot through your clothes. She was wearing her black puffer vest over a long-sleeved white tee, but the wind still slipped in around the edges and made her shiver.

Inside the library the atmosphere was engaging and noisy, so different from what libraries had been like when she was a girl. She ushered the boys to the kids' area, which was bustling with children on school holidays. A man in a green ranger's shirt stood before a line of aquariums with frogs, tadpoles, tiny fish, turtles and crickets. He called for the children's attention and they scurried towards him, forming a waist-high mosh pit. In a corner, three stressed library attendants argued quietly among themselves as to the best arrangement of egg cartons and paint pots for the after-show craft activity. The ranger began to pluck out animals from tanks to show the kids.

Krystal perched on a vinyl seat at the periphery, her eyes on the four boys, watching their excited faces. Her body was here, trying to be a good mum and friend, but her mind was undeniably else-where, over at the cafe with Gabriella McPhee.

She'd spotted her easily enough, recognising her from the photo in the newspaper; her bright-red hair was an instant giveaway. Krystal had barely been able to order her coffee, so strong was her magnetic pull to the woman. From a table against the wall, she'd watched as Gabriella talked to another woman, one who looked quite similar and had the same red hair – her sister, she guessed. She watched Gabriella move about the cafe in her boho-style wrap dress, soft jersey material in muted autumn tones of caramels and earthy reds, all swirls and florals. She took in her knee-high brown suede boots. Her long, gold gypsy earrings. Her laugh, coming from deep in her chest.

Her chest . . . Krystal could barely breathe imagining what lay beneath.

Squeals erupted from the children as a green frog leapt from the presenter's arm and onto the carpet. He rushed to snatch it up before it could be trampled by little feet. Jasper followed, eager to help, his eyes bright with excitement. She hoped he wouldn't turn out to be one of those boys who loved frogs and reptiles. She really couldn't cope with snakes and lizards in their apartment.

She pressed her hand to her forehead as the children cheered, her mind spinning with memories of Gabriella McPhee.

What was she going to do now?

Roxy arrived at Krystal's apartment at five o'clock, wearing black jeans and boots and a maroon velveteen jacket. Her spiky bleached-blonde hair showed dark roots. Her grin was a mile wide.

'That was just the best!' she said, throwing herself on Krystal again. '*You* are the best! I ate duck, chicken liver and kangaroo and I've never eaten any of those before in my life. I wasn't even squeamish. And that was just the entrée! I had beef for the main.'

'So, you basically ate a whole farmyard of animals,' Krystal said, laughing and beckoning Roxy inside.

Roxy spun around with her hands on her cheeks. 'And oh, lord, the cheese board!'

'I'm so glad. You really deserved it.'

'Hi, boys!' Roxy called to the kids in the lounge room. They called back cheery hellos but didn't stop playing their game of *Operation*. Olly was obviously struggling, judging by the sound of the buzzer and his disappointed wails.

Krystal ordered pizza via Uber Eats, fed the ravenous small people, then let them return to their game while she and Roxy ate more slowly.

'I'm really not sure why I'm eating at all,' Roxy said, biting into a slice of Meat-a-tarian. 'I'm already so full.'

'It's your birthday.' Krystal shrugged. 'You may as well go the whole hog.'

'I think I may have done exactly that by the end of today. There'll be nothing but trotters left.'

Kyan had taken centre stage in the middle of the lounge, entertaining the younger three by acting out horrible Viking tales. He had a particular love of Viking history, the more bloodthirsty the better.

It made Roxy cringe but she nevertheless scoured second-hand shops and brought home boxes of books describing battles and massacres to indulge his passion, good mum that she was. The Wise People said that, with boys, it was important to get them reading and keep them reading, and to let them read *anything* they wanted to, just as long as they didn't give up.

'But what if they want to read about, I don't know, heinous crimes, or how to shoot and butcher your own cow, or porn?' Krystal had once wondered.

Kyan roared savagely, and the three young ones squealed and fell back against the blue couch that had seen better days. Krystal closed the lid on the remains of the triple cheese pizza in the box in front of her. Suddenly, her mood fell. As much as she loved Roxy and their combined brood of boys, and the welcome company they provided, her mind was like a terrier on the hunt for rats – obsessed.

Roxy must have noticed. 'Tell me what happened yesterday,' she said quietly, shoving the pizza box out of the way to give Krystal her full attention.

'It's nothing.'

'It's not nothing.'

'It's your birthday.'

'And I've had a great one. Your turn. Spill.'

Krystal took a deep breath. 'I think it's her.'

Roxy raised a dark eyebrow. 'How do you know?'

'I just do,' Krystal said, shrugging.

Her friend eyed her levelly. 'Did you speak to her?'

Krystal shook her head. 'I couldn't. She came towards me but I panicked and took off.'

Roxy gave her a small, sympathetic smile but waited in silence for more.

'I want to go back there,' Krystal said, not even having to think about it. 'I have to go back there. I'm *burning* all over with a need to . . .' She swallowed. *To get close enough to Gabriella to touch her* was what she was thinking, but to say that out loud would make her sound mad. 'I barely slept last night. It was all I could think about.'

'That's understandable. The kids are back at school next week. You could go back then. Make a time to see her and have a proper chat.'

'I could,' Krystal agreed. She crossed her arms over her chest and rubbed her upper arms. 'I'm itching, literally, like a complete nutjob. I want to go there now, even though I know the cafe will be shut, even though I know she won't be there.' She paused, trying to untie all the knots in her mind. 'That's how messed up I am about this woman. I know it sounds crazy.' She felt tears sting her eyes and blinked them away. She needed to *do* something. She needed to open the valve on the pressure cooker of unanswered questions in her head.

'If you really feel like you have to go now, I can stay here with the kids,' Roxy said. 'It wouldn't take you long to get over there at this hour.'

'I can't leave the kids,' Krystal said, lowering her voice.

'Of course you can. You've had them all day while I've gone and wined and dined myself – the best date I've had in decades, by the way.' She nodded towards the kids. 'I don't think they'd even notice.'

Krystal looked over at them, giggling and playing happily, with full bellies. If she put on a DVD they would probably simply fall asleep. But it was nuts. All that would happen was that she'd get there and she'd crawl the car past the cafe and it would be locked up for the night. She didn't need to see an empty cafe; she needed to catch a glimpse of Gabriella, or hear her voice. She needed to know if she had a husband or kids of her own. She wanted to see her walking around, to see her moving, to sense the life she was leading. She could already see herself in her mind, pulling over to the side of the road, letting the Holden idle, staring at the cafe, wishing it would spring to life before her eyes and Gabriella appear from thin air.

But the cafe would stay dark and silent and give nothing away, just like everything about the night Evan died.

'No, it's okay,' she said, breathing out. 'You're a star for offering. But I've got to try to keep my head about this, no matter how hard it might be.'

3

'Do you want to see a picture of my new man?' Pippa said, her smile lighting up her green eyes.

Irish eyes, their father liked to remind them. Monty was deeply and embarrassingly proud of the fact that the McPhees were of Irish descent. *Australian, Dad!* Pippa would say. *Just Australian now.* The sisters' near-identical colouring came from their mother, though Lottie's red hair had been a rusty grey when she passed away swiftly last year from a stroke, just a couple of months after the opening of The Tin Man. Lottie had been an enthusiastic supporter of the business venture and was the one to suggest that Gabby could use the family home as security against the bank loan.

'What are you talking about?' Gabby failed to hide her shock as she pulled up a chair. This was a big leap from their conversation at the cafe two days ago. Also, she was thrown. She'd come here to talk to Pippa about the disturbing vision. She wasn't sure she could handle an excited declaration of an extramarital affair right now.

They were in her sister's rather fabulous 'She Shed' in the garden, the feminine equivalent of a Man Cave, positioned away from her husband and children. It had to be fabulous: it was Pippa's work-from-home office and sometimes her clients visited her here. With four children, she and Harvey had needed a big house and Ringwood was an affordable location, but not exactly one known for its trendiness. The She Shed gave Pippa a decidedly chic space to make her own. The decor was styled on French boudoir colours and furniture, with pale blue walls and white trims, an ornate distressed white writing table, a chandelier and duck-egg blue textured pillow shams.

Pippa's personal appearance was also, as usual, flawless. Today she was wearing a drool-inducing sleeveless 1950s-inspired dress. Beneath the deep V-neck, a fitted panel showed off her gym-toned waist and the skirt flared over her hips in structured box pleats. Blue and white diagonal stripes gave the feeling of yachting somewhere exotic. A bolt of pure envy flashed through Gabby. Once upon a time she could have worn that dress too. The sisters were so alike that they'd shared clothes from their late teens on, when Pippa had almost caught up in height. But these days Gabby's weight fluctuated so much depending on the medications she was on and the resulting inflamed skin and fluid retention, that she now collected loose, bohemian style clothes that could accommodate anything from size twelve to size sixteen. She cast an eye down at her dark brown maxi dress with elasticised waist and 1970s orange floral print, feeling vaguely disappointed. Before her operation, she'd worn more structured clothes. Now everything seemed to hang shapelessly. At least she could still indulge in good boots.

It wasn't just Pippa's clothes that she coveted. Gabby sighed audibly with relaxation every time she climbed the two steps to the tiny porch of the She Shed. It poked at the occasional pang she had to have her own space again one day, away from her childhood home and out from under her dad's feet. Not that she wasn't thankful. Truly, she couldn't *be* more grateful, but, nearly two years post-transplant, she was starting to hope that she was finally okay and could be trusted on her own with the kids. Besides, Charlie would be sixteen soon. It was unfair to expect him to be responsible for the girls, but it did give her more confidence to know that an almost-adult would be in the house with her if anything did go wrong. Plus, there was the dog, a trained service animal after all.

On the other hand, Monty was in his mid-seventies and his eyesight was diminishing. He'd never quite regained his spark after Lottie had died. Gabby often found him staring vaguely into space. He was thinner, his skin looser, his face paler. Her parents had been her carers for years but soon she might need to be her dad's, and she certainly owed him that after everything she'd put them through. When the virus had attacked her heart, it had attacked them all.

'I didn't expect to fall in love so quickly,' Pippa admitted, a small flicker of doubt pinching her forehead. 'But he's so fabulous. Look!' She thrust her mobile phone at Gabby to show her the photo.

Gabby took the phone, holding it out at a bit of a distance, an automatic gesture these days as her eyesight changed with age. She was only forty-one but she felt like a granny every time Celia held up a picture or book for her to look at and she had to recoil from it just to pull her focus into line. She was rather disgusted, actually, at this outward, bald sign of ageing.

Except, of course, she was happy to be ageing at all. Happy to be alive to even experience the disappointment of failing eyesight. Sometimes she simply forgot and Old Gabby would raise her disgruntled head.

'Have you booked an appointment with an optometrist yet?' Pippa teased.

Gabby glared at her. 'You just wait. It'll be your turn next.' She refocused her attention on the phone. What she saw on the screen was not what she'd expected. She gaped at Pippa. 'This is a surprise.'

'I know!' Pippa squealed, clenching her fists with glee. 'He's stunning, right?'

'Yes, he is,' Gabby agreed, still wondering how this had all come about so quickly. 'Pure black?'

'Part Andalusian! And he's a dream ride!'

'You've ridden him already? When?'

'Last weekend. I told Harvey I had to meet a new client and that she could only meet on the weekends because she worked full-time.'

'Do you feel bad, lying to him?'

Pippa lifted one shoulder. 'Not much. We don't really speak enough for me to get the chance to lie,' she said bitterly. 'But it had to be done. I've signed the papers and paid the money. He's mine.'

'And Harvey still doesn't know?'

'No!' She looked horrified. 'He can't know! He wouldn't approve at all.'

'But how are you going to keep this a secret? He'll cost a fortune and you'll come home smelling of horse.'

'My business has a separate bank account and I do all the books. I'm going to keep my riding clothes in a bag in the car and shower at the gym on the way home. Please don't look at me like that. I need this. My marriage is falling apart and I need something that's just mine. The children – bless them, I love them, but they take everything, including my time, thoughts, emotional energy, and half the time, my bed. I need joy and distraction and exercise and sunshine and if . . . if this marriage does all fall apart, it will give me something to go on with. Some kind of joy.'

Gabby nodded and handed back the phone, then poured herself a glass of lemon water from the jug Pippa always had handy on a side table. Right now, this horse was a precious, shiny bubble of hope for an overworked, overstressed mother whose world was on the brink of collapse.

'I understand. I really do. I hope you'll both be very happy together.'

'Oh, we will be.'

'I can't wait to meet him.' She and Pip hadn't ridden together since they were teenagers. 'When you find your agistment for him, there might be another horse there I could ride. One that's terribly old and slow, with any luck. We could go out for a trail ride together.'

Pippa clasped her hands together, a beautiful rosy glow on her cheeks. Then she took one more look at the photo of her horse, inhaled a deep, satisfied breath, and put the phone next to her laptop, where a logo for a hair salon was displayed onscreen, repeated several times in different colours as Pippa tried to find the right balance. Gabby was always in awe that her sister could take someone else's idea and vision and turn it into an image. Pippa had designed the logo for the cafe, a greyscale image of the Tin Man from *The Wizard of Oz* holding a bright red heart in his hands. Somehow, she'd managed to get such emotion into the Tin Man's face, such vulnerability. She'd also designed the signage for the shopfront, which was simple but elegant.

'Where are all your children?' Gabby asked, suddenly realising how quiet the yard was, considering it was school holidays.

'They're at Harvey's parents' for a couple of nights.' She sighed, relieved. Then she seemed to remember that Gabby had asked to come over this morning and focused her thoughts. 'Sorry, I just hijacked your news. What's happening?'

Gabby adjusted her position in the wooden chair, which was

pretty but not comfy. 'A woman came into the cafe when you were there the other day. There was something about her.' She was wary of sharing this with Pippa, knowing it sounded crazy. 'I think . . . I feel like . . . maybe she was searching for me. She kept looking at me, and when I looked at her she turned away. Then I went to go up and talk to her and she just fled.'

'Why would she be looking for you?'

'I'm wondering if she has worked out who I am.'

'And that is . . .?'

'The person who has her loved one's heart.'

Pippa frowned and distractedly played with a pleat in her dress. 'What makes you think that?'

Gabby hesitated, not ready to share the awful things she'd seen in her mind and felt in her body, almost as if she'd been momentarily possessed. 'Just a gut feeling.'

Pippa looked unconvinced. 'Perhaps you should go and see the counsellor at the hospital.'

Gabby gave an empty laugh. 'You think I'm crazy.'

'No, of course not. But whatever you're going through, you need to talk to someone.'

'Funny, I would have thought the same applied to you and Harvey,' Gabby said, a touch miffed. She had hoped she could talk to her sister.

Pippa glared at her, then looked away. A wind chime tinkled at the front door of the She Shed and a dog barked a few doors down. Somewhere in the street, a game of Marco Polo was happening in a pool, which Gabby fervently hoped was a heated one given the chill in the air.

'If she is who I think she is, what do you think she wants?' Gabby pressed on, moving past their awkward moment as only sisters could. She was desperate to know, to have Pippa even hazard a guess, despite her disbelief.

Pippa shook her head. 'I have no idea. How would she even have found you? The security around the recipient's identity is watertight.'

'The newspaper article, remember?'

Pippa groaned. 'Belly and balls! I forgot about that. Do you know, other mums at school ask me what I got up to on the weekend and I can't recall a single thing. Every day just seems to fly past and mean nothing.' She flopped back in her chair.

'I know the feeling,' Gabby said.

Pippa took a deep breath and brought her attention back to Gabby's situation. 'It would actually make a lot of sense, if she was looking for the recipient and then your transplant date conveniently turned up in the newspaper.'

'She's going to come back for me. I can feel it.'

They were both silent for a moment, each of them considering the multitude of possibilities for how that next meeting might play out.

From within her oversized handbag, her message tone sounded. It was Cam.

> R u at home? Summer's got
> gastro. I need to drop the
> other two back with you.

Gabby frowned, staring at the screen.

'What's up?' Pippa asked.

'It's Cam. Summer's got gastro.'

'Nasty,' Pippa sympathised.

'He wants to bring the other kids home early.'

'Again?' Pippa sounded disgusted. 'Why?'

Gabby and Cam's parenting arrangements were shared equally, in theory. Two weeks without the kids had seemed an eternity when they'd first separated, but they'd agreed that a week-about schedule was too disruptive. Gabby couldn't say she would ever enjoy it being this way, but so much had happened in the past five years that any sense of normality had been blown to pieces and she'd had to quickly accept a new type of normal. Ever since Cam and Meri had had a new baby, however, his commitment to his first three children had been steadily decreasing.

'What's going on with him?' Pippa said.

'I have a theory,' Gabby muttered.

Fine, I'll be home in half an hour, she texted. She stood, hauling her bag up to her shoulder. 'I better go.'

The first time Gabby met Meri was when she'd been sick as a dog in hospital and Cam had brought the kids to visit. He and Meri had been together for some time but his former wife and future wife hadn't yet met. Gabby had looked at the (slightly younger) woman's kind eyes and full cheeks and thought, *Thank god*. Someone – a mother figure – might be there for her children, to wrap them in cosy arms. Meri was a social worker, which gave Gabby confidence that someone responsible would be there to keep an eye on Cam.

This gastro situation would be a nightmare for Cam and Meri, sure. It was the last thing anyone needed when they had a six-month-old baby in the house. But Cam knew he had to keep Summer with him. Any infectious illness posed a serious threat to someone with a suppressed immune system like Gabby. It was a tightrope she had to walk. She loved her kids. She wanted to be with them and hug them and make them dinner and hear about their days. The doctors all said, *You've been given the gift of life, now go live it*. A transplant recipient had to be careful not to take risks that could lead to infections, but also, ironically, take some risks in order to keep their sanity and live their life. It was the constant battle between becoming a petrified, paralysed germophobe and loving the guts out of life. She'd developed rules for herself, like she wouldn't go to someone else's house if she knew there was illness, but she would never stop herself from holding her children when they were ill.

She got into her car and texted Cam again. *Can you get Summer to call me, please?* At thirteen, Summer didn't yet have a mobile phone, though it wouldn't be long. Soon, Gabby's mobile rang and she put the call on speaker while she drove towards the family home in Camberwell.

'Hi, Mum.'

'Oh, sweetie, you don't sound well.' Summer's usually cheerful voice was flat and wobbly. 'Have you had some electrolytes or something?'

'Not yet. Dad's going out to get me some soon. Don't worry about me. I'll stay here till I'm better. I don't want you getting sick.'

Tears filled Gabby's eyes but she bit her lip. Still, her daughter read the delay in response for what it was.

'Don't cry, Mum. It's fine, really. I've got Netflix. I was supposed to go to that sleepover at Freddie's tomorrow, which is a bummer, but I'll see her at school next week.'

Gabby's middle child was blessed with a huge circle of friends and optimism for life. Gabby swung between thinking Summer would either become leader of the free world or a weather reporter on the nightly news.

'Call me, any time you want,' Gabby said at last, wiping her eye with the heel of her hand.

'I will.'

'Or use your iPad to message me, you know, about anything, even just to send me selfies of yourself ghastly green and flaked out in bed.'

'Okay.'

'Or if you want to watch *Ninja Warrior* with me over the phone, we can do that.'

'Okay, stop now. You're being clingy.'

'*Ninja Warrior* is too far?'

'Yep.'

She was being clingy, it was true. Had she always been this needy? Or was it one of those 'before and after' things, the line in the sand – the fracture line that ran through her life, the one that said that the old Gabby was gone forever and a new one was here. Sometimes, the two lives got muddled.

'Bye, Mum. Love you,' Summer said, with what Gabby thought was a slight wince of pain.

'Love you too, sweetie.'

Cam and the kids arrived not long after Gabby entered the house. He must have really been in a rush to get them home. She tried to give Cam the benefit of the doubt. Maybe he just didn't want Charlie and Celia to get sick too. Maybe it had nothing to do with his increasing inattentiveness since baby Mykahla was born – the unwashed lunchboxes, the lateness in picking up the kids, the way they looked ruffled and a bit sad when they came home.

Charlie was first out of the car, his ginger hair glinting in the afternoon light. A duffel bag of clothes was hoisted on one shoulder, his school bag on the other. Even during the holidays he was working hard on his assignments. He was heading into the final term of Year 10 and feeling the pressure, while also struggling to choose subjects to study for the Victorian Certificate of Education in his senior years. His head was lowered, leaning forward against the weight on his back. The sight pinched Gabby somewhere inside her chest – when had her little boy grown up into a young man with the weight of the world on his shoulders?

'Hi, Mum,' he said, kissing her on the cheek.

'Hi, baby,' she said.

He rolled his eyes to the sky, exasperated.

'Sorry,' she said quickly, putting a hand on his arm as he passed by. 'Not baby. Big boy.'

'That's not better,' he sighed, disappearing down the hall towards the staircase, where he would dump his gear on the floor until he went up to his room later. But first he would check the fridge. He was always checking the fridge, even if he wasn't planning on eating anything. It was some sort of touchstone ritual he had, perhaps to know he was home safe again, or some kind of caveman thing where he had to check on the supplies at regular intervals to know whether or not he needed to go hunting.

'Big man, then?' she hollered after his retreating back.

'Nope!'

'Young man?'

'Hi, Mum,' Celia said, throwing herself against Gabby's hip and wrapping her arms around her.

'Hi, baby,' Gabby said, kissing the top of the brunette head. Thank goodness there was at least one of them she could still call her baby. 'Are you feeling okay?' she asked, placing her hand on her daughter's forehead.

'Yeah, I'm fine,' Celia muttered, her breath hot against Gabby's ribs. 'Grandpa home?'

'No. Grandpa's doing a shift at the club.'

Monty still worked a couple of days a week, at their local RSL club. Not because he needed the money – *Though you always need more money*, he would say – but because he'd read studies about people who retired only to die a short time later and he didn't want to be a statistic. Which was determined, Gabby thought, considering his wife had passed away a year ago and she'd still been working too.

'Hi,' Cam said, rolling Celia's small suitcase across the weathered concrete path to the front door. His hair was swept to the side and particularly curly today.

'You need a haircut,' Gabby said, without thinking.

Cam snorted.

'Sorry! Old habits die hard,' she said, waving a hand in the air, while surreptitiously checking to see if his eyes were bloodshot. They were, a touch. But lack of sleep could do that too. 'Your hair's fine. Perfectly okay. Are you growing it?'

'No. Just too busy to get a haircut.'

'In the school holidays?' Gabby teased. Cam was a special-needs teacher and, usually, he adored kids, other people's and his own, which was one of the reasons why his falling levels of attentiveness to their own kids was making her so suspicious.

'I'm still working,' he grouched. 'There's always so much to do.' He rubbed at his forehead in a classic gesture of overwhelm.

'Sorry,' she said, placatory. 'It was only a joke. I know you work hard year-round for your students.'

He took a deep breath and adjusted his glasses on the bridge of his nose. 'Nah, it's not you, it's me.'

'It's okay, we're already broken up,' she teased again.

He laughed then, his Adam's apple bobbing in his throat, the same way Charlie's was starting to do. 'It's the new baby thing. It's really wearing me down.'

'Sleep deprivation?'

'It's killing me,' he said, staring into the middle distance as though he had shell shock – which, if her memory of having babies served her, he likely did. 'There's a lot to be said for having kids when you're young.'

Celia released Gabby from the hug and reached for her suitcase to take it inside. 'I'm going to find Sally,' she said.

They watched her disappear inside. Gabby teetered on the edge of lecturing Cam about how he could improve his parenting of their three kids but made herself bite her tongue. He'd already confessed he was struggling. And he was looking after Summer while she was sick to help keep Gabby safe from what could be, for her, a potentially deadly bacterial infection or virus. Perhaps she should cut him a bit more slack, just for a while longer.

'It will get better,' she said. 'One day, Mykahla won't want your constant attention and she will be riding around with boys on bicycles and smoking in the toilets.'

'Gee, thanks. And I still won't be getting any sleep,' he groaned.

'True.'

'Right, I'll be off. I'll drop Summer back as soon as she's right to go.'

Just like that, all of Gabby's feelings of generosity disappeared. He couldn't wait to get Summer out of his house.

4

All four children wanted the meatball wrap at Chuckle Park, the funky laneway cafe and bar in Little Collins Street.

'Well, that's easy,' Roxy said, taking the menu from Kyan, who had been reading out options to the younger three. She took their drink orders too – four glasses of juice. 'What would you like?' she asked Krystal.

'I think I'll have the mushroom sanga.'

'And to drink?'

Krystal cast her eyes over the menu. She had an unexpectedly strong craving for an espresso martini. She could almost taste the burn of the vodka, the hit of the caffeine and the thick cream on top. But that was crazy. She'd never been a big drinker, and never during the day. She shook the feeling away. 'The *peppermynthle* tea sounds good, thanks.'

She stayed with the kids at the wooden tables – two square ones pushed together, all of them crowded around on fire-engine red metal stools – while Roxy ordered at the window of the caravan parked at the end of the lane. An abundance of synthetic leaves and flowers cascaded from the top of the van in pinks and greens. More colour spilled from similar installations on the walls above them. Fake grass lay beneath their feet. Burnt-orange glass lanterns swung from electrical cords crisscrossing the laneway above their heads, and blue sky peeked at them through awnings and corrugated iron shades. Dark multi-storey buildings towered above them on either side, with Chuckle Park a riot of colour and charm squeezed in between.

Roxy returned to the table and handed over her phone for Kyan to play a game, and Krystal did the same for the three younger boys to share. The laneway wasn't big enough for kids to be running about and shrieking. They would have plenty of time to run themselves ragged at the museum after lunch.

'How's your fella going without you?' Krystal asked.

'He's gone through two temporary carers already,' Roxy griped.

'In two weeks?'

'He's a bloody grumpy old bugger,' Roxy said, a small smile emerging. 'He yells at me every time I turn up, too, but I just seem to have a way with him and he's eating out of my hand by the time I leave.'

'You're the whisperer,' Krystal said, picturing Roxy as some sort of lion tamer. 'I'll bet the agency will be happy to have you back on board next week.'

Roxy widened her eyes. 'I dare say they will.'

'Might be a good time to ask for a pay rise.'

Roxy shook her head. 'I wish. No one goes into this line of work for the money.'

'Such a shame. It must be an awful thing to be so vulnerable and have strangers coming into your home every day. We'll probably all end up that way eventually.'

They were quiet a moment at that sobering thought. A man with an enormous grey wolfhound on a thin leash walked past the pink and white picket fence and entered the cafe through the wooden archway. Krystal watched the dog for a moment as the man sauntered down the lane to order at the caravan.

A sound of excitement from the boys hailed the arrival of a young woman with lolly pink hair, a nose ring and a smart chocolate-coloured apron to deliver their food and drinks. The boys set upon their meals and Krystal and Roxy spent some time urging them to slow down, hold their wraps with two hands and watch out for falling sauce, and handing them serviettes when it inevitably went wrong. When the first frenzy had passed, Roxy and Krystal turned to their own food.

'Any news?' Roxy asked, then took a bite of her pulled pork roll with apple and cabbage slaw. 'Is there any way you can find out for sure if Gabriella has Evan's heart?'

Krystal swallowed her mouthful before she spoke. 'No. All that information is locked away.' She cast an eye towards Jasper, who was getting to an age where she had to be careful what she said in front of him; he'd started listening in and asking questions. She had so many unanswered questions herself about Evan's death . . . and so much guilt. She wasn't sure she was ready to explain a heart transplant to her son.

'How did you and Evan get together?' Roxy asked, changing the subject. She and Krystal had met at the boys' school when they'd dropped Austin and Jasper off for their first day, and had comforted each other in the carpark as they both shed tears. They'd been friends ever since, but Roxy had never asked many questions about Evan. Krystal assumed she simply sensed how difficult it all still was, and she appreciated that Roxy was the kind of friend she could go out with for coffee and they could read newspapers and magazines together without having to talk the whole time.

Now seemed as good a moment as any to share a little about her life with Evan.

'We met at Cinque restaurant, where we both worked. I was a waitress and he was the sommelier.'

'Tell me the story,' Roxy encouraged, so Krystal put down her sandwich and let her mind drift back to that time.

She first laid eyes on Evan the day she'd gone to the restaurant for an interview. Cinque's owner was meeting with several prospective new employees that day and Krystal had been the last one, at three o'clock. Evan had been behind the marble-topped bar, checking through the day's arrival of wine crates, when he happened to look up just as she was watching him. She was sitting next to the expansive glass windows, the view of the city far below, and the sunlight fell across her shoulders, warming her. The look on Evan's face when their eyes met was one of surprised delight.

He'd paused, bottle in hand, simply to admire her. She'd smiled back at him – friendly, not flirty – then turned away, knowing instantly that a man like that was out of her league. He had an upper-class aura about him. He was handsome and clean cut, his clothes were expensively made, and he held himself so confidently.

The restaurant's owner, on the other hand, was a charismatic guy who was clearly not above letting everyone know he was always up for a bit of fun. Krystal's long hair was tied up on the crown of her head, exposing her pale neck, with soft wisps tucked behind her ear, and his eyes drifted to her cleavage a few times. She sighed quietly, weary of men like this, but absolutely not afraid. She'd grown up having to fend off men's attention, and she was capable of taking care of herself. From the way they were bantering, she knew she had the job.

She glanced over at Evan again, and he returned her gaze. To her embarrassment, the owner noticed.

'Evan's our sommelier,' he said. 'I'll introduce you in a minute.'

'Lovely, thanks.' She snapped her eyes back front and centre, feeling her cheeks burn.

Over the next few weeks she saw Evan almost every time she was working, though she made no effort to connect with him beyond polite greetings or necessary work discussions. This was the best job she'd had since moving to Melbourne from a small town in the Dandenong Ranges. She was twenty-two years old and for the past two years she'd been working as a cleaner or cashier or kitchenhand, anything to earn a bit of money. This was her first big step up. While serving diners, she was polite and efficient and had a knack for anticipating needs. Older women loved her, as did the older men, and younger men, but with the latter she maintained a careful distance. She and Evan exchanged small talk now and then, but she wasn't prepared to jeopardise her role at the restaurant in any way, especially not by flirting with him.

Then, as she was setting tables late one afternoon, the sky turning a dusky pink above the city towers, the warm glow of the pendulous lights and the chandeliers making the silverware sparkle, she spoke to him as he walked past carrying a blackboard listing the day's specials.

'Evan?'

He stopped, seemingly surprised. 'Yes?'

'How does someone become a sommelier?' She shrugged. 'You know, just out of interest.' She didn't want him to think she was after his job, or to make anyone think she wasn't grateful to be waitressing, but she was curious as to where she could progress from here.

He rested the board against the chair nearest to him. 'There are a few different paths but there are some clear stages. The first stage is really all about self-education.'

'Drinking a lot of wine?' she said, laughing.

'Absolutely.' He grinned at her. 'Doing some wine appreciation courses, going to wine tastings, subscribing to wine journals, visiting vineyards, and learning about the great wine regions of the world, including those here in Australia, is really important. Then there's formal study – paying for an industry-recognised course – which is helpful. You don't have to do one, but I think it does give you an edge.'

She felt her face fall and she returned her attention to the napkin she'd just folded, pulling it open and refolding it. 'That all sounds like a rich man's game.' Wine – particularly good wine – was expensive.

He seemed at a loss as to how to respond to that and she regretted giving away her weakness – she didn't come from privileged stock and didn't have money to invest in her education. He stepped closer to her and she felt her breath hitch in her throat. 'There are other ways to get a start in the industry. What you're doing here, right now,' he said, indicating the table, 'is already helping you. Part of being a sommelier is knowing exactly how to set tables, how to present wine, open wine, pour wine, and the right order of serving. Don't dismiss the fact that just by working here, you're giving yourself a good grounding. You can work your way towards being a sommelier entirely through hands-on experience.'

That cheered her. 'Thanks.' She gazed up into his face. He was about a head taller than her. His thick hair was tamed into shape by some sort of wax. He was clean-shaven and smelled faintly of an aftershave that could have been made from the ocean itself.

'You're welcome.' He added, rather hopefully, 'Of course, I'm happy to help you too, if you'd like.'

She held his gaze for a moment, trying to decide if he was genuine or not, trying to decide whether or not to trust him, then gave him a nod. 'Sure, maybe one day.'

From then on, whenever they were working together, Evan took it upon himself to show Krystal something new either before the diners arrived or later on, when the last ones were lingering and the staff were focused on cleaning up. Half-drunk bottles were the perfect opportunity for him to introduce her to a variety of wines. She could recognise all the main types of grape easily enough, but when they started to look at the more unusual ones she got cranky and impatient.

'I'll never get this,' she'd moan, resting her forehead in her hand. 'Half of them are in a different language.'

When he'd tried to show her the differences that came about when wine was aged in oak barrels, or toasted oak barrels, or pine barrels, or cherry wood, or cedar, she threw her hands in the air. 'Forget it. I give up.'

He watched her a moment, then said, 'It does help to have a particularly good sense of smell. I'm just lucky, I guess.'

'Big nose,' she said, then clapped her hand to her mouth. 'Shit, I'm so sorry! I didn't mean you have a big nose!' But he did have a big nose, and he knew it. Her skin seared.

To her relief he simply roared with laughter. 'Well, I have to have some sort of flaw to make me interesting. If I were perfect, you wouldn't like me.'

She laughed, both because she was still so horribly embarrassed and because he'd suggested that there was some attraction here.

'You tell the truth,' he said, suddenly serious. 'I like that. For most of my life, that's been a rare thing.'

He definitely had her attention now.

'Come out with me on Wednesday,' he said. He knew they both had the day off.

'What?'

'Spend the day with me.' He kept his eyes on her. She looked down at the floor, furrowed her brow in confusion, looked back at him and opened her mouth to refuse – an automatic response – then paused. He grinned, sensing her hesitation. 'Come on. We'll have some fun. Nothing serious. Just two night-workers from the hospitality trade soaking up some sunshine and fresh air for a change.'

'You make us sound like vampires.'

'Sometimes it feels a bit like that, doesn't it? Getting home after midnight when the streets are cold and quiet?'

He'd hit a nerve – she *was* lonely. She shrugged, as casually as she could manage. 'Okay. I've got nothing better to do.'

'Where would you like to go?'

'Surprise me.'

A loud crack brought Krystal out of her reminiscences. Olly had knocked a glass off the table and it had hit the ground, breaking into several pieces. She jumped off her stool to pick them up, relieved that the fake grass had cushioned the fall a little and stopped the glass from spraying in every direction.

Olly stared at the ground, frozen.

'It's okay,' Krystal said. 'It was just an accident.'

A bearded man arrived with a dustpan and brush, wearing a similar apron to the one the woman with the pink hair had worn. 'You all right, buddy?' he asked Olly.

Olly nodded silently.

'Thanks,' Krystal said, placing the glass into the dustpan. 'Sorry about that.'

'No big deal. Happens all the time,' he said cheerily.

She straightened and gave Olly a squeeze. 'Have you finished with your lunch?' She picked up a piece of meatball and held it in front of his face but he shook his head and went back to watching Jasper and Austin play a train game on the phone. She sat down again next to Roxy.

'I liked that story,' Roxy said, pulling her denim jacket tightly across her chest against a stiff wind that had just shot down the laneway. 'I'd like to know more about Evan.'

Krystal huffed, her mood swiftly swinging from the fond past to the bitter present. 'Yeah, so would I.'

Roxy frowned. 'What do you mean?'

'The thing is . . .' Krystal took a deep breath. 'Evan wasn't here when he died.'

'Here, in Melbourne?'

'Yes.'

'Where was he?'

'In Sydney.'

'Why?'

'That's the problem. I have no idea why, and no one could explain it. He told me he was going to work at the restaurant here in the city, kissed me goodbye, and the next time I saw him he was on life support in intensive care at Sydney Royal North Shore Hospital. I never got to speak to him again.'

Roxy crossed one leg over the other, tapping her Dr Martens boot in midair as she digested this new information. 'And you haven't been able to find out anything?'

'I've come up with a dozen explanations, none of them good. I mean, what possible reason could he have had to lie to me if he wasn't covering up something he didn't want me to know?' For a man who'd said he valued the truth, he sure was hiding a lot of secrets.

Roxy cast her eyes upwards, obviously trying to think of something credible that would ease Krystal's mind. But she came up blank. 'Is this why you're so . . .' Here she paused, searching for the right word. '. . . *interested* in Gabriella?'

'Yes,' Krystal said carefully. 'It's like I have all these missing pieces surrounding Evan's death but knowing where his heart ended up . . .' She dropped her voice, glanced at the boys, then leaned closer to Roxy. 'It would just be one less question.'

'I get that.'

But it was more than that. It was also about her own guilt in the matter. If she could just speak to Gabriella, then maybe – just maybe – she could have some idea of whether Evan could forgive her for what she'd done.

'Come on,' Roxy said, getting to her feet. 'Let's get these wild ones to the museum. Then we can work out a way for you to meet Gabriella.'

5

Sharp pains shoot up my legs with every heavy footfall on the bitumen.

    Cold air rasps down my throat.

    'Stop!' The call cuts through the night air.

    Bright, white light sears my eyes. It is blinding.

Gabby woke with a start, gulping for air, confused. Street-lights speared through the white plantation blinds beside her bed. Bright lights, so luminous they hurt. She stumbled out of bed and slammed her palms against the blinds to shut them, her heart racing. What the hell had just happened?

From the other side of the bedroom door came a frantic scratching sound.

She opened the door and Sally pushed her way inside, leaning in to Gabby and nosing at her hands, whimpering slightly.

'It's okay,' Gabby said, and sank to the floor, her back against the bed. The golden retriever climbed over Gabby's legs, planting her front feet on one side and her back feet on the other, offering support.

'Thanks,' Gabby whispered, hugging the dog to her chest and resting her head against Sally's shoulders.

Technically, Sally was Celia's dog. They had crowdfunded an assistance dog for her when Gabby had first got sick and Celia was just seven years old. It was a terrible time for them all, but Celia had struggled the most – outwardly, at least. Gabby and Cam still expected repercussions from the emotional toll it had taken on their other two children to surface later. But Celia's panic attacks and generalised anxiety led her to withdraw so much into herself that they had been frightened their daughter might stop talking altogether and they'd lose her to a dark place. She'd struggled at school, and eventually refused to go. Medications were trialled, but then Gabby's donor coordinator at the hospital had suggested an assistance dog. They'd needed more than ten thousand dollars for a fully trained and accredited dog, but they'd successfully raised the funds, and Sally had changed all their lives for the better.

Lately, Sally seemed to have transferred her attention to Monty – whose bedroom was right across the hall from Gabby's – shadowing him and pushing her head up into his hands. Now she was here.

'You're a clever girl,' Gabby whispered. She stroked Sally's long fur, soft as feathers, and her breathing and heart rate slowed. As much as she might have wanted to believe that the vision that had happened at the cafe was a one-off, the dream that had just woken her was proof that it wasn't.

Her alarm went off at seven o'clock and the memory of the disturbing dream rushed at her. She felt edgy, not knowing if that would be it or if more of the intense flashes would follow. Sally was still snoozing, stretched out on the floor beside the bed. Luciano was rostered to open the cafe this morning, so Gabby could sleep in a little. She sent a text message to Cam asking him how Summer was feeling today, then headed to the kitchen.

The McPhee house was a perfect rectangle, a standard 1920s brick home. It had been renovated over the years, her parents adding a second floor in the 1980s, ten years after they bought it, to accommodate more bedrooms and a second bathroom. Then as now, Gabby's bedroom was at the front of the house, closest to the road, with the open-plan kitchen, dining room and family room at the other end of the house.

The kitchen was lovely and modern, all white surfaces and stainless-steel appliances, with honey-coloured polished floorboards that added warmth to a space that might otherwise have been stark. The fridge door was covered in school notices and timetables, photos, and bills to be paid. The surface of the island bench was always littered with library books, school projects, handbags, scarves and car keys, no matter how much she tried to create systems for those things to be kept elsewhere. Potted colour in the form of violets or orchids sat on benches or small sideboards in the living room, enjoying filtered light from the morning sun. The words *Love, Laugh, Life* hung in sparkling pink letters above the window overlooking the backyard.

Camberwell was one of Melbourne's most desirable locations. People might think the McPhees must be mega wealthy to live in this 'tastefully renovated' five-bedroom home in a 'leafy tree-lined avenue', rubbing shoulders with the poshest of the posh. In reality, Gabby's parents had bought a (then two-bedroom) suburban home for the then average Melbourne house price of thirty-five thousand dollars. They'd held onto it and now the house was valued at around one hundred times what they'd paid for it. Lottie and Monty McPhee had won the Australian property market lotto.

She was surprised to find Charlie already up and making coffee. 'Morning!' she said, squeezing his shoulder. She'd have preferred to kiss him and hug him but was making strong efforts not to come across as needy and smothering.

'Hey, Mum,' he said, focusing on the milk he was heating. They had their own espresso machine, which had been tax deductible, thankfully. A good espresso machine for the cafe cost up to thirty thousand dollars. This one – shiny red and silver – was about a tenth of that. Charlie was a bit of a whiz as a self-taught barista. He'd been watching videos on YouTube about how to create coffee art with the foam and had perfected the love heart and the tulip, but was still working on the trickier rose.

'Want one?' he asked, looking over his shoulder.

'Yes, please.'

She padded to the double doors that led out to the patio and opened them for Sally to go out, shutting the door behind her against the chill. 'You're still on holidays. Why are you up so early?' she asked, then went to the pantry to pull out her tray of medications. She began to pop blister packs, collecting her many pills and vitamin supplements.

He shrugged. 'Woke up early.'

'Something on your mind?' She poured water from the filter into a glass and began to swallow pills, five at a time.

He grunted, noncommittal, and turned the dial to cut the steam. He banged the jug on the granite benchtop to settle the foam.

'Did something happen at your father's?' She steeled herself, ready for whatever he was going to say.

Charlie sighed and began pouring milk into the navy cup, which already held a shot of espresso. 'It doesn't matter.'

Gabby swallowed the last of her water and tightened the belt of her fluffy yellow dressing gown. Yellow wasn't a great colour for her complexion but she loved its cheeriness, so indulged in it with a robe that no one outside the house would ever see.

'It matters to me,' she said, restraining herself from losing her temper at Cam. 'Is it because he brought you back early?'

Charlie carefully carried the cappuccino over to Gabby. His brow was pinched, but whether that was from concentration or unhappiness, she couldn't be sure. 'It's just him, you know. He's different now.'

'Thanks,' she said, as he turned back to the machine to begin another coffee for himself. 'What do you mean, different?'

'Just since the baby . . . he's distracted and grumpy. It doesn't seem like he wants us there any more.'

Gabby could have cried. She felt Charlie's sense of rejection so intensely. She wanted to march over to Cam right now and shake him. How dare he make his son feel unwanted! Fierce anger rose in her – she wanted to hurt Cam as much as he'd hurt their son.

'I'm sure that's not true,' she said, trying to make Charlie feel better. 'Having a new baby is such a difficult time, but he'll get through it. I'm sure he's just exhausted.'

'Yeah.'

Celia's footsteps bounded down the stairs and she threw herself at Gabby for a morning hug. Gabby pulled her into her lap and kissed the top of her head. 'You should have slippers on. Your feet are freezing.'

'Where's Sally?' Celia asked, pushing away her mother's hand as she tried to smooth down the fluffy bits that were sticking up. Gabby loved her littlest girl's beautiful soft brunette curls, as yet untouched by the endless types of products Summer now used. She still marvelled that she'd ended up with one redheaded, one blonde and one brunette child.

'Outside.'

Celia sprang off her lap and went to the door to let Sally back in, and she fell upon the dog as though she hadn't seen her in months. They collapsed to the ground together for a love-in.

'Want a coffee, Seals?' Charlie asked, finishing the second cappuccino.

'Yes, please,' Celia said, kissing Sally on the head. The dog smiled and put her paw on her arm.

Celia had just started to drink weak coffees. Gabby didn't exactly approve, but it seemed everyone drank coffee these days, even children. A couple of weeks ago, two young boys in school uniforms, who Gabby and Ed had guessed must have been no older than nine, had ordered flat whites on their way to school. Ed had shot Gabby a look and mouthed, *Is that legal?* There were no laws against it, so what could they do? Gabby eased her conscience by telling herself that surely a weak coffee – and Ed had made sure it was weak – was better than a can of caffeinated so-called 'energy drink' they could have bought elsewhere. At least coffee came from a plant and not a laboratory. Besides, in Ethiopia, children were weaned onto coffee at just a few months of age, or so an Ethiopian cab driver had told her once.

'Can I have a cat?' Celia asked.

'I'm not up to cats yet,' Charlie said, putting his coffee to the side to start a new, weak coffee for Celia. 'I'm still on flowers.'

Monty disapproved of the kids drinking coffee, but it wasn't as if Gabby could take the moral high ground. She *did* own a coffee shop and was carving out a name for herself in the specialty coffee and roasting trade. This was the seventh business Gabby had owned, the biggest and best. It had often been said in their household – by her parents, mostly – that the only reason to build a business was to sell it for a profit. Not this one, though; The Tin Man was for her kids. She just hoped she was around long enough to build it into something amazing for them. But the statistics were sobering, with only sixty per cent of transplant recipients in Australia alive ten years after surgery – little more than half of all recipients. As of this weekend, she would have made it to two years.

She pushed that thought away and instead watched Charlie artfully swirling frothed milk. You needed steady hands for coffee art, something she no longer had. It had been more than six months after the surgery before her hands stopped shaking enough for her to be able to write legibly with a pen once more or hold a glass without fear of dropping it.

Margaret, one of her transplant friends, said it had taken her even longer. She said the whole experience was like being reborn. *You have to learn to eat, write, go to the toilet, and clean your teeth all over again.*

Gabby sipped her coffee. 'Mm, Charlie, you have a real talent for this.'

'Maybe I should come work for you.'

'I'd rather you went to business school and learned how to run the place,' she said. Her own studies in business had given her a solid grounding that she'd been able to call upon time and again.

'But I could still do coffee art for fun.'

'Of course you could. That's the great part about owning a business. You can do whichever bits you love the most.'

She turned to Celia. 'Seals, do you want to come to work with me today or do you want to stay here with Charlie and Grandpa?'

'Stay here,' Celia said, now lying on the floor alongside Sally.

Monty arrived in the kitchen then, looking thin, with white whiskers and wispy steel-grey hair sticking up in much the same way Celia's had done. 'We're going for a boat ride,' he said, joining the conversation. He had slipped a navy cable-knit jumper over his pyjamas, charcoal-coloured slippers covering the fine skin of his ageing feet.

'Can I bring Sally?' Celia asked, sitting upright.

'If she wears her official coat, yes,' Monty said, putting the kettle on to boil. He was a tea man in the mornings.

'That sounds like fun. Thanks, Dad,' Gabby said, smiling at him, grateful that at least one man in her children's life was still showing up for them.

'It's my absolute pleasure,' Monty said, and she knew that was the truth.

The air conditioning in the front area of The Tin Man was extra cool to compensate for the heat emanating from the steel roaster, which was in full swing on the other side of the glass wall. The aroma filled the whole cafe. Gabby waved to Ed, who looked smart in her biker boots and black jeans, and set some Colombian folk music to play through the cafe speakers after the current playlist finished. Then she wandered out back to watch Luciano in action.

She smiled and called hello; in return, he gave her a lifted chin and distracted nod, a picture of concentration, like the conductor of an orchestra. His almost-black hair was long at the front but combed to one side. He had about a week's growth of facial hair and wore a simple blue collared shirt with his jeans and Blundstones. It was probably a good thing he was aloof, because she suspected it would only take one genuine smile from him to turn him into a serious distraction.

Gabby settled herself on top of two unopened hessian bags of beans stacked near the fridge. They were stamped with the black and red logo of the Colombian farm. It was loud in here, with the roar of the gas as it pumped through the pipes into the roaster, and the spray of the beans as they peppered the sides of the rotating drum. It gave her a real thrill to watch over one hundred kilograms of green, vegetal-smelling beans transform into rich brown, flavourful coffee beans in as little as eight minutes. If they weren't sold as a single origin bean – and most weren't – they were blended with other types of freshly roasted beans, ground, bagged and sold to customers in-house, or to other cafes. There was something so elegant and yet robust about the process. It was a finely choreographed dance.

Luciano had his back to her most of the time, his eyes on the computer screen in front of him, watching the graph trace the heat and rotation speed for this particular blend's profile. The temperature had to be tightly controlled. The big black roaster – about the size of a small garden shed – generated heats of over two hundred degrees Celsius during a roast, and Luciano had to closely watch the rate at which gas pumped into the drum. He had up to three sets of roasts going at once, all at different stages: one lot roasting, one cooling and one de-stoning.

Luciano left his computer for a moment and hoisted up a big white bucket holding twelve kilos of green beans, lifted it high above his head and poured it into the hopper, where it would await its turn to roast. Then he strode back to the screen. A few beans had begun to pop now, like popcorn – this was the 'first crack'. Gabby loved this moment, which meant the beans were nearly there. The tension rose and all her senses were tuned in, waiting for the exact point for Luciano to cut the gas. More and more beans popped, like rain on a tin roof. Luciano, his brow furrowed and his jaw set in concentration, pulled out a metal pipe from the drum – the trier – and held it just below his nose. Steam rose from the brown beans, lifting the aroma profile to Luciano. He didn't have much time.

He thrust the pipe back into the drum and checked the graph on the computer again. From where Gabby sat, she could see the ascending blue and grey lines had nearly met, which would be the point of completion. She sat taller, holding her breath. If he was even moments too late, the beans would be ruined.

He pulled out the trier again, inhaling once more, his head tilted to the side, almost as if he was listening to the beans. There! He replaced the trier, went back to the control panel and snapped off the gas, then released the beans from the drum into the cooling dish below. The roar of the gas fell away, only to be replaced by that of the industrial fan below the cooling tray. A three-armed propeller swept through the chocolate-brown beans as air rushed at them from below, dropping their temperature as quickly as possible.

Gabby inhaled, letting the aromas soak into her, a smile on her face. It was like magic. She grinned at Luciano, even though he was still busy, running his hand through the cooling beans. He picked up a handful to smell, cracking one open with his teeth. He nodded once to himself in satisfaction. The beans were good.

Back to the computer he went, dropping the new batch of green beans from the hopper into the drum. They began to spin, tapping out a rhythm of sorts as the gas roared once more.

Gabby went to stand next to him, and stared at the coloured lines moving on the graph. The maths behind the science of roasting was still just a little beyond the reach of her permanently medicine-affected foggy mind. But her nose didn't lie.

'The beans smell amazing,' she said.

Luciano smiled, still gazing at the screen, but clearly proud.

'I'm so lucky to have you here,' she said.

He glanced at her quickly, confused. 'Why?'

'It's not like there's a raft of experienced roasters in the country just waiting for jobs to turn up. The specialty coffee business is such a small world.'

He turned to face her properly, and she felt his energy hit her. Felt the intensity of him. Felt her blood rush.

'Ironic, isn't it?' he said. 'We're part of a small world in Australia but we're only here because we're part of the huge world of coffee trade, with our beans coming from so far away. We're just the last in an exceptionally long line of hands.'

Gabby swallowed. She hadn't expected poetic reflections from her taciturn roaster. She felt an unusual sense of rapport with him and, heaven forbid, a definite attraction. She'd been given a second chance at life, against the odds – she really didn't believe it was possible to find love again too.

Love? Listen to yourself!

'I enjoy watching the beans,' she said, simply to have words coming out of her mouth instead of tiny whimpers, which she hoped had just been inside her head and not actually audible. 'The aromas seem so alive to me, so inspiring and exciting.'

Gabby was nearly the same height as Luciano, so their eyes held each other's evenly. Above the intense heat here in the roasting room, she could feel the warmth emanating from his body.

'Do you cup?' he asked, striding to the roaster. He placed a bin with a plastic liner under the cooling tray, then opened the chute to fill it with beans. From there he poured them into the de-stoning machine, a vacuum-like apparatus that sucked out foreign bodies such as stones, nails, corn kernels and other things that had contaminated the beans as they'd dried on the sides of roads in their country of origin. To much excitement in-house, last week the de-stoner had extracted two small white tablets from the Colombian beans.

'Yes. For the past year, I've been the only one cupping, to test the quality of the roasted beans we bought.' Gabby stared at the back of Luciano's olive-skinned neck, peeking out from the collar of his shirt. He straightened, heading back to her and the computer once more. 'Have you written up flavour profiles for these blends yet?' she asked, her heart beating hard enough for her to feel it in her chest.

'Not since the last lot. I need to do new ones.'

The beans in the roaster had just reached the Maillard phase, the point at which the flavours began to develop. They were turning yellow before Gabby's eyes through the peephole.

'Let's cup together on Monday,' she said. 'I'd like us to work together on the flavour profiles this time.'

'Okay. Sounds good.'

Leaving him alone to focus on the beans, she spun on her boot heel and swished her way out of the roasting room, the length of gold bells around her neck tinkling.

She was his employer, scheduling essential work – so why was she blushing as though she'd just asked him out on a date?

Keep your head, Gabby. Keep your head.

6

Krystal's racing mind woke her at four-thirty. It was Friday 4 October – the second anniversary of Evan's death, and the day Krystal was going to meet Gabriella McPhee and tell her who she was. Rain splattered against her bedroom window. She pulled the doona up tighter under her chin and tried to get back to sleep, but she was too nervous.

Instead, she threw off the covers, pulled on her ugg boots and went to the kitchen to make coffee. While the kettle boiled she looked around at the apartment, wondering how much it had changed since Evan's death.

There was the same blue couch with its worn pink and yellow cushions, though the couch itself was definitely worse for wear, having had two young boys eating and drinking on it. But she could still see Evan lying there, a baby asleep on his chest. He'd spilled red wine on it once and the stain was still there too, alongside Olly's 'painting' made with black and brown felt-tip pens.

When she and Evan had first moved here, Krystal had been fond of bright, Mexican-inspired colours and busy patterns, and Evan embraced them eagerly, saying he'd had enough of white walls and perfectly styled houses for one lifetime. 'I love the craziness and colour you bring to my life,' he'd said, while wearing a lime-green lampshade with burnt-orange tassels on his head.

She particularly loved their bedroom, with its wooden bedhead painted azure, pink cushions, a white doona with colourful flower accents, and a picture in a white wooden frame of a grey and white donkey wearing a wreath of bright flowers around its neck.

Where she'd come from, in the Dandenong Ranges, it was frequently cold and misty and rainy. But there was still so much colour to be found in the greens of the bushland and the patches of wildflowers, and a big blue sky above. Here in an apartment in the city, she'd needed to capture some colour and bring it indoors.

She wanted to tell Gabriella all of this, to let her know she had the heart of a man who'd embraced change, who'd been part of the Farner Seven legal team that had won one of the biggest cases in Australian history, but who'd then been brave and carved out a life for himself out of his family's shadow; a man who never once became cranky with one of his kids when they woke him up wanting to play with him, even if he'd only had a few hours' sleep after a late night at the restaurant.

But would she tell her the other things, like the fact that he'd lied to her about going to Sydney? What did that say about what he thought of Krystal? She had no idea.

She was standing in the kitchen, leaning against the bench while the water rumbled to boiling, when her phone rang in her bedroom. Her heart kicked. No one ever rang at this time of the morning except when dreadful things happened. She froze a moment, wondering who it could be. Was it about her mother? Or her sister? She pushed herself off the bench and went back down the carpeted hall to find her phone. It was on the rustic wooden bedside table, the screen glowing in the darkness.

She should have known. There *was* one person who rang at this time of day. Cordelia-Aurora.

She let it go to voicemail, carrying the phone back to the kitchen, where she finished making her coffee with a supermarket-brand coffee bag and milk that smelled suspiciously close to curdling. Finally, the phone tinged to let her know the long message was finished. She took a few gulps of her coffee first, fortifying herself for whatever Evan's sister had to say.

Cordelia-Aurora's voice, snippy and officious, explained that she was calling at this time of the morning because she was just *soooo* shockingly busy all the time and it was the only scrap of the day when she could ever make personal calls. She said the word 'personal' as if it was a dirty word.

'Apologies for the late notice, but I'm having an anniversary party for Evan at my house on Saturday afternoon. Tomorrow. How time flies! It's just the family and a few close friends, canapés and drinks on the deck – I was sure I'd invited you but it must have slipped through the cracks. I really should have got my secretary to do it. I've just been so snowed under with the Willisteen case, you've read about that I'm sure, it's been all over the papers lately – or maybe you haven't, I'm not sure what you read these days, we hardly ever see you or the boys any more – oh, and of course the boys are invited too. Anyway, I must rush, my personal trainer has just arrived and I need him to set me up for a great day in court. First drinks at two pm sharp, see you there, and don't bring a thing.'

Krystal's anger was swift.

. . . the boys are invited too . . .

Like a cocktail party would be fun for two children under the age of six. Could Ms Cordelia-Aurora Arthur pause for just a moment to reconsider the word *party*? Holy shit, the woman was from another planet. How on earth was Krystal supposed to explain to the boys the idea of a party for the anniversary of their father's death?

Then, with shock so great she had to put her mug down onto the bench, she wondered – would the boys even really care?

Jasper would, on some level, probably. But could a five-year-old actually remember anything from his life at age three? A set of three black-framed photos of Evan with Krystal and the boys hung along the hallway, placed deliberately low to encourage the boys to look at them, but high enough that they couldn't pull them from the hooks. Jasper knew who his father was, visually at least. And she told him stories about Evan, like the time when he spent fifteen hours putting together the flat-pack chest of drawers that was now in Jasper's room, all because he wanted to say he had built his son something. Or the way he would hold Jasper up over his head and fly him through the air, making him laugh and laugh, and one day he did it for so long that Jasper vomited all over Evan's head. Or the time when Jasper had a terrible fever and Evan had lain on the couch – that one right over there with the red wine stain – with his son on his chest, and Jasper had fallen asleep there, and Evan didn't move a muscle for two hours so Jasper could finally get some rest.

But did Jasper really remember his dad, or just the stories Krystal told?

And as for Olly . . . he'd been only one when Evan died. There definitely wouldn't be any memories there. Sense memories, maybe. Totally unconscious things, like the smell of his dad's skin. Or the way his little hand fitted inside Evan's. Maybe the sound of Evan's voice was stored somewhere deep inside Olly's brain. Perhaps one day in the future Olly would hear or smell something that evoked these traces of his dad, and he would feel a rush of warmth in his chest, and it would make him smile, but he would be completely oblivious as to why. It would be almost as though Evan's ghost had paid him a visit. Maybe that was what people experienced when they thought they felt the presence of a ghost. Maybe it was just their cells remembering something they didn't consciously recall, so they said it must be a spirit when all the while it was an electrical impulse deep in their subconscious.

But she couldn't explain this 'party' to the boys. A party to them meant cake, funny hats and Pass the Parcel. Candles to blow out. A celebration! This was not somehing to celebrate.

It's not a PARTY!

Her sister-in-law had no friends with children as far as Krystal knew. This would be an excruciating, stand-up, snobbish affair and the kids wouldn't be allowed to touch anything and would be bored stiff and complaining, and somehow Krystal would end up feeling like the one who was in the wrong and having to apologise, when it was her husband who'd died and left her all alone with two tiny children.

The last thing she wanted to do was go to that . . . event. But the problem was that her own mother and sister weren't in her life. For better or worse, Evan's family were the only family the boys had other than Krystal, and the only connection to Evan they had left. Except for Gabriella.

Roxy had advised Krystal to go to the cafe, ask to speak to Gabriella, and tell her calmly and honestly that she believed Gabriella had Evan's heart. 'Just keep it simple and remember to breathe,' her friend had said.

Krystal took a deep breath now. *Just keep breathing.*

She checked the time – still not even five o'clock. The boys would be up in an hour. She went to their room to make sure they were under the covers. As usual, Olly was sprawled horizontally across the bed, his zoo-animal-themed doona long since kicked off. She crept in and gently pulled up the cover to lay over him. He stirred a little and she froze, not wanting him to wake up. When he stopped squirming, she turned to Jasper, who was on his back, arms up by his head, also lacking his doona, which was adorned with Spider-Man, naturally. She pulled up his bedcovers too, then tiptoed out of the room. It was true what they said, that you always loved your kids a little bit more when they were asleep.

She decided to do some work while she waited for them to get up. Well, it wasn't really work so much as a hobby, but it gave her somewhere to focus her excess energy. She set up her laptop at the dining table and opened her music list, put her earbuds in and started playing Kelly Clarkson's song 'Stronger'. What doesn't kill you makes you stronger, the saying went. Kelly sang about it. Social media was full of it. People had repeated it to her often – strangers, workmates, anyone with an opinion on her heart's devastation.

Two years today.

She missed Evan's laugh, wanted to go back in time and record it on her phone so she could hear it now. They'd often recorded the children's voices when they were little, just learning to talk, giggling wildly or singing tunelessly in the back seat of the car. But never each other's. It had always been about capturing the moments of their children's lives, those precious, spectacular moments that they knew would only come once. The moments were fleeting, and their hearts ached with the beauty of this unique, irreplaceable instance and the sadness of its passing.

Motherhood, Krystal had quickly learned, was all about grief, over and over in tiny nicks and stabs. *Death by paper cuts*, Evan had said once. From the moment the babies left her body, it had been a parallel journey of joy and loss as they grew out of the triple-zero Bonds suits, as they began to lose their downy baby hair and grew toddler hair, as they got too heavy to hold in one arm, started eating solids, began to talk. They learned to crawl, and they crawled away. They began to talk, and the gurgles were gone. All these tiny pinpricks of sadness every day. The only consolation was that each loss meant the development of something new to enjoy.

She'd never foreseen the loss of her husband, or how she might find her own way forward in the aftermath. No bleeding paper cuts; just one gaping, gushing wound that would never heal.

These days she wrote to try to redirect the flow. She wasn't a proper writer, and this wasn't a proper job. At Jasper's school, where she worked three days a week, in that air-conditioned office with the fluorescent lights above her and the endless stream of children and parents and delivery drivers that came to the counter – as well as the odd police officer, which always added a good deal of interest and whispered conversation in the tearoom – and the ringing phones and the repetitive blips from the computer that announced the arrival of another email, *that* was where she did her real work. Honest, boring, grunt work. The kind of work people like her did. Not the kind of fancy-schmancy careers that Evan's family and friends had.

Janice was the full-time office administrator, and she gripped her authority tightly with her fake nails. There was another part-time assistant, Margie, and their days crossed over on Wednesdays. Krystal had started to enjoy midweek. Margie was a bubble of light and Krystal found herself drawn to her like a moth.

But on other days she wrote, if she could call it that. It wasn't like she wrote novels, or even short stories. Her word count was small. Sometimes just fifty words. Sometimes fewer. By utter chance, she'd landed herself a job writing for Millie May Cards, an electronic greeting card company, the kind that created small animated movies that people sent via email these days.

It had started simply because she had so much grief and so few people to talk to. She began writing letters to Evan. Long letters full of things that hadn't been said and should have been, or telling him what the kids had been up to, the funny things they did. Sometimes it was hardest to bear the good times, knowing she couldn't share them with Evan. Who else would have appreciated the combined humour and frustration of Olly's 'flour angel' phase, when he took flour or cocoa powder or sugar from the cupboard when Krystal wasn't looking and poured it on the floor, lay down on his back and scissored his legs and moved his arms up and down to make the most precious piece of art right there in the kitchen?

Many mums would be horrified, or angry. Sometimes she thought of those mothers who would have yelled at their small child, hit them, called them names or sent them to their rooms, and she just cried and cried. Couldn't they see it was a magical moment, one they would ache to have back if something happened to take their child away? They'd beg and plead and bargain with the world to have their child back tipping flour on the floor. Only Evan would have enjoyed Olly's art as much as Krystal did. So, she wrote to him, everything pouring out.

Sometimes she was angry with Evan too, more often early on, when the questions surrounding his death seemed the key to reversing time. If she could just figure out why he was in Sydney that night, alone, without having shared a word of his plans with anyone, if she could just solve that puzzle then she would know how she could have stopped him going, how she could have prevented this whole awful thing.

She wrote to him, asking him. He never responded, though she had dreams that he came to their home in the middle of the night and wrote answers across her notebook in his spiky handwriting, telling her what had made him do what he did, unravelling the mystery. But she could never read the pages in her dream. They blurred before her eyes as she tried to make out the words. Worse yet, sometimes the blue ink changed to purple and then red. Blood red. It ran off the page like his blood dripping onto the carpet, staining it forever, forcing her to walk over his blood every day on her way to the kitchen for a cup of tea or to make the kids' meals, forcing them to eat their fish fingers surrounded by the evidence of his demise.

Then, on the first anniversary of Evan's death, a distant cousin had sent her an electronic greeting card to say she was thinking of her. There was fine print right at the end of the little movie – something involving a pond and lilies and the setting sun. *Want to write for Millie May Cards?* it asked. Some sort of advertisement in exchange for a free card, she assumed.

She clicked on the link. She read the submission guidelines. It was simple to do. Name, address, email, PayPal account details and her written content. If her piece was accepted, she would receive twenty-five US dollars in her account. Almost out of defiance, she copied and pasted a chunk of her emotional outpouring to Evan.

Two weeks later she received an email from Millie May head office and the money appeared in her account. She laughed, thinking it was absurd. Then she submitted more, and the same thing happened. Naturally, she specialised in grief, loss and remembrance.

Today, though, she was lost for words. She must have sat there for nearly an hour, with nothing to show for it. Jasper got up first, and Olly was not far behind. Right, it was time to get ready to go. She made them scrambled eggs for breakfast, wanting something substantial in their bellies before they made their way over to The Tin Man to see Gabriella.

But then Jasper said he felt sick. Then Olly said he felt sick. Then Jasper vomited. Then Olly vomited. They must have picked up some sort of bug.

All her hopes and plans for the day were ruined.

7

'Harvey, you can't leave marinated chicken unattended or it will burn,' Pippa snapped.

'It's called chargrilled,' Harvey replied wearily, sipping from his glass of red wine and ignoring the flames that licked at the sweet-and-sour sauce. 'It's an actual thing, you know.'

Pippa all but growled in exasperation and turned to head back inside Monty's house.

Gabby braced against the strain of tension between them. Roughly twenty years of marriage had withered down to this. Their kids had taken to looking at the ground, anywhere other than at their parents chipping away at each other.

Monty came to the aid of the chicken then, snatching the tongs from the side of the grill and turning the kebabs over. Gabby shared a knowing look with him. Her father's cheeks were flushed; he always hated public displays of disharmony. Her parents had seemed to be unfailingly kind to each other. She wondered if they'd really, truly been happy all the time or if they'd just been better at not letting the cracks show, and for Pippa's sake she wished Lottie were here to help her through this.

Pippa returned from inside the house holding a pavlova square the size of a small country, topped with strawberries and cream.

'That looks amazing,' Gabby said, glad to be able to change the focus.

'The antioxidants in the berries negate all the badness of the sugar,' Pippa said, laying it down on the outdoor dining table.

'I like your theory.'

'It works for me,' Pippa said, licking cream from her finger.

The sisters stood for a moment, surveying the backyard.

'Back to school on Monday,' Pippa said, sounding relieved.

'Yes, though the end of the holidays always makes me a bit sad,' Gabby said. 'There's so much less pressure in the house when we're not all slaves to timetables.'

'Is Summer coming back today?'

Gabby raised her eyebrows at Pippa in annoyance. 'She was due back this morning but Cam still hasn't shown. I texted him and he ignored me. I phoned and it went to voicemail.'

Pippa shook her head. 'Not good enough.'

'Not by half.'

Celia had set up the white linen teepee on the lawn and several of the younger children were crowded in there. Sally had her head poked in the door, with her tail wagging like a metronome outside.

Pippa's kids ranged from nine to fourteen years of age. If they had lived in the same neighbourhood they would have gone to the same schools as Gabby's kids. Gabby and Pippa had gone to Camberwell South Primary, which Celia attended now, and then to Camberwell High, where Summer and Charlie were.

Camberwell was spoiled for choice for amazing private schools, but Monty and Lottie had always argued that state schools were just as good, that you already paid for them in your taxes, and you saved boatloads of money over thirteen years. Pippa's kids were also enrolled in state schools, over in Ringwood.

Tori, Pippa's second youngest, affectionately wrapped her arms around Gabby's waist. 'Happy translation day,' she said.

'Transplant day,' Pippa corrected.

'Transplant day,' Tori tried again, then pointed to the huge red, glittery heart on the front of her T-shirt. 'I wore this for you.'

'I love it,' Gabby said and kissed the top of her niece's head before she skipped away. Then she turned back to her sister. 'You look amazing, by the way.' Pippa smiled secretively, her eyes bright and eager. 'In fact, you're positively glowing. You look like . . . you're in love.'

Pippa giggled and touched her hair, checking the position of her hairclip. She was wearing another apron dress today, this one forest green, over a long-sleeved white tee and black tights. 'I *am* in love,' she whispered, leaning in towards Gabby. 'I have a new man, remember?'

'Harvey still doesn't know?'

Pippa shook her head, frowned and mouthed, *No!*

Their hungry children were getting noisier by the minute and a flurry of activity followed. Children running on the lawn. The two eldest boys taking over the barbecuing when Monty's thick spectacles got too clouded with steam. The three youngest girls crawling in and out of the teepee. Felix – twelve, and the quietest of them all – sitting down on the grass to play with Sally, who rolled onto her back to beg for belly rubs. Monty discussing a new app Harvey was co-creating for the health fund he worked for. Pippa sorting out the salads.

Gabby soaked it up. This life, it wasn't perfect. Cam should have brought Summer over by now. Her mother was gone. Gabby was two years post transplant and the reality was that time was against her – the dog would probably outlive her. And Pippa and Harvey's marriage was falling apart. But today of all days, she was grateful to have hers at all. Where there was life, there was still hope.

The sun began to lower in the sky, people reached for jackets and Gabby brought out a mohair rug for Monty's lap. He momentarily looked as though he might wave her away, but then she gave him the stern eye and he nodded and allowed her to lay it across him, tucking it around his ribs. The chargrilled feast had been devoured, along with the entire island of pavlova. The six kids had disappeared inside – Summer *still* wasn't here – their activities carrying them to different parts of the house.

The oldest boys were holed up in Charlie's room doing whatever it was their generation did on their phones. Not that Gabby was too concerned; Charlie's best mates were also studious and level-headed. They were different from other kids Gabby saw at the school, not loud and pushy like so many of the footballers, or foul-mouthed and jittery like the basketballers who sat on the brick wall at the school gates. She kept thinking that girls would pop up on his radar at any moment, but thankfully not yet. He was self-possessed – her illness had forced him to grow up quickly – and she needed to trust him.

In the middle of the outdoor table was a huge vase filled with the most gorgeous, exquisitely fragrant white lilies. They were a gift from Monty, who'd signed the card from *Mum and Dad*, which had made Gabby cry with longing for her mother. The scent moved around them, coming and going like a silk scarf dancing on the breeze. Gabby had all but given up alcohol after her surgery in an effort to keep her new heart healthy, but today she held a rare glass of bubbles and sipped slowly, savouring the taste, silently identifying the flavours of woods and berries.

Thank you.

She'd lost count of how many times she'd said it today.

Thank you to my donor, thank you to my donor's family, thank you to science, thank you to the doctors and nurses, thank you to the incredible luck of the draw that granted me more years here with my beautiful family.

Thank you to *him*. She'd always felt her donor was a man.

She'd written to her donor's family almost two years ago, as each recipient was encouraged to do. She'd been extra lucky in that she'd been permitted out of hospital just two weeks after the operation. Another member of her transplant support group had been in hospital for three months, with several serious bouts of rejection, and kidney failure too. She said the setbacks had affected her mental health so badly, with no fresh air or sunshine, endless noise, no privacy or independence of any kind, that if she'd known how awful it would be she wouldn't have gone ahead with the surgery at all. She would have chosen to die. But Gabby's surgery had gone well and all indications were that her body had accepted this foreign entity as its own, with not a single episode of rejection. She'd got off lightly indeed.

Her surgeon was George Thanos, a man she had been relieved to observe had woolly tufts above his ears that were decidedly greying, indicating a lot of experience under his belt. She didn't think she could have been so optimistic if the surgeon had been younger than she was. George was shorter than Gabby and wore glasses, the one thing that made her slightly nervous about him – could he see everything properly? Not that she had much choice, of course; it was either George or die. She chose George.

George had seen her soon after the surgery, maybe even the next day, though the early days in ICU were a little hazy. But he'd stood next to her and smiled. She remembered that because it was a big, confident, winning smile, one that told her they'd done well.

'It's a great-looking heart you've got yourself in there,' he said, raising his eyebrows and grinning with glee as if they'd got away with something akin to a casino heist. 'Very good. It went in nicely. If I was a betting man, I'd wager my house that you and that heart will have a long and happy life together.'

'How do you know?' she'd croaked, her voice still raspy from the breathing tube that had been down her throat while she was under the anaesthetic.

He'd opened his mouth as if to speak with well-worn authority, then paused. 'Do you garden?' he asked.

'What?' She was highly medicated and rather confused.

'Have you ever gardened? Roses? Vegetables?'

'Oh.' She'd had to pull her mind back to the days before the virus, back to when she'd been able to breathe properly and been active. 'Yes, a bit. Flowers and herbs mostly.'

He nodded. 'Then you know that feeling you get when you're planting a seedling and it goes in just right? It's like the roots have taken before you've even finished covering it with soil. It looks strong and vital and you know when you go out to water it the next day it will probably have grown a new shoot overnight. Do you know what I mean?'

'Yes, I do.' She'd had that experience and she'd had the opposite too, when a seedling just didn't come out of the container cleanly, she'd felt the roots break away and seen the little plant droop almost immediately, and no matter how carefully she built it up with soil and watered it she'd known it had simply lost the will to live and wouldn't make it.

George's eyes glinted behind his glasses. 'They don't call it a trans*plant* for nothing.' He patted her arm. 'You're going to be just fine.'

Writing the letter to her donor's family had been incredibly difficult. Nothing sounded good enough. She couldn't possibly express the depth of her gratitude or the sadness she felt for their own loss, or the empathy for how emotional a decision it must have been for them.

She felt guilty in so many ways: for living when their loved one was dead, for not being able to make the words on the page say what she wanted them to say, for eating a chocolate muffin (was that *really* taking care of her heart as she'd mentally promised them?), and most of all for truly not knowing whether, if the situation had been reversed, if it had been *her* child lying in that bed on life support, with no chance of recovery, that she could have made the same choice to donate.

Somehow, after dozens of attempts, and consultation with Pippa and her parents, she'd got something down on the page. Less was more, they all agreed.

'Keep it simple,' Pippa kept saying, slashing through words with a glittery green pen.

'Tell them about your children,' her father had advised from the corner of the lounge room, the financial pages of the paper open in front of him.

'I can't,' Gabby said. 'No personal details are allowed.'

Monty had flicked his paper to the side to gaze over his reading glasses at her. 'Not even that you *are* a mother?'

'Nope,' Gabby sighed.

'That's ridiculous. What family wouldn't want to know that their donation had saved a mother's life for her three young children?' he grumped.

'But what if the donor had been a young woman too?' Pippa chimed in. 'What if she'd been a mother herself? That actually might make them feel rather shitty, that Gabby is here and their daughter or mother or wife isn't. Sorry, Gab.'

'Well, what's left to say?' Lottie had said. 'I'm sorry for your loss, and thanks for the heart.'

Sally had come and leaned her body against Gabby's legs at that moment and Gabby had realised – as had her sister and parents – that this conversation was causing her stress. The golden retriever's presence was a large, visual indication that Gabby's heart rate and cortisol levels had risen. Everyone backed off immediately. Gabby took a deep breath and stroked Sally's ears.

Pippa was probably right – the shorter the better. Besides, the hospital would edit it and remove anything that might give away any personal details.

Four months after the operation, it was done.

Aside from my unending gratitude, the only thing I have to offer you in return is this: that I will look after my new heart with the care that it deserves, and together I hope we will live a long and healthy life.

'So, Gabby,' Harvey said from across the table, his humour having been improved by a few glasses of wine. 'How are you feeling about your transplant today?' She was surprised: it was unlike Harvey to raise potentially emotional topics. Monty and Pippa turned to Gabby to wait for her answer.

'I feel bloody lucky.'

'As do we,' Monty said, raising his glass. 'To Gabby.'

'To Gabby,' echoed Pippa and Harvey.

'Hello?'

Gabby looked up to see Summer standing at the back door of the house. She was wearing jeans and a light grey jumper, her blonde hair pulled back into a long ponytail and shimmering like something from a shampoo commercial.

'Sweetheart!' Gabby pushed back her chair and went to hug her. 'How are you feeling?'

'All good. Twenty-four hours since the last symptom,' she assured Gabby.

Gabby squeezed her again. 'I'm so glad you're home.'

'Hi, everyone,' Summer said, waving at the others, who all welcomed her warmly. Then she turned back to Gabby. 'Dad's still outside. He wants to see you.'

'Okay, sure,' Gabby said lightly, while inwardly thinking, *I bloody well want to see him too!*

She walked through the house and stepped out the front door. The gardens were always cared for and the lawn always mown, her father disciplined in maintaining its appearance, though the narrow concrete footpath from the road to the front door was decades old, narrow and greyed with age.

She found Cam out in the street, sitting in his beaten-up blue sedan. He'd run into a pole in a supermarket a couple of years ago and had never fixed the long scrape down the passenger side. She went to the driver's window.

'Hi,' she said, restraining herself from launching straight into him.

'Hi.' He was unshaven, and his T-shirt had a stain of some sort on it. Baby sick, maybe. He looked down at the dashboard and picked at something Gabby couldn't see.

'What happened? Why are you back so late? I've been worried.'

'Stuff, you know, baby stuff. I just couldn't get out the door before now.'

'That's not good enough,' she said, firmly.

He ignored that. 'Can I leave the kids with you for a month?' he said, in a tone that suggested it wasn't actually a question as much as a foregone conclusion.

'What? Why? What's happening?'

'It's back to school this week –'

'Yes, I know. We have three children in school,' she said, barely even trying to control her derision.

'– and I've just got lots on.'

'You've got lots on?' She was almost lost for words. Since when did that make a difference? *She* had lots on too. Everyone had lots on. That was *life*. When Cam didn't respond, she challenged him head on. 'Being busy isn't an excuse for not being a parent, Cam.'

'Don't be like that. When have I ever asked for time off?'

Her head spun. On the one hand, it was true, he'd never tried to get out of an entire fortnight. A weekend, or a day here and there, sure. He'd been late many times and had skipped extracurricular activities. But on the other hand . . .

'*Time off*? It's not a job. They're your children. You don't get "time off". Everyone knows that! That's the deal you make when you have kids. They come first.'

'Well, stuff changes,' he said lamely, shrugging like a teenager.

'What stuff?' She glared at him through the open window but he wouldn't meet her eye.

He sighed and then groaned. 'You know how hard this has been for us since Mykahla arrived.'

Us? Her hackles rose. Was this coming from Meri? And if it was, why would Cam be so weak as to let her dictate his relationship with his three older children?

'What is it that you are saying, exactly? Please be specific.' There was a long pause while she waited with a hand on her hip and her eyebrows arched.

'I need a break from the kids.'

He may as well have slapped her.

'I love them, you know that,' he went on quickly. 'But I'm just not coping.'

She moved her hand to her forehead and tried to ignore the panic that was tumbling through her. 'Are you smoking again?'

'No!' He turned to glare at her then, his chin raised defensively.

She didn't believe him. Cam wasn't perfect but this was definitely out of character for him, and she knew all too well that odd behaviour from Cam went hand in hand with marijuana use, one of the biggest contributing factors to their break-up. 'Well, you don't get to have a break from your children,' she said through gritted teeth. 'End of story.'

'I have to go,' he said baldly, and turned the key in the ignition. He pulled away from the kerb, leaving Gabby to jump out of the way of the wheels. In the two years since her operation she hadn't had one episode of rejection, but today rejection had found her and her kids anyway.

Gabby lay alone in bed, awake in the dark, staring at the ceiling, wondering if yet another vision or dream would come to her tonight, wondering how frightening it would be, how awful. Would something new happen? Something that might add more information to the scene that kept playing out? Her pretty, French provincial-style room – she and Pippa shared a taste in decor – should have been a sanctuary, but now the nights made her anxious, worrying about what was to come.

Instead of waiting for it, she flung off the duck-egg blue and white bedspread and opened the drawer of her bedside table. Inside, curled at the back, was a stethoscope. She hadn't felt the need to use it for a long time. When she'd first come home from hospital, she would fall asleep every night listening to this new heart beating inside her, willing it to keep going, to keep her alive. Some of the nurses told her to speak to the heart, to send it good wishes and welcome it into her body, to help make it feel at home and lessen her body's fight against it – ultimately, to lessen the chance of rejection.

Rejection. The word they all feared most.

She snuggled back under her doona, placed the earpieces in her ears and lay the chestpiece over her heart.

Lub-dub . . . lub-dub . . . lub-dub.

There it was, beating away, pumping her blood, keeping her alive. Someone else's heart. A heart full of nerve cells that had lived inside another human being from not long after conception to their time of death. A heart that might have travelled the world. Fallen in love. Been betrayed. Been educated. Indulged. Danced. Lied. Cheated. Gambled. Recovered. Swum in foreign oceans. Rock climbed. Painted. Loved horror movies. Craved friendships. Felt, seen or experienced a million things that Gabby never had.

'Who are you?' she whispered, closing her eyes.

Lub-dub . . . lub-dub . . . lub-dub.

'I'm listening, if you want to talk,' she said, this time feeling more than a touch foolish, but needing to tell him that she was open to what he had to say. He'd been trying to get her attention, after all. He wanted to share something with her; he wanted her to listen. On this day, even more than any other, she owed him that at least.

Lub-dub . . . lub-dub . . . lub-dub.

The room began to spin.

His heart rate increased. *Lub-dub lub-dub lub-dublubdublubdub.*

Fear sizzled.

Her first reaction was to pull back, to make it stop, but she knew she had to find out what was on the other side. It was her duty to listen. She squeezed her eyes shut, holding the stethoscope to her chest despite the rapid rise and fall in her breathing, despite every instinct that told her to push it all away.

She was running. It was the same cold, dark street she'd seen before. Night-time. Her feet stung as they hit the ground. Her breath rasped in and out, the air painfully cold.

Gabby wrenched the stethoscope away, sweat beading across her forehead, her rapid breaths dizzying, on the verge of hyper-ventilation.

Sally was at the door again, scratching and whining. Gabby jumped out of bed and let the dog in, calling her up on the bed, pulling her body against her own, holding her tightly while her heart rate and breathing slowed and then returned to normal. She stroked Sally's soft fur, then spooned with the retriever for the rest of the night.

8

The only way Krystal was going to make it through Cordelia-Aurora's offensive celebration of Evan's passing was to have a drink before she went. The boys appeared to have finished vomiting – some kind of twenty-four-hour thing – though if they managed to vomit over Cordelia-Aurora's Italian leather couch, Krystal didn't think it would necessarily be such a bad thing. She poured a shot of vodka into her glass of orange juice, a trick she'd learned from her mother, and something she tried now to pretend she wasn't replicating. But this was an emergency.

Roxy texted.

> Thinking of you today, having
> to go to that awful party. x
>
> Thanks.

Krystal sipped her drink, thinking how lucky she was to have Roxy. With her mother out of the picture, Krystal might have been able to rely on her sister, but Liesel had moved as far away from their mother as she could, taking up residence in Norway more than ten years ago. Liesel had emailed, offering condolences, but the last time the sisters had talked on the phone was at the start of the year. As for her father, he was a serial cheater who had ruined his wife's and daughters' belief in men, all of which made Evan's deceptions on that final night that much worse.

> Good luck. I'm here if you
> need me. x

Krystal gulped down the rest of her laced juice while the boys were distracted by the television, ignoring the voice telling her she was no better than her mother and should be ashamed of herself. 'Don't worry, I am,' she replied to the voice. But it wasn't as if she was an alcoholic; she was just trying to get through this awful day. And it was only one drink. She could still legally drive.

When they were young, Liesel had named Carol's phases of sobriety 'blooms' because, just like lovely flowers, they would burst into colour and vibrancy and bring joy to everyone around them. When their mother was blooming, the sisters were treated to glorious times that involved baking, packed lunches, clean clothes and arriving at school on time.

But the blooms didn't last. Inevitably they withered, browned, died and rotted. Without warning, the girls were alone again, fending for themselves.

That was why she was taking the boys to Cordelia-Aurora's stupid party. For better or worse, she and the Arthurs were all the family her children had left. If anything ever happened to Krystal and her kids were orphaned – something that once upon a time she'd never have believed possible but now knew otherwise – well, at least the Arthur family was sober. At least the kids wouldn't end up in foster care. If a minimum standard of care was the only option, the boys would be better off with the wealthy, snooty family of their father than with strangers. She hoped.

'Krystal, come in,' Cordelia-Aurora purred, opening the door wide. 'Hello, boys!'

Krystal took a moment to take in her sister-in-law's appearance. With her near-black hair rapidly greying – something the forty-year-old welcomed, as she felt it gave her more gravitas in the courtroom – her sharp cheekbones, wide jaw and heavily drawn-on eyebrows, the woman never failed to remind Krystal of Cruella de Vil. Adding to the impression, it wasn't unusual for her to be draped in coats and wraps, some with faux-fur trims; at least, Krystal *assumed* they were faux fur. She wouldn't have been entirely surprised if Cordelia-Aurora turned out to be the owner of a fur farm.

'Hi, Aunty Cordy,' Jasper said, clasping his Superman figurine to his chest. At his informal use of her name, Cordelia-Aurora stiffened noticeably and the fake smile on her face faltered.

'Say hello,' Krystal prompted Olly, who was holding her hand tightly and leaning into her leg.

'Hello,' he all but whispered.

Behind Cordelia-Aurora, people gathered in tight groups and classical music played from an invisible source.

Cordelia-Aurora lived on the forty-fifth floor of one of those appalling, snobby central Melbourne towers, with a depressing colour scheme that Krystal thought would have suited a prison – lots of greys, black and browns, nothing that could offer interest of any kind. It was the sort of apartment block that had a full-time concierge, a gymnasium, a heated swimming pool and a rooftop bar overlooking the city. It might have impressed Krystal, just a little, if it had views over the city centre, or over the botanic gardens and the river, but Cordelia-Aurora had lucked out and taken a south-facing apartment with views over bland grids of buildings sprawling out towards Port Phillip Bay. Either Cordelia-Aurora couldn't afford the apartments with the truly great views, or she had simply missed out and not got the best – both possibilities made Krystal a teensy bit happy, she was somewhat ashamed to admit.

Inside the apartment, the decor was just as bad – silver-framed black-and-white sketches and bland furnishings, all in nothing colours that expressed zilch about the person who lived there. Photos on the wall? No. Brightly coloured cushions? No. The odd smiling Buddha or even a smidge of green in a miniature bamboo plant? Nope. Krystal was certain that one day, stylists would look back on this decade's tastes and cringe at the depressing awfulness – *Abandon all hope ye who enter here!* – just as everyone now cringed at the oranges and browns of the 1970s. She imagined psychologists might probably blame the stark minimalism of the era for inducing crazed gunmen to commit mass killings.

They followed Cordelia-Aurora into the apartment and the door closed behind them with barely a whisper – there'd be no being woken up in the night by the neighbour's front door *thunk*-ing loudly into place and the chain being latched. There was no need for safety chains here. To the left, the sleek kitchen was bustling with caterers dressed in black waistcoats over long-sleeved white shirts, the women with their hair tightly pulled back into tiny buns. Krystal smiled at them, feeling more at home in their corner of the world than she would with anyone else here. But the caterers merely nodded solemnly at her and busied their hands. The dining table was set up as a bar, with a young bartender behind rows of silver ice buckets and shiny glasses, poised to take Krystal's order.

There was a young, stylishly dressed woman seated on the couch, feeding a bottle of formula to a baby in her arms. Krystal felt great relief; at least one other person in this room might talk to her, if only because they had children in common. But the woman didn't return her smile.

'Everyone's already here,' Cordelia-Aurora said. Krystal wasn't sure if she was imagining the implied criticism that she was late. 'Mum and Dad are out on the balcony, the waiters will bring around food and you simply ask for whatever you like at the bar and Malcolm here will help you,' she said, motioning to *the help* with a wave of her hand.

Just when Krystal was wondering how long she actually needed to continue talking to Cordelia-Aurora, her sister-in-law left her, heading back to the balcony where the majority of guests were clustered, teetering in high heels or swathed in Armani suits, emitting an occasional burst of pretentious laughter. Coming back through the doors as Cordelia-Aurora left was Evan's brother. He caught sight of Krystal and came over immediately.

'Krystal, lovely to see you,' Rupert said, striding to her and kissing her on the cheek. Oh, the sight of him – he looked so much like Evan. She was momentarily speechless. 'How are you?' he asked. He even sounded like Evan.

'Yes, fine, thank you,' she said, remembering to say *fine* and not *good* and *thank you* instead of *thanks*, then was annoyed at herself for trying to be anything other than her real self. Her stomach was a mound of knots and all she wanted to do was flee, but she was determined to play nice today, maybe exceed nice and land on congenial, for the sake of her boys.

'Hello, lads,' Rupert said, bending down to hold out his hand for them to shake. They both stared mutely at him.

'How about a high five for Uncle Rupert?' Krystal said, smiling at the boys to encourage them to go along with it.

Jasper suddenly grinned and jumped to slap at Rupert's hand. Rupert feigned injury. 'Wow! You're stronger than Superman,' he said, pointing to the figurine in Jasper's hand.

'No one's stronger than Superman,' Jasper said, shaking his head as though Rupert must be dense. 'That's why he's *Super*man.'

'Good point,' Rupert conceded. 'You'll make a good lawyer one day.'

Krystal stiffened at the implication that her boys would go into the Arthur family business, rather than perhaps the hospitality industry that their father had enjoyed so much more, but told herself to let it go. Jasper didn't know what a lawyer was and had lost interest anyway, wandering over to a waiter who was bending down to his height, holding out a plate of some kind of fancy-looking prawns on spoons.

'Now, how about you, Oliver?' Rupert said, holding up his hand again. Krystal managed to stop herself rolling her eyes in exasperation that Evan's family insisted on calling her younger son *Oliver* even though he'd been nothing but Olly since the moment he was born. But Olly just clung silently to her leg, staring at Rupert, a tall man in a charcoal-coloured business suit with a glinting silver watch that Krystal suspected cost more than her car.

'This weekend must be awful for you,' Rupert said to Krystal, pressing his lips together just as Evan would do.

She swallowed hard. 'It's not much fun.'

'No,' he agreed.

'Nor for you, I imagine,' she said, acknowledging a moment too late that Evan's family – as much as she disliked them – had lost a loved one too.

Rupert shrugged, noncommittal. 'Come and have a drink.' He motioned towards the temporary bar. 'You'll need one to face all of them out there.' He flicked his eyes towards the balcony.

Krystal laughed. Had Rupert always been this nice?

'Cabernet merlot, please,' she said to the barman.

'Same here,' Rupert added.

Krystal realised that Olly had detached himself and gone off after his brother. They were meandering through dry-cleaned trouser legs, following waiters like dogs sniffing out food.

She turned to look at Rupert, to ask him about work and make polite conversation, and that was when she noticed the gilt-framed black-and-white photograph of Evan perched on the corner of the dining table, a single tea-light candle flickering in front of it and a perfect white rose by its side. She froze. It was a shock to see his face. He was happy, relaxed, staring straight into the camera, the background blurred, though it looked like he was outdoors.

Krystal's eyes connected with her husband's and she stopped breathing, for how long she couldn't say. But then oxygen flowed again, and following fast on the heels of the impact of seeing him was confusion, because this was a photo taken of Evan when he was younger. Much younger – before he met her.

'Here you go,' Rupert said, handing her the glass of red wine.

'What?' She snapped out of her daze. 'Oh, thanks,' she said, taking the glass.

Rupert turned to look where she'd been focused. He too stared at the photo for a moment. Some other guests came to the bar and Rupert took Krystal's arm and guided her gently out of the way, stepping them closer to the photo. Still he said nothing. Krystal was vaguely aware that the children must have located their grandparents, because she could hear Ivy's patrician voice making a fuss over the boys, telling them how tall and handsome they were, and Wyatt's deep, stern voice warning them not to go too close to the edge of the balcony.

'He was so happy then,' Rupert said.

'Happy?' she repeated.

'He'd won the Farner Seven case. It was huge. He'd been working on it for nearly two years.'

'Yes, I know,' she said, annoyed at his assumption that Evan hadn't shared with her this part of his life. Of course he'd told her about it. He had led the team of himself, Cordelia-Aurora and Wyatt for the defence of the giant chemical company Farner Seven, in a high-profile class action in which a community had tried to sue for damages, alleging that chemical contamination of their water supply had led to multiple cancers and other illnesses. But, Evan had told her, there was simply no proof that it was true. It wasn't a popular outcome – everyone wanted the battlers to win over the giants – but the lawyer's job was to ensure the right legal conclusion was reached. She knew he'd felt sympathy for the sick people, but the case had also garnered the Arthur family empire legendary status in the legal world. They were now top-tier corporate defence lawyers.

Despite the victory, it had also been the end of Evan's legal career. He'd not enjoyed helping the giant company succeed and it had seriously damaged his relationship with Cordelia-Aurora. They'd fought the whole way through, he'd told Krystal. At the end, he wanted nothing more to do with the family firm.

It was also a time when he was engaged to another woman, someone with the sort of breeding and education and snootiness Krystal would expect to find here today. Evan had told her he'd wanted out of the relationship for a long time, but the pressure of the Farner Seven case meant he simply couldn't afford any disruptions. Delaying the break-up wasn't something he was proud of, yet this was how his family wanted to remember him – as a successful barrister engaged to the right woman. It wasn't an accident they'd chosen to display that photo today.

They had no respect for the fact that he'd left their firm and decided to swim upstream and find his own way in life. Everything that came after the day that photo was taken – his bravery in leaving the family business, his leap of faith to follow his passion to be a sommelier, his love for Krystal and his two adored sons – didn't even rate a mention with them. It never would.

'He wasn't happy because he'd won that case,' she said, latent anger rising. A voice somewhere in her head told her to shut up, to just leave it alone and keep the peace, that she was here for the sake of her boys' future and whatever these people thought of her didn't matter any more. But it was too late, the dam had burst.

'What do you mean?' Rupert asked. His chin lifted just a touch, his shoulders setting.

'The reason he was so happy when the case ended was because he knew it was his last day of that life,' she hissed. The people who'd come to the bar for a drink were eavesdropping. She glared at them and they at least had the decency to stop staring at her, though she could tell they were still listening.

'He couldn't wait to get away from your family, to get out from under your father's thumb, to leave the beautiful but emotionally spineless woman your mother had set him up with, to stop working in a career that was breaking him down.'

'What is going on?' Cordelia-Aurora was at Rupert's side, speaking quietly but firmly, her jaw set and her eyes boring into Krystal's.

'Oh, don't even try to pretend you didn't know what you were doing with this photo,' Krystal countered, waving her hand and slopping red wine onto the grey carpet. There was a collective shocked intake of breath.

'I don't know what you're talking about. Are you drunk?' Cordelia-Aurora said, loudly enough to make sure everyone within earshot could hear.

Rupert took the glass from Krystal and placed it on the table, near Evan's photo.

'You'd like to just wipe me from history, wouldn't you?' Krystal said.

'That's ridiculous. You're *here*, aren't you?'

'What on earth is the problem here?' Ivy hissed, arriving swiftly to impose her matriarchal power to hush up the inconvenience in the corner. The woman was a Barbara Walters lookalike, wearing a suitably mother-of-the-dead navy pantsuit and pearls.

'The problem is that you always wanted me gone,' Krystal growled at Cordelia-Aurora. 'You always thought Evan belonged to you and he couldn't possibly make any decisions for himself. *The problem* is that you forced me to sign those organ donation papers. You butchered him.'

Several eavesdroppers gasped at that. Ivy's hand rose to the pearls at her throat.

Then the boys were back at Krystal's side. 'Mummy, what's wrong?' Jasper asked. She took a breath and held it a second, willing herself to calm down. But the memory of that night was too much for her to handle, especially here, in the lion's den.

'You were there, Krystal,' Cordelia-Aurora said. 'You had the legal authority to sign those papers, no one else.'

'And you hated that, didn't you? Finally, I had power over Evan's future that your family couldn't touch and you just couldn't accept that, so you took advantage of me at my most desperate moment, my weakest, most vulnerable moment. You bullied me and coerced me into signing those papers even though you knew I didn't want to, knew that I was totally against it, because you couldn't possibly believe that I knew Evan better than you did.'

'That's enough.' Wyatt was in the fray now, tall, white-haired, big-nosed.

Cordelia-Aurora narrowed her eyes. 'Krystal, I am cautioning you to consider what you are saying *very* carefully. You are in a public space, in front of no fewer than ten lawyers. If you're not careful, you might find yourself being sued for defamation.'

'You'd love that, wouldn't you?' Krystal rolled her eyes at her sister-in-law, gathered her boys to her side and stalked from the apartment to the elevator. Jasper pushed the call button for her, then silently took her hand in his. Olly leaned against her leg as the softly lit capsule zoomed them down to the ground floor and away from the icy hell above.

9

The kids were back at school for the first day of the last term of the year and Gabby was still reeling from Cam's bombshell that he was taking a break from his children. She hadn't told them yet, not able to bear the thought of what it would do to them, instead firing off an angry text message to Cam this morning telling him he needed to deal with his drug habit and return to the world of functioning adulthood. He'd ignored that, of course, and it had only made her stroppier. To cheer herself up a little, she'd brought her big vase of perfumed lilies into the cafe, placing them on the counter where they drew endless comments of appreciation from customers, many of whom looked as though they could use a bit of cheering too as they kicked off a new work week. She'd also brought Sally in, wearing her special red coat that identified her as a service dog.

She moved to the room behind the glass wall, telling Sally she could lie down and have a nap beneath the cupping bench, and prepared herself for the session with Luciano, checking they had everything they needed. To join him in a cupping session was really laying her professional cards on the table: she wanted to prove her abilities and gain his respect. She only hoped she'd be able to pull it off.

Next week, The Tin Man would start offering free cupping events to customers on Sunday mornings. It was a fantastic way to spread the word about the cafe, leading to ongoing media opportunities, and Pippa was working on a sharable poster for the sessions. Teaching consumers about coffee profiles and the differences in taste would strengthen their commitment to buying the high-quality products The Tin Man sold. Ultimately, it would drive interest, word-of-mouth, customers through the door, and sales.

The Tin Man sourced beans from El Salvador, Guatemala, Colombia, Ethiopia and India. From these, Luciano made three different blends, which Gabby had named following the *Wizard of Oz* theme – Moody Munchkins, Vanishing Wizards and Flying Monkeys. They also offered single-origin beans in-house for real enthusiasts to taste.

The Ethiopian and El Salvadoran beans were quite different and caused a lot of chatter at the counter, though generally customers preferred a blend over a single origin. There was nothing more dismaying than a customer who came in and decided to be brave or adventurous (or sometimes just pretentious), ordered a single-origin coffee, didn't understand the flavour profile, disliked it and walked away unhappy.

Luciano, looking his usual slightly rugged but handsome self – and today with a red-and-white neckerchief that added colour to his outfit – was helping Ed at present, a sudden rush of customers creating a long line of yellow order tickets. Gabby laid out three white cups on the wide multi-purpose wooden bench, her boots making small thuds as she moved about, her gypsy bells tinkling pleasantly. She was nervous. This was a chance for her to find a real connection with Luciano. Regular cupping was crucial for them to know the quality of the beans they had bought, and today Gabby could show him just how good she was at this.

'You ready?' Luciano came through the swing doors, casting his eye over the cups, the colourful poster of the coffee flavour wheel and the box of synthetic scent tubes. He smiled at Sally under the table, who thumped her tail on the floor in return.

'Almost. Just need the grounds.'

'I'll get them.' He ran three lots of beans through the grinder and returned with small plates holding pyramids of coffee. He hummed quietly, the most relaxed Gabby had seen him, and she quietly rejoiced at finally breaking through his barriers. He tipped a portion of grounds into each cup then pulled out his tatty notebook from the back pocket of his jeans. 'Let's do this.' His enthusiasm was contagious.

First, they assessed the dry matter, looking at the size of the grounds and their colour, with some nearly black and others the colour of treacle. Then they stood side by side at the bench, in front of the first of the three cups, and assumed the cupping position with their hands behind their backs. Luciano went first, bending at the waist, his nose over the cup, sniffing rapidly in and out like a dog, the standard way to inhale the aromas. Gabby followed, doing the same, feeling slightly silly as she always did. But when she closed her eyes, the aromas bloomed like fireworks through her nose and she could see them in her mind like colours. A smile broke over her lips.

It was working! She made some notes and they repeated the process for the next two cups. 'You did a great job with these,' she said. She carefully poured a small amount of just-boiled water into each white cup, over the grounds. They 'broke' the coffee – using spoons to push back and forth across the top of the cup. Then they 'cleaned' each cup, removing the froth and any floating bits, like skimming of the surface of soup.

'Let's start,' Luciano said. 'Ladies first.'

Gabby began at the first cup, using her spoon to lift small amounts of coffee to her lips and slurping it in as loudly as possible, to oxygenate the liquid and release more flavours. 'Mm, good,' she said. She continued onto the second and third cups, with Luciano following her, slurping each one. They each paused a moment to write notes, then started over with the first one. This time, with the coffee cooling, the flavours had developed just that little bit more. Gabby adjusted her notes for the second blend. Luciano did the same.

When Luciano had finished writing, Gabby spoke. 'Shall we share what we've written?'

'Ladies first,' he repeated, grinning.

He grinned!

'All right. I'll start with Moody Munchkins. This is a sweeter, darker roast with a strong brown-syrup flavour, with hazelnut and malt the predominant notes, but also accents of vanilla and even smoke.'

Luciano lifted his chin, seemingly surprised but also impressed. 'That's exactly what I wrote.' He handed over his notebook so she could check his inky writing.

She couldn't help but smile with satisfaction. Although she knew her nose was special, she'd still been anxious to show Luciano what she could do. 'Okay, let's look at Vanishing Wizards. This is a complex roast, one that has retained acidic, fruity attributes of cherries and peaches, but also warmer spice notes of cinnamon.'

Luciano ran his hand through his hair and rubbed the back of his head. 'Same,' he said. 'Though I also noted clove.'

'Clove?'

He shrugged, as if not wanting to appear to be challenging her too much.

Gabby slurped the blend once more, swishing it around her mouth, tasting again. 'I agree there's something else, but I would say it was anise.'

'Anise?' He went to the large, laminated flavour wheel on the table and studied the picture. Gabby went to the sensory profile kit and pulled out a tube of anise and a tube of clove. She handed them both to Luciano and he slurped more coffee, swallowed and opened first the tube of clove, waving it under his nose, then the tube of anise. He stilled. His eyes flicked to hers. 'You're right; it's anise.'

Gabby nodded silently, holding back her triumphant grin as much as she could, trying to be cool. 'They're very close. It's an easy mistake,' she said generously. 'Shall we look at the last?'

'Yes.' He replaced the tubes into the kit.

'Okay, Flying Monkeys is an exciting blend, I think, with definite floral notes of rose and jasmine, and a fresh apple chaser,' she said, thoroughly enjoying herself now.

Luciano just stared at her. 'Yes,' he said. 'You're right. You are one hundred per cent right. How did you . . . I mean, where did you learn . . .'

'Oh,' she said, vaguely. 'It's just a bit of a gift.'

He squinted at her as though trying to figure her out, and she suddenly felt self-conscious and vulnerable. This gift was a complicated thing and she wasn't sure she should share where it had come from.

'This has been great fun,' she said, carrying the cups to the sink to be washed.

'It has,' he agreed. 'I rarely come across someone who can match my cupping expertise.'

She turned away from the sink to face him.

'Or my arrogance,' he said, closing one eye, appalled at himself.

She laughed.

'Sorry, that made me sound like a right tool.'

'It's okay. You *are* gifted.' They stared at each other a moment and it was as though the ground beneath Gabby's feet shifted. This attraction to Luciano was problematic on many levels, yet the feelings brought with them fresh hope. Hope for a future she was almost too scared to consider.

'Well,' he said, 'I guess I better get back to work.' He moved towards a bag of the Flying Monkeys blend and lifted out a scoop of beans.

'Wait – I was thinking we should begin checking out some other cafes around the city. What are you doing for lunch?' She heard the words coming from her mouth but could hardly believe she'd uttered them. Still, she ploughed on. 'Can I shout you a bite to eat and a coffee somewhere?'

He paused, holding the scoop, and considered her a moment. 'Okay.'

'Great.'

'Do you like seafood?'

'If it's cooked, yes.'

'Have you been to Bar Carlo?' he asked, tipping the beans back into the bag.

'Not yet.'

A ten-minute cab ride got them there easily. Bar Carlo sat in Meyers Place, a somewhat dingy laneway of concrete, corrugated iron and roller doors, off Little Collins Street in the CBD. In contrast, the interior was dark but warm. Rustic charcoal-coloured wooden tables and soft lighting took the edge off the colour scheme of black, red and white. Living greenery softened the industrial edges of the space. They eased their way through patrons propped on stools at tables and at the bar, past rows of amber, orange and golden liqueurs illuminated behind the bartender, and found a seat at the back.

'Is this a favourite of yours?' she asked, studying the menu, which oozed Italian charm. She saw *cicchetti* – savoury snacks served on boards and plates – being delivered to others around them, and her mouth watered at the sight of the cured meats with crostini or bread rolls, figs, prosciutto, olives, cheeses and pastries.

'I love this city for its authentic Italian food,' he said, studying the chalkboard nearby. 'My mamma's face lights up whenever she connects with other Italians. I grew up spending a lot of time in these eateries.'

'Were you born in Melbourne?' she asked, putting her menu clipboard down.

He nodded. 'My parents migrated here with their parents after the war.'

'Have you been to Italy?'

'Many times. There is so much family there. You can't escape them,' he said, with a small, amused smile that said, *What can you do?* 'Everyone wants to show you the best of Italy.'

'Sounds wonderful,' she said, dreaming of sun-drenched valleys, Roman architecture and mountains of food, glorious food. 'I'd love to go.'

'You should,' he said. 'It's the birthplace of the Australian coffee scene.'

'Unfortunately, travel is more complicated for me than for most people. The potential for illness and so on.'

And just like that, reality hit. His face fell. 'Oh, of course.'

Silence lingered between them.

'How did you first get into roasting coffee?' she asked, changing the topic.

'Just one of those things, growing up with so many foodies around. One thing led to another. I was a barista first, then a friend decided to start a boutique roasting gig in his parents' backyard and I helped him out. He taught me the basics and I got hooked. I worked my way around, did a course, started attending conferences. It's very much a learn-on-the-job skill.'

'But there's real art in it,' she said. 'There is skill you can learn but then there's another level of something like intuition that comes into play.' She could see him soaking up her appreciation and his shoulders visibly relaxed.

'What about you? Who taught you to taste?' he said. 'That's quite a nose you've got there.'

'Surprised?'

'A little, to be honest. I guess I thought you were more of a businesswoman than an artisan.'

Gabby noticed how much his assessment of her pleased her. Was it just her feeling this vibe between them? She was decades out of practice. 'Well, it's an odd thing, something I haven't actually shared with anyone else.'

He cocked his head, intrigued. 'Go on.'

'It's a bit out there,' she confessed. 'Do you think you can handle it?'

'Okay, you have to tell me now.'

'All right. Soon after my transplant, lying in the hospital bed, a strange thing happened.'

Luciano rested his elbows on the table, watching her intently. She wasn't totally sure why she was sharing this, except perhaps because of the weird flashes that had been happening lately, and that she needed to tell someone and she didn't want to upset anyone in her family. She'd once tried to talk to Lottie about this when it first happened, but her mother either hadn't believed her or didn't want to know.

'I was lying there, a mainline in my chest and six lots of drips running into me, and I was suddenly overcome by an aroma. It was intense and it was some sort of food. It made me think of my childhood but I couldn't pick it. I decided it must have been something they were serving for lunch and thought no more about it, just accepted it as one more hospital odour among the antibacterial soaps, iodine and disinfectant. But it came every day, in waves.'

She paused, remembering that it made her feel calm, but in a totally different way from the sedatives the doctors kept her on, which just made her feel numb to what was, in reality, genuine horror that her heart – her very own heart, the very core of her – had been ripped out and a stranger's sewn into her chest.

'But after I went home to my parents', the aroma followed me.' She had Luciano's undivided attention, the chatter and bustle in Bar Carlo fading to the background. 'I knew what the smell was.'

'What was it?'

'Hotdogs.'

'Hotdogs?'

'I'd probably eaten a hotdog twice in my life, both times when I was a kid. The combined aroma of fried onions, warm bread rolls and the sharp tang of tomato sauce was clear. But I hadn't eaten one in thirty years.'

'Was it a craving?' he asked.

She shook her head. 'No. I suddenly knew, with crystal clarity, that it wasn't *my* memory I was experiencing. It was someone else's. It was *his*.'

To her relief, Luciano didn't look at her like she was crazy. Instead, he looked utterly intrigued. 'Your donor's?'

'Yes.'

The owner of that memory was a man. She'd felt it in her bones. She felt it, physically, in her chest, this strong, muscular heart beating away.

'It was frightening. I wanted to escape. But where could I go? He was *inside* me. He would go wherever I went. So, I increased my sedatives, hoping to block the feeling of his presence. But it was short-lived and selfish; my children needed me to be present for them. I wanted to be present for them – it was the whole reason I'd been through the heart transplant ordeal in the first place. I stopped the sedatives and steeled myself for an onslaught of insights into his life. I just wanted to get them over with, to face the monster in the house, so to speak.'

'What happened?'

She shrugged. 'They didn't come. The insights stayed away, and day by day I grew more confident that everything I'd experienced had either been in my mind or had been induced by the barrage of medications. I got on with life – taking the kids to school, going to physiotherapy, watching swimming carnivals and music eisteddfods, taking medications, visiting the hospital. The aroma of hotdogs never came back. But I *was* left with something else – a gift. Inexplicably, I'd developed a sommelier's nose.'

Luciano held her gaze.

She shrugged, unable to explain it any more now than she could back then. 'That's what you saw in action today.'

10

Krystal pulled the cling wrap tightly around the Vegemite-and-cheese sandwiches and tucked them alongside apples and crackers into the lunch boxes – a red Spider-Man one for Jasper and a blue PJ Masks one for Olly. It was the first day back at school and she was running late. She opened the fridge to put the butter away and spied the half-empty bottle of white wine in the door. She had drunk the first half by herself last night once the kids were in bed and now she felt shame creeping up her body. But why? She pulled out the bottle and read the label. Seven-point-seven standard drinks in a bottle, so she'd had about three and a half drinks. That wasn't too bad, was it? Lots of people in this country drank that or more on a daily basis. She put the bottle back and shut the door.

'Jasper, can you go and change into your school pants, please?' she called. The boys were slumped on the couch eating breakfast – cornflakes for both, but cow's milk for Jasper and soy milk for Olly, who was dairy intolerant. When he was a baby, Krystal only had to put a drop of milk on his cheek for him to break out in nasty eczema.

She took the boys' water bottles from the draining rack on the sink and filled them, her eye darting to the clock. She had the morning ritual down to within minutes and knew they weren't going to make it, which meant she'd be late for work too.

Jasper brought both bowls to the sink, still wearing pyjama pants.

'Jasper, pants!'

'All right,' he grizzled, in a tone she really should have picked him up on but simply didn't have the time or mental space for this morning. Her mind was well and truly busy elsewhere.

Gabriella McPhee has Evan's heart.

Or maybe she didn't. Krystal had to confess that it was just possible that she *wanted* to know for sure where Evan's heart was, wanted it so much that she might be leaping to conclusions. According to the newspaper, Gabriella's transplant date was one day after Evan died – but then, it had been nearly midnight when she'd signed the papers. His heart couldn't have got to Gabriella until the next calendar day, especially because he was in Sydney.

Sydney.

The very word conjured up dark and monstrous images in her mind.

She'd known the organs could be flown anywhere in the country, or even over to New Zealand. It was kind of poetic that it had ended up back here in Melbourne; almost as if he'd wanted to come home.

That was, *if* it was his heart.

She would go back to The Tin Man this afternoon after she finished work at the school. Roxy was taking the boys home with her, which she and Krystal often did to give each other an afternoon off, so her boys wouldn't think anything was wrong. She had to go back and see Gabriella.

She rinsed the breakfast bowls, thinking about the scar that ran down Gabriella's chest, imagining what it might look like, wondering if it was straight or jagged, an ugly purple or fine white. She wanted to see it. It would be an exquisite horror, a breathtaking pain, to see the line, the incision, and know that Evan's heart was just there, centimetres below. Krystal craved that pain. It was sick, clearly. Probably something like deliberately cutting herself with a knife.

'Olly, it's time to go,' she said, turning off the television, then held out a hand to him to encourage him up. Her youngest wasn't always compliant with the idea of day care. 'It's soccer day,' she said, inspiring him.

'Soccer! I wub soccer!'

'I know!' she said, smiling widely. 'Let's go.'

He rolled off the couch and walked towards the front door, where Jasper was already waiting, thankfully wearing his long navy school pants. He was playing with the door, repeatedly opening it a fraction and letting it bang back into place. Krystal groaned at the noise but ignored it.

She cast an eye up at the clock again. Shit. She cursed herself for letting her mind drift, for allowing herself to obsess over Gabriella McPhee and all the memories she brought back to life.

'Okay, let's go,' she said, grabbing her keys off the side table. The elevator dinged. 'Quick, the lift is here!' She bustled the boys out into the hall and the heavy front door banged shut behind them.

After seeing Jasper to his classroom, Krystal hurried into the administration office.

'Sorry!' she said, breathless. She tossed her leather backpack to the ground, and sat down quickly in her chair.

Janice looked up from her own workstation, opened her mouth as if about to call her out for her lateness, but then closed it again. Krystal knew she'd been employed in this role as a bit of a charity case, some sort of social service from the school to one of their own – the widowed, single mother of a child in their care. She wasn't afraid of hard work. She'd spent years working as a cleaner, waitress, checkout operator or delivery woman before she'd landed her job at Cinque, where she'd met Evan. It had actually been the position of cleaner she'd applied for here at the school. But the principal saw something else in her.

'Can you type?' she'd asked, peering at Krystal through half-moon glasses. Candice had a mop of cherry red curls, mismatched with pink lipstick, and wore a canary yellow top, a combination Krystal found intriguing. 'Answer phones?'

'Well, yes,' Krystal had said, confused.

'I think you should consider the position of administration assistant instead.'

'I haven't done that before, though,' Krystal said, her mind racing to find some sort of relevant experience somewhere in her past.

'Look, you're a mum. Mums are working administration officers from the word go. Give yourself a leg up. The job's yours if you'd like it.'

Truthfully, the role had never held much appeal. But she was smart enough to know that it would look better in her work history, the principal was right about that. Evan had life insurance, so she was far from destitute, but she knew she'd still have to work and, more than that, she knew she needed some sort of structure and responsibility to keep her focused so she didn't slide into dysfunction. She didn't want to end up like her mother.

Now, she settled herself at her desk quickly, longing for coffee but deciding to wait until Janice's frostiness abated. She concentrated on the school newsletter that was due to go out this afternoon. Janice collated each item but it was Krystal's job to double-check all the dates and payment requests and send out the email. Low, dark clouds had gathered outside. She could hear Mrs Giannopoulos's voice droning on about long division, and Mr Roberts playing his guitar in his classroom, to much shrieking and applause. In the sick bay, little Bo Wei was crying softly on and off, waiting for his mum to come back and pick him up.

Krystal rubbed at her eyes, aching for that cuppa.

'Coffee?' Janice suggested from her desk.

'A double shot would be nice,' Krystal said, thinking miserably of the instant coffee in the tearoom. It was one of Krystal's jobs to order tea and coffee supplies, and she bought the stuff in one-kilogram tubs, along with raw sugar and long-life milk.

'Maybe one day,' Janice said, her mood seeming to improve. 'We should raise it with the P & C to ask if they'll at least fund us for a pod machine. Not that pods are real coffee, but they're a darn sight better than instant.'

'It's the packaging,' Krystal said. 'The environmental leader, what's her name, Siobhan? She won't like pods because of the waste created by all those tiny plastic packets.'

'Maybe we should petition for a coffee van, then, to visit us at regular hours and make us all sorts of fancy coffees.'

'That's a great idea.' Krystal swivelled her chair around to study Janice, somewhat buoyed by this sudden spurt of conversation. Janice looked especially nice today, in a black pencil skirt, white blouse and matching jacket. Her red fingernail polish gleamed, reflecting the fluorescent lights above them. Her steel-grey hair was short and spiky, her thick-rimmed glasses edgy. Krystal wondered what her supervisor had been up to on the weekend.

Sex?

Antiquing?

Sex *and* antiquing?

Krystal studied her own cheap black pants and T-shirt with cable-knit cardigan and considered that she could use a wardrobe update, something to compete with Janice here in the office.

'Maybe two teaspoons of coffee will help,' Krystal said, getting up.

'Did you have a bad night?' Janice asked, her fingernails continuing to tap across her keyboard and her eyes peering straight ahead at her screen.

'I didn't sleep very well,' Krystal said, pausing mid-stride. 'Why do you ask?' She was on edge now, her new, warm feelings towards Janice quickly cooling.

'Just that you look like you could use that coffee,' Janice said, her eyes still on the screen.

Krystal closed her eyes in frustration – she'd thought they'd been making social progress – and tucked her cardigan around her tighter. 'I'm sure you're right.'

Finally, the school bell rang. Krystal met Roxy – today wearing a patchwork coat that made her look like a friendly scarecrow – at the classroom door where she was collecting Jasper and Austin. She kissed Jasper goodbye.

'Good luck,' Roxy said, carrying both boys' bags like a Sherpa, while they raced ahead of her down the verandah.

'Thanks.' Krystal hurried away, her boots clunking along the wooden boards, down the stairs and across the concrete, weaving through kids in yellow and navy uniforms, out to the car and on her way to The Tin Man.

The slow end-of-school traffic made her twitch with nerves. All she could think about was Gabriella.

Gabriella, Gabriella, Gabriella.

If she could just *be* there, next to a piece of Evan, maybe she could move on somehow from the mental nightmare she'd been in since his death. She inched her car through school zones and past buses, debating with herself, giving herself the chance to back out. She could take more time to think about it. She could try talking to someone at the hospital, though she knew that would be a waste of time. All information was sealed.

By the time she arrived in South Yarra and found a parking spot, she had almost no memory of the actual drive there. Her mind had been completely consumed with thinking about Gabriella, Evan, Cordelia-Aurora and everything that had happened that night in Sydney.

She stopped momentarily at the fountain in the courtyard outside the cafe, took a steadying breath, then forged on. Inside, the cafe was an oasis of beauty and she felt her spirits rise just being here. The aroma of coffee and vanilla wafted through the air. She stilled, taking it all in, getting her bearings. Frank Sinatra played over the sound system. To her left was the green wall, ivy and potted plants covering the bricks, that she'd sat beside the first time she'd seen Gabriella. In front of her was the cabinet of drool-worthy cakes and pastries. Behind the counter was a dark-haired, heavily whiskered man, probably in his mid-forties, scowling and working the coffee machine. He briefly looked up at her, then went back to his work. A huge bouquet of white lilies on the countertop exuded a thick, sweet fragrance.

Krystal swept her eyes across the tables and lounges. In the furthest corner she spotted a more intimate nook, with a few dark brown cowhides lying on the floor between the heavy, stuffed lounges, and pink carnations adorning a low glass table. Her breath caught in her throat. Seated at one of the lounges was Gabriella McPhee, her long red hair loose, dressed today in a ruffled off-the-shoulder white shirt and maybe . . . was that just the hint of a scar showing at the neckline? She was working on a laptop, which balanced on her knees atop a long, layered denim skirt. Incongruously, there was a dog at her side, a creature with golden blond hair so beautiful it should have been in a pet food commercial. It wore a red service jacket and sat up quite straight, as though on guard.

Krystal almost lost her nerve then and took a step towards the counter with a view to ordering a coffee and gathering her wits. As she moved, the dog's head snapped towards her and it fixed Krystal with a stare. Her step faltered; then Gabriella looked up, following the dog's gaze, and their eyes collided.

Time stood still. It was as though she could see Evan's essence behind those eyes and her urgent need to get close to Gabriella thundered in her ears. Gabriella's hand lifted to her chest and even from where Krystal stood it was easy to see shock register on her face.

She knows!

A hurricane of emotion swept through her, from her toes to her hair – excitement, grief, anger, desperation. Without thinking, she marched towards Gabriella, holding her gaze. She stopped at the edge of the table. All she could hear was her own breath – in, out, in, out. She needed to speak, to say something. Her eyes dropped to Gabriella's chest and her white shirt, rising and falling with every breath.

Then Gabriella coughed. Her hand flew to her mouth and her eyes watered as if she was choking on something. She leaned forward, hurrying to get her laptop onto the table in front of her.

'Are you okay?' Krystal asked, making a move towards her. The dog growled.

Krystal froze. The dog was statue stiff, one side of its top lip twitching like Elvis Presley's famous sneer.

Gabriella straightened in her seat again, but beads of sweat had broken out on her forehead. Krystal didn't know what to do. She couldn't go towards Gabriella because the dog was in the way, but she wanted to make sure Gabriella was okay, and there was so much pressure inside her, the words she needed to say trying to force their way out.

Gabriella coughed again and blinked her eyes, then took a big breath. She was okay. Krystal took her chance.

'I'm sorry for interrupting, but my name is Krystal Arthur. I think you might have my husband's heart.'

Gabriella stared at her, some kind of realisation crossing her face. 'It's *you*. You're the one doing this.'

'Doing . . . what? What do you mean?'

'That one was new.' Gabriella said it quietly, almost to herself.

'What was new?' Krystal stood stiff with tension.

The dog growled again. Gabriella looked surprised and reached out her hand to place it on the animal's neck. In the back of her mind, Krystal considered that this type of canine behaviour could precede an attack. But it was a trained golden retriever, not a stray frothing at the mouth.

'I don't understand,' Krystal said. 'Maybe I should start again. You're Gabriella McPhee, aren't you? I only need a few moments. I just need to talk to you about something . . .'

The dog got to its feet, its growling intensifying. Then the man with the dark hair was at her side. 'Excuse me, I'm going to have to ask you to leave the cafe now.'

Krystal spun to glare at him, a loud buzzing inside her head. She needed this all to slow down. She needed time to explain who she was.

'As you can see, you're upsetting this dog.' He kept his dark eyes on her but gestured to the retriever, who had drool dripping from its lips now, its eyes still boring into Krystal. She'd have to rethink that idea about retrievers being harmless. 'This dog is a service animal and is on duty. If she feels you're a threat, I'm guessing you probably are.'

'Luciano . . .' Finally Gabriella spoke, as if she was going to tell him everything was okay.

But Luciano held out his hand to Gabriella and addressed Krystal. 'Let's just call it a day, okay. I can send for a cab, or make you a coffee . . .'

'I'm not drunk,' Krystal hissed at him, the guilt of last night's wine fresh in her mind and now horribly aware that the cafe chatter had quietened as customers turned to stare. Her skin flamed.

Still, Luciano hadn't taken his eyes off her. Neither had the dog. Fierce, stubborn pride and anguish fought to get her to hold her ground. She couldn't lose now, not when she was so close she could almost touch her goal.

'Please, Gabriella, I only need a few minutes of your time.'

The dog barked – a single, piercing shot of sound that made them all jump.

'Let's go,' Luciano ordered.

Searing with humiliation under the eyes of the whole cafe, Krystal hurried to the door and just made it outside before she burst into tears.

11

Gabby paced the floor of the storeroom, Sally trailing after her, licking at her hand every now and then. Luciano perched on a pile of three bags of Ethiopian coffee beans, the smell of hessian in the air.

'What just happened?' he asked.

'All this time I was thinking it was him, my donor, but it's not – it's her!' Gabby could feel how wide her eyes were and purposely relaxed them so as not to look like a madwoman. She *might* be a bit mad, granted, but she didn't need to look the part.

'Do you know that woman?' Luciano asked, his finger tugging at his red neckerchief, and even in the midst of all this craziness she felt a flash of attraction to him. The way he had come to her rescue out there would be enough to confuse her on a good day, let alone now.

'Not exactly.'

Luciano waited, holding her gaze.

'She thinks I have the heart of . . .' she trailed off, biting down hard on her lip, suppressing a sudden bubble of emotion.

'Her husband,' he said.

'Yes.'

'That's big.'

'It is.'

'Do you think it's true?'

'I do. I've been having these insights – flashes. They're him – well, they're me, but it's not me, you know? It's like a dream but it's real. They're terrifying and I know it's him and he's trying to . . . I don't know, show me something? And I just thought this was like the thing with the hotdogs, something coming from him, but when I see her, I feel him. It's like she's the key to unlocking him.'

She stared at him a moment, digesting her own words. 'I sound completely bonkers, don't I?'

Luciano tilted his head to the side and gave her a sympathetic smile. 'Maybe a little.'

She stopped pacing and Sally gratefully sat down beside her leg, panting gently in the overly bright storeroom. 'The first day I saw her here in the cafe I had this vision not long after she left. It was night and cold and I was running in a street. Just now, when she stood in front of me, I smelled smoke. I smelled it like it was curling up from embers right below my nose.'

'What do you think it means?'

'I have no idea.' Gabby rubbed Sally's head. 'I have to go. I'm so sorry for dumping all this on you. You must think I'm a right nutter. We'll never speak of it again, I promise.'

She fetched her handbag from where it sat on top of a bucket of roasted beans, pulled out Sally's leash and clipped it on. Luciano got to his feet and thrust his hands into the pockets of his jeans, watching her. She straightened and gave him her best carefree smile. 'I'll see you tomorrow.'

He nodded. But as she turned to leave he said, 'I believe you, you know. I don't think you're nuts.'

She turned back to face him. 'Why on earth not?'

He rocked his head from side to side. 'Let's just say I've had a few crazy experiences of my own.'

'Really? Like what?'

He smiled, and his eyes lit up with something like relief. 'Another time.'

Gabby's thoughts were a whirlwind as she and Sally disembarked the Toorak Road/Burke Road tram and began the ten-minute walk home. But she calmed when she reached the entrance to the house. In the kitchen, she found the doors to the outside entertainment area wide open. Summer had brought Freddie home from school and the girls were having cappuccinos and croissants at the table, still in their blue and green uniforms. Gabby poked her head out the door and Sally stepped down onto the pavers and went straight to the girls' sides, checking for food. Technically she wasn't allowed to beg; but, in fairness, she was off duty now.

'Hi, girls, how was your day?' Gabby asked, remaining in the doorway. Unlike Sally, she knew when she wasn't wanted.

'Good,' they both chimed, and Freddie handed Sally an entire croissant. Sally's eyes widened to saucers, and she took it carefully in her mouth and walked across the grass to lie down and have some quiet time alone with her treat. The girls seemed to be in a good mood, Summer smiling widely, flashing her braces. She flipped her long blonde hair over her shoulder and giggled.

'Well, let me know if you need anything,' Gabby said, and went to turn away.

'Oh, Mum,' Summer called her back. 'I need to do a project for school on recycling so I need some of your used coffee grounds from the cafe.'

'Okay. What are you doing with them?'

'Growing plants in them.'

'How much do you need?'

Summer wrinkled her nose. 'Maybe enough for six small plants?'

'We'd have enough here at home for that,' Gabby said. 'I'll start putting it aside for you.'

'I need jars too.'

'There are heaps of recycled jars in the cupboard. Help yourself. That sounds like a really cool idea,' Gabby said, hiding her excitement that her daughter had a project that Gabby could help with. She also knew that saying cool wasn't cool. She thought she'd heard *epic* being used these days but she couldn't be certain. She decided to leave them to it before she embarrassed herself any further, and made her way to the lounge room, where Celia was snuggled into the brown leather couch with popcorn, watching *The Princess Diaries*. Retro flicks were all the rage among her peers.

'Hi, Fairy Cake,' Gabby said, kissing Celia on the head and rubbing her shoulder.

'Hi!'

Gabby grabbed a handful of popcorn and chewed carefully, already regretting it as she felt the sharp kernel husks wedging between her teeth. It just smelled so good! Salty and buttery and warm. 'Hey, what's this?' Gabby picked up a new artwork off the carved wooden chest that served as the coffee table, and flopped down on the couch next to Celia. It was a large poster, painted with a blue background, with six recycled CDs glued on, shiny side up, and fins, scales, eyes, lips and tails painted on to turn them into rainbow fish.

'We made them in art today. I made it for Mykahla for her nursery,' Celia said, pulling herself over to Gabby to lean on her shoulder and point out all the different fish.

'Oh, sweetheart, it's beautiful.' Gabby wrapped her arm around Celia and pulled her close for a hug, and in return got an overly tight two-arm bear squeeze. 'Whoa! When did you get so strong?'

Celia just shrugged. 'I can't wait to give it to her. Maybe we could drive over to Dad's so Mykahla can have it now?' she said, grinning, expecting Gabby to agree to the impromptu plan.

'Mm.' Gabby froze for a moment. Cam still hadn't responded to her, so his silence was the only thing she had to go on as to whether he'd meant what he said about the kids. Was this the moment to break it to her child that her father didn't want to see her right now? Or should she fob them off a bit longer in the hope Cam would come to his senses and see that his first three children still needed him very much, and get himself back on track before they knew anything was wrong?

Then again, her children weren't fools. They would know something was up. Besides, she was a terrible liar and they'd see through her sooner or later, and then they'd feel betrayed by her too. Charlie had already admitted to feeling unwanted because of Cam's grumpiness. She was so angry with Cam for putting her in this position. Surely it should be up to him to tell them he wanted a break, not her. It was his mess; he should clean it up.

But life was rarely neat or fair, and she and Cam had always told the kids the truth – about their separation, about her illness, about the transplant. The only thing they'd never discussed with the kids was his marijuana use, because they thought that would send the wrong message; although Cam was in favour of legalising marijuana, he still didn't want to encourage his kids to use it. His stance didn't make sense to Gabby but she was happy to go along with it, being firmly in the 'no drugs' camp herself.

'Listen, Fairy Cake,' she said, putting her hand on Celia's narrow shoulder, a shoulder too small to have to bear the weight of her father's failings. Celia's smile faded and her smooth brow puckered with worry. She was expecting this, Gabby realised. They probably all were. 'Your dad's going through a bad time right now and he needs a rest.'

'From me?' Celia squeaked.

'Not from you. He loves you! But he's struggling with all the everyday things he has to do, like going to work and looking after a small baby. Life gets really messy when you're an adult and things build up.' She couldn't say she was enjoying defending him, not one bit. 'Sometimes, people just need a bit of space to catch up on sleep and concentrate on one thing at a time.'

Celia touched one of the rainbow fish with her fingertip. 'Doesn't he want to see us?'

Oh, if Gabby's heart hadn't already been torn out and replaced with another it would have ripped in two right there. 'He loves you,' she repeated. 'He just has a lot on his plate right now and needs a rest. He'll be back soon, I promise.'

She didn't like promising that. She had no control over what Cam did. But Celia's eyes had started to well up and she would say anything to make her daughter's pain stop. She tucked Celia's brown hair behind the slightly-too-large ears that she would one day grow into. 'Until then, how about we pop this in the post for Mykahla, and you can write a card or a letter to go with it?'

Celia wiped her eyes. 'Okay.'

After Summer had waved goodbye to Freddie and Charlie had come home from swimming training, and after Monty had made

113

them all butter chicken and rice for dinner and they'd filled their bellies, she repeated the same conversation for the benefit of her elder two children.

'He doesn't want to see us?' Summer said, screwing up her face in disbelief.

'I knew it!' Charlie said, shoving his plate away and pushing back his chair.

Beside Gabby, Monty sat quietly, looking murderous, occasionally tapping the table with his knuckle in what she knew was calculated thought. She glanced sideways at him, nervous at his silence.

'I know he loves you all,' Gabby said, again attempting reassurance.

'Just not as much as Mykahla,' Summer said, her face bright red with suppressed emotion.

'I promise you that's not true,' Gabby said, and meant it, though she noted that she'd again made a promise on Cam's behalf and she really should stop doing that. It would be so much easier if she could just explain to them that Cam was on a bender and needed to spend time in meetings for addicts and concentrate on getting himself well again. In some ways, she realised now, she was actually relieved he'd made the call, as she didn't want the kids exposed to his habits and she needed him to be a fully functioning caregiver. Still, that small mercy aside, she was furious he'd let this happen at all.

'Whatever,' Charlie snapped, in a rare display of temper. He left his plate where it was and stormed from the table, and they all sat in silence for a moment as they listened to his big feet clomping up the stairs to his room. It was an awful time for Cam to do this to Charlie, who'd be turning sixteen at the end of the week. Arguably, he needed his father now more than ever before.

'I'm done here too,' Summer said, getting up from the table and also heading up the stairs, though more sedately than Charlie.

Monty turned to Gabby, his jowls hanging low with contempt for Cam. 'That went well.'

Gabby shook her head and rolled her eyes to the ceiling, feeling her lips pinching tight against words she wanted to say. Sally came to the table and laid her head in Celia's lap, and the little girl flopped over to hug her. At least the dog was faithful to her.

It was a relief to drag her weary body to the sanctuary of her room later that evening, after everyone else had settled into their bedrooms. Charlie and Summer would be awake for a while yet, she knew, but she needed to lie down. It had been an enormous day. She stretched out across her bedspread, lamplight glowing gently beside her, and took some deep breaths, processing everything, from the cupping session and her progress with Luciano, telling him about the sense memories, to the woman in the cafe and the smell of smoke her presence had brought with it, and now her children's reactions to the news about Cam. She groaned quietly and covered her eyes with her arms. She knew she had done as much as she could for the kids tonight and they would need some time to work through their feelings, so she let her mind go back to the woman in the cafe.

The woman's presence had triggered the first vision and then a new one today. She was the key. Gabby sat up and pulled out her laptop, propping herself up in bed with fat ruffled pillows at her back. She opened the laptop and searched for 'weird things happening to organ donor recipient'. She quickly came across the term *cellular memory* – the theory that an imprint of the donor's living experiences was held within the cells of their organ. She'd never heard of it.

She read further, then stopped short: *Heart transplant recipients seem to be the most vulnerable to taking on the donor's memories, sensations and personality traits.*

Gabby stared at the screen for a moment, then clicked on more links. As she read the case studies, a surreal feeling of knowing settled into her bones. A part of her had already known it, though she'd managed to cultivate some robust denial. Yet it made sense. Your heart was everything, wasn't it? People said to follow your heart, or speak from the heart, or open your heart. We were encouraged to live our life from the heart. Some ancient cultures believed the human spirit resided in the heart, and that it was an organ far superior to the brain.

An organ recipient's essential immunosuppressant medications might actually make them more able to receive imprinted messages, as the body's natural defences against outside influences are already lowered.

It felt true. At the same time, it was undeniably creepy. No one in their right mind would actually want to take on a dead person's living essence. She followed the links to the sources that refuted the case study evidence. They argued that most of the reported changes in sense of smell, or taste, or preference in music and so on could be explained by other things, like the major trauma the patient had been through, or a side effect of the medications.

She thought back to the others in her support group who'd gone through the process at the same time as her. Margaret had lost her appetite for meat and become vegetarian overnight. Eunika had loved pop music but now listened to classical all day long, even taking up piano lessons. Lars had weird, frightening dreams and developed a phobia of water, even struggling to stay calm in the shower. And there was Gabby, with her odd memories of hotdogs, and now vivid all-too-real flashes of someone else's life.

She read case after case of patients knowing things they couldn't possibly know about their donor – things that the donor's family had later corroborated. Most of the cases came from America, as Australia had fewer examples of donor families and recipients being able to meet with each other. But when she got to the story of a young child who'd helped the police find the killer of the little girl whose heart was now in her body, Gabby shut the laptop.

It was a sickening and terrifying concept.

Her first instinct was to make sure she never saw this woman again. Then, maybe, the visions would stop. But how could she keep the woman away? She could go to the hospital to see her donor coordinator and ask her to intervene, to talk to the woman and tell her to go away, but that would mean the coordinator would have to confirm that Gabby was indeed the donor recipient the woman had been looking for, and there was no way the coordinator could do that. A breach of privacy and ethics of that magnitude would cost her her job.

A restraining order? Ha! On what grounds? The woman hadn't done anything other than try to talk to her, and that wasn't a crime. It wasn't an option for Gabby to stop going into work. Young businesses were like small children – they needed constant attention.

Then she realised the woman already knew her name. She could find out where Gabby lived. She could turn up on the doorstep at any moment. She could phone her at work or even find her personal phone number. She could contact her via the cafe's email address. There was no way Gabby could hide from her. She couldn't stop the woman from coming back.

If she couldn't make her go away then she really only had one option, and that was to face her, though the thought of another weird vision erupting in her made her feel queasy. Maybe if she *did* speak to her, though, the woman would say her piece and move on, and take the visions with her, and Gabby could stop fearing her. Maybe she needed to see this woman in order to make it all stop.

With that, she reopened her laptop, trying to remember the woman's name. Katy? Carla? Damn her useless short-term memory. She'd be able to search for her on Facebook if she could just remember. Kylie? And what about the surname? Anders?

No matter how hard she tried to recall it, the name had slipped away. Instead, she set up a simple blog and new Facebook profile with her transplant date and location, and explained that she was looking for her donor's family. For many reasons, transplant teams discouraged recipients from searching for donor families. She knew she was opening a can of worms. What if they wanted money from her as payment? What if they judged her for the way she lived her life? What if they stalked her? What if they were smothering and possessive and bought a house to be near her and expected her at all their family gatherings?

It was a risk worth taking. She needed to find this woman, not only to make the visions stop, but also to help her. The woman had donated her husband's heart so that someone – Gabby – could go on living. She owed her. Maybe through meeting her she would finally be able to let go of some of the guilt that went along with knowing she was only alive because someone else had died. And maybe then this heart in her chest could rest easily once more.

12

During her lunch break on Wednesday, Krystal jumped in her car and headed down to St Kilda Beach to clear her head. She found a park easily, kicked off her boots and wrapped her lightweight camel-coloured cardigan tightly around her against the breeze. The sand was cold underfoot, palm trees swaying and seagulls ducking, diving and cawing. She and Evan had come here often, hiring bicycles and riding the coastal track before the boys came, and later playing in the sand with their sons. She felt close to him here.

She began to walk, the sun high in the sky, her sunglasses barely blocking out the bright white glare off the water's surface. She'd been so close to connecting with Gabriella on Monday but the moment had been ruined, and she wasn't even sure what had happened. All she knew was that Gabriella was saying odd things about 'a new one', and the dog had thought Krystal was some kind of threat, and she'd been hustled from the cafe. The humiliation still burned.

She'd thought speaking with Gabriella would somehow ease the pain of her loss. But now she was more confused than ever. She realised that she'd harboured some sort of fantasy that Gabriella might hold the answers she needed. She had no idea why a policeman had phoned her late in the evening and summoned her to urgently get on a plane with her two tiny, sleepy, grumpy children in tow. No idea what Evan had been doing running down an alley in the dark when the car had struck him. And no idea why he hadn't told her the truth.

She bent down to pick up a particularly beautiful shell, almost in the shape of a heart, a rainbow of purple and blue and pink spilling through it. Was it a sign from Evan? He'd been good at finding beautiful things in the world, something she'd once believed was a birthright of the wealthy, until Evan showed her differently.

For their first date, Krystal and Evan met at Rippon Lea Estate in Elsternwick, a late-nineteenth-century mansion on the outskirts of the city. It was a bright, blue-skied day in spring, the wind still cool enough to make jackets necessary, but the sun gorgeously warming on their backs. The mansion itself – dark brick with mustard-coloured trimmings – made her jaw drop. She'd never seen anything like it. There were two storeys above ground, with stone pillars, moulded ceilings, gilded wallpaper, wide staircases and landings, plush carpets and curtains, and more rooms than she could count.

They joined a tour group alongside tourists from America, England, Japan and Germany, as well as a couple of Jewish men wearing mink hats and black silk coats, with long beards, who may well have come from the orthodox Jewish community just outside the estate's gates. Together the motley group moved through the mansion, gawping at the formal drawing room, sitting room, dining room, bedrooms, bathrooms. There was a glass conservatory overlooking the magnificent grounds. Stained-glass windows to rival great cathedrals. Marble fireplaces and bronze statues. Below ground, there were a wine cellar, butler's pantry, wood cellar, coal cellar, scullery, laundry and kitchen. It was simultaneously breathtaking and infuriating. All that money! For one family!

Then there were the gardens. Pathways meandered through the sixteen acres of lawns, waterfalls and rock tunnels. A broad lake boasted waterlilies and quacking wood ducks. There was a boathouse extending out across the water with purple froths of wisteria behind it. A steel windmill cut a striking figure against a backdrop of white puffs of cloud. The arched bridges were impossibly romantic.

With every step their surroundings shimmered with greenery and pops of blues, pinks and orange. Blooming beds of purple pansies. A magnificent old oak tree near the stables showing off its flush of seasonal green. They walked through an orchard of heritage apple trees, their boughs laden with pink and white blossom. Inside the domed fernery, dappled light rained down through rainforest species that towered above them. It was nothing short of magical.

They walked until their feet ached, and somehow the peace and tranquillity soothed Krystal's ruffled working-class feathers. They rested for tea and a selection of tiny sandwiches at the old gatehouse, sitting outside below a tree, filtered light dancing across their hands.

Surprised by how much emotion this place had stirred in her, Krystal attempted to deflect it. 'It's a bit much, isn't it?' she teased, glancing at their surrounds. 'Imagine all of this belonging to one family. It's obscene.'

Evan put down his sandwich and levelled his attention on her. 'It doesn't mean they were happy, though.'

Now it was her turn to squirm. 'Well, no, of course not. But it helps, doesn't it? All this wealth! I mean, you'd have to be trying not to enjoy yourself.' She attempted to laugh off her criticism. Over the course of the day she'd found herself enjoying Evan's company more and more, and now she hoped she hadn't put him off with her envious words.

Evan nodded slowly and wiped his hands on his serviette. 'My family is well off,' he said, straight to the point.

'Really?' She didn't know why she was surprised. Evan spoke like an educated man. He was deeply knowledgeable about wines of the world. He'd brought her here, to this place of excessive wealth.

'They're all lawyers. I was one too.'

'You're kidding. And now you're a sommelier?'

He nodded, smiling a little, obviously pleased he'd surprised her.

'Why on earth would you leave a job like that?'

He laughed again, heartily this time. 'Because it made me miserable.'

'Oh.' She didn't know what she thought about this. She felt ridiculous for just moments ago having allowed hope to swell in her chest that there might be something between them. How could she have thought he might be interested in her?

'Money shouldn't make you miserable,' he said.

'Sadly, I have no relevant experience to be able to offer an opinion on that.'

'The thing is, though, all of this –' he gestured around them – 'the only reason it's even here for us to enjoy today is because someone donated it to the National Trust. Louisa Jones gifted it all, despite having children she could have passed it on to. She was motivated to protect the grounds and the history for future generations.'

Krystal thought back to the tour guide's words. She vaguely

remembered the tour guide saying something about this, but she hadn't really paid attention, too preoccupied running scripts in her head about how unfair it was that some people had so much while others had to struggle for everything.

'People with money can be generous too,' Evan said. 'So, promise me you won't hold it against me that my family have money?'

'Okay,' she agreed. 'I promise.'

Evan's lovely warm eyes took on a cheeky glint. 'But do feel free to hold it against *them* that they're priggish, selfish bores.'

She burst out laughing. 'All right, will do.'

Krystal turned around on the sand and began to head back to the car. Memories like this one were a precious gift but they were also like being stabbed through the heart all over again, not just with grief but with the betrayal. In his final hours, her husband had been lying to her and she had no idea why.

She grieved the Evan she knew – her husband, the boys' father, her best friend, her lover, her lifelong mate. But then she hated him too. For what could he have possibly been doing in the streets of Sydney? She didn't even know if it had been the first time he'd gone to Sydney without her knowing. He worked long hours in the restaurant; it wasn't unusual for him to be gone eight hours or even twelve, coming home in the early hours of the morning. How many other times had he flown to Sydney without tellng her?

By the time Evan died, she no longer worked in the restaurant. She didn't work anywhere outside of the home. She had a one-year-old and a three-year-old and could barely keep track of the days of the week, let alone worry about keeping track of Evan. He'd taken advantage of her commitment to their family.

In her most optimistic moments, she told herself he was there for something wonderful, organising some sort of marvellous surprise for her birthday or a long-overdue holiday. But she knew in her gut that wasn't it.

The most logical conclusion was that Evan had a mistress in Sydney.

Then, sometimes, she went to even darker places. She wondered if he'd had links to organised crime. In her more hysterical moments, she even wondered if maybe he'd had a secret he was ashamed of, like being a drag queen or something.

All of this not knowing tainted their whole relationship; every single thing she'd thought was real between them was brought into question. Had their life together been a lie? She'd gone over everything again and again, trying to recall a conversation or hint that would have alerted her to what was going on. There must have been a clue there somewhere; she'd just missed it, too buried in the depths of child-rearing and sleeplessness. She'd phoned the police many times in the past two years, hoping for an update or a breakthrough in their search for the hit-and-run driver. But they'd had next to no leads. It had been late. The street was dark. It wasn't the first time a driver had panicked, sped off and never been identified, and it wouldn't be the last.

She checked the time and climbed back into her car, already counting the hours until she could go home and go to bed.

'Shh!' Margie pulled Krystal into the kitchenette of the school office.

'What's going on?' Krystal whispered, already smiling because Margie had a glint in her eye that was as bright as a diamond.

'We've got a new toaster,' Margie said, nodding to the unopened box on the bench, then pushed the kitchenette door closed behind them. The hot water tank on the wall ticked as the thermostat kicked in, and the strip light above their heads buzzed aggressively.

'Okay,' Krystal said, trying to work out the catch. Margie's amusement was electric in the air. Her straight blonde bob and demure work clothes were a total ruse; Margie was bad to the bone.

'Quick, get it open before Janice comes back.'

Krystal did as she was told, ripping open the box and extracting the appliance from its plastic wrapping while beside her Margie carefully wrote a note with a thick black marker. Then she whipped out a roll of sticky tape and broke off a piece with her teeth. Krystal plugged in the toaster and Margie spun it around so that the lever and controls were hidden at the back against the wall, then taped her note on the side facing outwards.

Please note: Toaster is voice activated. Speak loudly and clearly.
"Toast!" *to begin toasting.*
"Pop!" *to end toasting.*
~ Thank you ~

'Oh, you're terrible, Margie.'

'I know!' Margie agreed gleefully. Then she placed a fresh loaf of bread right next to the toaster, ready to go. 'Let's get out of here.' She opened the door and checked both ways for Janice. Finding the coast clear, they hurried to their workstations and assumed postures of industrious labour, each occasionally breaking into body shakes as laughter rippled through them.

Soon enough, Janice returned, carrying a fistful of jangling keys and oozing self-importance. Krystal and Margie stared at their screens, tapping away in silence.

'Nice to see you both hard at work,' Janice said.

'Thank you,' Margie said sweetly. She had totally missed her calling in the theatre.

Krystal admired her so much. Like Krystal, Margie had come from a small town in Victoria – Marysville – but almost ten years ago, ninety per cent of her town was wiped out in the Black Saturday bushfires. She lost both her parents and many friends. She and her brother relocated to Melbourne to start over with nothing to their name and their lives shattered. Yet here she was, alive and smiling and fizzing with humour. She was inspiring.

The clock at the bottom of Krystal's computer screen said ten minutes to one. Janice took her lunch at one on the dot, leaving whoever else was in the office to deal with kids coming in during the lunch break looking for lost property, or injured and needing sticking plasters, or wanting someone to call their parents to pick them up because they were sick. For the next ten minutes, Krystal focused her attention on typing up the swimming carnival heat lists for each age group for this coming Friday.

Ten minutes later, Janice pushed her chair back from the desk. 'Right. Lunch.'

Krystal glanced sideways at Margie, whose lips were firmly pressed together, showing only the slightest hint of dimples.

Janice exited to the kitchenette. There were a few moments of silence. Margie kept typing. The seconds dragged on in taut anticipation. Krystal's nerves twanged.

Then they heard the unmistakable rustle of the bread bag and the sound of heavy slices being dropped into the toaster.

'Toast,' Janice said, tentatively.

Margie began to laugh and covered her mouth to hold it in.

Janice cleared her throat. 'Toast!' she said again, with more authority now.

Krystal bit down on giggles, her cheeks heating up. Margie doubled over, her body racked with silent guffaws.

'I said, Toast! Toast! *Toast!*' Janice growled and stomped a heel on the linoleum in fury.

Margie leapt up and scurried from the office towards the toilets.

Janice burst out of the kitchenette, her face puce. 'What the hell's wrong with the new toaster?' she demanded, and as Margie was nowhere in sight, Krystal was forced to reply.

'Um, what do you mean?' she asked, trying for innocence, but there must have been a waver in her voice because Janice narrowed her eyes and her lips twisted into a sneer. She turned and went back to the kitchenette. Krystal heard her rip off the note and spin the appliance around. A second later, she was back.

'Who did this?' she demanded, her voice low and menacing.

Krystal was about to guiltily admit that it was Margie – and herself, too, she supposed – when she felt a rush of solidarity towards Margie and contempt for Janice's stronghold over their workspace. She wasn't *that* superior.

'It was just a joke,' she said, as lightly as she could. 'It was a bit of fun, that's all.'

'Well, I'm not laughing,' Janice said, and screwed up the note in her hand. She went back to her desk, reached under it for her crocodile leather handbag and stalked from the office.

Margie returned a moment later. She caught sight of Krystal's dismayed expression. 'What happened?'

'She wasn't too impressed,' Krystal said. 'I told her it was just a joke but she'd already lost her cool.'

Margie grimaced. 'Is she very mad with us?'

Us? Krystal opened her mouth to correct Margie, to remind her that it had had nothing to do with Krystal at all – she'd just been an unwitting accessory – but she knew Margie hadn't meant any harm. She'd been trying to bring a bit of fun into their dull little desk jobs. She gave her friend a smile. 'Don't worry about it. I'm pretty sure she thinks I was responsible.'

'Oh, sorry,' Margie said, clutching her hands to her chest.

'Really, it's not a big deal.'

'Thanks, Krystal. You're a good mate.'

13

'Your project is due tomorrow?'

'Yes, so I need an audience to practise in front of,' Summer said, setting up her slideshow presentation in the television room, connecting her laptop to the screen with a cable.

'Didn't you only just start this on Monday?' Gabby asked. On the carved chest in front of them sat six glass jars containing a combination of potting mix and coffee grounds with lovely fat green herbs growing from them. Obviously they hadn't been grown from seeds.

Summer shrugged. 'Yeah.'

Gabby decided not to voice her disapproval that this last-minute effort might actually be cheating. Her daughter was a great student and her ability to pull things together quickly had worked for her so far through school, but she was bound to trip up at some stage if she didn't get more organised. Gabby would have a chat to her about that after she'd handed in this assignment; now wasn't the time to upset her.

Gabby, Monty and Celia huddled together on the couch and gave Summer their undivided attention. Charlie was upstairs in his room studying. She could hear the wheels of his chair rolling around above them. Summer cleared her throat. She was wearing a grey Lorna Jane tracksuit and looked gorgeous. Just the sight of her made Gabby want to cry.

That was how she was these days. Cracked open. Cracked open from the actual, very real, cracking open of her chest. The genie had been let out of the bottle and with it had come a tendency to weep: at a yellow daisy struggling to grow between pavers; at her youngest daughter's fierce love for the dog; at the dog's devotion in return, lying across Celia's legs as she slept at night; at her son's broadening shoulders and the fluff on his upper lip; at the slackening in her dad's jowls; and at the homeless girl who sometimes slept outside the entrance to the cafe at night. It was as though when they sewed and stapled her back up, tiny holes had remained. Emotions simply kept rising like water, finding their way through.

'Each year, Australians throw away about one billion takeaway coffee cups,' Summer began, using her most serious voice, the one that Gabby always thought would serve her daughter well in the political arena. Summer clicked a button on the keyboard of her laptop to move the slideshow on to a picture of a garbage dump. 'These cups end up in landfill, where they contribute to methane gas production and an increase in greenhouse gases.'

Gabby shifted uneasily. She did have some knowledge of the environmental cost of takeaway cups, but the hectic pace of building her business had involved so many other practical and financial needs to be met that she'd put the whole environmental thing on the backburner for the time being, till she felt she had more time to deal with it.

'An average cafe throws away three and a half tonnes of used ground coffee each year.'

'Really?' Gabby asked, horrified. This was terrible. She did see it. There was no way she could miss the huge bags of waste that went out the door each day. Again, it was one of those things she'd just blocked out, intending to get to it once the critical phases of business building were done, but now she could see she'd let it go too long. She was practically an environmental vandal.

'Shh!' Celia said, looking at her mother earnestly, leaning on Monty's shoulder. 'Go on, Summer.'

But, as Summer's presentation showed, there was some hope, with new business ideas and research happening around the world, focusing on profiting from recycled spent coffee. 'Options include pelleted garden fertilisers that smell like coffee rather than animal manure, laundry detergents, biodiesels and even road base material.'

'That's fantastic,' Monty said.

'Shh!' Celia said again, enthralled by her big sister's presentation. Gabby smiled at Monty over the top of Celia's head.

'Unfortunately, while the research is promising, we haven't even scraped the surface of the business opportunities for spent coffee grounds,' Summer said.

Monty stood up and thumped his right fist into his left palm. 'Eureka! Summer, you're a genius.'

Summer stopped. 'I am?' She beamed, flashing her lovely white teeth beneath the clear braces.

'Yes! Gabby, this is a wonderful opportunity for you to diversify your business portfolio,' Monty said, rubbing his chin.

'Here we go,' Gabby said, smiling. She knew a flare of business passion from a McPhee all too well and it was a welcome sight in her father, who seemed sad more often than not these days. A project would be wonderful for him.

'Your business is a veritable goldmine,' Monty went on, running his hand across his mouth and beginning to pace. He pulled up his trousers under his small pot belly.

'Erm, maybe,' Gabby said. The information Summer had shown them was fascinating, but Gabby already felt at maximum capacity running one business. She didn't feel anywhere near ready to start another one yet.

'Don't worry,' Monty said, holding up his hands as if reading her mind. 'You just let me and Summer take care of it.'

'Really?' Summer said. 'We'll share the profits, right?'

'Of course we will,' Monty said. 'But only if you share the risk too. That's how it goes, my girl.'

'Oh, all right,' Summer said, sighing.

'I'll get the Ideas Book.' Celia got up, her pink track pants and matching top making her look like a young, miniature version of a cool old granny who went out power walking along the river with hand weights.

'Here, show me that pie chart again,' Monty said to Summer.

Gabby congratulated Summer on her project then left them to it, warning Celia that she should be in bed in ten minutes when Grandpa said so, and urging Summer not to stay up too late even though she still had to print labels for her jars. She then retired to her room, hoping for a good night's sleep free of unpleasant visitations.

But it didn't go that way. Around midnight, she woke gasping from a terrible nightmare of being lost in blackness, unable to feel her body, unable to talk, being trapped in limbo, hearing voices from a distance but not able to connect. She opened her mouth to call for help, to ask someone what had happened, but nothing came out. It was as if she'd been put in a dark bubble somewhere and no one knew where she was. Almost as though she'd died but had nowhere to go, lost in unending emptiness.

She pulled herself from bed at five-thirty in the morning, sleep-deprived and groggy, and staggered to the shower. She couldn't go to work, she was certain of that. Luciano was opening the store, and while she'd planned to be there to go through stocktake with him, it would just have to wait. She was in no condition to play the role of leader today.

Instead, she pulled on her soft, tattered jeans and a long-sleeved tee and messaged Pippa to see what she was up to. She needed company. A few messages later, they had a plan.

It was the smell that greeted Gabby first as she stepped out of her small, red, long-in-the-tooth Barina – manure, hay, wood shavings and eucalyptus. Pippa's horse Hercules was kept at a private agistment property at Kilsyth, about twenty minutes' drive from Pippa and Harvey's house, and it was here that Pippa had convinced Gabby to meet her, saying they could go for a ride to blow away all the stress. She pulled her denim jacket around her and released her long, unruly ponytail from being tucked inside the jacket. The time on her phone was a quarter past nine. They'd agreed to meet after the school run.

While she was waiting, she checked to see if any messages had come through to her blog overnight, and found two responses.

I think you might have my father's heart. He died after a car accident in the outback on the thirtieth of September two years ago.

Gabby shook her head. Hearts only lasted six hours at the most.

My sister died from head injuries after she fell from her rooftop while cleaning the gutters. She was thirty-five. She has two young daughters and was a high school teacher. She lived in Adelaide and died on 5 October 2017.

That one was more feasible. The woman would need to have died just past midnight, as Gabby's operation was early in the morning on the same day. But she still wasn't certain they could have done the retrieval and flown the heart the hour and a half from Adelaide in time. It *could* be it, but she had her doubts.

She put her phone away and looked around the property. She'd pulled up near the stables and tack room, under the shade of a gum tree. It was beautifully quiet, with just bird chatter in the air. A horse let out a loud snort and she went to the white wooden railing of the nearest paddock to see if she could find Hercules. She didn't have to look far. As soon as she approached the fence, the big black horse in the yard looked up from where he was chewing, pricked his ears, whinnied at her and trotted to the fence.

'Oh, aren't you handsome!' she said, holding her hand out over the railing. He came straight to her and she closed her fist for him to sniff – a horseman's handshake – which he did, his warm breath caressing her skin. She leaned to the side to peer past his huge bulk, just to check she had the right horse before she fell completely in love. Finding no other black horses in sight, she let her heart be swept away by his huge dark eyes, long thick forelock and mane, shiny coat and calm presence. Until this moment, she'd had her doubts about Pippa's sanity in keeping a secret horse, but now she was head over heels for him too.

Pippa's old and shabby blue Corolla wheezed up alongside Gabby's car – no one in the McPhee family had ever put much value in cars – and her sister jumped out, her fierce frown disappearing as soon as she clapped eyes on Hercules.

'Isn't he gorgeous?'

'Yes, he really is!' Gabby hugged Pippa, noting the squinty flesh around her sister's eyes that suggested Pippa had been crying.

Hercules gave a throaty nicker to Pippa.

'I'm coming,' she said, releasing Gabby to open the passenger door of her car and fish in her handbag. 'The kids have been getting a lot of cut-up apple and carrot in their lunchboxes,' she said, opening a sandwich bag and pulling out treats for Hercules. He took them delicately from her outstretched hand.

'Do they wonder why?'

'No. The sugar cubes got a few queries, though.'

Pippa was joking, Gabby was almost certain.

'All right, big man,' Pippa said, running her hand down his neck. 'I need to get changed.' She was wearing clothes suitable for school drop-off and client meetings – a dress, tights and pointy flats.

Pippa went to the boot and retrieved her gym bag, which happened to have jodhpurs, a polo shirt, three-quarter-length riding boots and a helmet stashed inside. Then she pulled out another bag, this one a small suitcase on wheels, the size of carry-on aeroplane luggage. 'This one's for you,' she said, the wheels grating over the bumpy ground as she wheeled it to Gabby. 'I often carry around work stuff in this bag to take to clients, so the kids didn't bat an eye at it.'

'Thanks. Did you borrow some gear?'

'No. I decided to get you an early Christmas present,' Pippa said. 'I went on a bit of a shopping splurge at Horseland straight after I organised agistment here and I got you a full set at the same time as I got all mine.'

'No, Pippa, you can't,' Gabby said, bending down to unzip the suitcase.

'Yes, I can and I did. Nothing brings me more pleasure in my life right now than this, so please don't spoil the fun for me. Just say thank you,' Pippa said wearily.

'Are you okay?' Gabby asked, putting her hand on Pippa's arm.

To her alarm, Pippa's eyes filled with tears and her face crumpled. 'What's happened?'

Pippa shook her head and waved a hand at her. 'Just Harvey stuff,' she said.

'What stuff?'

'I think he gave me an ultimatum last night,' she said, her voice cracking.

'Which was?'

'He wants more sex. And if he can't have more sex, then he doesn't want to be in this relationship any more.' Pippa broke down, leaning her elbows on the wooden fence to support her head.

'What the hell?' Gabby was furious. 'He can't just demand sex! Doesn't he know anything about women? What did you say?'

'I said if he paid half as much attention to me as he does to his job then there might be a chance of building intimacy.'

'And what did he say?'

'That we should simply have sex and then we would have intimacy!'

'Oh, for god's sake.' Gabby sighed, rubbing Pippa's back. She stayed silent for a few moments, enjoying Hercules's snuffling attention and calm vibe as he hung out with them at the fence. 'What are you going to do?'

Pippa wiped her face and shrugged. 'No idea.'

'Have you thought any more about counselling?'

'I honestly don't think it would make a bit of difference,' Pippa said sadly. 'I think we've just come to the end of the road. It feels like we're both just waiting for someone to make the call. Besides,' she said, nodding towards Hercules, 'this is my therapy, right here.' The horse blew out a long, contented breath and flicked his tail lazily at a fly on his side.

'Okay, let's get our counselling session started, then,' Gabby said. She went back to the suitcase. Inside, she found two navy polo shirts, a pair of taupe-coloured jodhpurs – fortunately in a generous size – ankle boots and a black flocked helmet. It would have cost a small fortune. She looked up to rebuke Pippa again, but her sister's face had already brightened, her cheeks regaining their colour. It was clear this really was bringing her great happiness.

'Thank you,' Gabby said instead. 'I love them.'

'Yay!' Pippa clapped her hands. 'Let's get changed.'

They got dressed in the stable the same way they'd done as teenagers, standing in the wood shavings, avoiding the damp parts, the seductive aroma of horse in the air. Hercules came in to watch, shoving his nose inside their bags, looking for treats or something to chew on. He picked up one of Gabby's boots just as she was hopping on one foot to get to it, and made to escape before Pippa caught him and brought it back.

They were laughing so hard that Gabby forgot about her nightmare last night and instead felt completely free of responsibilities. The rest of the world – the kids, The Tin Man, the woman in the cafe, her medications, even the awful news that Pippa's marriage really did seem to be on the edge of collapse, and everything that meant in relation to the future care of Gabby's kids – all just fell away.

At last they were ready. Pippa put a halter on Hercules. The brass buckles were shiny and new, and jangled as she adjusted it at the side of his face.

'Who am I riding?' Gabby asked.

'Did you see that Appaloosa a few yards away?' Pippa asked, picking up a brush to clean her horse's already near-perfect coat.

'No. I didn't get any further than nuzzling your little pony here.'

'Do you know, I almost don't notice his size any more but when I'm up there –' Pippa nodded towards his back – 'I feel untouchable.'

'Lifted up,' Gabby said.

'Exactly.' They fell silent for a moment, with just the soft sound of brushstrokes in the air. 'Anyway, the Appy belongs to the woman who owns this place and she has difficulty riding these days due to a knee problem, so she's happy to lend him out for rides.'

'Is he safe? I'm far too old to be falling off horses.'

'I saw someone else ride him the other day and he seems pretty quiet, a bit slow if anything.'

'Good.'

'Come on,' Pippa said, flinging the brush to the corner of the stable. 'Jump on and I'll give you a ride over to the paddock.'

'I can't get up there!'

'Yes, you can. There's a mounting block just outside. I'll dink you.' She grinned.

'No, it's fine, I'll just walk.'

'Come on, it'll be fun. Please?'

Gabby groaned. 'What if I fall off?'

'You're not going to fall off. We're walking about a hundred metres! It will take you back to our childhood.'

Gabby hesitated but agreed.

Pippa led Hercules alongside the plastic moulded mounting block and stepped up onto it, throwing his lead rope over his neck as she did.

'Stand still, baby,' she said, placing her hands on his back. She jumped on the spot a couple of times to get propulsion then sprang up, landing with her torso across his back and then kicking wildly with her legs to try to wiggle her way up to sitting, but she couldn't make it. Gabby laughed.

'Stop it!' Pippa squeaked, trying not to laugh herself. Neither of them had been bareback on a horse in decades.

Gabby helped Pippa up, grabbing her lower leg and giving her a boost until finally she was up and sitting, triumphant.

'There!' Pippa said, puffing. 'Your turn.'

Gabby couldn't stop giggling. This horse had sent them back in time and it was absolute bliss. She was young and strong again, in her other life, the life 'before', somewhere on the other side of the dividing line down the centre of her chest, the weight of her worries nowhere in sight.

'Come on,' Pippa urged.

'You had the easy bit,' Gabby countered. 'His rump's a lot higher, so I have to jump further than you did.'

'But you're taller. That's how it works.'

Gabby put her hands on Hercules's back. He was behaving himself perfectly, having barely moved while Pippa had flailed about, only shifting one foot to account for her weight landing on him. She began to bounce, psyching herself, but the giggles kept coming.

'Pippa, I don't have the bladder strength for this any more,' she said, suddenly serious. 'What if I leap up and wet myself?'

That just made Pippa laugh more, which in turn made Gabby collapse again too. They were having the wildest time and they hadn't even begun to ride. At last, Gabby coughed and took some deep breaths. 'I need to focus. I might be able to jump, and I can laugh, but I'm not sure I can do both at the same time.'

'Serious face,' Pippa said, waving her hand over her face like a magician, setting her mouth. But the mirth was just below the surface. All Gabby had to do was catch her eye and it sent them into peals of laughter.

'That's it, I give up!' Gabby stepped away from Hercules. 'I'm going to walk.'

She stepped down off the block and held out her hand for the rope, which Pippa handed over. Gabby led Hercules to the other paddock, grinning, all the weight magically lifted from her mind and spirit. Between her dog and this horse, they might just be able to solve all the problems of the world.

14

'Hi, Janice, it's Krystal. I can't come in to work today, sorry. Coming down with something. I'm going to drop Jasper off and head back home. See you Monday.'

Krystal disconnected the call, glad that Janice hadn't answered her phone and she could just leave a voicemail. It was raining and the temperature had dropped again, a retreat to winter weather, and the darkness of the clouds seemed to fill her small apartment and drag her mood down further. She couldn't deal with Janice's power suits and heels today, nor sorting endless lost property, printing out head lice warnings or collating permission slips for the swimming carnival. Some days, it was just all too hard.

She rugged up her boys in long fleecy pants and jumpers, and hustled them into school and day care before driving numbly back home. After flopping back into bed and staring at the wall for nearly an hour, she forced herself to get up. She made some instant noodles and ate them. Then her thoughts turned to vodka. It was nearly eleven o'clock. That wasn't too bad, was it? Sure, pubs didn't open before midday, but it wasn't like she was going to drink all day. She wasn't some kind of drunk.

'Pull yourself together, Krystal.' She took her bowl to the kitchen and washed it, then forced herself to turn away from the cupboard above the fridge where the alcohol was kept and do laundry instead. Forced herself to think of all the terrible things her mother used to do when she was drinking, of all the ways she let her children down.

She folded clothes and put them away. Put a batch of muffins into the oven for school lunches. Found the missing library books. Scrubbed the awful mouldy bits from around the bathroom taps. Threw away the odd socks that had been sitting in a pile in the laundry room for months. Made a shopping list.

'Just be a good mum. That's all you have to do.'

But, oh, the ghosts were haunting her today. The memories of Evan. Thoughts of Cordelia-Aurora and the Arthurs at that horrible party. Of being escorted out of The Tin Man.

She looked around the apartment. The only reason she and Evan had bought an apartment here in St Kilda was because they'd both been working in the restaurant nearby. It had no view, except of the walls of the neighbouring buildings. But she'd left the restaurant when she was six months pregnant with Jasper, and now the boys were getting bigger. They were so active. The walls had scuff marks from shoes and soccer balls, and their squeals and chatter ricocheted around the small space. Life was moving on without Evan.

Maybe she should move out to the suburbs. Evan's life insurance had paid off the apartment and given her a little bit to put away. Moving further out would mean more space for the boys and a bit more money in the bank to play with.

She touched the flags that stretched across the window looking out onto the apartment block next door. They were made of rough jute and dyed in bright colours that cheered even the greyest of outlooks. She and Evan had bought them at a stall at the Queen Victoria Market one scorching hot summer's day. She liked it when Evan was hot and flustered, red and sweating, without any of the traces of haughtiness that sometimes filtered through from his upbringing. He was just a limp, damp mess like the rest of society, eating ice cream and guzzling water from plastic bottles that were never cold enough.

There were so many memories here in this apartment. She'd already lost so much of Evan; she wasn't sure she could lose this too.

Her dark mood swirled to anger. That ridiculous party last weekend had reignited her resentment at years of rejection by the Arthur family, especially Cordelia-Aurora, from the very first day they met.

Six months into their relationship, when Krystal was still only twenty-two years old, Evan had taken her to meet his family. She'd been anxious that his delay in introducing her had meant that he didn't see a future for the two of them, but he assured her it was more to shield her from them.

'They can be difficult,' he'd said. 'Especially my sister.'

'She's mad at you for leaving the firm.'

'That, and other sibling stuff.'

The date was set for Christmas Day, possibly the worst day in the history of dating for a new addition to meet the family, but as Krystal didn't have anywhere else to be and Evan felt compelled to see his parents, she insisted she go with him.

'It has to be one day. Why not today?' They were at her place – a tiny one-bedroom apartment above a Chinese takeaway, where the smell of fried onions and soy sauce clung permanently to the air-conditioning vents, and each afternoon before they left for work they heard Mrs Kravitz next door crying into her chicken and sweet corn soup as she watched the news. She was only young, still in her thirties, but had lost her husband six months ago after a short and vicious illness; they'd had no children, and Krystal couldn't imagine anything worse.

'Because I'd rather stay here with you,' he said, his voice husky, kissing her nose and lowering the bedsheet to reveal her naked body and lay tiny kisses across her chest.

'Come on,' she said. 'How bad could it be?'

'Bad, trust me,' he said, inching his way down between her breasts.

He murmured, getting back to delighting in her body for the third time since coming home late from the restaurant. They were both always so wired from the intensity of service that it took them ages to come down. It didn't matter though. They slept in late each day, rarely rising before midday, and lived their lives in the nocturnal hours.

'Well, it'll be a quick trip then,' she said, and broke out into squeals of pleasure as his tongue traced her hip bone, and the next little while was spent most definitely not thinking about the Arthur family.

But Christmas Day awoke hot and angry, and Krystal and Evan endured the slow crawl down to the peninsula to the white-pillared home of his parents, which in the future she would come to think of as The White House and to dread visiting more than having her wisdom teeth out.

She'd worn a simple yellow dress with red sandals, and brushed her long hair till it was shiny and put it up in a high ponytail. She was bringing Ivy and Wyatt a fruit cake which she'd made herself, having looked up a recipe online and bought all the ingredients and a square baking tin, and burned herself on the boiling mixture. She'd smothered the cake with thick white icing because it had broken just a little when she'd flipped it out of the tin.

She'd been very proud of her cake, tying a silver ribbon around it and adding a decorative piece of holly on top and covering it carefully with a triple layer of cling wrap for the drive down.

'You really don't have to take them anything,' Evan had said several times, looking anxious, and she'd assumed it was because he knew her cooking skills were limited. She'd taken it as a challenge to show him she could be thoughtful and clever and lovable.

'I know, but I want to,' she said.

Finally, he stopped trying to talk her out of it and simply kissed her on the forehead. 'You're so sweet.'

She knew Evan's family were well off, but she was utterly thrown by the magnitude of wealth on display. The white pillars and walls of the house were blinding in the light and there were so many rounded layers it looked like a ghastly wedding cake. A heavily manicured lawn sparkled with tiny rainbows from invisible sprinklers in the ground that were sending out mists of water droplets. Evan parked alongside lush topiaries. Aside from the fountain in the centre of the circular driveway, all was silent.

Back in her mother's fibro shack in the Dandenongs, Christmas Day hadn't been a barrel of laughs, but it was anything but silent, with the throaty revs of motorbikes, her mother's latest boyfriend's tools hitting the concrete floor of the carport with loud clangs, music blaring from car speakers, clinking beer bottles, whining dogs and bursts of drunken laughter.

Evan put his arm around her shoulders, squeezing her to him, not saying a word but, she thought, able to sense her plummeting courage as her soft footsteps neared the house. It was Cordelia-Aurora who met them, just after Evan pushed open the front door. Not a moment after he'd called hello she was there, gliding across the tiled floor as though she didn't even need to walk, but invisible servants just picked her up and carried her wherever she needed to go.

'Evan, darling, you look too thin,' she purred, kissing him on the cheek.

'Hello to you too,' he said, stiffly.

Krystal stood with a stupid smile plastered on her sweaty face, waiting for Evan's big sister to acknowledge her, or at least glance in her direction, but Cordelia-Aurora's eyes were locked firmly onto Evan.

'How was the drive? Was it terrible?' she asked him. Not even a flicker of an eye movement in Krystal's direction.

By now, Krystal's smile had waned and she could feel the corners of her mouth wanting to draw down hard. Her cheeks flared with the embarrassment of someone who'd brought a homemade cake to this freaking palace.

'I'd like you to meet Krystal.' Evan forced Cordelia-Aurora to look at Krystal.

Cordelia-Aurora sighed . . .

She sighed!

. . . and slid her eyes to Krystal's, nodding at her.

'It's lovely to meet you,' Krystal said, and thrust out her hand.

Cordelia-Aurora looked down, very slowly, as if considering whether or not to touch the thing that was hovering between them. Some kind of finishing school manners must have kicked in because she roused herself, took Krystal's hand (though didn't squeeze it), tilted her head and said, 'Pleasure. Thank you for coming.'

Krystal held up her cake plate. 'I made a cake to give to your parents.'

'She's worked so hard on it,' Evan said, nodding, encouraging Cordelia-Aurora to play nice.

'Oh, lovely,' Cordelia-Aurora said, sounding genuinely pleased.

Krystal's hopes soared. She'd done the right thing! All that sweating in her stuffy apartment and burns and stress had been worth it. Cordelia-Aurora held out her hands for the plate and Krystal proudly handed it over, then looked up at Evan, who winked at her.

Cordelia-Aurora turned on her heel for them to follow and spoke as she walked away. 'The caterers have everything sorted for our lunch today but the staff have all just gone for their tea break so I'll give this to them. They don't expect anything fancy from us so this will be just the thing.'

Evan sucked in air between his teeth and reached for Krystal's hand, squeezing it hard. *Sorry.*

She smiled at him. *It's fine! It's nothing!*

But it wasn't nothing, and she knew then that Cordelia-Aurora was going to make trouble for her till the day she died.

She took her hand away from the flags at her apartment window. Cordelia-Aurora would make trouble for her till the day she died . . . or the day Evan did.

It was Cordelia-Aurora's fault that Evan's heart had been ripped out and given to someone else. Krystal never wanted to do it.

Could she sue Evan's sister for emotional distress after she forced her to sign the consent forms? She laughed out loud. Imagine suing one of Melbourne's elite legal families. It would be like trying to sue the Mafia! It was completely outrageous.

Except it wasn't *completely* outrageous, was it?

There had to be another law firm in the city who would just love the chance to take down the Arthurs. She simply had to find them. She would throw herself into this vendetta – oh, what a delicious word – and forget all about the woman in the cafe who might, or might not, have her husband's stolen heart. Instead, Cordelia-Aurora would pay, if not in money then certainly in reputation.

She found a list of injury claims lawyers in the city and phoned a few until she found Trentino Cossa, who could see her after lunch.

'If he can't help you, no one can,' the receptionist chirped cheerfully. 'He hasn't lost a case in over three years.'

Her heart bursting with hope, Krystal pulled on a black skirt suit left over from her days at the restaurant – she was thrilled to find it still fitted – and paired it with a soft white blouse, pantihose and demure heels. She wanted to be taken seriously and to be respected as the grieving widow that she was.

She treated herself to a cab, not wanting to fuss with parking or deal with public transport in the rain. At the firm, the receptionist ushered her into Trentino Cossa's office, which boasted a two-metre-long aquarium of colourful tropical fish.

'Please, take a seat,' Trentino said, eyeing her through his Buddy Holly glasses and gesturing to the plush leather chair opposite his desk. 'I'm very sorry for your loss, Mrs Arthur. I met your husband once or twice but knew him mostly by reputation. He was quite the young lawyer to watch. I know my partners would have been happy to entice him over into our firm if they could have.'

Krystal swallowed. That was a version of Evan she'd never met, but she was still touched. 'Thank you.'

'Please, tell me how I can help.'

She clutched her sweating hands together and told him everything that had happened at the hospital in Sydney, everything Cordelia-Aurora had said to her, the blackmail she'd threatened, how she'd taken advantage of Krystal's shock and devastation, and Krystal's distress at feeling forced into signing the donation papers. Trentino took plenty of handwritten notes, allowing her to talk. When she finished, he put his engraved silver pen down, lifted his stormy-grey eyes to hers and said, 'You won't win.'

His bluntness was like a slap in the face. She wondered if she'd heard him right, or indeed if he'd heard *her* correctly.

'What do you mean?' she said, trying to sound calm, curious even, as though what he'd said was worth a discussion.

'Look, to be blunt, Mrs Arthur, there wouldn't be a lawyer in Melbourne willing to take on a case against Cordelia-Aurora. The Arthur family are legal royalty in this city.'

'Right,' she said, hope buoying, because maybe there was still a chance that a law firm *outside* Melbourne would take on the case.

'But even if you could take away that hurdle, I don't think you have a leg to stand on. You were Evan's next of kin and you signed the papers. A whole world of legal process surrounds organ donation, and hospitals have to ensure that everyone is informed before signing.'

Maybe she could sue the hospital?

'But you wouldn't get anywhere with the hospital either.'

She blinked back tears, ignoring the pain in her throat.

'The courts wouldn't look favourably on your situation. There would be a media storm around the case and the public wouldn't be on your side. Even if by some miracle you did win the case, your name would be mud.'

She could put up with that. She'd do it for Evan. Evan deserved justice and this was how she could do it. This was how she could make what she'd done right.

'No firm in their right mind would take this on a no-win no-fee basis, because the chances of winning are slim to none, so you'd be made to pay up front. The legal fees would bankrupt you while the Arthur family would simply find ways to keep stringing it out through the courts for years and years, which they'd legally be able to do, and it wouldn't cost them a cent.'

'Oh.' She hadn't thought of that.

'My advice to you,' he said, more gently this time, 'is to take good care of the money you received from Evan's life insurance payout, invest it wisely, get some counselling, enjoy your kids, live a good life, and try to move on.'

Rain slid down the cab's window and the windscreen wipers thumped from side to side. She couldn't process the depths of her disappointment that there was no way to make amends for what had happened to Evan.

Her thoughts flicked to Gabriella McPhee the way she imagined a former smoker's mind must jump, unbidden, to cigarettes. She pulled out her phone to distract herself and went to Facebook to look up The Tin Man, as she'd done before, reading through posts, looking for clues about Gabriella's life, looking for photos, looking for one of Gabriella where she might be able to see the top of the scar. Then she entered Gabriella's name in the search function, wondering why she hadn't done it before. And there was her profile, accompanied by a smiling photo of her with her three children – a boy and two girls. But also listed in the results was another account. *Gabriella McPhee Heart Transplant.*

Krystal's pulse quickened. She clicked on the profile. *Heart transplant 5 October 2017, Melbourne. Looking for donor family.* There were a number of responses on the page, some as recent as this morning. It looked as though the profile had only been there for a few days – since Monday, when they'd met at the cafe. She read through the posts, her own heart in her throat, hoping someone wouldn't say something that sounded convincing enough to cut Krystal out of the race. But mostly, there were only awful responses on the page.

Against God's will . . .

Leave the dead in peace . . .

Greedy . . . you already got their heart, now you want their family too.

Zombie . . .

Zombie? Krystal gasped with disgust on Gabriella's behalf. How could people be so horrible? Suddenly, she felt a wave of sympathy for Gabriella when all she'd felt before was weird jealousy, desperation and even anger. It wasn't Gabriella's fault that she had Evan's heart. Well, Krystal *thought* she had Evan's heart. There was no way of knowing for sure, but she still had this urgent need to meet her and find out somehow. For the first time that day, she felt like she was on the right path. She messaged Gabriella privately.

It's me again. From the cafe. I don't know what happened the other day with your dog; it was all very confusing. Can we meet? I have Fridays off. Is tomorrow any good? Krystal

15

> Any chance we can move our
> meeting with Marco to my
> house today?

Gabby read Luciano's message while pulling on her brown suede boots. She had been just about to leave the house and head in to The Tin Man for the meeting with the coffee trader. Her mind raced with questions.

Their trader, Marco, travelled the globe constantly for his work, going into dense jungles and unstable political environments to meet with growers. He had the carefree nature of someone who was used to plans going awry. She didn't think he'd mind where they met him.

> I'm sure it would be okay with
> Marco. Is everything all right?

All good, I'm not sick or
anything. I'll message Marco.
See you soon.

Intriguing. A small thrill of excitement ran through her at the prospect of seeing the enigmatic roaster in his home environment.

The sun was out again after yesterday's downpour and she was wearing her brightest maxi dress, a decidedly tropical pattern, deep navy with large green ferns and colourful parrots and flowers; she knew the green intensified the colour of her eyes. She added a cream wool shrug for a bit of extra cover, and hopped into her car, feeling confident in her appearance while also telling herself to get a grip. Even *if* Luciano was interested in her, she wasn't exactly a great catch – the baggage she brought with her was enough to sink a ship. Besides, he was an employee.

Over in Coburg, she passed shop after shop offering mouth-watering food and fantasised about all the multicultural treats she could pick up to take home to her family – falafel wraps, haloumi pies, spinach tarts and European cheeses. Lebanese, Egyptian, Greek, Italian. Coburg had it all. She should have brought an esky with her.

She found Luciano's house in a wide street of older, family-sized properties. The homes were bathed in bright sunshine, small lawns at the front behind old-fashioned fences. His was an art deco house with latte-coloured rendered walls and extra-wide architraves around the doors and windows.

An abundance of sweet-smelling jasmine in bloom spilling over the front fence stopped her in her tracks. The aroma was practically visible, like a halo. Her whole body flooded with optimism as each note spun and sparkled through her senses. In parallel beds through the lawn, mature roses dazzled in shades of blush, candy cane, claret and sunshine, with equally powerful fragrances to match. She beamed with delight – the front yard was like a lolly shop for her nose. Up two concrete steps, she rang the buzzer at the metal grille door.

Luciano appeared inside the house, wearing jeans and a pale blue polo shirt, the curves of his biceps peeking out below the sleeves. His hair was a bit more dishevelled than usual – a few uncontrolled curls – but his whiskers were the same as always. He wore olive green loafers on his feet. His gaze drifted down her colourful dress and he stumbled slightly as he said hello, which simply added to Gabby's joy, already ignited by the fragrant garden.

'Come in. Sorry to do this to you at the last minute.'

'That's okay,' she said, crossing the threshold into his home. 'Stuff happens in life that you can't control – like ex-husbands, for example.' Luciano gave her a curious look, and she shook her head. 'Never mind.' She followed him down the tiled hallway lined with family photographs. In the lounge room a tennis racquet lay abandoned on the grey carpet and a young girl's denim jacket studded with pink sequins hung over a chair; also strewn about were some kind of monster truck and stacks of schoolbooks. An antique, rounded green couch sat in front of her, perfectly matching the style of the house. Sitting at one end was a young girl. With her long dark hair, delicate chin and caramel skin, she was a smaller, feminine version of Luciano. Gabby quickly connected the dots to conclude that Luciano must be married, which well and truly dampened her fizzing joy from moments ago. She chastened herself for getting carried away. This was a good thing and would make it easier to let go of her ridiculous fantasies.

'This is Antonia,' Luciano said.

'Hi, I'm Gabby,' Gabby said, smiling at the girl, who looked up from the book she had open on her lap, her pen poised.

'Hi,' Antonia mumbled. She didn't smile. In fact, she had the same dark brooding thing going on that Luciano did so well.

'Antonia is sick today and couldn't go to school. Normally my mamma would look after her, but she has gone away for a few days to visit my aunt.'

'It's all good,' Gabby said, smiling too broadly, trying to rapidly adjust to this new information about Luciano. She followed him into the kitchen, where he hurriedly moved some dirty cereal bowls off the bench and into the sink.

Marco was already there, sitting at the wooden table, wearing his trademark white turtleneck skivvy and jeans. He stood to greet Gabby, kissing her on each cheek, his greying beard tickling her face. Marco was always on a tight schedule, taking more than a hundred flights a year and a good number of trains and buses in between. He reminded Gabby of a sailor, popping into their port every now and then.

She took a moment to look around. The kitchen had big windows and lots of filtered light, and hanging from the walls and filling all available bench space were pots of delicate ferns and blooming orchids, in whites, pinks and oranges. 'This is beautiful,' she said. 'It's like sitting inside a greenhouse.'

'It is,' Luciano agreed. 'But I can't take credit for it. My sister-in-law set them up.'

Gabby was dying to ask more but the two men were taking their seats and Marco began his rundown of his recent travels and what was happening out in the world's coffee countries.

'Ideally our sources of coffee would remain the same; but unfortunately, gang violence, corruption and climate change are making things unreliable,' Marco explained. 'Leaf rust has been rampant through El Salvador this year and yields are down by as much as sixty per cent.'

'Oh, that's terrible,' Gabby said. El Salvadoran beans were her particular favourite.

'Producers are telling me over and over that climate change is their biggest problem.'

'Next time you're in the cafe, I should introduce you to Ed – Edwina – my head barista. She's studying meteorology and climate change is her big thing. I'm sure she'd love to hear about your experiences.'

Marco went on to outline alternative options for South American beans. Gabby tried to concentrate on all the figures – millions of kilos of green coffee produced each year, altitudes and profiles – but she was distracted by Luciano, whose knee had just bumped hers, and whose house she was sitting in, and whose daughter was on the couch in the next room. Before she knew it, Luciano and Marco had agreed on a plan for their next shipment and Marco was on his feet. She stood too and he kissed her farewell on each cheek.

'Till next time, *addio*.'

'*Addio*,' she said.

On his way out, he stopped to farewell Antonia, saying something in Italian that made the girl smile, and then he was gone, onto his next adventure.

'Well,' Gabby said, turning to Luciano. 'That man knows how to live, doesn't he? I don't think there's a corner of the earth he hasn't seen.'

'Maybe Antarctica,' Luciano said. 'I don't think there's much coffee grown there.'

'True. Marco is driven by the bean, that's for sure.'

There was a small pause then, as they hovered at the doorway to the lounge room, watching Antonia flicking through her maths workbook. Gabby couldn't help but pry. 'What kind of illness does your daughter have?' she asked, wondering suddenly if she should be worried about catching whatever disease was floating around in the air.

Luciano indicated with a flick of his head that she should follow him back to the kitchen, where they resumed their places at his rustic table. 'She isn't really sick. At least, I don't think so.' He frowned. 'I don't know what to think most of the time.'

'What do you mean?'

'She isn't my daughter; she's my niece,' he said, lowering his voice.

'Niece?'

'My brother and his wife were killed six months ago in a boating accident.'

'Oh, god, I'm so sorry.'

'In their will, they had appointed me as guardian of their three children if anything ever happened to them.'

'Oh, Luciano.' Tears sprang to her eyes, leaky sieve that she was.

Luciano stared towards the lounge room but the faraway look in his eyes suggested his mind was somewhere else entirely. 'They would never have really believed anything would happen to them. I don't even know why they chose me. I'd never settled down. Much like Marco, I was travelling all the time, with a girl in every port.'

To Gabby's disgust at herself it stung to hear him say that, but Luciano didn't seem to notice her discomfort.

'This is their house – my brother and sister-in-law's. I moved in here so the kids could stay in their home.' His eyes roved around the kitchen. 'I've taken over the mortgage and now I'm raising three kids. Just like that.' He snapped his fingers. 'Everything changed overnight.'

She gave him a sympathetic grimace, knowing that feeling well.

He went on, 'Antonia's not really sick, as in she's not *ill*. She's . . . tired.' He shrugged helplessly. 'Grief is exhausting.'

'For you too, I bet.'

'I still can't believe they're gone. It was Sergio's birthday last week. He was younger than me. He would have been forty.' He stared into the middle distance for a moment and she waited for him to continue. 'Now I'm my mamma's only son left and I went from playboy to dad-of-three overnight.'

'How old are the kids?'

'Antonia's the oldest; she's ten.'

'Same as my Celia.'

'Olivia is eight and Cooper is six.'

Wow. No wonder the man seemed distracted so much of the time. He was carrying the weight of the world – three worlds, really. Three important, difficult, precious and excruciating worlds.

'I never sleep any more,' he said.

Despite herself, Gabby laughed. 'That's completely normal, I'm afraid.'

A tiny smile played at his lips. 'So now you see why I need to work with coffee. I can't live without it.'

'Spoken like a true parent,' she said, and squeezed his arm. His eyes went bright for a moment but he swallowed hard. 'So, the other day when I was describing my visions, those crazy moments you mentioned you'd had . . . were they to do with your brother?'

He blinked and gazed at her intently, then folded his arms at his chest. 'One day I was driving the car – Sergio and Lucy's car, because it's a family car and I only had a two-door – and I stopped at a set of traffic lights and looked over at the passenger seat and he was there, just sitting beside me, smiling. He had the chipped tooth from when he'd fallen off his bike as a teenager. He even smelled of garlic, because he loved the stuff but, geez, it didn't agree with him.' He shook his head, remembering. 'He was only there a second and then he was gone. But it was real, you know?'

'Yeah, I think I do.'

He scratched at his whiskers. 'Anyway, there have been a few moments like that, living here in their house, everything still vibrating with their presence. Cooper, the youngest, I hear him talking to them at night, laughing even, sometimes. It really sounds like they must be there.'

'I don't think we can logically explain everything, especially anything to do with death – the greatest mystery on earth. You'd drive yourself mad,' she said.

'Yep, been there.'

'Me too.'

They smiled at each other, tentative smiles, and Gabby's thoughts again turned to the woman in the cafe, the woman she needed to find, the woman whose heart had been broken when she'd lost her husband. Gabby could help her, she just knew it.

Back out in her car, she checked her phone for Facebook messages and almost leapt out of her seat when she saw a new message, from a Krystal Arthur. *That* was her name! She replied quickly. *Yes, today is great. I'll be at the cafe in half an hour. I'll wait for you, whenever you can get there. Gabby.*

She let go of her plans to stock up on multicultural foods and instead drove too fast back towards The Tin Man, sweaty and jittery. Her heart, as if knowing it was going to meet up with Krystal, was jumping around too. She hoped Krystal got the message soon. She hoped she wouldn't make Gabby wait a long time, or worse, back out entirely. But by the time she got to the cafe, Krystal had sent another message and confirmed she would be there soon.

It was happening.

She didn't know what to do with herself. Ed was working at the coffee machine, Lin was alternating between plating up cheesy croissants and clearing dishes, customers were coming and going, but no one seemed to need Gabby. Should she claim a quiet corner of the cafe for her and Krystal to talk? Or should they go off site? What if another vision came and it was even worse than the others? She paced the floorboards, picking up an empty coffee cup here or there, folding throw rugs over the backs of the chairs, changing the water for the lilies, which were still going strong a week later.

Her belly was flipping but she didn't know if she should eat something to calm it down or if eating would make it worse.

Then Krystal was there, standing just inside the entrance, wearing flared trousers, boots and a snug black top, staring straight at Gabby. Her nose twitched, as though she was unsure if she should approach. Gabby reminded herself to breathe, then smiled reassuringly and moved towards her.

'Krystal?'

Krystal nodded, seemingly unable to speak. Then her eyes dropped to the neckline of Gabby's tropical dress and Gabby's hand went there automatically, touching the top of her scar.

'Sorry,' Krystal said, her hand on her forehead, looking away at the ground.

'No, it's okay,' Gabby said. 'Please, come and sit down.' She led Krystal to the brown leather wingback chairs in the corner closest to the courtyard, with a view of the fountain outside. They both sat stiffly, perched on the edges of the chairs, as if one of them might need to leave at any moment.

Gabby crossed her arms over her body, then released them again. What was she going to say to this woman that wouldn't make her sound crazy? Her brain was unwilling to figure out how to approach this conversation. She was waiting to *feel* something, for another vision, or for a bolt of lightning to confirm what she suspected. But nothing came.

Damn you, she cursed him, the one who'd been haunting her, turning up in the middle of the night to terrify her but absent now when she was trying to solve a puzzle. Then she wondered if maybe that was the point. His absence might mean she was on the wrong track completely. Confusion and doubt began to spin. Maybe she'd imagined the whole thing after all – not the visions, they were real enough, but their connection to this woman.

The silence between them stretched past awkward.

'I'm sorry . . .' Krystal began, at exactly the same moment as Gabriella spoke.

'I know this will sound crazy . . .'

They both stopped.

'You go first,' Gabby said.

'Okay,' Krystal began. 'Firstly, I just want to say sorry for the last time I was here. I upset you and your dog and, well, I'm just so embarrassed and I didn't mean any harm . . .'

'It's fine, really. I think Sally, my dog, just sensed something unusual. Please, let's start again. I saw you here a couple of weeks ago. You were sitting over there –' she pointed to the green wall – 'and you were wearing a pink shawl.'

Krystal looked over to the wall, then chewed her bottom lip.

'I was going to introduce myself but you left before I got the chance.'

Krystal remained silent for a moment, and Jack Johnson's mellow voice filled the cafe. Then she looked straight at Gabby, took a breath and said, 'I think you have my husband's heart.'

Gabby nodded. 'I think I do too.'

16

This was the moment Krystal had been waiting for. Now it was here, she had no idea what to do. Gabby's head was lowered and she was almost peeking at Krystal from below her ginger lashes. Krystal was vaguely aware of the group of Scandinavian-looking tourists who'd just burst into laughter at a nearby table. Vaguely aware of the grind of the coffee machine. Vaguely aware that someone was wearing too much perfume. And vaguely aware of her own heart beating in her chest.

Evan.

Gabby waited patiently for her to come to terms with this news. At last Krystal swallowed, needing to say something.

'Why do you think you have his heart?'

Gabby interlocked her hands around her knees, then released them and leaned back, then switched which leg was crossed over the other. 'That's a really good question,' she said, and laughed self-consciously. She tucked her hair behind her ear. 'It's a long story, so maybe before I go into that, we should start at the beginning.'

'Okay.'

'What date did your husband pass?'

'Evan died on the fourth of October 2017, just before midnight.'

Gabby flinched, waited a moment, then said, 'I'm so sorry for your loss. I can't even imagine.'

Krystal felt her nostrils flare with the effort of suppressing her emotion. 'Thank you.'

'My transplant date was October fifth, and the operation was early in the morning, so that fits. But you live here in Melbourne, don't you?'

'I do.'

Gabby frowned. 'The thing is that I know my gifted heart came from interstate. I shouldn't know that, but one of the nurses let it slip. I guess that rules out your husband.'

Krystal felt ill. 'Evan was in Sydney when he died.'

Gabby uncrossed her legs and inched forward in her chair. 'So, if it *was* a match, it wouldn't have taken long for the retrieval team to get his heart to me. A flight from Sydney is only about an hour.'

Around Krystal, the world shrank down to nothing except the small space connecting her to Gabby. 'Yes.'

'But there's no way we can possibly know for sure,' Gabby said, knitting her hands together on her lap.

'There is that,' Krystal admitted. She rubbed at her forehead, an intense headache developing behind her eyes.

'Unless . . .' Gabby drummed her fingers over her mouth, eyeing Krystal, seemingly nervous, almost cringing.

'What?'

'What did Evan look like? If you don't mind my asking, of course. I don't want to upset you.'

'It's okay.' Krystal pulled out her phone and selected a photo of Evan to show Gabby. She leaned forward and Gabby did the same until their heads were quite close, staring at the man on the screen.

Gabby drew in a sharp breath.

'What?' Krystal looked at her.

'It's him,' Gabby whispered.

'What do you mean? How can you tell?' Krystal's voice rose a notch.

Gabby retreated in her seat again.

'What is it?' Krystal asked.

'There's really no easy way to say this.'

'Go on.'

'I've been having . . . visions, I guess. Memories, perhaps.' Gabby closed one eye to look at Krystal, almost apologetic. 'Looking at him now . . . it's like looking at me.' She pointed to the phone in Krystal's hand.

Krystal froze.

'They're kind of like flashbacks. The first day I saw you in the cafe, the day I tried to introduce myself, it was as though your being here triggered the first one. I've had weird dreams and, look, I know it sounds nuts, but I feel as if he's trying to tell me something. I feel like he wanted us to meet.'

Krystal's hands had begun to shake and she twisted them together. 'What can you see?'

'Mostly,' Gabby said carefully, 'I'm running in a cold street at night. I hear someone yell out, "Stop!" There's a blinding white light.' She paused. 'And then pain and darkness.'

'You can see that?'

Gabby nodded.

A single tear rolled down Krystal's cheek. 'Evan was hit by a car in a backstreet in Sydney. I imagine that blinding light you see is from the headlights just before he was hit.'

162

Gabby closed her eyes, as if only now truly believing that what she'd seen was real. 'I'm so sorry.'

'How is it even possible that you are seeing this?'

'There's a theory about something called cellular memory. The people who believe in it say the cells of an organ carry the imprints of memories that an organ recipient might then be able to access.'

'And you believe this?'

Gabby shrugged. 'I don't have any other way to explain it.'

It was a shocking notion. The idea that this total stranger might have access to her husband's memories when Krystal herself didn't was piercingly cruel. For a second, she wanted to flee. She stood up, took a few steps, spun in a circle, then sat down again.

'What about the smoke?' Gabby said. 'The second time you came in, I was overwhelmed by the smell of smoke.'

Krystal shook her head. 'I have no idea what that was.'

'Oh. Well, I guess the memories could be from any time in his life, right? Even from before you met him.'

Before she met him? Krystal took a moment to digest this. Not only could Gabby see Evan's memories from the time that Krystal knew him, but before that as well. It was insane. Except it wasn't, because her description of him running in that street was all too real.

'Have you had any other visions? Like, from his childhood maybe? Or anything about me or our boys? We have two sons.' She was hungry now, desperate for as much as possible.

'No. Sorry. I don't know for sure what brings them on, other than that they seem to be connected to you.'

'But there's nothing now?'

Gabby shook her head.

Krystal's mind was spinning. If Gabby could access those memories, of the car, and the smoke, then she might also be able to access the ones that Krystal needed the most. Finally, she might find out exactly what Evan was doing in Sydney that night.

'Gabby, I need your help.'

'And she agreed?' Roxy asked, paying for the tickets for the enormous Twin Dragon at Luna Park. She was escorting their three eldest boys onto the ride.

'She's coming over on Tuesday when the boys are at school.'

'What are you going to do?'

Krystal shrugged. 'I have no idea.'

Roxy shepherded the boys to the ride's entrance and waved goodbye to Krystal.

'Me too, me too,' Olly wailed, throwing himself at Krystal's leg, grabbing at her jeans with his fists.

'You're not tall enough yet,' she said, again. In truth, she was vastly relieved to have an excuse to sit this one out. She felt queasy just watching that ride. Even swings in the parks made her nauseous and dizzy. The enormous pendulum swing of this piece of 'amusement' would be sure to make her ill. She took Olly over to watch the pretty horses go up and down on the carousel instead.

Loud music pumped from nearby rides and screams pierced the air from the Scenic Railway, the world's oldest continually operating roller-coaster. It thundered past, rattling the rails. Gaudy colours and lights shone from the tightly packed array of rides and experiences. Loudspeakers echoed, bells rang, seagulls squabbled over dropped chips, and the sound of the gulls took her back in time to the day of Wyatt's sixty-fifth birthday.

Evan's father had thrown himself a live jazz soiree in the pillared house down on the peninsula. Less than two hours in, Krystal had

had quite enough of Cordelia-Aurora's glares at Jasper running too close to the white walls and squealing with excitement. Still, it was Evan's father's birthday so she gritted her teeth, determined to stick it out. But when Krystal caught Evan sighing for the third time, his polished fake smile firmly in place while his toffee-coloured eyes dimmed with every tuxedoed waiter that passed bearing a silver tray, she'd scooped up Jasper and taken Evan's arm and spirited them away and down to the water for something to eat that was sizeable enough to actually fill their bellies.

She whinged long and loud about her sister-in-law. 'Why does she still insist on trying to get you to come back to the firm?' she complained, shoving another chip into her mouth and flicking her foot at an overly aggressive seagull whose red-rimmed eye was firmly set on the potato scallop in Jasper's hand. Grease slid down his chubby hands and chin.

'Because my family values what someone does more than they value who they are as a person,' Evan said resignedly, dipping a chip into tomato sauce.

'Why do you let her get away with it?'

Evan leaned back on his hands, his shirtsleeves rolled up to reveal the dark hair on his arms, something she had always fancied. 'She knows where I stand,' he said simply. 'It eats her up that she's lost this battle with me. She always had the killer instinct, much more than either Rupert or me, and that's made her a valuable asset in the firm. She thinks she's failed because she couldn't convince me to go back again. I know I did the right thing, so I simply choose to let her have her tantrum while I can smugly be the bigger person.'

'Doesn't it get to you, though? Sometimes?' Krystal had witnessed Evan having terse, hushed conversations with Cordelia-Aurora, though they were always too refined to air their grievances in public, and he often seemed unhappy and distant afterwards.

'Sometimes, yes. But I think she's sad,' he said, his eyes meeting Krystal's above the fish and chips. 'Don't get me wrong; she's a horribly flawed person. But still, sad.'

'Sad?' she asked, pulling her tone back to something akin to concern.

Evan's dark chest hair peeked out above the starched white of his formal shirt, the two top buttons also now undone. She felt an astonishing rush of lust for him then. The man looked good in a suit. Not that she didn't see him in a suit often. As a sommelier in a fine restaurant, he wore a suit to work every day. But not a tuxedo. No, this was another level of cool entirely. Like James Bond.

'She's all alone,' he said, licking salt off his fingers. 'Look what we've got.'

Jasper was wiping his greasy hands down his overalls with glee and wiggling his toes in the afternoon light. Krystal thought about lurching after him to stop him ruining his new outfit (purchased especially for today), but his utter joy at this spontaneous dinner by the water was too good to spoil. Just like that, she felt her forehead soften and she breathed in gentle, briny air as best she could over the bulge in her belly. Olly. He'd be with them in a couple of months' time.

She supposed Evan might be right and Cordelia-Aurora *could* be sad and lonely. Still, Krystal thought her husband was a saint for putting up with her, even if she was family.

'I love you,' she said, reaching for his hand.

He smiled at her and took her hand, and they laughed at the discomfort of the salt and grease on their skin. 'I love you too.'

Then Jasper was on his feet and running after a seagull and Evan pushed himself up to catch him before he got to the water. 'Hold on, buddy!'

*

'Dadda.'

Krystal blinked, returning her focus to the noisy bustle of kids and parents around her. She looked down at Olly. 'What did you say?'

Olly looked up at her with his big brown eyes and long lashes. He was wearing dark, soft denim overalls today with a bright red shirt underneath, and his fair hair was brushed. He looked like he could be in a catalogue for children's clothing, so adorable that she could swoon from the love he invoked in her.

'Dadda,' he said again.

Krystal froze. Had he been reading her thoughts? She'd heard people say that kids were more intuitive than adults. When both her boys were born she'd looked into their eyes and they'd seemed like the oldest souls, from another place entirely and not totally here on earth yet. How long did they hold onto that?

'Why did you say that?' She looked around, wondering if there was someone who looked like Evan that Olly might have connected with the photos in their house, or indeed if Evan's spirit had somehow just materialised in this moment.

'Gull!' Olly cried, pointing to the seagulls cawing and chasing each other.

'Yes, seagull.' She had no idea if he was randomly pointing to the birds or whether he was again referencing her memories. Or maybe it was *his* memory; he had been there, after all, even if it was in her belly. Research showed that babies could hear sounds and even see quite a bit of light when they were in utero. Did they retain those memories too?

'Where's Dadda?' she asked him, trying again. 'Is he here?' She held her breath, waiting.

'Heaven,' Olly said, and moved off to chase a gull.

She watched Olly running in circles, laughing, the grey and white birds fluttering around him. *Heaven*. That was what she told the boys, though she had no idea if she believed it or not. The reality was she had no idea where Evan was.

Roxy and the boys returned from their ride, smiling, the boys making jerky superhero moves with their arms and legs and loud *pow-pow* sounds.

'You made it!' Krystal said, touching Jasper's hair.

'That was epic!' Jasper screeched. 'It went so high then *whoosh*, so low, and I thought I'd fall out!'

'Mum screamed,' Austin said, his dimples lighting up his face.

'It's true, I did,' Roxy confirmed, fluffing up her hair with her fingers. She was wearing a purple coat today and if she'd had a top hat to match she would have been the spitting image of a female Willy Wonka.

'I'm hungry,' Kyan complained. 'Can we get something to eat?'

They ordered dagwood dogs and beer-battered chips and sat at a bright blue wooden picnic table with bench seats, the same colour as the sky, to devour their hot, greasy food.

'Can we do the Scenic Railway next?' Kyan asked through a mouthful of chips.

'Let's go for something Olly can do first,' Roxy said, pulling out a wet wipe from her backpack and wiping Austin's slick fingers. 'He won't be tall enough for the Scenic Railway,' she said to Krystal.

'How about we do the carousel and the Ferris wheel,' Krystal said, 'then you can go on the Scenic Railway and I'll wait with Olly again.'

'No, you should definitely go on the Railway,' Roxy said. 'I'll wait with Olly. You have to do at least one ride.'

'I'm doing two,' Krystal objected.

'The carousel and Ferris wheel don't count!' Roxy teased.

Krystal shoved a piece of batter into her mouth. She rushed to finish before the boys pulled them away again. 'This is perfect hangover food,' she muttered.

Roxy continued to chew but raised an eyebrow, questioning. She'd never seen Krystal with a hangover.

'I know, I know,' Krystal said, taking a sip of water. 'But after the day I had yesterday, can you blame me?' She'd been so wrung out after her conversation with Gabby. Far from answering her questions and making her feel better about everything, knowing that Gabby could see Evan's memories had only stirred up a hornet's nest of questions. She couldn't sleep, so she'd found a way to calm down.

'No, I can't blame you at all. It's like you're living out a movie script or something.'

The boys finished their food and jumped to their feet, pulling Krystal and Roxy with them. On the carousel, Krystal and Roxy sat next to each other, Krystal on a white horse, Roxy on a black one, the horses' heads tossed high, manes adorned with colourful flowers, legs prancing in midair. As Krystal's horse went up, Roxy's went down. The boys were in front of them where they could see them. Kyan, big for his eight years, had grumbled about having to go on the baby ride and looked suitably bored, but the other three laughed.

'What do you think is the appropriate food and beverage to offer someone when they come to your house to try to access your dead husband's memories?' Krystal said.

'Oh, good question. Let's see ... maybe something with a pinch of toad and an eye of newt? Something from a cauldron, obviously.'

Krystal smirked and gripped tightly to the golden pole in front of her, not because she was afraid of falling but simply to give herself somewhere to focus her anxious energy.

'Sorry, I'll be serious. Maybe just some tea and biscuits? Keep it simple. You'll be stressed enough as it is, I should imagine.'

'True.' What if Gabby saw something really awful, something Krystal later wished she'd never known?

'I know this is a delicate question,' Roxy said, as quietly as she could given the noise around them. She leaned over from her horse towards Krystal. 'But does Gabby know you never actually wanted to donate Evan's heart?' Her brow was worried into wavy wrinkles.

'No, I can't tell her. That would be just . . .'

'Horrible – for her, I mean. Obviously you had your reasons,' Roxy added quickly.

'Yes.' Krystal had shared with Roxy a little of that time in ICU in Sydney, but she'd never told anyone the full story. 'Aside from that, how likely would she be to want to help me then?'

'Not very, I would think.'

Roxy's horse rose, Krystal's descended.

'None of this is her fault,' Krystal admitted. 'It's mine.'

17

On Saturday afternoon, Gabby finished the almond-milk golden turmeric latte that Kyle had made for her, chewing thoughtfully on a couple of tiny bits of ginger and enjoying the warming spices as they settled in her belly. She needed to speak to Cam but he'd been ignoring her calls. She went to the storeroom and called him from The Tin Man's phone instead. To her surprise he answered, which made her simultaneously relieved and furious, knowing that the only reason he'd picked up the phone was because it wasn't her name that had shown up on the screen.

'Hi, Cam, it's Gabby.'

There was a short pause before he rallied. 'Hi, how's it going?'

How was it going? He was avoiding their kids; how did he think it was going?

'I know you're . . . having time off,' she said carefully, pacing between the hessian bags, trying hard not to let her fury push him away. Now that she had him on the phone, she didn't want to lose him. 'But I was hoping we could talk about Charlie's birthday.'

'Oh, right,' Cam said, as if he'd forgotten all about it.

Gabby could hear Mykahla screaming in the background and cringed. It was never a good time to try to talk to a parent with a crying baby nearby. But she pressed on. She had to. 'We're doing our usual birthday breakfast thing and I'm hoping you and Meri and Mykahla will come over too,' she said brightly. 'It would mean a lot to Charlie.' She was completely prepared to guilt-trip him if she had to.

More wailing from Mykahla and shushing noises from Meri. Cam covered the phone a moment and said something to Meri, then came back on the line. 'Can I call you back in a minute?'

'No,' she said firmly. 'Cam, you've been avoiding my calls, I've had no real answer from you as to why you aren't seeing the kids, they have no idea what's going on, and you left it up to me to tell them and defend you when I don't know what's got into you.' She lost her cool. 'You have four children. Four. Yes, I can hear that your youngest is challenging right now, but the other three need you too. You can't just abandon them.'

He was silent in return and she wanted to pick up a white coffee cup from the bench in front of her and fling it at the storeroom wall.

'For fuck's sake, Cam, they need you, and *I* need you too. I need to know you're still in this. You may have forgotten this in your sleep deprivation and stoned fug, but I have a seriously reduced life expectancy and I need to know you are here for our kids.'

'I can't do this now,' he said, angry.

'When, then? When can we talk about this? And will you be there tomorrow, for Charlie? Can you at least do that?'

Cam sighed and she imagined he was rubbing his hand through his hair in frustration. 'I'll try,' he said, and hung up.

'Is he coming?' Pippa whispered, hugging Gabby while looking around for the birthday boy.

'He'd better be,' Gabby muttered. 'I've messaged him enough times.' She'd even messaged Meri, something that was tacitly understood to be a breach of boundaries, but she really needed Cam to show up for their son this morning. She released Pippa and bent to hug all four of Pippa's kids, who were complaining loudly about how hungry they were. 'Go on through. Grandpa's got the pancakes on already.'

She ushered them down the hall and into the kitchen, where colourful streamers and balloons swung from the windows and cupboards. She'd stayed up late last night until after she was sure Charlie was asleep so she could surprise him with them when he woke.

'Happy birthday!' the kids screeched, hugging Charlie one at a time, even Hunter, who, at fourteen, might have chosen to play it cool. Gabby exchanged a sentimental look with Pippa, both of them proud their teenage sons were still happy to hug their cousins.

'How are my favourite grandchildren?' Monty boomed while flipping pancakes.

'Hey!' Summer and Celia protested.

'Oops, sorry! I forgot about you lot,' Monty joked, winking at them.

The kitchen bench had turned into an overflowing breakfast bar, with stacks of plates and cutlery, orange juice, batch-brew coffee, baskets of sweet pastries and plates of toppings for the pancakes – berries, bacon, lemon juice, sugar, syrup, chocolate chips, banana slices, yoghurt and even a tub of ice cream.

Come on, Cam.

As if reading her mind, Charlie looked up from a gift he was unwrapping – a new shirt from Pippa – and caught Gabby's eye, then glanced over to the clock on the oven. He looked back at her and she gave him a sympathetic smile.

'Right, let's eat,' Monty said. Wearing his fancy navy and white tartan apron that Lottie had given him one Christmas, he stood tall and proud, loving the role of cooking for his family. He delivered a mound of fluffy pancakes to the benchtop and everyone lined up to serve themselves. There were too many of them to all sit together so they sat at bar stools at the bench, at the dining table, and some kids spilled outside to eat alfresco in the still chilly morning air.

Gabby and Pippa sat at one end of the dining table, while Monty sat at the other, regaling smaller McPhees with a tale of him and Lottie eating pastries in Paris while pampered dogs sat in chairs at another table with their own plate of food. Celia dropped hunks of pancake to the floor for Sally to gobble up, not even bothering to try to hide it. Gabby sighed. That dog – that ten-thousand-dollar dog – had come with a strict rulebook so the family didn't break her, but everyone had long since given up any pretence of being strict enough to enforce it.

'What's Harvey doing this morning?' Gabby asked quietly, cutting into her pancakes covered in maple syrup, ice cream and chocolate pieces.

Pippa swallowed a mouthful of berries and ice cream and rolled her eyes. 'He's gone fishing.'

'Fishing? Since when does he fish?'

'As of today, apparently. Some guy from work invited him to go out on his boat.' Pippa adjusted the cream chiffon scarf at her neck. 'We had a fight last night,' she whispered. 'He slept on the couch.'

Gabby winced and took a sip of her affogato.

'We've turned each other into the worst versions of ourselves,' Pippa said, her voice breaking on the last word before she shoved a forkful of pancake into her mouth.

Gabby patted her knee under the table.

'Any words of wisdom for break-ups?' Pippa asked.

Gabby almost choked on her coffee. 'I'm probably not the best person to ask right now.' Grimly, she looked over at the clock, each minute that slid by with no sign of Cam another moment of shared anguish with Charlie. The birthday boy came in from outside for another helping of pancakes and Gabby took the opportunity to leap from her seat and hurry to her room to pull out her surprise.

She returned to the kitchen carrying an enormous and rather ghastly yellow hat with red and green trimmings and red fluffy pom-poms that hung down around the brim.

'What is that?' Charlie asked, with a mouth full of bacon.

'This is the new family birthday tradition,' Gabby said. 'It's the birthday sombrero!' She guided him to a bar stool while the others cheered and laughed. The gaudy hat really didn't do much to enhance his red hair, red flushed cheeks and freckles. But, of course, the hat wasn't there to make him look good; it was there to be ridiculous. A dose of frivolity could only be a good thing for her kids right now. She tightened the string under his neck.

'Don't you dare take photos,' he grumbled.

'Too late!' Pippa sang out. 'I'm already posting them to Instagram.'

'What are you doing to me? I have a reputation, you know. This is so messed up,' he said, though Gabby could tell he was happy beneath the complaint. At least, she hoped he was, just a little bit.

Gabby lit a sparkler and handed it to him to hold while they all sang a raucous, off-key rendition of 'Happy Birthday'. Charlie tried to look unimpressed but she knew he was soaking it in. They ended with a big cheer and applause, and Hunter found some Mexican music online and set it to play on his phone, leading to an eruption of the Mexican hat dance. Even Monty had a go, though he didn't swing himself vigorously around his partner like the others did, but tiptoe-jogged instead. At the end of that, they cheered some more.

Everyone was in high spirits when Celia's voice broke in. 'Where's Dad?'

The chatter and laughter fell away.

Gabby rubbed Celia's back and kissed the top of her head. 'I don't know,' she said. She was tempted to fill the silence with platitudes like *I'm sure he's still coming* or *I'm sure there's a really good explanation*, but the truth was she had no idea. It was unforgivable. Gabby's eyes slid sideways to Charlie, who pulled off his sombrero and handed it to Pippa's youngest, who wanted to try it on. His shoulders slumped dejectedly. She gave him an apologetic look and he shrugged it away, but she could see that the little boy inside his elongating body was wounded.

'Eat some more,' she said now, handing him the plate he'd earlier been loading up with second helpings.

He took it from her. 'Thanks.'

'Have you finalised your elective choices?' she asked, as nonchalantly as possible. Tomorrow was the day for him to return his preferences for senior subjects next year. It was another reason she'd been hoping Cam would turn up, so Charlie could make his final announcement to them both.

He nodded and chewed. She waited for more information. Monty was now wearing the sombrero and sidled closer, also waiting.

Charlie smacked his lips, swilled some juice, then said, 'I've decided to do theatre, art, music, physical education, the easy maths and English. I realised I had my thinking all wrong. I need to utilise my creative strengths.' He picked up his cup and gulped coffee.

'Well,' Gabby said, 'that sounds great.'

What?!

Charlie had been struggling with the choices and felt such pressure to get them right, but this was the first she'd heard about art, music and theatre. 'Creativity' and 'Charlie' were not words she would use in the same sentence, with the possible exception of his latte art. Still, she couldn't challenge his decisions here, on his birthday, not when his dad had just stood him up, and especially not while her father was wearing a sombrero. No one could have a serious conversation while someone was wearing a sombrero.

'Physical education sounds good,' Monty said encouragingly. 'Does it include swimming?' Gabby could tell he was trying to be tactfully supportive by singling out the subject in which Charlie had demonstrated interest and talent.

'Yep.'

Gabby exchanged a slightly alarmed look with her dad. In her previous conversations with Charlie about his studies, he'd talked about taking practical subjects that would help him in future business endeavours – like Accounting, Chinese as a second language, and Economics. He wasn't much into sciences or abstract maths. He had practical intelligence, like her. All her embarrassing dreams of teaching her son how to run a business with the hope of his taking over The Tin Man one day had just fallen in tatters at her feet, replaced with visions of him singing and dancing in suburban theatres. She wanted Charlie to pursue his passions, of course. But she had assumed he would follow in the McPhee footsteps and go into business. It turned out she was a horribly clichéd parent after all. An awkward silence drifted between them.

'Mum,' Summer said at last, her dimples flashing as she licked her fork clean. 'He's joking.'

'What do you mean?' Gabby said, flooded with relief but trying to hide it.

'Gotcha,' Charlie said, with a small smile. 'Don't worry, I'm still doing all the business subjects we talked about.'

'Oh, I knew that,' she said unconvincingly, ashamed she'd been caught out not supporting his dreams . . . even if they were fake dreams. Cheeky bugger.

After Pippa and her kids had left and Charlie had headed off to a mate's place for the afternoon, Gabby grabbed her car keys. Fuelled by maternal rage, she drove straight to Cam and Meri's place, half an hour's drive east. They lived in a partially renovated, rendered-brick house, with a newish kitchen but a horrendous bathroom. The bedrooms for the kids were small but functional and a strip of backyard offered some lawn where they could sun themselves.

Gabby arrived in the early afternoon, determined to thrash things out with Cam. She opened the gate and it swung back out of her hands and clattered into the catch. She hurried up the path and knocked on the old wood door.

Meri answered it, her hair in a messy ponytail, no make-up, baby puke on her shirt and the offending puker, baby Mykahla, on her hip.

'Hi,' Gabby said, smiling, making an effort to save her wrath for Cam. She waved at Mykahla and gave her a huge smile. 'Hello, gorgeous girl.'

'Gabby,' Meri said, surprised, looking over Gabby's shoulder as though searching for the kids. 'What are you doing over this way?' She was cautious but not hostile.

'I know it's poor form to drop over unannounced, but I really need to talk to Cam,' Gabby said. 'It's about the kids. Specifically, about missing Charlie's birthday this morning.'

'Right,' Meri said, moving Mykahla to sit on her other hip. The baby frowned and beat her fist on Meri's chest in protest.

'Is he home?' Gabby persisted.

'Um, yes, come in,' Meri said, standing out of the way of the door. 'He's just having a lie-down.'

'Oh?' Gabby was taken aback. 'Is he sick?'

'No,' Meri said, distracted, putting Mykahla down on the brightly coloured mat beneath the play station arching above her. The baby immediately began swinging at the hanging stuffed animals with glee. At least Mykahla was in a good mood. 'I'll just get him.'

Meri disappeared through the lounge towards the bedrooms, and Gabby cooed at Mykahla and cast her eyes around at the mound of unfolded washing on the dining table, the line of ants crawling across the kitchen bench, the highchair, bouncer and playpen taking up valuable space in the small house. All in all, perfectly normal for a home with a baby.

Meri reappeared. 'He'll be out soon. Would you like a tea?'

'No, thanks. I'm all good.'

Meri eyed the washing and hurried to fold towels.

'Here, let me help you,' Gabby said, picking up a sheet and flicking it out to fold it. 'Trust me, I remember only too well what these early months are like.'

'I'd like to refuse, but I'm just too tired,' Meri said, and gave her a thin smile.

'How is everything going?' Gabby asked, as casually as possible. 'Are you missing work?'

Meri scoffed. 'Gosh, no.' Her most recent posting had been within the state's foster care system, placing children in homes and providing reports on their progress and the birth parents' ability to have the child back in their care. It must have been a terribly stressful role. 'The only thing I miss is sleep.'

'Yeah. It's a killer.' Gabby placed the folded sheet on the table and picked up a towel. 'And what about Cam? How's he coping, really?'

Meri shot her a look. Gabby knew that this was a line they couldn't easily cross, but she was getting desperate. Meri opened her mouth to speak, just as Cam entered the room.

'Gabs, hi.' He stood in shorts and a tee, his hair too long and messed up, his face unshaven. His shorts hung off his hips and she could see the hollows in his cheeks.

'Hi,' she said. His appearance shocked her. But then anger shot through her. The only time she'd ever seen him look this bad was when he'd been at his worst smoking pot. She'd thought it had all stopped once Meri was on the scene, but it looked as if the arrival of Mykahla had sent him back to his old ways.

'What are you doing here?' He smiled and waved at Mykahla and blew a raspberry at her, and she grinned in delight and rolled onto her tummy, kicking her legs out behind her like a frog.

'She'll be crawling any minute,' Gabby said.

The three of them watched Mykahla for a few moments while the baby tried to work out how to roll the other way, till she began to complain and Cam helped her return onto her back where she could see the dangling animals once more.

'I have news,' Gabby said, drawing his attention back to her.

He stood up. 'Hm?'

'It looks like Pippa and Harvey are breaking up.'

'Huh.' He didn't sound shocked.

She stared at him, waiting for more. But his eyes were empty, his mind not even here. Clearly he'd been smoking today, and that was what had kept him from Charlie's breakfast, the selfish prick.

'It's obviously sad for them,' Gabby went on, narrowing her eyes at Cam. 'But it's more than that, isn't it? Pippa and Harvey were my – were *our* – backup plan to take care of the kids if I die.' She said it bluntly; she'd meant to. She wanted to shock him. Behind her, Meri had stopped folding washing and was standing still.

'And?'

'What do you mean, *and*? This obviously makes me very anxious because you have been ignoring our children –'

'I'm not ignoring them.'

'– and you couldn't even pull yourself together long enough to come to your son's sixteenth birthday!'

Cam sighed, petulant. 'Jesus, Gabs, I'm taking a break.'

'See, that, right there, that is what I don't get. Charlie's turning into a man and he needs a role model. He needs you now more than ever. You're not done yet. You can't take a break from your children!' She was shrill. She took a deep breath. Behind her, she was aware that Meri had picked up Mykahla and taken her away. She would feel bad later, she knew, for having a go at Cam in front of the baby, and would have to apologise, but right now she needed him to talk and tell her what was going on.

Cam screwed up his fists and rubbed at his eyes. 'Yes, I can!' he shouted. 'And I have to, or I'll . . .'

'What? *What?*' Gabby was furious. 'What, Cam? What will you do? Hit them?'

'No! I would never hurt them.'

'Yell at them?'

'I just can't do it right now.'

'These effing drugs,' she said, shaking her head in disgust. 'Look at you! This is how you looked when you were at your worst. Does Meri know? Of course she knows. She's a flipping social worker, she couldn't not know.' And she was probably mortified, Gabby realised, distraught that she couldn't stop her husband from descending into the gutter, embarrassed that this had happened on her watch. 'Are you going to meetings? Have you spoken to your doctor?'

Cam collapsed into a chair and put his head in his hands.

She wanted to hit him, throw something at him, shake him till his teeth rattled. He didn't get the luxury of doing this now, not to her and their kids, and certainly not to Meri and Mykahla. Selfish bastard.

Still, she felt a small, grudging amount of respect for the fact that he knew he was unfit to be caring for the kids. It was far from ideal, but she would rather the kids were with her than with him right now.

'Clean yourself up,' she said, finding stern calm. 'Both of your families need you and none of us has time to wait.'

18

About five minutes before Gabby was due to arrive, Krystal had to physically stop herself from messaging her to call the whole thing off. The only way she'd managed to do that was to down two quick shots of vodka.

Under what circumstances had she ever imagined she could deal with the woman who had her husband's heart coming here, to their home? It felt sordid, like Gabby was the other woman in a twisted threesome. Gabby's presence here might take something away from what Krystal and Evan had, leave a stain on their love story.

But then, what sort of love story was it if he'd been able to lie to her so easily and convincingly?

Off to work, gorgeous. The restaurant's fully booked so it'll be a late one. Don't wait up. He'd leaned over the back of the couch, his black jacket slung over his shoulder, and kissed her on the cheek.

Bye, she'd sung through a mouthful of toast, while the boys played with pots and pans on the floor.

Bye, boys. Be good for Mama. He waved at them. Then he was gone.

Now, with her own heart thumping obtrusively in her chest and Gabby moments away, that memory burned.

He'd betrayed her.

She threw her hairbrush across the bathroom, where it banged against the yellow wall, denting the plaster, then clattered to the ground and spun across the blue and white tiles. She leaned on the basin, biting down fury.

In a cruel twist of fate, the only way she could discover the truth about his actions that night was to seek the help of the stranger she'd never wanted to have his heart in the first place. Gabby's revelation that she could see some of Evan's memories had left her in deep shock. Then that dense, pleasantly numbing fog – like emotional anaesthetic – had worn off, leaving throbbing pain in its wake. She could see why people turned to drugs and alcohol to deal with pain, and almost felt something akin to empathy towards her own mother. That numbness was such bliss, such respite.

There was a quiet knock at the door.

She was here.

Not only did Gabby have Evan's heart, she had his memories too. His memories! The one thing that should have been exclusive to Krystal was her memories of Evan and of their lives away from his interfering family or his toffy friends or even the friends they'd shared at the restaurant. The one thing she had to offer her children were memories. And now a stranger – another woman – could lay claim to them.

Krystal paused in the hallway and stared at a photo of Evan at the botanic gardens, sitting on a picnic blanket, holding baby Olly in the crook of his left arm, his right arm wrapped around Jasper's waist, both Evan and Jasper laughing. Such joy. If she'd known it would be mere months before he was gone, she'd have done something. Anything. Put them on a plane and gone to live in New Zealand, maybe. Anything to make sure he wasn't in Sydney that night.

It was grossly unfair and she should never have been in this position, and yet she wanted those memories. She'd do anything for them.

Knock-knock-knock.

'Coming!' Krystal called. She arranged her features into something she hoped conveyed gratitude rather than misery, and opened the door to see Gabby standing self-consciously hugging an enormous bunch of dark red gerberas wrapped in sepia-coloured paper. She smiled when she saw Krystal, and thrust the rustling bundle towards her.

'Hi! These are for you.'

Krystal stared at the flowers.

'I just wanted to say thank you,' Gabby said, still holding them out.

'W-what for?'

Gabby laughed nervously. 'For saving my life!' Her voice faltered on the last word.

Krystal still hadn't reached for the flowers. She knew she should, but she was stuck. Stuck in a time warp.

'Is something wrong?' Gabby withdrew the offering. 'Are you allergic?'

'How did you know?'

'Know what?'

'Evan always gave me gerberas.'

'Oh.' Gabby seemed taken by surprise.

Krystal took the flowers and stepped aside for Gabby to come in. She picked up her rusty red, flowing skirt as she crossed the threshold, even though she didn't need to. Krystal was rattled by the gerberas and took a moment to pull out a drawer in the kitchen to find a vase. With shaking hands, she cut the string holding the stems together and arranged them in the wide-mouthed green vase, then placed it on the dining table.

Gabby was staring at the photos in the hallway.

'Would it help if you looked at them?' Krystal asked.

'Would you mind?' Gabby asked, tentatively, obviously feeling as out of her depth as Krystal did.

'Go ahead.'

Gabby approached the photos, her arms crossed over her white button-down shirt. 'He's handsome,' she said, turning to smile at Krystal.

Krystal joined her in the hall. 'Yes.'

'And I can see how much he loved the boys,' Gabby said, her voice tightening. She waved a hand near her face. 'Sorry.'

Krystal felt her own throat tighten. 'He was a great dad.'

Gabby turned away, her face crumpled, and went back towards the dining table. She took a deep breath and touched the gerberas. 'Did Evan like hotdogs?'

Krystal stared into Gabby's green eyes. 'He loved them. Why?'

Gabby smiled, first at Krystal and then at the photos of Evan. 'After the surgery, I kept smelling hotdogs. I thought it was coming from somewhere in the hospital to begin with, then realised it was inside me, but it wasn't my sense memory. It was someone else's.'

Krystal felt a curious mix of dread and excitement. 'They were his guilty pleasure,' she said. 'His family are such snobs. They wouldn't dream of eating something as low-class as a hotdog. Evan did still have high-class tastes but he said he'd always "go to the dark side" for a hotdog.'

'I wonder why hotdogs were the first thing that came to me.'

'Maybe he'd eaten one just before he died,' Krystal said, but the idea raised more questions than it answered.

'Maybe.'

They were silent a moment and Krystal's mind went to all the things she wanted to know. She forced herself to be patient. 'Would you like a tea or coffee? I'm afraid I've only got supermarket teabags and powdered coffee mixes.' She went to the kitchen and pulled out her stash of packets. 'I've got instant cappuccinos, hot chocolates – oh, there's a coffee bag from somewhere, I can't remember where that came from.'

'A cappuccino would be great.'

'It's ridiculous offering *you* – a boutique coffee roaster – a powdered cappuccino. I mean, they're rubbish, obviously.'

'Really, it's fine.'

Reluctantly, Krystal tipped the packet mix into a mug and poured boiling water into it, stirred it and handed it to Gabby. She made herself a tea with milk and they sat at the dining table, the gerberas standing tall beside them.

'It's a great location you're in,' Gabby said, making conversation.

'Thanks. We moved here to be near work.' Krystal told Gabby how she and Evan had met. 'He'd been a lawyer but then he had what he called a "clean change", as opposed to a sea change or tree change, taking a straightforward, honest job doing something he loved.'

'As a waiter at the restaurant?' Gabby asked, sipping her drink.

'No, as a sommelier.'

Gabby choked on her coffee, hurrying to get her mug to the table. She spluttered disconcertingly for a few moments, her eyes watering.

Krystal waited, poised to leap up and slap her on the back if necessary, and imagined what an awful thing it would be to have

Gabby die right here in front of her, Evan's heart failing on the floor at her feet.

'Sorry,' Gabby squeaked. 'That went down the wrong way.' She gave a final cough and cleared her throat. 'Well, how wonderful for him that he found something he loved so much.'

'Yes, it was. He made life as a lawyer sound like a soul-destroying death march through bleak, snow-filled trenches.'

That was why the photo Cordelia-Aurora had chosen for the 'party' was so inappropriate. If she'd really understood her brother at all she'd have seen that the true ecstasy he'd felt that day was knowing he'd been released from the prison he was in, not because it had been the pinnacle of his career before he'd thrown it all away on a fanciful job with wine and a girl from the sticks.

'I think I've had a "bean change",' Gabby said. 'Everyone else in my transplant group went off coffee after their operation. They couldn't even look at it, let alone smell it. But I was the total opposite. Suddenly, I couldn't get enough of the stuff.'

'Evan was a bit of a coffee snob, too,' Krystal said, watching Gabby.

Gabby raised her eyebrows and smiled.

'So, what should we do now?'

'Do?' Gabby toyed with the fob watch on a long gold chain around her neck. Her dangly crescent-moon earrings swung daintily when she cocked her head in query.

'To . . . retrieve his memories,' Krystal said, trying to keep her tone light, though each word stung. She was asking another woman how she could get close to her own husband.

'Oh.'

'How does it work?' Krystal pulled at the loose cotton threads on her ripped jeans. 'You said that I had triggered something in you the day you saw me at the cafe. Was it something I did, specifically?'

Gabby looked crestfallen. 'I have no idea, I'm sorry. Things just happen, without me trying. Or he comes to me in dreams.'

Krystal stiffened.

'I'm sorry,' Gabby said, and briefly put her hand on Krystal's. 'This must be so difficult for you. I wish I could give you more definitive answers. I really want to help you and I was hoping that perhaps just being here with you, talking to you for a while . . .' she trailed off and looked around, '. . . or that if I were in Evan's home he might make an appearance.'

'But there's nothing at all,' Krystal said, dismally.

'Not yet,' Gabby said, sounding hopeful. She pushed her mug away. 'But, look, this is already crazy enough so I might as well go ahead and say it . . .'

'What?'

'What if I close my eyes and you . . . talk to me?'

'As if you were Evan?'

'Yes.'

Krystal stared at Gabby, not having a clue how to respond. There was no handbook for this.

'Sorry!' Gabby held up a hand in apology. 'That's super weird, isn't it?' She laughed hollowly. 'Forget it. It's probably stupid.'

'No.' Krystal took a deep breath. She wanted this to be over. She wanted answers from Evan. 'It's not stupid. I mean, there's nothing to lose, right?' Except perhaps her sanity, dignity and self-respect. 'It's the best idea we've got right now.'

Gabby smiled gratefully. 'Okay.' She settled herself on the chair, closed her eyes and folded her hands in her lap, almost as if in meditation or prayer.

Krystal waited, aware now of the ever-present sound of the ducted air conditioning, the heavy thump of a door closing down the hall and the *ting* of the elevator a moment later. She wondered how long she'd have to wait for Gabby to do whatever it was she was doing. She chewed on a nail to distract herself.

A moment later: 'All right,' Gabby said quietly.

Krystal stopped chewing her nail and dropped her hand to her lap. She studied Gabby's face. It was calm, her ginger eyelashes resting above her freckled cheeks. Her breathing was gentle. She didn't look like Evan. Obviously, she didn't expect that Gabby would disappear and Evan would zoom into her place as though he'd just stepped through a portal or anything. She'd wondered if she would be able to see some sort of shimmer or aura, but there was nothing.

She swallowed hard. 'Can you feel anything, or see anything?' she asked, feeling like a total knob. If her mother could see her now she would knock her into the next room.

Gabby shook her head slightly but otherwise remained unmoving.

'Okay.' Krystal tried to muster more commitment to the task. She found herself taking a deep breath too, trying to reach a place inside herself of inner quiet, or stillness, or folk magic or woo-woo, anything that might help.

'Evan,' she said, fumbling for the right tone in which to address the dead. 'I . . . hope you can hear me.' She stared at her hands, now folded on the tabletop, and tried to concentrate on Evan, not on Gabby. 'I . . .' She was about to say *I miss you*, but her throat squeezed shut on the words, damming a torrent of emotion that would have gone with them. 'I'm confused,' she said, instead leaning more into her anger. Unlike sorrow, anger would hold her together. 'Why were you in Sydney? What were you doing there?'

She waited, continuing to stare at her hands. But when no response came from Gabby, Krystal peeked up at her face. Lines creased Gabby's forehead. Her entwined fingers squirmed in her lap. Did that mean she was seeing something she didn't want to see? Was it something awful, just as Krystal had feared?

She tried again, blurting out the thing she wanted to know most of all. 'Do you forgive me?'

Across from her, Gabby tilted her head as though querying this.

Krystal flicked her gaze around the room, again checking for a visitation of sorts, but there was still nothing. Impatient, she spoke to Gabby. 'What can you see?'

Gabby opened her eyes and took a deep breath, then shook her head. 'Nothing.'

'Nothing?'

'I'm sorry.'

Krystal felt like a total idiot. 'It's not your fault. The luck just wasn't with us today,' she said, trying to sound flippant.

'I'd better go,' Gabby said, standing up suddenly, looking more upset than Krystal would have expected. After all, Krystal had the most at stake here. She slung her big bag over her shoulder. 'But we can try again another time.'

'Sure, okay,' Krystal said, wondering why Gabby's mood had changed so swiftly.

'I'll message you.' Gabby was moving backwards towards the door, a smile plastered on her face. Then she waved goodbye as though they were new friends who had met at a fancy yoga class and taken their relationship to the next level, and would now be meeting up for steamed greens and yerba mate tea.

Krystal closed the door behind Gabby and rested her forehead against its cool, firm surface, her eyes closed, wondering what the hell had just happened. Maybe, she told herself with a flash almost of relief, Gabby didn't have Evan's heart after all. The alternative – that her own husband didn't want to talk to her – was too excruciating to contemplate. No, it was far more palatable to believe that she and Gabby simply had this all wrong.

Back in the kitchen, she stood on tiptoe to reach the bottle of vodka in the top cupboard and rested it on the bench while she pulled the shot glass she'd used earlier from the dishwasher where she'd hidden it out of Gabby's sight. She unscrewed the cap and was just about to pour when there was a knock at the door. She froze, wondering if she could ignore it. But then a voice called out.

'Krystal, it's Gabby.'

'Coming!' She put the cap back on the bottle and returned it to the cupboard and swept the shot glass back into the dishwasher, then opened the door.

Gabby's arms were crossed and she swayed from side to side uneasily.

'What's happened?'

'Can I come in?'

Krystal stood aside and waved her in, then closed the door.

Gabby paced in a circle, rubbing one hand over the other. Then she stopped and faced Krystal. 'I did see something.'

Krystal's stomach plunged in dread. 'What was it?'

'A woman.'

Krystal closed her eyes. She'd been expecting it, of course. It had always been the most logical explanation.

'I didn't want to tell you. I freaked out, sorry. But it's your right to know. You asked me to help and I can't lie to you. I owe you so much . . . the truth is the least I can give you.'

Krystal moved to the table and sat down. 'What did you see, exactly?'

Gabby dropped her bag and sat down too. 'It was just a flash, you know. Not much. The two of them sitting in a house. It was more the feeling that went with it.'

'And what was that?'

Gabby swallowed. 'Guilt and shame and . . . fear.'

'Fear of being discovered?'

'I think so.'

So it was true. The simplest answers were usually the right ones. 'I need more information,' Krystal said to Gabby, her voice shaking. 'Promise me you'll keep trying.'

Gabby nodded. 'I promise.'

19

That night, Pippa brought the kids over for dinner.

'I'm avoiding Harvey,' she said, tossing her jacket and bag onto the kitchen bench.

Monty put his arm around her shoulder, looking worn and sad. Her parents had never loved Harvey, but both Monty and Lottie had appreciated his upstanding character and essential goodness. 'I'll get the pizza bases out of the freezer,' he said.

'Thanks, Dad.'

Gabby made them tea while their combined seven children dispersed throughout the house and yard, then she took Pippa to sit in the corner of the lounge room in the floral-upholstered chairs with a small low table between them. The 'tea nook' was perfect for holding private conversations. It made Gabby feel like a lady from the Victorian era who had to sit and do needlepoint while exchanging the latest tittle-tattle of the day, and she always found she rather enjoyed it.

'Do you want to talk about it?' she asked, crossing one leg over the other and smoothing her skirt.

'Hell, no,' Pippa said. 'I'm sick to death of it all. Tell me something interesting instead.'

Gabby blew out a heavy breath. 'Well, I definitely have a few things to share that will take your mind off your home life.'

'Oh, good!' Pippa's face lit up. 'What is it?'

Gabby told her about the visions, her online research into cellular memory, her meetings with Krystal, and the other woman. Her sister sat with her mouth ajar for most of the conversation, completely shocked.

'Drink your tea before it gets cold,' Gabby said, motioning to her untouched teacup.

Pippa took several gulps of her extra-milky Lady Grey. 'Why didn't you tell me this sooner?'

'You know why. You've had enough of your own drama to deal with. And I wasn't entirely sure what was going on, to begin with.'

'Shit. This is huge.'

'Yeah, it is.'

Pippa took a moment to process, then said, 'What does she mean she doesn't know what he was doing in Sydney? How can you not know where your husband is?'

'It's amazing what someone can keep from their partner, isn't it?' Gabby said, feigning surprise.

'A secret horse isn't the same as a secret trip interstate.'

'I'm not sure about the logic of that,' Gabby said. 'But Krystal said Evan left for work, and some hours later the police called to tell her he'd been in an accident and she needed to get to Sydney's Royal North Shore Hospital as soon as possible.'

'Oh, that's awful.' She replaced her blue and white teacup on its matching saucer and lifted the pot to top it up. 'More?'

'Thanks.' Gabby held out her own cup for a splash more and gazed out the glass doors into the backyard.

'What are you going to do?' Pippa asked.

'I don't know. I can't exactly make the visions happen.'

Pippa opened her mouth to speak, then closed it again, looking torn.

'What? What were you going to say?'

'I don't like the idea of this,' Pippa lowered her voice, 'but have you tried actually asking him what he wants?'

'I have. But sometimes it feels like he's haunting me.'

Pippa sat bolt upright. 'Haunting you?'

'Shh!' Gabby widened her eyes in alarm, aware that Monty and a fluctuating number of children weren't far away, over in the kitchen preparing pizza toppings.

'Maybe this is what he wants; he wants me to help his wife,' Gabby said.

'But you can't help her at the expense of your own sanity or safety.' They both paused a moment, considering her words. 'You don't think he would actually try to hurt you, do you?' Pippa asked. 'Can't some ghosts do that?'

'Poltergeists, I think.' Gabby's knowledge of the supernatural realm was limited to a few scary movies she'd watched when she was younger.

'I'm sure I've heard that some can throw things, or lock you in cupboards, kill you or assault you in your sleep or abduct you.'

Gabby flinched, unnerved. 'I think the latter is aliens, not poltergeists, and I don't think he – Evan – is like that.'

'How do you know? You don't know anything about him! He's already scared you. And now he's all but admitted he was having an affair.'

'Maybe.'

'Just tell her you're sorry but you can't help any more. You haven't got anything further from him. Tell her you're happy you met her and you wish her well but you don't owe her anything.'

'Don't I? I have her husband's heart, a heart she gave to me. She wanted someone to have that heart, to live a life that her husband no longer had. That is beyond generous.' Gabby felt her eyes well. 'I wouldn't even be here today if she hadn't had the grace to think of someone other than herself at the worst moment of her life. Can you imagine?'

Pippa sighed. 'No, I can't imagine. But you don't know that's true. If it wasn't her it would have been someone else.'

'Not necessarily. It was a game of roulette I was lucky enough to win. And it *wasn't* someone else who donated the heart, it was her. I owe her. More than that, I owe Evan.'

Pippa closed her eyes a moment, as if she simply couldn't believe the foolishness of her older sister, then picked up her cup again to sip thoughtfully while they listened to Sadie and Celia pull a pile of paper and pens from the craft corner of the kitchen and spill them across the dining table. 'So, what are you going to do now?'

'I don't know. I don't like the way we left things. She still doesn't know why he was out in that street that night.'

'You could just lie, you know. Make up a reason – a good, lovely reason. Tell her you got the affair thing wrong. Tell her he was planning a surprise holiday or something. Let's face it, if he lied and told her he was going to work but was secretly going to Sydney then it was for something he really didn't want her to know about. Having a mistress is probably the best outcome, really. He could have had a gambling problem, or a drug problem, a secret family, or worse. So, tell her this reason – the lovely one – came from Evan, give her some peace of mind and let her go on her way.'

Gabby scoffed. 'And anger Evan, and provoke him into even more hauntings?'

'I don't think you've got much to lose,' Pippa said reasonably.

'I can't do it, Pip. I will never be able to repay her for wanting someone to have Evan's heart and giving me more time with my children.'

Pippa leaned back, defeated. 'I suppose.'

'I'm going to try to get more information for her. Best case scenario, Evan shows up, Krystal gets her answer and he leaves me alone.'

'And worst case scenario?' Pippa prompted.

To that, Gabby had no answer at all.

'Can you smell smoke?' Gabby asked, taking coffee cups from Ed and securing lids to them for the woman in sky-high heels and a belly-low bright red dress who was busily double-thumb tapping on her phone screen.

Ed lifted her unmade-up face and sniffed the air. 'I don't think so.' She continued to heat milk, unperturbed.

'Skinny flat white and double-shot long black?' Gabby looked at the customer expectantly. The woman nodded, continued to tap the screen with one hand and reached for the coffees with the other. Gabby stared at her a moment, waiting, but when the woman didn't bother to stop what she was doing, she put the coffees down and reached for a takeaway tray to secure them. 'There you go,' Gabby said, handing over the tray.

'Thanks,' the woman said, reaching blindly for the tray. She took it and promptly dropped it, hot coffee exploding over her bare legs and several customers nearby.

'Ow, shit!' the woman screeched, dancing from side to side as coffee ran down her legs and into her shoes.

Gabby rushed around the counter with a wet cloth and handed it to the woman first, then found more for the unhappy bystanders who now had coffee rivulets down their jeans and suit pants. Kyle hurried over to help from the other side of the cafe where he'd been delivering food and drinks to a group of backpackers, each of whose packs took up a seat of its own.

Gabby straightened. 'Thanks,' she said to Kyle. Then she caught the smell again. She hadn't imagined it.

She ran towards the roasting room behind the glass wall, her boots landing loudly on the wooden floor of the front of house, then dully on the resin floor of back of house.

'Fire!'

She knew where the fire would be because it wasn't the first time it had happened and it wouldn't be the last. When the beans were roasting they shed their husks, which were as fine and light as bees' wings. Cooking at around two hundred degrees, and being sucked out of the drum and piled together with hot air swirling through them, they could easily combust.

Luciano had his back to her, watching the computer screen. Coffee beans popped in the drum, right on first crack, the most delicate moment in the roast. Luciano's full attention would be on the moving lines on the graph on that screen. At the same time, the de-stoner was in action, pellets of roasted beans clattering through the metal pipes.

'Fire!' she called, louder this time.

Luciano spun to look over his shoulder, one hand still on the dials. 'What?'

Gabby was at the husk bin now, bending down to turn the tap on the wall. It was stuck hard; Luciano must have turned it off and she couldn't shift it. She felt something pop inside her hand, and pain splintered through her fingers and arm.

Luciano must have smelled the smoke now too. He abandoned his precious roast and rushed to where she was, brushing into her on his way past. With a flick of his wrist, he snapped on the tap. They heard the sprinkler spit to life from inside the pipe above the husk bin, and water doused the flames.

Gabby clutched her injured hand to her chest. Luciano turned off the tap again and charged around the floor-to-ceiling metal roaster, back to his computer. He cut the gas and pulled the lever to drop the beans onto the cooling tray, but they were already blackened. He growled in frustration. The fan below roared into life but it was too late. Tendrils of smoke rose from the charred beans. He came back to her side, scowling, crouched down to his haunches and opened the side door of the husk bin. He reached in and pulled out a metal bin now heavy with water and soggy, burned husks.

'What a mess,' he muttered. He straightened, hands on hips. 'Are you okay?'

Gabby poked her hand gently. 'I think I might have sprained something.'

'You need ice,' he said, and went to the double-door stainless-steel refrigerator and pulled out a first-aid ice pack, wrapped it in a tea towel and brought it to her. He placed it tenderly on her hand.

'Thanks,' she said, pressing the pack into the palm of her right hand and closing her fingers around it. 'The tap was turned off so tightly and I was rushing to try to get the fire out.'

'I couldn't smell it.' He looked at her, a glint of admiration in his dark eyes. 'But you smelled it from front of house?'

She shrugged. 'I have a good nose.'

'I've noticed,' he said, and looked at her nose a moment with such admiration she almost thought he was going to kiss it.

'What happened, Luciano?' a small voice asked.

Gabby peered around the silver roaster to see a young boy appear from the storeroom, carrying a toy dog in his hand, his lapis-blue eyes excited beneath his blond fringe.

Luciano smiled warmly at the boy. 'Uncle Luciano has been

making a big mess out here.' He bent down to the boy's level and pointed to the blackened beans in the cooling tray. 'See those beans? They're all ruined.'

The boy screwed up his nose at the scorched smell in the air. 'It stinks out here.'

'Yeah.' Luciano turned to Gabby, sheepish. 'This is my nephew, Cooper.'

'Hi, Cooper. I'm Gabby.' She gave him a big smile then raised her eyebrows at Luciano, questioning.

'Cooper wasn't feeling too good this morning and he didn't want to stay with Mamma, so . . .' He shrugged, helplessly.

'It's okay,' she said. 'I get it.'

'You were supposed to be helping me roast, mate,' Luciano teased him. 'What happened? Look at my beans!' He gestured to the ruined batch spinning in the cooler.

Cooper grinned, clearly unperturbed.

'I'm going to have to clean up this big mess now,' Luciano went on. 'Want to help me?'

'No way!' Cooper erupted into giggles. 'It's your mess so you have to clean it up,' he said, clearly mimicking a line he'd heard many times before. Sadly, it was probably his mum or his dad who'd said it, Gabby assumed.

'Good point,' Luciano said, his hands on his hips.

'Do you like dogs?' Cooper asked Gabby, holding up his palm-sized brown and white dog on a keyring.

'I do. I have a dog at home. Her name is Sally.'

'Are you for real?'

Gabby laughed. 'Yep. She slept in my bed last night.'

'Whoa! Luciano, did you hear that?' Cooper asked.

'Yeah, I heard,' Luciano answered, and by the tone of his voice, Gabby was pretty sure this was a frequent topic of conversation between them.

'Do you have a dog?' she asked.

'No, I'm not allowed. But I want one more than anything.' He scowled at Luciano, who tousled his nephew's hair before setting to work cleaning out the husk bin.

'Well, maybe one day,' Gabby said.

'I'm saving up my pocket money and everything. I have a collar and lead already and a water bowl too.'

'Sounds like you're organised,' Gabby said, taking the ice pack away from her hand and tentatively stretching out her fingers to see how much damage she might have done. It felt like the joint below her middle finger had been hurt the most.

'Can I come and visit your dog?' Cooper asked, glancing over his shoulder at his uncle.

Luciano looked up from the cooling tray, where he'd positioned the chute to dump the beans. 'Coops, Gabby doesn't need us invading her house.'

'But, please, oh please, oh please, oh pleeeaaase!' Cooper sing-songed, dancing on the spot. The child was completely adorable.

'You're welcome to come and visit Sally,' she said. 'Any time you like.'

'Do you have a photo of her?' Cooper asked.

'Um, yes, on my phone. Follow me.'

She led the way to the other side of the room and to her enormous bag – big enough to hold all her medications, dental floss, creams for various skin flare-ups, antiseptic ointment to quickly treat small cuts that could become infected, random paraphernalia belonging to her children – put the ice pack on the benchtop and lifted out her phone, finding the photos she'd taken of Sally playing with the kids on the lawn last weekend.

'Oh, look at her!' Cooper said, grabbing the phone with both hands. 'She's a golding retriever, right?'

'A golden retriever, yes.'

'She's beautiful,' he said softly.

'She is,' she agreed, thinking how many times Sally had helped her out recently.

'How old is she?' he asked.

'Four.'

'How much does she weigh?'

'Er, about twenty-eight kilos, last time she stood on some scales.'

'That's about right,' he said, nodding, his brows knitted in concentration.

Gabby had to stop herself from giggling at his intensity.

'Sometimes I bark at school,' Cooper said, flicking through the photos. 'But the other kids call me weird.'

'Oh. How does that make you feel?' she ventured.

He shrugged. 'They don't understand how much I love dogs and how awesome they are. Did you know that dogs have three hundred million factories in their noses to smell with?'

'Factories?' It was Gabby's turn to frown. 'Oh, you mean olfactory receptors! They're the bits that receive the smells.' She wondered if she'd somehow got more olfactory receptors from Evan, or whether she had just become better at using the ones she already had.

'Yeah, and their brains can smell invisible stuff like fear and sadness.'

'They can smell fear?'

'Uh-huh.'

Well, that would explain why Sally rushed to her bedroom door when Gabby was having a nightmare.

'I'm impressed you know so much about dogs, Cooper.'

'I have a lot of books,' he said. 'Aw!' He was looking at a picture of Celia and Sally in the teepee together, Celia reading a book and lying with her head resting on Sally's belly.

'That's my daughter Celia. Sally is really her dog but she shares her with the rest of us. I'm sure she'd be happy for you to visit.' Gabby looked up to find Luciano watching them, his eyes soft and a look of love on his face so pure it melted Gabby to her core.

'Luciano, if you're free on the weekend, maybe you'd like to bring your three kids to my place, and they could have a play and Cooper could meet Sally?'

'Oh, please, oh please, oh please!' Cooper sang again, bobbing up and down next to Gabby.

Luciano swallowed – she could see the muscles in his neck flex – but he took a moment to speak. 'That sounds great,' he said, his voice quiet and gravelly.

'Yay!' Cooper screeched and ran to Luciano, flinging his arms around his uncle's waist.

Luciano patted him on the back gently and smiled at Gabby. 'Thank you.'

'You're welcome,' she said, already counting how many sleeps it was until they visited.

20

Krystal sat at the table at the far end of the staffroom. She was pretending to listen to Janice's team meeting ramblings, but all she could think about was Gabby's revelation of the other woman in Evan's life. Although she'd suspected it, hearing it spoken was like being shot through the middle with a cannon. A hole gaped where her innards should be and all that was left was the shell that looked like her.

Her eyes drifted longingly to the door at the other end of the light-filled room, over near the teachers' pigeonholes, as she wondered how much longer she'd be trapped here. She noticed that the specialist teachers were having a meeting over that side of the room but that their gathering included iced cream buns and regular bursts of laughter. She sighed and focused her attention on Janice's fingernails, freshly lacquered red with gold tips.

Janice checked her diamante-encrusted gold watch. 'I'll have to wrap this up soon as I have a meeting in the principal's office to go through the extensive list of jobs coming our way for the organisation of all the various Christmas parties and break-ups happening before the end of term,' she said, then scribbled a note to herself in her large executive diary.

Margie had once said that if Janice were a man then the size of her diary would be screaming to the world that she was compensating for inadequacies in other areas of her life. Krystal flicked her eyes to Margie now and her colleague returned the look with a smirk and a tiny eye roll. Janice held these meetings once a month on a Wednesday, when both her underlings were present. Normally, Krystal welcomed the break from the humdrum at her desk even if it meant she had to listen to Janice drone on. Today, though, she just wanted it to end so she could get back to pretending she was a functioning person when all she really wanted to do was lie down in bed and stay there.

'One more thing,' Janice said. 'As of next year, the two part-time roles that you both occupy will be consolidated into one full-time position.'

Now Krystal forced herself to concentrate. It sounded very much as if Janice had just said that one of them would lose their job.

'I'll email you a position description and instructions for applying when we get back to our desks. You have ten days to submit your application, which the principal and I will consider. If necessary, we'll advertise the position to the public. But, obviously, your previous employment in this role means we'd prefer to keep one of you on.'

Yes, that *was* what Janice was saying. Someone would be let go.

'Do either of you have any questions or comments?' Janice peered at them over her glasses and closed her diary with a finality that made it clear no one was to offer any other words. That was fine with Krystal; she'd had nothing to say all morning.

'I think we have everything we need, thank you,' Margie said, and Krystal felt herself bristle ever so slightly at the tone of her friend's voice. She wrinkled her nose at her to say, *Oh, you big suck-up!* but Margie slid her gaze away. They walked in silence back to the admin building and to their respective desks.

'I can't believe they're going to ditch one of us,' Krystal muttered. But Margie just tutted noncommittally and stared straight ahead at her screen. 'I mean, this is a bit awkward, isn't it? Both of us having to compete for the one job?' She wanted to get it out there as soon as possible. Margie was her friend.

'It doesn't have to be,' Margie said calmly, continuing to click with her mouse.

'What do you mean?' Krystal rolled her chair closer to Margie. 'This is not good. One of us will lose her job.'

Margie considered Krystal briefly, gave a small smile and shrugged. 'What will be will be,' she said, and turned away again.

Krystal had been so obsessed with thoughts of Evan's betrayal this morning that she'd failed to notice Margie's new navy shirt dress with a brown belt to match her mules. She'd put a colour through her hair, too.

'Have you got a new man?' she whispered.

'What? No. Why?' Margie said, frowning.

'New dress?'

Margie continued typing. 'I just thought it was time for a change.'

Krystal waited a beat but when Margie offered nothing further she just said, 'Okay,' and turned back to her own desk. She couldn't help but think that it was rather fortunate timing that Margie had chosen today – the day Janice announced that they would have to compete against one another for a job – to improve her working wardrobe.

*

Traipsing into the foyer of her apartment building with her two boys by her side, Krystal found a yellow manila envelope sticking out of the letterbox. She was distracted by Olly tugging on her arm, wanting to get up to his room to play with his PJ Masks headquarters, and Jasper asking if they could have ice cream for dinner and refusing to accept that dessert was not dinner and no, they couldn't have dessert every day anyway because it wasn't good for them. She pulled out the envelope, opened the box with her key and collected several more letters, and shoved them in her handbag.

With both boys bouncing and spinning in the elevator, she began flicking through the fistful of envelopes – a phone bill, a body corporate notice, an electricity bill, a roadside assistance renewal notice (why did all the bills always come at once?), and then the big yellow envelope. She flipped it over and paused at the sight of the return address stamped on the back. It was from the law firm of Trentino Cossa. Her heart skipped. Had he found a way for her to sue Cordelia-Aurora after all? She tore the envelope open. Inside was a law journal with a handwritten note from Trentino paper-clipped to the front.

Krystal, here is the latest issue of this journal, which arrived at my office last week. There is an article on page 16 that I thought you would be interested in. Best, T.

How odd. Then, with growing excitement, she wondered if perhaps the journal contained something that might help with a potential lawsuit against the Arthur family.

She hurried the boys inside, tossing their bags on the kitchen bench, ignoring their lunchboxes and water bottles for now.

'Boys, go to the toilet and wash your hands for afternoon tea,' she said, and shooed them in the direction of the bathroom. Olly was still learning to pee standing up and Jasper was taking great pride in showing him how to do it. Sadly she'd have to clean up their efforts later.

She flicked on the kettle to boil water for tea and leaned against the bench, flicking the pages of the journal to get to the article. And there was Cordelia-Aurora staring out at her. She was dressed as usual in black, seated against the backdrop of a tall bookcase filled with leather-bound law books, her hands clasped in her lap.

The gift that keeps on giving

On the second anniversary of her brother's death, leading Melbourne barrister Cordelia-Aurora Arthur, of the firm Arthur & Arthur, says it was 'a natural decision' to offer her services to Australia's organ donation authority.

Ms Arthur's younger brother was Evan Arthur, a Victorian barrister best known for his work on the Farner Seven case, and whose life was claimed by a tragic accident. She says that the family's decision to donate his organs was 'simple' and that it gave her great comfort to know a part of him lived on.

'He was such a good person, such a generous individual. It's what he would have wanted and it was both our duty and our privilege to carry out his last wishes.'

Ms Arthur says that the statistics show that the majority of people in Australia support organ donation yet only a small percentage ever register their intent or talk about it with their families. 'This has to change.' She is putting her passion to good use, now serving on an advisory board to the country's organ and tissue donation authority, advocating for laws to fill the gap between a person's intention and the family's final say.

'We were lucky in that the family was in total agreement. But that's certainly not always the case and it's in those murky waters of consent that I hope to best use my legal expertise to achieve the vital outcomes.'

Krystal stopped reading, feeling bile creeping its way into her throat. How dare Cordelia-Aurora use something as tragic and painful as Evan's death to drum up more business for herself?

Total agreement? Nothing could have been further from the truth. *The family's decision?* It wasn't the family's decision that mattered, it was *hers*, as his wife and legal next of kin. *What he would have wanted?* No one could say that for sure. He'd never registered his intent and he'd never discussed it with Krystal. No one had any idea what he wanted.

The article didn't even mention that Evan was a father and husband. No mention of the three people who mattered most. It was all about scoring goodwill for the Arthur empire.

'Mum!' Jasper called from the bathroom.

'Yes?'

'Olly's wee'd on the floor again.'

Krystal blinked quickly and closed the journal to return to later when she'd stopped shaking from the lies, the deception, and the omission of the fact that the only reason Krystal had signed those consent forms was because Cordelia-Aurora, upstanding citizen and barrister, and now champion of The Cause, had blackmailed her broken, vulnerable, distraught sister-in-law into doing so.

Within two months of their first meeting, Cordelia-Aurora had confronted Krystal face to face. Although she'd overheard snatches of whispered bickering between Evan – defending his girlfriend – and Cordelia-Aurora, Krystal had always managed to shake it off. Never for a second had she imagined that her mere presence in Evan's life would trigger such out-and-out hatred. But then, one summer evening, on the balcony of Evan's apartment during another attempt by Evan to encourage his snooty relatives to warm to Krystal, everything changed. In a moment when almost everyone happened to leave the balcony at the same time and it was just Krystal and Cordelia-Aurora overlooking the lights of the city, the full shock of Evan's big sister's hatred hit her.

Cordelia-Aurora rose from her chair like a serpent readying to strike, placed her wineglass on the table between them, and made a direct line for Krystal. Krystal looked up from her seat, surprised and apprehensive. Cordelia-Aurora didn't speak to Krystal voluntarily – only under the scrutiny of Evan.

'I know what you did,' she said flatly, glaring at Krystal.

'What?'

Cordelia-Aurora leaned down so their faces were close and her body cast a shadow over Krystal. 'You do realise I'm a barrister, don't you? One with many powerful connections?'

Krystal scoffed. 'So what?'

'So that means I only had to ask the right person for a favour and I was able to get a full criminal record check on you.'

Krystal was stunned into silence, frozen, just as she'd been as a little girl when one of her mother's boyfriends began to look at her the wrong way. She was trapped.

'I know what you did,' Cordelia-Aurora hissed again. 'I was going to take the information to Evan, but right now he is so . . .' Her eyes flashed, reflecting lights from inside the apartment. 'Well, there is an indelicate word for it, but I'm too civilised to go to that level so I'm going to say *enamoured* of you, that I know it would only make him deaf to what I have to say.'

Krystal swallowed hard and was ashamed when her voice came out shaky. 'I-it's not true. I was innocent.'

Cordelia-Aurora barked out laughter. 'Spoken like a true criminal.'

Krystal was angry now. 'It's the truth.'

'But you just said it wasn't true,' Cordelia-Aurora countered, baiting her.

Krystal gritted her teeth. 'If you'd read on, you'd have seen that all charges were dropped.'

'Oh, I did read on. I read everything.' Cordelia-Aurora paused, her gaze moving over Krystal's face and down her body. Then she straightened and smoothed her hair. 'Your mother has quite the history herself.'

Krystal could hear the others inside. Ivy was complaining about the lack of suitable venues in the city for an upcoming fundraiser auction for the hospital charity whose board she served on. Then Rupert suggested they hold it at their white house, as a tea party out on the lawn, which sounded lovely to Krystal but the explosion of laughter from Evan's parents indicated that it was out of the question.

They'd be back out here any minute and then Cordelia-Aurora would stop this game. Krystal just needed to wait her out.

'The thing is, as a barrister, I know that charges are dropped all the time, and it's rarely because of something as simple or as direct as someone's innocence. Cases go to court based on the admissible evidence, not on the truth.'

Krystal could hear her own breathing, feel her nostrils flare and her skin burn with humiliation. She wanted to screech at Cordelia-Aurora and also to rush to Evan and stop him from hearing all this.

Footsteps and voices were coming closer to the balcony.

Cordelia-Aurora got in one final sentence. 'I'm just letting you know that I know your secret, and the second you put a foot wrong, the moment I see a crack in Evan's faith in you, the very instant the winds of change blow in my favour, I will reveal your dirty little secret to everyone.'

Then she'd turned, painted a huge smile on her face and joined her parents and two brothers, leaving Krystal in her seat, trembling with rage and injustice.

*

212

Now, having cleaned up the bathroom, put a frozen pizza in the oven for dinner, lined up a set of plastic bowling pins and an inflatable ball in the hallway for the boys to play with and uncorked a bottle of wine for herself, Krystal leaned against the kitchen bench, seething. When would Cordelia-Aurora be out of her life forever? Right now, all she wanted to do was take the boys away, maybe up to north Queensland, the very opposite end of the east coast of Australia, and never have to communicate with anyone from the Arthur family again. But then the boys wouldn't have any grandparents to speak of, and they wouldn't have their uncle Rupert who, on the whole, was a reasonable sort of person, and she couldn't say for sure that the boys wouldn't need him to step up one day and patch some of the gaping holes left by Evan's death.

His death.

In Sydney.

Her fury swung back on itself and now launched a full-throttled attack on Evan. 'What did you see in that woman?'

The bowling pins smacked against the walls in the hallway, eliciting triumphant squeals.

'Mum, did you see that?!' Jasper shouted, running in, his delighted smile and shiny eyes drawing her attention.

'I heard it! What a great shot,' she said, holding up her hand for a high five. He jumped up and smacked it hard.

Olly came running in holding the yellow ball. 'Jasper, back up, back up!' he complained. He wasn't yet coordinated enough to stand up the pins without overbalancing them and needed Jasper to do it. 'My turn!'

Jasper groaned and let his head fall back dramatically. 'Oh, all right,' he said, with a long sigh. 'Come on, Mum.' He took her hand and pulled her out into the hallway.

Krystal watched as Jasper set up the pins and Olly tried to help but only got in the way and knocked them over, and Jasper growled at him and told him to stay back. She couldn't believe where the years had gone. Her anger at Evan turned around again and came back as desperate, aching grief. 'You've missed so much,' she whispered to him. And it was only a tiny fraction of all he would miss. If she could just turn back time, if she could just have him back, she'd forgive him. They'd work through it. They'd sort out whatever had gone wrong that she didn't even know about and they would make it all better.

Please come home.

She glanced at the front door, knowing it was insane and impossible but still fantasising that he might suddenly open it and walk through, tired and weary from his long night shift but still happy to see them.

But he wasn't talking to her. Not back then, keeping his very large secret tucked away from sight, and not now. Now, he was talking to Gabby. For as long as she'd known Evan, there'd been a woman between them. First, Cordelia-Aurora. Then the mistress. Now Gabby.

Talk to me, Evan. For god's sake, talk to me.

21

Gabby woke. She was hot and sweaty, the light in her room an eerie blue. She couldn't tell what time it was. Silence gathered close around her, tacky against her skin, pressing her into the mattress. She strained her ears to listen for something that would either indicate what had woken her or give her some sense of the time. But the silence persisted, everything too quiet, as though she'd stepped through a doorway into another world.

She tried to lift her hand to wipe at her eyes, but her limbs were heavy and unmoving.

All she could do was lie there, resigned to her immobility. Listening. Waiting.

For him.

He was here, just out of reach, somewhere behind the veil that separated life and death.

Then something shifted – the tiniest puff of air across her neck. She blinked.

He was there at the foot of her bed, a man as fully alive as any she'd ever seen.

He didn't smile.

His Roman nose was slightly too big for his face but was balanced by waves of thick curly hair and broad shoulders. She was fascinated. This was the man whose heart was inside her. She dropped her eyes to his chest, clothed in a white business shirt. She stared at the smart black buttons done up neatly. He wore silver cufflinks.

Then the light in the room transformed, the dark blue intensifying into indigo and then into black.

Her heart rate – *his* heart rate – kicked up a notch. She was falling, as though she might slide right off the edge of the bed. The light fixture on the ceiling began to flick backwards and forwards as nausea kicked in and the room began to spin. She closed her eyes, panicked, willing it all to stop, but she spun and spun, as though on an awful amusement ride she couldn't get off. She whimpered, unable to speak.

Fear whiplashed through her. She began to cry, the whole room roiling from side to side like an enormous sea vessel in a terrifying storm. *Please, make it stop*, she begged him silently.

She tried to fix her gaze on something solid in the room but the only thing motionless was him. She stared into his eyes. They were cold and unmoving, pits of black.

He's here to kill me.

And then she saw the blood, oozing through the buttons of his shirt, the massive wound beneath it from where his heart was taken, flowing, now gushing, blood pouring from him while all around them the room spun, faster and faster into a whirlpool of colours. She screwed her eyes shut, holding on for dear life.

*

Pippa's She Shed was adorned with multiple vases of fragrant pink roses, which had all burst into spring bloom. The aroma was heady, instantly soothing Gabby's distress from her other-worldly experience during the night. 'It smells amazing in here,' she said, pulling up the wooden chair next to Pippa's desk.

'They're too beautiful to let them rot on the bushes,' Pippa said, pushing the plunger down in the coffee press. It was Gabby's Flying Monkeys blend, and the notes of rose and apple in the brew were intensified by the floral scents dripping from the air. It made Gabby slightly giddy with pleasure.

Pippa handed Gabby the coffee in a cream-coloured hand-thrown mug. Her sister had recently started collecting pieces from a local potter who dug his own clay from the surround-ing area and used a kick wheel to spin the clay the way they did before electricity, as well as using fire to drive the intense heat of the kiln. Each piece was unique and cost a bomb, so she was building up her collection slowly.

'Are you okay?' Gabby asked, studying Pippa's face. She looked effortlessly elegant as always, her make-up immaculate, but her eyes and cheeks pulled downwards. At her words, Pippa's eyes filled with tears. She hurried to put her own mug down on her desk and place her fingers under her eyes to catch the tears and avoid messing her mascara.

'It's over,' Pippa said, giving up on trying to stem the tears. She whipped out a couple of tissues from a box and held them to her eyes, leaning her elbows on her desk.

'What happened?' Gabby asked, putting down her coffee and laying her hand on Pippa's back.

'Harvey and I were fighting last night. It was awful. We tried to lock ourselves away in the bedroom but we just lost it and started yelling at each other. The kids could hear us. Sadie came in crying, asking what was wrong.'

'Oh, shit.' Gabby put her hand on Pippa's arm.

'Then Felix came in and told us to stop yelling. Then Hunter came in and demanded to know if we were getting divorced, and Harvey ...' – she paused to hiccup a few times – 'Harvey just blurted out, *Yes, we are!* then stormed out, grabbed the car keys and left.'

'He left you alone to deal with the kids?'

Pippa nodded through her sobs.

'What happened then?'

'I had to sit them down and tell them that we both loved them very much and nothing would change that, and that Harvey and I did still love each other too, but sometimes ...' She hiccupped some more. '... Sometimes people grow apart and can't live together any more.' She rolled her eyes. 'You know, the usual tripe you hear on television all the time.'

'How did they take it?'

'Hunter stormed off to his room and slammed the door. The other three cried themselves to sleep.'

'That's really crap, Pip.' Gabby hugged her.

'I just wish we'd had the time to get ourselves into a good state and go through everything calmly with them. We should have got over ourselves and gone to counselling so we could show a united, supportive front for them, rather than exploding into the bloody natural disaster they're now having to wade through.'

'That would have been ideal, sure, but it's not too late. You could still all go together as a family. It would help now as you move through the stages of separation.'

'You think?' Pippa looked up, her eyes red, desperate to cling to some sort of hope.

'Definitely. Would you like me to help you find someone to make an appointment with?'

Pippa nodded and Gabby took over in front of the computer

to search for a family counsellor who could help them as soon as possible. Twenty minutes later, they had an appointment booked. Even if Harvey refused to go, it would still help Pippa and the kids.

Pippa pulled herself together and finished her now-cold coffee. She put her hand to her cheek. 'I must look a sight.'

'Actually, you still look beautiful even when you're soggy.'

Pippa gave her a small, grateful smile. Then she took a deep breath and turned her attention to Gabby. 'What brought you around this morning, anyway?'

It was Gabby's turn to take a deep breath. She told Pippa about the awful nightmare she'd had. 'At least, I think it was a nightmare, but I also felt like I was awake. I really have no idea if it was real or not.'

Pippa groaned. 'I don't like this at all.'

'Well, then you might not like the reason I'm here.'

Pippa raised her eyebrows at Gabby, waiting.

'I've decided I need a psychic.'

'You're kidding.'

'No, I'm not. We're trying to communicate with a dead person. A psychic seems like the most logical person to help.'

'I'm not sure you can use the words psychic and logical in the same sentence.'

'So, I found one online.' Gabby paused.

'And?' Pippa blew her nose.

'And she's not far from here. I was hoping you'd come with me.' Gabby grinned at Pippa expectantly.

Pippa looked aghast. 'But I don't believe in psychics.'

'It doesn't matter. I've never been to one either. For the purpose of today, I just need some . . . support, I guess. This whole thing is undeniably a bit creepy, but I need it to end. Evan wants something from me, Krystal wants something from me, and I want to repay them for what they did. They saved my life.'

The guilt-trip worked. 'All right, all right, I'll come. I'm probably not in any fit state to work today anyway. But, for the record, I don't think this is a good idea. I don't think any of it is a good idea.'

'Your objection is noted. You are absolved from any responsibility.'

Miss Melba's Reading Room was in the backyard of a small brick house, surrounded by tall, gnarled trees that looked like they belonged in an Enid Blyton story. Actual toadstools grew in the lawn and small, gilded fairy doors sat against the trunks of the trees. Fairy lights dripped from branches; in the overgrown grotto, their light was actually rather charming, even in the middle of the day. Gabby and Pippa followed the pebbled path around the side of the house and found a purple door with a dreamcatcher hanging at head height. Knee-high hunks of rose quartz crystal sat either side of the doormat, which proclaimed *Peace* to the world. Gabby paused, exchanging a look with Pippa, who shook her head slowly with derision.

'Come in!' Miss Melba called from inside, making them both jump.

Gabby pushed open the door and they entered a softly lit one-room hut, with more fairy lights strung around the walls. Thick claret-coloured curtains were drawn across the windows. It was like being inside a gypsy caravan.

'Welcome,' Miss Melba said, shuffling cards and beckoning them over with a tilt of her head. 'It's a pleasure to meet you,' she said to Gabby, seeming to intuit that it was Gabby who was there to see her. But then, Pippa was hanging back with her arms crossed, so perhaps no special insight was required. She smiled at Pippa. 'Come in, dear. I don't bite.'

The sisters pulled out heavy wooden chairs, which scraped over the blue wooden floor, and sat, adjusting purple sateen cushions at their backs.

Miss Melba's age was not easy to guess. She wore heavy make-up and her black hair was mostly covered with a green scarf. The skin of her face was plump but her hands, expertly shuffling a worn deck of tarot cards, were spotted and veiny. Strings of coloured beads and crystals plunged down her chest and disappeared into her shelf of bosom. Other than that, she was dressed entirely in black.

'Have you come to see me about a man?' she asked suddenly, piercing Gabby with a stare that unnerved her.

'Yes, sort of. Probably not in the way you think, though.'

Miss Melba nodded and pulled out a card, flipping it over in the centre of the table.

Out of the corner of her eye, Gabby could see Pippa giving her a hard stare. She had been adamant on the drive over that Gabby shouldn't give Miss Melba any details at all. 'If she really is psychic she shouldn't need any information,' she'd declared knowledgeably.

Miss Melba studied the card, then put it back into the deck and continued to shuffle for a moment, then closed her eyes, her hands slowing in their rhythm.

Gabby's scalp tingled.

'The man you've come to see me about,' Miss Melba began, her eyes still closed, her voice low, 'he's crossed over, hasn't he?'

'Yes,' Gabby said, casting her eyes around the small room, looking for any sign of Evan.

'You two have unfinished business,' Miss Melba went on.

'Yes.'

Miss Melba nodded slowly, tilting her head to the side as if listening. Then she frowned and shook her head. 'There is something different about this. He is trying to talk but the ...' She clicked her fingers as if trying to find the right word. 'The *vibration* is off, somehow.'

Beside Gabby, Pippa rubbed her forehead, perhaps feeling tense and sceptical, or perhaps afraid of where this was going. Gabby wasn't sure if she should help Melba by telling her about the transplant or just wait it out. Before she could decide, Melba spoke again.

'I need something of yours,' she said, opening her eyes. 'A piece of jewellery or something like that. Something you wear a lot. Or even your phone will do. Just something that holds your vibration.'

'Oh, okay.' Gabby reached into her bag for her phone, which she'd turned off before coming in, and handed it to Melba, who took it with both hands and held it to her chest, her eyes closed once more in her listening pose.

Gabby chanced a look at Pippa, who merely raised her eyebrows and lifted a shoulder to suggest she had no idea what was going on.

'You and he were very close,' Melba said. 'No, wait. You are still close?' She opened her eyes and stared at Gabby, perplexed. 'But he *has* crossed over, yes?'

'Yes.' Gabby swallowed. 'I have his heart.'

Pippa *tsk*ed.

Melba furrowed her brow.

'I had a heart transplant and his heart is now in my chest,' Gabby clarified.

Melba looked relieved. 'Ah, yes, I see that now. That makes sense. That's why the vibration is confused. His spirit is here but so too is a physical piece of him.' She smiled as if this was the most interesting reading she'd done in a long time.

'He's been hanging around,' Gabby said. 'Haunting me, I guess.'

Melba frowned. 'And you want to know why?'

'I think he wants me to speak to his wife. She has questions for him. But when we tried to talk to him together, it really upset her because I didn't have enough information. I thought maybe *you* could speak to him? I'm not a psychic . . .'

'Everyone has psychic abilities, but it's like a muscle: you have to use it or you'll lose it.' Melba's tone was encouraging.

'That might be true,' Gabby conceded, 'but I don't think I have time to start from the beginning. We need a professional to talk to him.'

Melba took a deep breath, rubbed Gabby's phone between her hands, and once again closed her eyes to listen for Evan's spirit.

Gabby waited. Pippa wiggled her foot. Melba breathed.

Finally, Melba handed back Gabby's phone. 'All right, Evan says –'

Gabby's face burst into a smile. Pippa's mouth fell open. *Evan.* Melba knew his name! She had to be the real thing.

'– that this is a journey for you and his wife to take together.'

'What?' Gabby was shocked.

'He says he wants you to help her. There are things she needs to know.'

'Then why can't he just tell you now, and you can tell me and I can tell Krystal?'

Melba nodded. 'That would be easier for us to cope with, wouldn't it?' She smiled sympathetically. 'Here on the earth plane, we want things finished and we want things now. We don't want to wait. And we also always want to know why, why, why. But out there, on the spirit plane, they aren't so concerned with providing reasons or following timelines.' She shrugged. 'We don't know exactly what they do out there but they aren't always available to come to the phone, as it were.' She chuckled gently at her own joke.

Gabby sighed in frustration. 'So, what do I do?'

'You're just going to have to keep trying.'

Now Gabby was cranky. She'd had to pay for this reading up front – one hundred dollars through PayPal – and this was all she was going to get? Apart from the emotional stress this whole fiasco was causing her, the lack of sleep and the potential threat to her physical wellbeing, she had an ageing father to keep an eye on, an AWOL ex-husband to marshal and a business to run. All this time away from the cafe, while doable in the short term, was going to start affecting it soon. She might not be needed on the floor, but she played important roles in providing guidance and boosting morale, rostering, balancing the till, banking, paying bills, ordering stock, meeting with the growing number of buyers of their roasted beans, scheduling maintenance checks, and organising quarterly tax returns, ongoing marketing and more. Her mind needed to be fully committed to the job, not constantly distracted by worries that some sort of vision was going to strike her.

'How am I supposed to do that?'

'Evan says you're going to have to work that out with Krystal,' Melba said. 'It's the only way.'

'Nothing she said was true,' Pippa said, sliding into the passenger seat and tugging on the seatbelt. 'She didn't give you anything valuable, she just put it all back on you because she was clearly out of her depth. Total fraud.'

'What are you talking about? She knew his name!'

'Lucky guess.'

'There are about a billion names in the world. How lucky do you think she is?' Gabby all but squealed, pulling out into the suburban street. 'How could she possibly know that?'

'I have no idea, but it's like magicians – all smoke and mirrors. I'm telling you, she's a fake and you shouldn't listen to anything she had to say.'

Gabby sneaked a glance at her sister and saw Pippa's blue eyes were set, uncompromising. Perhaps Pippa was right and Miss Melba was a fraud. It was a crushing thought, quickly followed by an even worse one. What if none of what she'd been experiencing was real and she was simply hallucinating all of this?

'Maybe I should get my meds checked,' she muttered, rubbing her temple.

'Best idea you've had all day,' Pippa concurred.

But then, she couldn't have imagined all of this. Krystal had validated so much of what she'd seen.

'No, wait!' Gabby thumped the steering wheel in excitement, remembering something the psychic had said. 'I do know what to do! Melba *did* give me the answer after all.'

22

'Why did you send me this?' Krystal held out the law journal, then took a seat in a heavy chair near the tropical fish.

Trentino Cossa folded his hands together and rested them on his belly. He scratched at his tight steel-grey curls a moment. 'Your visit the other day . . .' He paused, searching for the right words. '. . . Moved me.'

Krystal swallowed the lump that had been lodged in her throat ever since Gabby had told her about the vision of Evan in another woman's house. A lump formed by emotion so strong she didn't dare let it out lest it destroy her. How could she reconcile her need to get justice for Evan with her overwhelming desire to throttle him? Did the fact that he'd been having an affair change what they'd had together? Well, yes, because she'd always thought she was different, special enough for him to turn away from his stiff, chilly family and choose a life of colour with her. But she hadn't been enough after all. He'd still wanted something else, something more.

'When that journal arrived, it seemed like a sign of some sort,' Trentino said, shaking his head a little at the absurd notion.

'A sign?'

'I still don't think there's any way we can help you right now, let me be clear on that. But it irked me to read Ms Arthur expounding about how the family had decided to donate his organs, conveniently ignoring your existence at the same time. I don't like it when lawyers go rogue,' he said, distaste dripping from his words.

Despite herself, Krystal smiled.

'Gives us all a bad name,' Trentino said, frowning behind his thick-rimmed glasses. 'In general, people think badly of lawyers.' He sniffed. 'But some of us do what we do because we are driven to serve. I admired your husband. I'd like to help you, if I can.'

Krystal held his gaze, waiting, considering that she had also harboured disparaging thoughts about lawyers and the only reason she'd come to see him was because she thought she needed someone just as tough and brassbound as the Arthurs. Trentino gave off a stern but fair, fatherly vibe, and she couldn't help but like him.

'So.' Trentino sat up straight and folded his hands together once more, this time twirling his thumbs around each other in a thinking gesture. 'Where does this leave us?'

'I have no idea,' she admitted, and smiled, because oddly she felt a tiny bit better.

'Time,' Trentino said. 'I usually find that people give up all their secrets, given enough time. Ms Arthur abused her power with you that night. One day, that will come back to haunt her. When it does, come see me.' He stood and held out his hand for Krystal to shake. 'Stay in touch, okay?'

'I will. Thanks.'

He nodded at her confidently and Krystal turned to leave, tucking the law journal back into her bag. She had no real idea what had just happened, but nonetheless she felt better knowing there was one more person in the world who was on her side.

As it was Friday, her day off, and she still had a couple of hours before she had to pick up the kids, Krystal walked a short distance from Trentino's office to hop on a tram to take herself for a fancy tea at the Hopetoun Tea Rooms in the lavish Block Arcade in Collins Street. The tearoom had a permanent line outside behind a rope barricade, which gave Krystal plenty of time to soak in the atmosphere.

Both the arcade and the tearooms dated back to the late 1800s, and were designed in a French Renaissance style. Tall pillars, arches, skylights, stained-glass windows, and that floor! The full width of the arcade floor was made up of intricate floral mosaics, so precious that they were covered with carpet during the Second World War so that soldiers' boots didn't damage them. All around her were the warm colours of burnt orange, chocolate brown, charcoal and cream. Just standing here was therapy in itself.

To her right the shop's exterior, dark stained wood with black signs and gold lettering, framed a sensuously lit window display of the most gorgeous cakes and pastries on crystal platters. A pyramid of coloured macarons. Strawberry tarts dusted with icing sugar. Fluffy cream-filled sponges covered in edible pink petals. Hummingbird cake. Coffee rolls. Thick, creamy cheesecakes. Her eyes took them all in, and she had no idea which one to treat herself with because they all looked so enticing. On the other side of the display she could see patrons sitting in plush chairs, with gilded mirrors on the walls, silver high tea stands and delicate teacups in front of them.

The line moved steadily but still her mouth was watering by the time she was seated at a table next to the heritage green and gold wallpaper on the back wall. She ordered the now famous lemon and elderflower sponge cake – inspired by Harry and Meghan's royal wedding – and a pot of English breakfast tea. She couldn't remember the last time she'd taken time out like this on her own, to enjoy something so special and delicate.

Her cake arrived, four layers of sponge with cream, topped with a spray of yellow and white flowers, and she'd just poured her tea and picked up her fork to have her first mouthful when her phone rang. Her dreamy, pleasure-filled state vanished immediately. She couldn't ignore it – knowing it could be the school or day care centre to tell her one of her kids was sick or injured – so she braced herself and fished around in her bag to find it.

It was Gabby.

She momentarily considered letting it go to voicemail, aching to hold onto the peace she'd just found here in the tearoom, but at the last moment she answered it.

'Hello?'

'Hi, Krystal, it's Gabby.'

'Hi.'

'Do you have a moment to talk?' Gabby sounded as though she was at The Tin Man. Krystal could hear a man calling out orders to go and music in the background.

'Yeah, okay,' she said, her appetite for this gorgeous cake already fading as she wondered what devastating new piece of information Gabby might have for her.

'Great. Look, I know this will sound a bit out there . . .' Gabby said, then snorted. 'But then again, I think we've already passed "out there", haven't we?'

'Yes, probably.'

'Right, well, I wanted to try to get more information for you.'

Krystal's insides swirled. Here it came . . .

'So, I went to see a psychic.'

'Oh.' She wasn't expecting that.

'And she knew Evan's name.' Gabby spoke quickly, either nervous or excited. 'Which was pretty amazing, and makes me think she knew what she was doing and, anyway, she said something that made me think.'

'What did she say?'

'Well, she couldn't get much out of Evan, but she said that he said that you and I needed to "take this journey together".'

'What does that mean?' Krystal looked sadly at her cake, wishing she'd had the time to enjoy it before this conversation.

'That's why I'm calling.' Gabby took a deep breath. 'I think we need to go to Sydney, together, to see if we can unlock some more of Evan's memories to get the answers you need.'

Krystal's mouth fell open. She hadn't been to Sydney since Evan died. There was a long silence, which Gabby eventually broke. 'Krystal? What do you think?'

'Um . . . let me think about it. I'll get back to you.'

Krystal disconnected the call and sat perfectly still, staring at the swirly wallpaper beside her. Someone had taken a gold marker and written across a gilt-framed mirror: *Where there's Tea there's Hope.*

Was it a sign, like Trentino had said?

There was a pot of tea in front of her. Gabby had phoned with an opportunity. Although it made her feel sick and shaky, not having a clue what, if anything, they would find in Sydney, she knew she had to do it. She messaged Gabby.

Okay, we can go. When?

> How about Monday afternoon?
> We can visit the street where
> Evan was hit by the car
> that night. Sorry, I know it's
> probably not something you
> want to do. But I really want to
> help you and I think this is the
> best way.

Gabby was right: the thought of walking that street filled Krystal with dread. But she needed to be strong. She needed to know what he was doing there that night. For better or worse, she had to know.

> Okay.

'Want a piece?' Gabby asked, settling herself in the aisle seat next to Krystal while the flight attendants checked that everyone had their belts buckled and their bags stowed.

Krystal looked at the packet of chewing gum Gabby held between her thumb and forefinger. 'Is that . . . is this some sort of Evan thing?' she asked tentatively.

'What?' Gabby looked at the chewing gum, confused.

'That's my favourite brand, that's all,' Krystal said, and reached up to direct the air vent onto her face to cool herself.

'Oh.' Gabby frowned. 'No, it's just a post-lunch thing. I carry it with me all the time. Dental hygiene's really important after you've had a transplant – all that bacteria in your mouth is apparently quite dangerous.'

'Sorry. I'm a bit wired, heading to Sydney, leaving the boys with Roxy overnight, having to call in sick tomorrow.'

Gabby put the gum in her mouth and began to chew. 'I hear you,' she said. 'My kids are a bit vulnerable right now too.'

They paused in their discussion to watch the safety demonstration as the plane rolled across the tarmac, heading for the runway. When the demonstration had finished, Krystal spoke again, turning her body away from the man in the window seat on her other side. 'What do you mean, vulnerable?'

Gabby pulled the hairband from the nape of her neck and used her fingers to untangle her curls, draping them over her left shoulder. 'My ex-husband has decided he wants a break from them,' she said, clearly disgusted.

'What does that mean?'

'I have no idea. They've been a bit mopey and reactive, understandably. I'm most worried about my eldest, Charlie. He just turned sixteen and seems to have taken Cam's rejection particularly personally.'

Krystal clucked sympathetically. 'Boys need their dads,' she said, thinking of her own kids.

'He has a mobile phone now, and I sneaked a look at his call list and found several calls in a row to Cam's mobile. Cam didn't even answer them.' Gabby shook her head sadly. 'Almost broke my heart,' she said, then winced. 'Sorry, that's such a clichéd statement, and one that's especially awkward when you've had a heart transplant. Even more so when you're sitting next to the woman who gave you that heart.'

Krystal manoeuvred her legs in the tight space to cross one over the other, further distancing herself from the man at the window. 'It's okay, really. I'm sure I'm as freaked out about this as you are.'

The plane manoeuvred itself to point straight down the runway.

'We'd make a great headline for a trashy magazine,' Gabby said. '*The Women Who Shared One Man's Heart!*'

'*The Other Woman: Life After Death.*' Krystal shuddered at her attempt at a joke. It was the first thing out of her mouth but it cut a bit close to the bone. Thankfully, Gabby didn't seem to notice.

The plane began to rattle, accelerating along the runway, forcing them back in their seats.

'*Saved by a Married Man!*' Gabby said, waving her hand in an arc through the air as though conjuring up the title.

Krystal smiled and nodded but said no more, taking advantage of the natural moment to cease conversation as the plane roared and ascended into the air. Instead she racked up the facts silently in her mind.

My husband speaks from beyond the grave. My husband's sister forced me to cut out my husband's heart.

Didn't she?

My final betrayal.

They landed in Sydney at three o'clock in the afternoon, the sky blue with genteel puffs of cotton-ball clouds lazing about. Sydney was a few degrees warmer than Melbourne, and the brightness of the day shimmered around them as their cab whizzed them into the city, easing Krystal's nerves. They hailed one of the special black cabs, just like the ones in London, and directed the driver to take them over the Harbour Bridge. They gazed out at the magnificent blue of the harbour, white sails of boats bobbing about and the view of the Opera House extending out over the water. A huge cruise liner was stationed under the bridge, glittering and festive, a small nation on the water.

'Here, I want to show you my kids,' Gabby said, pulling out her phone and tapping at the screen. 'I want you to see them, because your choice to give me Evan's heart didn't just save me, it saved all of them too.'

Krystal closed her eyes for a moment, steadying herself, feeling deeply ashamed of the secret between her and Gabby.

'I took these on the weekend,' Gabby said happily. 'This is Celia, she's my youngest, only ten.'

A pretty girl sat on the grass, her arms around her knees, and smiled into the camera, all teeth and shining eyes in the sunlight.

'She's gorgeous,' Krystal said.

Gabby swiped the screen. 'And this is Charlie, he's sixteen.' A tall boy with bright red hair and striking freckles pulled an embarrassed photo face, reclining in a wooden outdoor chair, a coffee cup in his hand. 'He's got a real thing for coffee.' Krystal could hear the pride in her voice.

'And who's that? Is that . . .' She trailed off, remembering the first time they'd met.

'Luciano. Yes, you met him the day you tried to talk to me at the cafe. He's my coffee roaster.' Gabby's tone betrayed her affection for him.

'Are you two – together?'

'No,' Gabby said, a bit too quickly. 'Just . . . I don't know. Maybe one day?' She lifted a shoulder and let it drop.

'Look at you,' Krystal teased, glad to have sidestepped past the fact that he'd escorted her out of the cafe. 'You've gone all red.'

Gabby blushed further and put a hand to her cheek. 'It's very early days. I'm trying not to get my hopes up.'

Krystal wanted to ask her why not, but then remembered that they weren't really friends and probably never would be. She'd always find it difficult to be in Gabby's presence, knowing that if she'd got what she wanted back there in the ICU, Gabby most likely wouldn't even be alive today.

'And this is Summer, my middle child. She's thirteen and still lovely and happy, though I'm expecting that to change at any moment.'

Krystal smiled. Seeing those kids, knowing that they wouldn't have their mother right now if Krystal hadn't done what she did, despite not wanting to, shifted something in her. She felt real happiness for them. Relief. Maybe one day all the horror inside her would transform and grow into something peaceful.

Gabby kept swiping, looking for more good photos. 'Oh, and that's our dog, Sally. You met her, of course.'

'And are they your kids too?' Krystal asked, pointing to two other girls and a young boy.

'No, they're Luciano's kids. Cooper is desperate for a dog. That's why they came over, so he could meet Sally.' Gabby swiped again to show Krystal a photo of the cherubic child with blond hair and blue eyes, with his arms wrapped around Sally as she sat beside him.

'Adorable.' Krystal wondered again if she should move her boys out of the city. Maybe they could have a dog too.

Gabby's phone sprang to life in her hand and she took the call. Krystal turned to look out at the view, wishing the cab would slow just a touch so she could take it in properly, and tried not to listen, though it was impossible not to overhear with Gabby sitting an arm's length away.

'Hi,' Gabby said warmly. 'What's Grandpa making you for dinner?'

It must have been one of her kids.

'Oh, isn't he feeling well?' Gabby's tone changed to one of concern. 'Oh! That's no good . . . Okay, give Grandpa a kiss for me. Have fun. Ask Summer to call me when she's home. And Charlie too! Okay, bye, baby.'

'Everything okay?' Krystal asked.

'That was Celia. She likes to chat and tell me about her day. My father's looking after them tonight but apparently he was at work today – he does some shifts at the local RSL behind the bar – and dropped a glass and cut his hand.'

'Did he need stitches?' The traffic had slowed now and looming office buildings shadowed their passage through the northern suburbs.

'No, apparently not, but he's not cooking tonight so they're having a frozen lasagne.'

They were nearing their hotel; Krystal could see it on the destination map of the satellite navigation system on the dash.

'I worry about my dad,' Gabby said, still clutching her phone in her hand. 'My mum died about a year ago and he's never really been the same. I miss her fiercely; I can't even imagine how difficult it is for Dad.'

'How long had they been married?'

'Forty-five years.'

'Wow.' Krystal wondered if she and Evan would have made it that far, especially if she'd known about this woman in Sydney. The other night she'd wanted to believe it, though now she wasn't so sure. 'That must have been really hard on him.'

Gabby shook her head sadly, as though she still didn't quite believe it. 'It was. It still is.'

They arrived at the hotel and Krystal paid the driver. Gabby tried to give her some money but Krystal waved it away. 'It's my husband who's haunting you,' she said, trying to joke.

'True!' Gabby smiled, closing the door behind them. The cab drove off, leaving the smell of exhaust lingering in the air. 'But I owe you.'

Krystal felt another stab of guilt but put on a smile. 'Forget it. Let's check in and have a rest before we go and look for some dinner. I need to call my boys and it sounds like you've got a bit to catch up on too.'

'Okay, let's meet down in the lobby at seven?'

'Sounds good.' They had agreed to go after dark to capture the mood of the surroundings at the place where Evan had been hit by the car. The idea of it made her sick, but they were determined to get the answers they needed.

After checking in, Krystal went to her room and collapsed onto the bed. She had a harbour view, which seemed ridiculous. She was here to uncover buried secrets, things she might then wish she'd never known. It was obscene to have such a gorgeous view of the water outside her window, charming her into thinking she was on some sort of adventure, when the night loomed ahead, dark and dangerous.

23

The trunk of a tall, stately gum tree glowed ghostly white against the velvety sky on the corner of Ritchie Lane and Upper Almora Street in the affluent waterside suburb of Mosman, which was where Krystal had asked the cab driver to drop them off. Gabby exited the vehicle first, taking a moment alone to get her bearings while Krystal sorted the fare, then Krystal appeared at her side and the taxi zipped away, its vacancy light turned on.

'Here we are,' Krystal said, slinging the strap of her small purse diagonally across her body.

'Here we are,' Gabby repeated. Without further discussion, they began to walk.

Ritchie Lane was a narrow one-way street lined on one side with three-storey apartment blocks and modern, geometric balcony gardens sporting trimmed hedges, and on the other with houses behind six-foot-high rendered fences abutting the footpath and white agapanthus flowers reaching up into the night air. It was dimly lit – just one streetlight about halfway up. Wheelie bins stood like sentries, lined up along the kerb. Not a scrap of litter in sight. No loud music or televisions. An occasional yappy dog or a car a street away were the only real sounds.

'What was he doing here?' Gabby asked, then instantly regretted the absent-minded question. If anyone had any clue at all, it was most likely to be her.

'No one knows. Some people who live in this lane heard the screech of brakes and the –' Krystal's voice faltered – 'the impact.'

Gabby blanched.

'A man came out but only saw the colour of the car as it drove away. He couldn't give any details, the model or the numberplate. He wasn't wearing his glasses and it was dark. But he called the ambulance.'

'So, it was probably a hit and run?'

'The police investigated but never found the driver.'

They walked on in silence, and Gabby tried to imagine Evan here in this laneway – running, as she'd experienced in her visions. But why was he running? He'd been afraid, she knew that.

They were almost at the end of the lane when Krystal halted, staring at the bitumen beneath their feet. Black sky above. Black road below. Just ahead of them, the laneway swung sharply to the left.

'What is it?' Gabby asked, but by the way the hairs on her arms were standing up, as though they had suddenly become antennae to the dead, she knew exactly why Krystal had stopped.

Here. Right here was where Evan had hit the ground.

Krystal didn't answer. She was breathing erratically, and just as Gabby stepped towards her, Krystal buckled at the waist and fell to the ground. On her knees, Krystal placed her palms on the road, moving them about as if trying to find the exact spot, the exact moment when everything had changed.

'Ritchie Lane, just before the intersection with Beach Lane – that's what the police told me,' she said, still moving her hands over the rough surface of the road. Gabby swept her gaze across the ground for clues, hoping for a vision, but there was nothing yet.

Just then, a jogger rounded the corner, coming straight towards them, his shoes slapping, his breath bursting from him in raspy puffs. Both women recoiled and Krystal staggered to her feet.

'Watch it!' he called, leaping to the side but not pausing in his stride. 'Idiots.'

Startled, neither of them said anything for a moment. Then Krystal gathered her wits and hurled some abuse at his retreating back, for which she was rewarded with a middle finger raised in the air as he pounded along.

'Wanker,' she yelled at him. 'Wanky Wank from Wanksville!'

'Good to see the gravity of the moment hasn't diminished your fighting spirit,' Gabby teased, which made Krystal snort, the mood lightened.

'Come on,' Gabby said, starting to head back the way they'd come. 'Let's walk up the street again. You can talk to me about Evan and maybe something will come to me.' She put her arm lightly around Krystal's shoulder and while the other woman stiffened a little, Gabby was pleased that at least she didn't pull away. Maybe one day they'd be friends after all. Gabby dropped her arm and they walked at an easy pace back up the street. 'Tell me five random things about him.'

Krystal was silent a moment as she thought. 'Well, he was a big fan of the Australian Open. He took me with him one year before Jasper was born. He splashed out on really great tickets and we got to watch a fantastic match between Serena Williams and Victoria Azarenka.' Gabby could hear the smile in her voice. 'It almost converted me to being a tennis fan too.'

'But not quite?'

'No. I don't have the patience for it. But he just loved it. He wasn't into a lot of sports, thankfully, but he was mad for tennis.' They sidestepped a small pothole in the road. 'He also followed AFL – he was a Carlton fan, but didn't go crazy. He was pretty good at the footy tipping competition at work though.'

'At the restaurant?'

'Yes.'

Gabby was enjoying hearing more about the person Evan was. So much of her contact with him had been frightening or stressful or guilt-inducing. It was nice to think of him living his life.

'He got funnier as he got older.' Krystal's voice was warm with remembrance. 'We laughed, so much.'

They were almost back to where they'd started at the corner with the ghostly gum. Gabby looked at the tree and felt a tug in her chest.

There was something about that tree.

'He was a smoker when he was young, till his early twenties.'

Gabby couldn't speak. She had a smoker's heart inside her?

A swirl of emotions enveloped her. She felt cheated, and then ridiculous, because without this heart she would be dead anyway, and then angry because there would always be things she didn't know about this heart, and guilty for wanting not just a heart but a perfect heart, one that would give her the best chance to be here for as long as possible for her kids, and furious that young people were always so flippant about their lives. She'd read about a young woman in England, barely in her twenties, who received a new set of lungs, got on with her life and planned to marry her love, only to discover less than twelve months after her operation that her lungs had come from a man who'd been a heavy smoker and she had stage four lung cancer. She'd gone through all of that only to receive someone else's death sentence.

Would that happen to Gabby now too?

She wanted to ask Krystal other things – had he ever taken drugs, was he a big drinker, had he eaten a lot of saturated fat? – all things that were part of his lifestyle history and were now part of hers. But of course, she couldn't ask. She took a breath and put these things aside to think about them later. Or not. Sometimes, thinking was overrated.

She stopped at the tree, looking up into the sky, where its mighty branches swayed gently.

Beside her, Krystal was counting on her fingers. 'Is that five? I think I need one more. Um . . .' She stopped, looked up into the sky where Gabby's face was turned. 'What is it?'

'There's something here.'

'What do you mean?'

'I don't know, exactly.' Gabby stepped off the road and onto the footpath, her hand outstretched, and laid her palm on the tree. It was warm from the day's heat and pleasantly rough beneath her skin.

'Do you think something happened here?' Krystal joined her, also placing her hand on the tree.

Gabby shook her head. 'I don't know.' She stepped back and looked around. 'Here, come this way.' Her stride lengthened as she picked up her pace, passing big houses with big fences. They were heading downhill now, towards the water. They could see the lights on boats bobbing up and down. 'This way!' She turned down Superba Lane, driven by nothing other than instinct. Krystal jogged slightly to keep up as they passed a vacant lot on the left, bordered by commanding houses with views of the bay.

'What are you looking for?' Krystal asked.

'A house.' The words were out before she had time to think about it. Yes, it was a house she was looking for. They were jogging at a decent pace now, taking a sharp turn to the right, then to the left, getting closer to the water. She'd lost track of the street names, simply following her gut till she found what she was looking for – an aged brick home with whitewashed walls, blue trims and a red roof, squatting on the slope of the hill.

Gabby stood at the gate, hands on hips, trying to catch her breath.

'W-what is it?' Krystal puffed.

Gabby took in the details of the white wooden fence with blue trimmings and the archway over a stone path to the front door, a lush but rambling garden. The house was like a key that opened the lock to the memories she'd been unable to reach. She knew what was on the other side of that door.

It was a woman, the woman she'd seen in her vision and the woman she now knew had been running by Evan's side just moments before he was hit by the car.

'Gabby, what is it?' Krystal reached out and clutched Gabby's arms with both hands. 'Tell me,' she said, her voice low.

Krystal looked over her shoulder to the blue and white house, a lone light from one shuttered window over the garden. A bedroom, perhaps. Someone in there. Someone she needed to know about. Gabby allowed her mind to race through all the possibilities, from the ridiculous to the vividly realistic and sordid. A large possum suddenly dashed across the road and scaled the fence and the small tree just inside the yard, clinging to a branch that shook and swayed beneath its weight. Somewhere nearby, happy voices and a burst of laughter drifted out from the rear of a house. A new moon hovered behind a thick pelt of cloud, as though it too was waiting for answers before it would make an appearance.

'I –' Gabby started, then stopped. She needed time to think.

'I'm going in.' Krystal let go of Gabby and strode towards the gate.

'Wait!' It was Gabby's turn to reach for her arm, but Krystal shook her off, her boots landing with purpose on the pathway, loose pebbles crunching under her soles.

'Ro-ro-ro-ro!'

A booming bark came from inside the house and both women faltered. Security lights came on, illuminating the front garden.

'Krystal, I think we should wait, take some time to think about this, come back in the morning.'

But Krystal wasn't listening, too desperate to get answers. She rapped her knuckles on the metal frame of the grilled security screen, making it rattle loudly and aggravating the barking dog on the other side.

'Please, Krystal. Let's go. This is not the time to –'

Another light next to the door turned on. Gabby flinched against its sudden brightness. A deadbolt turned, the front door swung open into the house and the aroma of a lemon-scented cleaning product, or maybe a room spray, wafted out. Standing on the other side of the security screen was a woman, shorter than Krystal, wrapped in a red and white kimono, her long curly hair falling in soft waves to just above her breasts. Her chin was lifted, on guard. She clutched the open wooden door with one hand, while the other rested on the head of a Rottweiler emitting low, threatening growls.

'Yes?' the woman asked, her face in shadows behind the door.

'Who are you?' Krystal asked, the words rushing out.

'Who are *you*?' the kimono woman countered. 'And what are you doing on my doorstep at this time of night?'

Krystal stood mute.

'We're friends,' Gabby offered lamely. 'We mean you no harm,' she said, holding her hands chest-high in a pose of surrender.

Krystal came to life and rolled her eyes. 'Jesus, Gabby, we're not aliens that have just landed in a wheat crop.'

To Gabby's surprise, the kimono woman laughed softly.

'Okay, *friends*, how can I help you?' The dog had quietened but still watched Krystal stiffly, Gabby noted. Unlike Sally, this dog meant serious business.

Krystal hesitated. 'I'm sorry to disturb you,' she began carefully. 'My friend Gabby and I are up from Melbourne. We were out walking, and then we took a turn, and then another . . .'

'Are you lost?' the woman asked. 'Would you like me to call you a cab?' She'd half turned away from the door as though about to get her phone. The Rottweiler eased its muscles.

'No, it's not that.'

The woman inched back again, waiting for an explanation.

Krystal scratched at her temple, seemingly searching for a brilliant plan, but then groaned in frustration. 'My name is Krystal Arthur. Do you know who I am?'

The woman shook her head. 'No.'

Liar. Gabby squinted through the grille of the security screen and into the dim hallway, trying to wordlessly convey to the woman that she'd seen her with Evan. They were all quiet a moment until the roar of a motorbike in the distance broke through the stillness.

'Are you sure?' Krystal asked, her voice quiet, a small tremor in her words.

'Very sure.' There was an uncertain waver in the woman's voice too.

Krystal's chin lifted. 'I don't believe you.' The woman stared at Krystal from behind the door but said nothing.

'Krystal, let's go,' Gabby said, pulling at Krystal's arm, trying to break the tension.

'No, wait . . .' Krystal began.

'I'm sorry, I can't help you,' the woman said, beginning to close the door. 'Goodnight.'

'Please, can I just –' Krystal begged, but the door closed in her face, the deadbolt clunking into place.

Gabby put her hand on Krystal's elbow to guide her down the steps. 'Come on. Let's go.' They began walking back the way they'd come.

'You have to tell me what you saw that took us to that house,' Krystal demanded.

'I really don't want to lead you up the garden path with this. I need some time to sit with it and make sure I know what I saw. I could be completely wrong and I don't want to . . . to . . .'

Krystal stopped walking and turned to face Gabby. 'Upset me? Is that it? What you saw was bad, wasn't it? Was it more than an affair? Were they planning on getting married or something?'

'I just . . .' Gabby had no idea how to finish the sentence. She'd seen the woman running with Evan in that dark street before he was hit. She couldn't explain it.

'Just tell me, please. I know she's lying. She totally knows who I am.'

Gabby took a deep breath, forcing herself not to lose it with Krystal, who didn't seem to realise – or simply didn't care – that all of this was terribly difficult for her too, that having someone else's heart in her chest, having their cells speaking through her body and seeing someone else's memories was *fucking disturbing*.

She blew air out slowly. Krystal had a lot on the line here too, she knew that. And it was Gabby's duty to repay her gift of life in any way she could. Soon this would all be over and they could both go on their way. Up until this moment, she'd thought it possible that they might be friends, but now she could see clearly just how much her very presence upset Krystal. Before she'd met Krystal, she'd fantasised about one day meeting her donor family and about tearful reunions and that Gabby's life might be a salve for their loss, that the evidence of her living a great life would heal their lingering pain. But it was so much more compli-cated than that – like a marriage that was once forged with the best of intentions but had now come to a place of irreconcilable differences.

'Krystal, I'm really tired. It's been a big day . . .'

'Wait!' Now Krystal was excited, bouncing on the spot. 'Evan was taken from here to the hospital. There's one more thing we can do. We need to visit the ICU at the hospital.'

'*What?*' Gabby stared at Krystal in the dark, the whites of her companion's eyes glinting under the streetlights. Visiting the actual ICU where Evan had been was a ghastly notion.

'Please. If we go there, maybe we can trigger some more memories for you. Maybe his last hours were still fresh in his mind. We've come all this way.' Krystal reached out and took Gabby's hand in both of hers, pleading.

Gabby didn't want to open a doorway between this real life and the unknown of the spiritual world. She placed her hands over her eyes and squatted down on her haunches on the footpath to think for a moment.

They *had* come a long way. They wouldn't be back here again. She'd done hard things before this, she could do one more. She took a deep breath and got to her feet, mustering the last of her strength. 'Okay. Let's go.'

They entered the hospital through the accident and emergency door, Krystal visibly shivering as two ambulance officers burst in, pushing a gurney carrying an unconscious man with a banged-up face. The two women moved out of the way and then made their way unnoticed to the elevator. Krystal hit the button. 'ICU is on level six.'

'We can't actually go inside the ICU,' Gabby whispered, her belly dropping a notch as they zoomed up the floors. She'd spent far too much time in hospitals for her liking and was resistant to visiting any ICU, let alone the exact place where Evan had died.

'People are up all hours in ICU,' Krystal said.

'That's the point. What do you think we're going to do? Someone will stop us. You have to sign in to those places. We won't get far.'

'We just need to get close enough to trigger memories,' Krystal said, tapping her foot and chewing a nail.

The elevator glided to a stop and the doors opened with a ding. Krystal stepped out first, Gabby following, looking about nervously. Krystal seemed to be getting her bearings from her previous visit. But before they could take a step, a nurse with grey-speckled brown hair in a practical haircut approached them.

'Can I help you?'

'Ah, hi,' Krystal said.

'Are you looking for someone?' the nurse asked, pinning first Krystal and then Gabby with her stare.

'I –' Finally, Krystal seemed lost for ideas or a plan.

From down the hallway, Gabby could hear sobbing, the plastic rings of a hospital curtain being swept aside, a machine beeping. There was always a machine beeping somewhere in ICU.

'Do you have a relative in ICU right now?' the nurse asked, her patience gone.

'No,' Krystal admitted.

'Then you will have to leave, immediately,' the nurse said, pressing the call button on the elevator. The doors sprang open straightaway. It hadn't even left the floor yet.

'Yes, sorry,' Krystal mumbled. She and Gabby bundled into the elevator and the nurse stood watching them until the doors closed.

24

They rode in silence in the taxi back to the hotel. When they got into the lift, Krystal thought Gabby was looking worse for wear, her eyes bloodshot, her skin pale, deep lines extending down from the corners of her mouth. Krystal didn't feel so good herself. In the hallway outside the elevator, they said goodnight, neither making any plans for the morning.

'Thank you,' Krystal said, to Gabby's retreating back.

Gabby turned around and gave a sympathetic shrug. 'I wish . . . I don't know. We'll talk tomorrow, okay?'

Krystal was tempted to ask her to go on, to try to get one final detail from her, but she could see Gabby was spent. 'See you then.' She raised a hand to wave goodbye then returned to her own room. She went to the bathroom, washed her face and cleaned her teeth, then collapsed into the queen-sized bed with starched sheets and switched off the lamp. It was midnight and she was bone weary.

City lights sneaked in around the blackout curtains and small red and green bulbs glowed at her from various electrical appliances around the room. Her eyelids were heavy and dropping of their own accord, and she relished the idea of this whole day coming to an end and disappearing into the quiet of sleep.

But that wasn't what happened. Instead, her mind raced and raced, and propelled her back through time to the most awful night of her life.

Krystal was standing in a large ward with low lighting, just enough to see by. It was busy with people. Nurses. Clusters of distraught relatives, holding on to each other like life rafts. Blue curtains in semicircles around motionless bodies hooked up to machines. Tubes. Wires. Blips. Beeps. The air too cold.

In front of her was Evan, a white sheet and blue blanket over his body. His neck was in a brace. His eyes were closed. A thick, ropey tube was taped to his mouth. His lips were swollen and slack. A ventilator ticked and wheezed.

A doctor in a pressed shirt and name badge stood tall and grim, a folder under his arm, speaking to Krystal but also to Cordelia-Aurora, who was standing on the other side of the bed. He was the second doctor to confirm the awful news. Krystal pulled her green knitted cardigan around her and sniffed, the soggy tissues in her hand useless now.

Cordelia-Aurora was thin and stiff, her face paler than ever above her black crepe top and pants. She was nodding at him, saying words like, 'Of course,' and 'I understand.'

Krystal didn't understand a single thing. How was her husband here, unconscious in this bed, in Sydney, when just yesterday he'd been in their apartment, active, warm, humming with energy?

The doctor finished what he was saying, dipped his head

slightly, and left, pulling the curtain closed behind him to give Krystal and Cordelia-Aurora some privacy.

Cordelia-Aurora stepped towards Evan and put her hand briefly on his, then pulled it back again and crossed her arms.

Krystal stood motionless, staring at her husband, deep shock keeping her upright and breathing, slowing her mind. She could sense the pain – a great ocean of it somewhere below – but knew that if it were to force its way out of her body it would break her into a million pieces. She had children here, in another room with Evan's parents – fractious, weepy and exhausted children who needed her. She couldn't fall apart. Not yet.

Cordelia-Aurora turned to face Krystal and spoke. 'It's time to let him go,' she said, quietly but firmly.

Krystal dragged her eyes from her husband's body and regarded her sister-in-law. It was as though she'd never seen this person before. She shook her head. 'No.'

'The doctor has explained this. He's not here any more. He's brain dead.'

'Don't say that,' Krystal said, grinding out the words. 'What a horrible thing to say.'

'Two doctors have done the tests. Both have come to the same conclusion. To let him continue on life support is cruel for everyone, including Evan. He can't stay like this forever.'

Krystal wove her fingers into her hair and scratched at her skull.

'He's dead.'

'I need more time,' Krystal said.

'Time? What do you need time for? He is *brain* dead.'

'Shut up, please.'

'He's never coming back, Krystal. The least you could do, the thing you must do, is give him his dignity.'

'I need you to stop talking. I need more time to think.'

'There are people out there who need organs, who are going to die without organs. It's selfish to keep them waiting. This is something he wanted to do.'

'He never told me that,' Krystal said firmly, her jaw jutting.

'Well, he told me,' Cordelia-Aurora countered. 'You're not the only one who is suffering here. Mum and Dad and Rupert will be back in a few minutes and they are going to want to move this forward.'

'Move this forward? What does that even mean?'

'You asked the doctor if they could leave Evan on life support to see what would happen. Do you even remember what he said?'

Krystal's mouth opened as if to respond, but it was as though the words that were supposed to make their way out simply didn't exist. She wasn't sure she recalled the conversation, exactly. She hadn't slept for two days.

'He said there was a chance, as time went on, that his extremities would start to decompose. Fucking hell, Krystal.' Cordelia-Aurora's shoulders slumped then and she pinched the bridge of her nose, taking a deep breath.

'Hell is exactly what this is,' Krystal said. She picked up Evan's hand and held it in her own, swallowing hard, squeezing her eyes shut. His hand was warm, his wedding ring, warm. 'My husband is . . .' Krystal couldn't finish the sentence.

'Yes, *your* husband. You have all the legal rights here, a system that I don't mind telling you is highly flawed. You two might have been fighting day and night and about to be divorced but as his wife you would still have legal rights above and beyond what his birth family – his first family, his real family – have. If I could change that right now, I would. I could take you to court, but that would obviously take time, which we don't have. Evan needs your help. If you are half the wife you've always claimed to be then you will get over yourself and your issues with our family, and do the right thing by your children and the man you proclaim to love.'

'Proclaim?' Krystal repeated, her voice shrill.

Cordelia-Aurora gave her a warning look, signalling that there were others just outside the curtains. 'This is a tragic, awful accident, but don't let his death be the defining moment of his life. He would want to save other people's lives. Let him do that and let his gift of life be the act he is remembered for.'

Krystal pulled up a chair and collapsed heavily into it, Evan's hand still in hers. She bent slowly and kissed his knuckles, and rested her cheek on the back of his hand.

Cordelia-Aurora looked away.

Finally, Krystal spoke, her voice heavy and damp with tears. 'You say he's brain dead as though that's the key to deciding his worth. You might have loved him for his brain, but I loved him for his heart.' She let the words hang in the air for a moment before continuing. 'And his heart will still be beating when they cut it from his body.'

Cordelia-Aurora's face twitched, but she composed herself quickly, resuming her expression of disdain. 'He's dead. The only reason his heart is still beating is because it has a pacemaker and because of that machine, right there.' She pointed at the ventilator. 'Turn it off and his heart will stop.'

'Maybe not for days,' Krystal said. 'Yes, I *was* listening. He could live for a week or even longer.'

'And what would be the point of that? The end result will still be the same, except he doesn't get to save any lives that way. What kind of legacy is that?'

'Legacy? Who cares about his legacy? I care about *him*, end of story.'

Cordelia-Aurora screwed her fists into white-knuckled balls. 'He doesn't need his organs any more.'

'Are you saying he's just a body now? We don't know what he can feel. We don't know if he'll feel them saw open his chest and cut out his beating heart. We don't know if he can hear us right now! What if he's inside there, screaming to be heard, begging us to give him more time, begging us to give him a chance.'

'The doctor said . . .'

'I don't give a flying fuck what the doctor said. I am the only person standing up for wherever Evan is now and wherever he is going from here. Do you get what an awesome responsibility that is? You're standing here complaining that you have no say, but you should try it from *his* end – he truly has no voice, and I have total responsibility for his life from this moment forwards. And if he wants to stay here, maybe hovering over us right now in this room, for an hour or a whole week then it is my responsibility, all alone, to make sure he gets his final wish.'

'He's *not* here. He's gone. He is brain dead. His broken neck severed the blood flow to his brain and it died. There is no return. His soul, or whatever you believe in, is gone. He's just a body now, so what does it matter?'

'What does it matter?' Krystal was on her feet again. 'We have all sorts of laws about how a body should be treated after someone has died precisely because it *does* matter. We are appalled by crimes that include hacking up bodies, or burning bodies, or dumping bodies. Yet here you are, suggesting it suddenly doesn't matter!'

'That's completely different! This is a hospital. Doctors, highly trained surgeons, are going to operate on him with the utmost respect and gratitude for the lives he is saving. Krystal, be reasonable! People are literally dying for you to make up your mind and get on with the job.'

Krystal shook her head repeatedly. 'No. I don't want to donate his organs. I don't want someone to cut him up while he is still alive.'

'He's *not!*'

'His heart is still beating,' she hissed, lowering her voice once more.

Cordelia-Aurora began to pace. 'Look, let me get the doctor and the organ donation coordinator back and you can go through all these questions with them again to make sure you understand.'

'It's not just all that,' Krystal said, fat tears rolling down her cheeks. 'I can see that you don't get this, but I don't want to know that there are bits of Evan out there in the world, roaming around. Please . . . I just want everyone to leave me alone with him, to let me hold his hand and let him take his last breath in his own time, as he crosses over or whatever he needs to do. It's a journey only he can take. I want to bury him as him, not as a scarecrow filled with stuffing. Don't you get that? Even a little bit?'

'What I see,' Cordelia-Aurora began, slowly, 'is that you are thinking of yourself right now and no one else. You aren't thinking of what the rest of his family wants – what everyone in the real Arthur family wants – you aren't thinking about what's best for your children, to have this brought to an end and not put them through days or weeks of terrible suffering, having to be hidden away, taken care of by Mum and Dad because you're completely incapable of looking after them, when what Mum and Dad really want is to be by their son's side while he is stuck in this terrible limbo, a limbo imposed upon him by *you*, selfishly clinging onto your legal powers as a way to stick it to us one last time.'

'That's not –'

'Well, I can see beyond that. I am thinking of your children.'

'What?'

'As well as sparing them all this suffering, you can give them a legacy to be proud of, one in which their father didn't die randomly on a street in Sydney but one in which he was a hero and saved many lives, in which he lived and died as a leader by example. It's a memory they'll need to rely on when they find out what their mother is really like.'

'What? What are you . . .?' Krystal stopped. She felt the blood drain from her face. 'Are you threatening me? Are you ordering me to sign the donation papers or you'll tell them about the arrest?'

'Of course I'm not threatening you! I'm an officer of the court. But it's inevitable, isn't it? The truth always has a way of floating to the surface, and just in case your children aren't as forgiving as you hope – teenagers are notoriously hard on their parents – I'm sure you would want them to be able to look up to at least one of their parents.'

'Have you lost your mind?' Krystal whispered, leaning across the bed. 'I'm talking about saying goodbye to my husband *forever*.'

Krystal pulled herself out of the hotel bed and ran to the bathroom, sobbing as she splashed water over her face, trying to wash the memories away.

In her room down the hall, Gabby lay curled in a ball after the long and awful vision, suffocated by her knowledge of the ghastly truth, that Krystal had never wanted to donate Evan's organs. Gabby was never meant to have his heart.

25

After a restless, teary night, Gabby pulled herself out of bed before dawn, needing to go home. She couldn't face seeing Krystal this morning. Knowing that she had never wanted to donate Evan's heart, had resented doing it, had even considered it a form of orchestrated killing of her husband, was a crushing blow.

Every organ recipient she knew struggled with the guilt of benefiting from someone else's loss, but the one thing that made it bearable was believing that it had somehow brought the donor family comfort to know that the person's death hadn't been for nothing – that something good had come of it, and that they had honoured their loved one's wishes.

Well, so much for that.

Of all the things the donor recipient handbook had warned her to expect – regular hospital visits for the rest of her life, possible rejections, thrice-daily medications, a long recovery, side effects of the pharmaceuticals, and a limited lifespan – this was not one.

She was tainted now, tainted by Krystal's muddied intentions and whatever nasty threats Cordelia-Aurora had held over her head. It wasn't Gabby's fault, yet here she was, caught in a tangled web.

She swallowed her handful of seven morning medications and washed them down with a few mouthfuls of water. She lifted her chin and stared sternly into her green eyes in the hotel's bathroom mirror.

Enough. No more guilt.

Today, everything would be different. This was the day her apologetic, guilt-ridden, bleeding heart hardened. Today, her bamboo backbone straightened into a steel rod. Today, her cracked-open chest sealed for good.

She certainly couldn't control everything in life; in fact, she knew from experience that there was very little she could control at all. Bad things happened to good people and there was rarely any rhyme or reason to it. She was a good person. The bad thing had happened to her and it had happened to Krystal too. But somehow, despite all the badness going on for Krystal and Krystal's children and Cordelia-Aurora and Evan's parents and brother, something good *had* then happened to Gabby.

She texted Krystal to tell her she needed some time to think and was leaving Sydney early. Then she looked into her own eyes once more. 'You've got this, Gabs. You've got this.'

Today was a new day. Today was a bloody miracle. And she wasn't going to waste one more second feeling bad about the way things had ended for Krystal and Evan. That was their life. This was hers.

She waited till she'd crossed the tarmac at Tullamarine and was inside the airport before she turned on her phone. She messaged

Krystal again, telling her she'd seen the woman with Evan in the street the night he was hit. She needed to wash her hands of her involvement and get on with her own life.

No sooner had she sent the text than her phone tinged with a message from Charlie.

> Car accident on the way to
> school. Grandpa cut forehead.
> Summer sore neck. Celia ok.
> At hospital to be checked
> out. Tried to call Dad but no
> answer.

Gabby upped her pace through the corridors on her way to the exit, pulling her overnight bag behind her, and called Charlie.

'Hi,' he said, sounding years older.

'What happened? Where are you? Is everyone okay?' she asked, ducking and weaving through passengers.

'I'm fine. Still at the hospital. One stitch for Grandpa and a big egg on his head. Summer has a neck brace. A bit of whiplash, they think. Celia's kind of . . .'

'Quiet? Withdrawn?'

'Yeah.' Damn. Celia still had hospital phobia after all the time she'd spent there while Gabby was sick.

'What about the people in the other car?'

'It was just one woman on her way to work. She's fine. Grandpa's car looks much worse than hers.'

'Well, I'm glad you're all okay,' Gabby said, sounding much calmer than she felt. She burst out of the airport and into the cool Melbourne air. She kept up the pace to wind through the taxi rank. 'I took an earlier flight from Sydney, so I'm on my way to the hospital now.'

'Too late. They're about to send us home.'

Gabby pulled open the taxi's door. 'Then I'll meet you there.'

There was much fussing over the injured and recounting of the accident before Gabby felt it would be okay to leave Monty and Summer at home for a short time while she took Charlie and Celia to school. But when she suggested it, both children baulked.

'Can I stay home today too?' Celia asked, throwing herself at Gabby and clinging tightly to her waist.

'And I've got an assignment I can work on,' Charlie said, his eyes sliding away. Perhaps they were more shaken up than she'd thought.

'Sure, why not?' she said, kissing Celia on the head.

Charlie went to the kitchen to make coffee and Gabby followed him. 'Tell me again what happened,' she said quietly. Monty was sitting at the table outside.

Charlie measured out coffee and tamped it down into the basket. 'Grandpa had been sitting at the lights for a long time. Traffic was bad. The light was green but he couldn't go because of the congestion. Then there was a gap, but the light had turned. I guess he just hadn't noticed that it had changed because he was concentrating so hard. He hit the accelerator and ploughed straight into the other woman's car.'

Gabby took a deep breath, imagining all the terrible things that could have happened to them, and with a horrible, dragging feeling of doom realised that her father's eyesight had deteriorated so much that he wasn't able to drive any more. She also felt bitter guilt that she'd left the kids in his care, lied to them about why she had to go to Sydney (to bring some cheer to a woman on the transplant list, so she'd said) and gone on a disturbing wild goose chase with Krystal when she'd been needed here instead.

'The police came and the ambulance and they did their thing, and they decided to send us to hospital,' he finished.

It was a good thing she'd left Sydney early. Clearly, she needed to focus on her family. With everything going on with Krystal, and Evan's visitations, she'd simply not been present enough. Her father wasn't as capable as he'd been two years ago. The tables had turned. Her mother and father had been her carers; perhaps it was now her turn to step up for her father.

Charlie muttered something, heating milk.

'What did you say?' she asked.

'Am I the man of the household now?' he repeated, his eyes firmly on the jug.

'What? No!'

'But Dad's MIA and you weren't here and Grandpa's . . . you know, not himself any more. So that leaves me, doesn't it?'

'No! Look, Charlie Bear, stop doing that a moment, would you?'

Charlie turned off the steam and set the jug down. Gabby reached out her hands to turn him towards her. He set his broadening shoulders and looked down at her seriously, prepared to take on the world if he had to.

My god. What a man he was going to be.

Tears threatened, of course, but she shooed them away. 'Look, if anyone is the father of this household, it's me,' she said, grinning at him. She flexed her muscles like Popeye the Sailor.

Charlie scoffed. 'You've got nothing.' He poked her tiny bicep with his forefinger. 'It's a chicken's instep, that's all.'

That was what her mother used to say. He smiled at her and she nodded, sharing the memory with him. She dropped her arm. 'You are enough, Charlie. Do you hear me? You're enough. You're more than enough. It's crazy how much of enough you are!'

He blushed then. 'Yeah, all right.'

'It's not your fault your dad's gone off the deep end and it's not up to you to fill the gap.'

He nodded.

She hugged him, unable to believe he was taller than her now. She patted him on the back and then he pulled away to finish his coffee.

'Good chat, son,' she said.

'Yeah, good chat, Mum.'

The house creaked quietly in the warming sunshine. Summer had gone to lie down and watch a movie in bed. Gabby phoned to make her a physiotherapy appointment for her neck then took her some painkillers. Outside, she found her father sitting at the table, a large red bump straining underneath the cut and stitch on his forehead. He was staring at the lawn. Sally rested at his feet but thumped her tail in greeting to Gabby.

'Hey,' she said, giving him a smile as she pulled out a chair next to him. He had a navy woollen vest over his short-sleeved shirt.

He looked at her quickly, but his brow puckered and he looked away, his eyes watery behind his thick glasses. 'I'm sorry,' he whispered.

'It's okay.' She reached over and put her hand on his arm.

He shook his head, setting his jaw. 'I'm done now. No more driving. That's it.'

Gabby wanted to tell him that he was just upset, that accidents happened to everyone, at all ages, that he was just in shock and overreacting. But maybe he was right. Maybe he'd accepted that he'd come to a new stage of life, that his old life as he knew it was done. She knew how that felt. It was a profound moment.

'What about your shifts at the RSL?' she said.

He worked his jaw, obviously not having considered this yet. 'There are buses.'

'True.'

'Or maybe I'm done there too,' he said, his voice pinched.

'Maybe. Maybe not.'

He huffed.

She sat with him and they watched small wrens flitting in and out of the bushes, enjoying the sun, Sally's heavy sleepy breathing filling the silence. Sometimes words just didn't help and all you could do was sit.

Celia decided to go into The Tin Man with Gabby, and when they got there they found eight-year-old Olivia had accompanied Luciano to work. Olivia was helping Ed unpack the latest shipment of cakes and display them in the glass cabinet. Gabby could appreciate why she was keen to help; the aroma was dazzling, with scents of honey, caramel, strawberry and citrus dancing through the air.

'Hi, Olivia!' Celia called, waving wildly, thrilled to see her new friend again after their first meeting at the house on the weekend. Celia skipped over to Olivia and they instantly started *ooh*ing and *aah*ing over the cakes, deciding which ones they would have for morning tea.

Gabby went out the back to find Luciano. 'Let me guess, it was Olivia's turn to be too tired to go to school?'

He muttered something in Italian and dragged a twenty-kilogram bag of green coffee beans to the corner of the storeroom, rotating stock before a new shipment arrived this week. 'I don't know what to do,' he said. 'And because Cooper got to come to work with me when he wasn't feeling well, Olivia simply refused to stay with Mamma today. She can't give any good reason not to go to school other than that she's tired. If I try to be stern with any of them, their eyes well up with tears.'

'Oh, that's rough,' Gabby said, perching against a stack of bags, taking a moment to enjoy watching him muscle his way around the storeroom, occasionally grunting as he lifted and dragged. 'If it's any consolation, Celia came in to work with me as well. She was in a small car accident with my dad this morning.' She shrugged. 'She's fine, more or less, but it seemed mean to force her to go to school.'

'At least that's a good reason,' Luciano said. 'Are my kids faking it?' He stopped and wiped his forearm across his forehead.

'Maybe?'

'What should I do?'

'Have you spoken to their teachers to make sure everything is okay in the classroom?'

'Do you think there's a problem? Like bullying or something?' His eyes widened in alarm.

'Not necessarily.' She tried to reassure him with a gentle tone. 'It's just always a good idea to keep them in the loop.'

'I spoke to them often when I first went to live with the kids. They've all been very understanding. At least the kids didn't have to change schools, so it's not like everything is brand new.'

Gabby nodded. 'True . . . kind of.'

'What do you mean?'

'Well, I know it's a totally different scenario, but for me, there is a fracture line in my life, with Old Gabby on one side and New Gabby on the other. In a lot of ways, *everything* is new. I'm sure that having continuity at the school has helped your kids, but in other ways it will challenge them, because they can no longer turn up to their same classroom with their mum or dad beside them. I imagine it's quite disturbing to be in the same place but for nothing to be the same again. They probably still have schoolbooks that their mum covered for them at the beginning of the year; her handwriting greets them every time they pick up the book. Their dad might have gone to parent–teacher interviews, but now it's you. No one makes their sandwiches exactly the same way any more. As you said, grief is exhausting.'

Luciano's face suddenly tightened with emotion. He turned away and continued hauling and stacking. She gave him a moment, then said, 'You might just need to ride it out. It's already the last term of school. All kids are starting to get a bit tired by now, yours probably more so. My advice is to go with it.'

'Give up?' He stopped again and faced her.

'No, not give up. Give in.' She smiled. 'Let it be what it will be. It's just one muddy, heavy, clumsy foot after another, one day at a time.'

He nodded and scratched the back of his neck. She saw the curve of his bicep under his shirt and had to look away. 'But for what it's worth, your kids are welcome here any time.'

'Thank you,' he said gruffly, and she left him alone to work off his worries.

Around eleven o'clock, Ed made Gabby a siphon coffee, which took some time, so they didn't do it often, but it was magical to watch. Gabby called Celia and Olivia over to observe too.

'This is real-life science,' she told the girls.

'Here,' Ed said, pointing to the Bunsen burner beneath the lower chamber, which was filled with water. 'Click that button, and you'll light the gas.'

Olivia jumped up and pulled her fleecy jumper off in a flurry, as if she was about to do something terribly energetic. Ed grinned and mouthed *So cute* at Gabby.

Olivia pressed down on the button a couple of times and a blue and orange flame burst to life below the water. In the top chamber, eleven grams of freshly ground coffee sat waiting. The water began to sway and bubble. Then it flowed upwards, through the glass tube between the chambers.

'Oh, wow!' Olivia breathed.

'Awesome,' Celia agreed.

Ed picked up a wooden spatula and began to stir the coffee grounds as the water soaked into them. 'This will make the coffee bloom.'

Gabby loved this part.

'What does that mean?' Olivia asked, leaning across the bench as far as she could without burning herself on the gas.

'I know!' Celia said. 'It means that when the water hits the coffee it kind of bubbles and releases gas and makes it taste good.'

'Excellent, Celia,' Ed commended.

When the last of the water rushed up the siphon and flooded the coffee in the top chamber, Ed clicked off the gas and pulled the burner away, then put the lid on the top chamber to seal in the pressure. By this time, a few customers had gathered to watch as well.

'Now the coffee will pass through the filter in the top chamber, so our liquid will be in the bottom and the grounds will be left in the top.' A moment later, like magic, the nut-brown liquid did exactly that.

'Whoa!' Olivia squealed and clapped her hands, and the eager customers murmured their delight too.

'What makes that coffee different from an espresso?' a young woman with a baby on her hip asked.

Ed smiled. 'Each way we make coffee gives it a different flavour.' She looked at Gabby. 'Shall we do a few demonstrations?'

'By all means,' Gabby said.

With Kyle working the espresso machine to keep orders ticking over, Ed seized the opportunity to educate their audience on the marvels of coffee. She distributed the siphon coffee into tiny test sizes – just a slurp or two in babycino cups – and handed them out to willing participants. 'Here you go. Try that.'

Celia grabbed one, and Olivia took one too. Olivia sniffed it thoughtfully, then sipped and swirled it around in her mouth. Luciano had obviously taught the kids how to cup.

'It's smoky,' Olivia said.

'And nutty,' Celia added, and Gabby and Ed could barely look at each other for fear of laughing at the adorableness of the two girls.

Luciano had come to the swing door and was watching, a small, proud smile on his face. He caught Gabby's eye and she gave him a look that said, *Aren't our kids amazing?* He tipped his head in agreement. She was overcome with happiness, momentarily imagining the two of them together with their six kids.

But the odds of her even being alive in just eight years' time weren't favourable. How could she possibly plan a life when she could hear the end point rushing towards her like a freight train?

26

Krystal woke at seven o'clock with a crushing headache and stumbled to the hotel's bathroom for a glass of water. What an agonising night that had been. She pulled off her clothes, wanting to cleanse herself of the emotional storm that had descended on her. In the shower she let the water gush over her hair, face and body. She let herself cry, safe for once from worrying about losing it in front of the boys.

This was the worst she'd felt in a long time.

Her only hope was that Gabby would tell her everything she'd seen and between them they might be able to put the pieces together. Maybe then she could know for sure that Evan forgave her for giving in and allowing them to cut out his heart and other organs. There might even be enough information for Krystal to go back to the kimono woman's place and confront her. She was in too deep now; she needed to know everything there was to know about their affair.

Back in the bedroom, she sifted through the clothes in her carry-on bag, disappointed she had to put her jeans back on. She really needed a totally clean start to this day if she was going to keep herself together. She buttoned up a light cotton paisley shirt, wound her wet hair on top of her head then found her phone. She'd force herself to record a cheery good morning video to send to Roxy to play for the boys, assuring them she'd be picking them up this afternoon. She couldn't risk speaking to them on the phone. If she heard their voices now she would crumble.

But she paused when she saw a message from Gabby already waiting for her, sent at five o'clock this morning.

> I've changed my flight and
> gone back to Melbourne early.
> I need a break from all of this.
> I hope you understand.

Krystal collapsed back onto the bed.

It was over. She couldn't do anything without Gabby.

She'd been so close. A tear slid from the corner of her eye towards the pillow. Was this it, then? So close yet so far. She'd never know why Evan was here that night.

She'd failed him, again.

After allowing herself to succumb to misery for a while, she pushed herself up off the bed, thinking. Maybe there *was* still a way to get the information she needed, even without Gabby's help. She grabbed some chocolate and nuts from the minibar, threw her belongings into her bag and headed down to the lobby. Outside, she hailed a cab and directed the driver to take her back to the kimono woman's house. She asked him to pull over a few doors down the hill so she could survey the house a little. Just as he did, a new message arrived from Gabby.

The woman in the blue and
white house was there the
night Evan died, in the street.
She saw it happen. But that's
all I know.

Krystal stared at Gabby's text message and nearly fell out of the cab. She stood motionless for a few minutes, reading and re-reading the text, long after the car had pulled away.

This new information was almost impossible to believe. The man who'd called the ambulance hadn't seen anyone else in the street. The police had never found any witnesses. They'd door-knocked. They'd appealed for information. If this woman was there with Evan, why hadn't she come forward?

Krystal headed up the slope towards the blue and white house, dragging her carry-on bag behind her, the wheels bouncing over the footpath. In daylight, she could see sparkling wedges of blue water from the bay peeking through trees and from behind houses. In any other circumstances, this street would be pretty and friendly, in the kind of delightful suburb where those with disposable cash chose to live. The morning was already warm, and men in suits reversed sleek black cars from garages. Women in designer dresses carried briefcases, talked into phones jammed between their ears and shoulders, and clutched eco-friendly reusable coffee cups. Schoolkids in blazers and hats with pointless ribbons and crests marched towards public transport.

In the driveway of the blue and white house, the kimono woman was talking to a young girl wearing a green and white uniform and polished black shoes.

Krystal stumbled slightly on a patch of uneven concrete in the footpath. The kimono woman – with fair hair, in the sunlight, and now in a black jumpsuit and gold accessories – looked up and spotted Krystal as she stood gawking at them. The girl stopped too, looking from Krystal to her mother.

'Who's that?' the girl asked. Then, to Krystal's surprise, her sweet little face smiled brightly at her. 'Hello!'

The woman frowned at her. 'Get in the car, sweetheart. We're running late.' She clicked the remote control and the car's yellow indicator lights flashed.

The girl shrugged and pulled open the car door and climbed inside. 'Can I have your phone?' she asked, holding her hand out to her mother.

The woman handed it over, then shut the car door. She stood and stared at Krystal a moment, turned to leave, then changed her mind and spun around and came to the fence.

'What do you want?'

Krystal approached her. 'I know you know who I am. My husband was – is – Evan Arthur. I know you were there with him the night he died. Please, you have to help me.'

The woman's face paled and her hand went to her stomach as though she was about to be sick.

'Please! I have to know what happened.' Krystal reached out her hand and grabbed the woman's forearm. 'I have no idea why he was here in Sydney that night. He told me he was going to work at the restaurant in Melbourne and the next thing I know he's here, dying. No one has been able to explain why. Please, *please*! I'm desperate! You're the only person who can help me.'

The woman, shorter and slighter than Krystal, took in a shuddering breath.

'I've got to take my daughter to school. Wait here. I'll be back in half an hour.' She didn't look Krystal in the eye. She pulled her arm away and walked back to the car, then reversed out of the driveway.

*

Krystal paced back and forth on the footpath, not daring to let the house out of her sight. She doubted the woman was really coming back to talk to her as she'd said, but since she lived here, she'd have to come back eventually. If Krystal had to camp here all day and all night, she would.

Roxy texted to say that the boys had had a great night and had gone off happily to school this morning, though she confessed to giving them hot chocolate for breakfast, which had probably made them slightly hyper. Krystal assured her it would be okay, stopping short of unloading all the crazy new information she had learned in less than twenty-four hours.

Then she texted Gabby, begging for more details. But Gabby remained silent.

She sat down on the footpath, her back against the fence. The dog must have been locked inside the house, thankfully.

When the white sedan returned, Krystal thought she might explode with relief and anxiety. She leapt to her feet and hurried to the car's door.

'You're back!' she said, as the woman climbed out.

'I said I would be.'

'Yes, but – I'm so grateful, thank you.' Krystal made a conscious effort to back off a little. The woman was here but she was clearly not thrilled to be speaking to her.

'Come inside.' The woman led the way to the front door and Krystal heard the fast clicking of claws on floorboards as the dog came to meet them.

'What about your dog?' Krystal asked, bracing herself.

'She'll be fine if you're with me.'

They entered the house, the woman disabling the alarm system and greeting the dog, Krystal trying not to make eye contact with it so as not to alarm it.

The woman led her down a short hallway and into a black

and white kitchen with red highlights, where she indicated that Krystal should sit at the round breakfast table. The dog hovered for a moment, then trotted to the couch to have a nap.

'Tea?' the woman asked.

'Okay, thanks. With milk, please.' Krystal would have been happy to skip the tea and get straight to the answers, but the woman was clearly nervy and reluctant, so she forced herself to slow down. 'Do you mind if I ask your name?'

The woman's shoulders hunched as she threw teabags into mugs; she didn't turn around as she replied. 'Rebecca.'

Krystal scanned through her memories to see if she could recall any mention of someone named Rebecca, but she came up blank. 'I don't recall Evan ever mentioning you.'

'He wouldn't have,' Rebecca said, fetching milk from the retro red Smeg fridge, her back still to Krystal. 'Our meetings were secret.'

This jolted Krystal. *Secret?* Her fears returned to the obvious. 'Were you having an affair?'

Rebecca scoffed. 'No.'

'Then why were you having secret meetings?'

Rebecca sighed and spun around, leaning against the kitchen bench, her hands on the edge behind her, propping her up. There was a gorgeous red and blue stained-glass window behind her, casting her in pink and indigo hues. 'He was helping me. In a legal sense.'

'Legal? But he'd given up practising.'

'Yes.'

Krystal ground her teeth, frustration and urgency tumbling through her. 'Could you use a few more words? I'm lost.'

The kettle boiled, Rebecca filled the mugs with water and milk and brought them to the table. She sat down opposite Krystal. 'I can't tell you everything.'

'Why not?'

'For the same reasons Evan and I were meeting in secret.'

'You were in trouble?' Krystal hazarded a guess.

'I thought my life was in danger. My life, maybe my daughter's life. Talking to you now . . . it still feels risky.'

'Then why are you talking to me?'

Rebecca raised a shoulder. 'Because you're here. Because Evan risked his life – no, he *gave* his life – trying to help me. Because two years have passed and I haven't seen the car again. I suppose I think I owe him.' Rebecca sipped at her tea then jiggled the teabag while she collected her thoughts.

'What car? Please tell me what happened.'

'I used to work for Farner Seven. Do you know who they are?'

Farner Seven. The name startled her, a ghost from Evan's past suddenly appearing here in this room. Of all the things she'd imagined had been going on between Evan and Rebecca, Farner Seven had not featured.

'Yes. It was Evan's final case before he quit. He didn't like the fact that he and his family had got them off the hook. He felt so bad about it that he decided to leave the law firm.'

Rebecca nodded; clearly, this wasn't new information to her.

'That's right. I'm a scientist and I used to work for them. They employed me as a contractor and asked me to research the effects of their chemicals on water quality. I bred generations of fish – carp, mostly, not that it matters – in water supplies affected by their chemicals. I did the same with mice, using the water as drinking water. In all cases, the offspring had developmental deformities and cancers.'

Krystal frowned. 'But I remember Evan saying that the reason the case against them was unsuccessful was because there wasn't any evidence.'

Rebecca smiled, sadly. 'I gave the evidence to Farner Seven, along with my report and recommendation that their chemical plant be shut down and relocated. But it was never used during the case.'

'Why not?'

'The evidence was destroyed. Evan went ahead with what they had in front of them, as any tactical lawyer would. But years later, you had your first son.'

'Jasper.'

'Evidently, it changed Evan. He truly realised what an injustice it had been for all those families and their kids who that had suffered because he'd been a part of helping the company. He wanted to make amends, and about a year after Jasper was born he approached me to help.'

A clock was ticking somewhere nearby and its rhythmic sound filled the moments while Krystal tried to piece this together. 'You were a whistleblower.'

Rebecca tapped the side of her mug absently. 'It wasn't something I ever imagined I would do. But, like Evan, I was full of guilt. I had spent years telling myself that it wasn't my fault, that I'd done everything I was supposed to do and that the result was out of my hands. I'd thought about blowing the lid on the case, but there are enough stories in the media about how whistleblowers' lives are ruined – how they are sent to jail for breaching confidentiality agreements, how they are threatened, attacked and even killed. I have a daughter to think of. But then there was Evan, persuasive and compelling.'

Krystal smiled despite the gravity of this news. When Evan was passionate about something it was hard to refuse him.

'The stress was terrible. So many times I almost cracked and pulled out, but Evan stayed strong and kept encouraging me. We were building a case of evidence against Farner Seven. I couldn't talk to anyone else about it, but he was my rock.' She paused, her eyes suddenly bright. 'Sorry.' She sipped her tea some more.

The idea that Evan had been another woman's rock in her time of need was unsettling for many reasons, but she couldn't afford to lose focus right now. She was here for the answers she'd been so desperate to find for so long.

'How did you end up in the street with him that night?' she asked, wanting to know and not wanting to know in equal measures.

'About six months into our meetings, I began to notice a black car with heavily tinted windows in the street. I didn't think anything of it at first, just that it must belong to someone who lived in this street or visited often. But then I started to notice it at other places, too – at my office and then at my daughter's school.'

'That must have been terrifying.'

'It was.'

'Did Evan know about it too?'

'Yes. He said Farner Seven must have caught on to what we were doing and wanted to intimidate us but we couldn't let them get to us. He helped me organise extra security measures about the house.' She pointed to the Rottweiler, now snoring on the couch. 'He also bought me a puppy.'

The thought of her husband buying a puppy for another woman brought up yet more confusing emotions for Krystal.

'He said we had to stay strong, for the sake of all those families and children, and that it would all be over soon enough. On the night of the accident, my daughter, Sarah, was at her father's place and Evan was here. We were sitting in the lounge room.'

Krystal remembered Gabby saying she'd seen Evan in a woman's house.

'I was falling apart under the pressure. He suggested we go for a walk and get some air. He checked at the window to see if the car was outside and said there was no sign of it.'

Krystal's gaze fell on the window over near the lounge, security bars bolted over it on the inside.

'I shivered while we walked, whether from the cold or fear I'm not sure, but I couldn't see the car either and slowly we began to relax. Evan kept telling me it would all be okay, that we just had to keep our eyes on the finish line, that we were nearly there.' Rebecca picked up her mug again but only got it halfway to her lips before putting it back down on the wooden table. The refrigerator gurgled then sighed, and the dog's tail thumped on the couch while he dreamed.

'We'd only been walking a few moments when I heard a car approaching slowly behind us.' She paused, closing her eyes as if not wanting to remember. She opened her eyes and when she spoke, her voice shook. 'I was terrified. We had no idea who was driving, but they didn't give up. Evan told me to look straight ahead. We kept walking but they kept following.'

The images Rebecca painted were vivid in Krystal's mind. She sat frozen.

'Suddenly Evan became furious and spun around to challenge whoever was in the car. I panicked and called out to him, but he kept going, charging straight towards it. It swerved away from him at the last moment and disappeared around a bend. "Come on," he urged, and we kept walking . . . But then the car returned.'

Krystal's heart raced, as though she was there at that moment and could somehow stop what was about to happen.

'I started to cry. He put his arm around me, half holding me up as we hurried along, looking for somewhere safe to go. But the faster we went, the faster the car followed. We broke apart and began to jog, with no plan or discussion, just needing to escape. We ran, one block, two blocks. Still the car followed. Evan pulled me behind a huge gum tree and the car flew past.'

The gum tree. Gabby had known there was something important about it.

'"Hurry!" he said, and we started to run again. We ran down Ritchie Lane and just when we thought we'd lost it, the car ambushed us from the front. It must have sped around the block to come from the other direction. We headed down a driveway to duck behind an apartment block. Evan was behind me, but then . . .' Rebecca raised her shoulders, as though she still couldn't understand what had happened. 'I guess he wanted to lure the car away from me, so he doubled back. I yelled out to him to stop but he jumped in front of the car. He leapt to get out of the way at the exact same time the driver spun the wheel to avoid him and he was hit.' She wiped at the tears on her cheeks. 'He flew through the air and landed on the footpath. I'll never forget the sound.'

Hearing Rebecca describe Evan's last night was horrendous but also, weirdly, a relief. Finally, Krystal could put pieces together. Not all of them, but a lot. She knew so much more now than just an hour ago. She could finally begin to try to understand.

It made sense. Though shocked, she was proud, too. Evan was a good man and he died trying to make a big wrong right.

'But why didn't you stay with him when the car hit him?' Krystal asked, fishing in her bag for a tissue.

Rebecca looked to the ceiling. 'I'd run down a driveway and Evan had turned back and had a head start on me. When the car hit him . . .' She paused, reliving the moment. '. . . A man rushed out of his house straightaway and got to him first. I saw him pull out his phone and call the ambulance. I panicked. I was terrified the car would come back for me, so I took my chance and ran as fast as I could. I heard the sirens moments later and knew he was being taken care of. It was days before I found out he'd died.' She swallowed a sob. 'I'd never have left him if I thought he was dying.' She took a shaky breath. 'He didn't deserve that.'

'No, he didn't.'

Rebecca told Krystal that she'd shared everything she could. She pushed her chair back and rose, waiting for Krystal to do the same. Krystal took the hint and picked up her bag.

'But what about the car?' Krystal asked. 'Who was it?'

Rebecca blinked. 'Farner Seven, of course. The scientific evidence I'd submitted had been destroyed during the trial – burned, Evan said. But they knew I could recreate it, which I did, and I gave it to Evan. It was one of the pieces of evidence we were putting together for him to call for the trial to be reopened.'

'But the car just stopped coming?'

'Yes. I haven't seen it since. I presumed they went into hiding to avoid the police. And Evan had the evidence. Once he was gone, they must have hoped I'd be too scared to do anything more, and they were right. They'd won.'

Krystal gave her thanks and left, shell-shocked, numb, and with no clue what to do next, except to board a plane to get home to her boys.

27

With Celia, Charlie and even Summer back at school today, and Monty still pensive but in better spirits than yesterday, Gabby headed into work with renewed optimism and an action plan. She was going to do something risky – well, risky for her. Butterflies fluttered in her belly as she entered the cafe, but her attention was diverted to the music. Brisbane indie band Sheppard was pulsing through the speaker system. Kyle looked over from the coffee machine and grinned cheekily.

'Don't give me that look, Gabs,' he said, frothing milk. 'Someone had to take control. There was discussion of an intervention but I said it could be a bloodless coup, so I took control.'

'Intervention? Bloodless?'

'The music's been sad and old lady-ish lately.'

'Has it?' Gabby halted, her hand on the strap of her handbag, trying to recall what she'd been playing recently. There'd been

Jack Johnson, John Mayer, Celine Dion and Adele. *Hm.* Perhaps he had a point.

'I distinctly heard John Denver the other day, and as much as I love myself a good country boy I just couldn't take it any more.' He banged the stainless steel jug on the bench to settle the froth as though he was banging a gavel and eyed her firmly.

'I see. But Jack Johnson's not old lady-ish. He's cool and hip. Isn't he?' she asked, taking off her bag and setting it temporarily next to the swing door.

Kyle began to pour milk into two mugs, using a spoon to hold back the foam till the cups were almost full. 'The very fact you used the words "cool" and "hip" illustrates my point.'

'Well, what's the right word?'

'Oh, Gabby, sweetie,' he said, shaking his head of green hair and passing her the mugs. 'These are for table twelve.'

'Remind me to fire you,' she said, taking the mugs.

'Right you are, captain.' He saluted.

'Love your pants,' the woman at table twelve said, taking her cappuccino. The woman looked particularly stylish herself, so Gabby took the compliment with pleasure. It reminded her why she'd taken so much trouble to find the right outfit today. She'd chosen soft chambray pants, with extra material fluttering down the sides like the petals of a tulip. She'd matched them with a white scalloped-edge blouse patterned with dark-chocolate blossoms, and mules and dangly earrings.

'Thanks. Enjoy your coffees,' she said to the woman and her friend. Then, before she could change her mind, she strode out back.

Luciano was well into a roasting session. The beans inside the drum rattled around in the heat, the gas hummed, the cooling tray spun with the fan roaring below it, and the scent of freshly roasted coffee was thick in the air. His head was bent over the computer watching the coloured lines on the graph, his fingers on the dials, dark curls gently caressing the olive skin of his neck, all the lovelier against his white collared shirt today. Lin was washing dishes and she waved to Gabby, and Gabby smiled and waved back as she passed on her way to see Luciano.

She stopped at his side. He looked up quickly and gave her an easy smile. He flicked his eyes back to the screen, frowning in concentration. First crack was just beginning, with one or two beans emitting small pops inside the drum. She shouldn't talk to him, not now. But after her momentary feelings of self-pity yesterday about her short life expectancy, she'd given herself a stern lecture. It was only yesterday morning in Sydney that she'd declared that this was her life now. Hers. She wasn't going to waste another moment in guilt or feeling sorry for herself. Stagnation wasn't an option. Neither was giving up.

She'd woken with an almost reckless desire to suck the marrow from this day and every day going forward. She'd been timid, she realised, hesitant to truly trust her heart, not feeling worthy of this incredible gift. But it wasn't a gift at all – not in the way she'd thought. In many ways, knowing Krystal's true motivations had freed Gabby to get on with her life instead of feeling indebted in a way she'd never be able to escape from.

So here she was. It was now or never.

'I wanted to ask you something.'

'Hm?' Luciano murmured, then spun to pull out the trier to smell the beans. The scent hit Gabby hard, but while in the past she may have been sentimentally reminded that this gift of smell had come with the gift of her heart, today she chose simply to feel grateful, not guilty.

Not wanting to distract Luciano when he might burn himself, she waited impatiently while he sniffed the beans, then placed the trier back in the roasting machine and adjusted the dials slightly.

'I know you are an employee and there are all sorts of guidelines about these things, so it's a risk to say something like this, and I want you to know that you are absolutely free to say no and there will be no recriminations of any kind.'

'Huh?'

She could tell he was struggling to concentrate on her words and on his roast, which was right at the critical moment, but she had to plough on. Energy was pouring through her today and it wasn't waiting for this roast to finish.

'Will you go out with me? On a proper date?'

'Um . . .' He flicked his eyes to hers, back to his computer, then back to hers, and left them there.

She resisted the urge to add qualifiers to fill the silence. *It isn't a big deal, we could just have a bit of lunch. We couldn't really go for coffee, ha ha, but maybe tea? Or a drink? You know, an alcoholic one?*

She bit them all down and waited.

Luciano's jaw loosened, then his lips parted, a sparkle hit his eyes, and he smiled. 'Okay.'

'Really?'

'Really.'

'You don't feel like you have to or anything, like you'll lose your job or something ridiculous like that, just to be sure.'

He laughed, grinning at her, causing a flash of attraction to zap through her. 'No. I can sign something if you like.'

'All right. How about lunch, today? My treat.'

'Done.'

'Great.' Relief flooded through her and she realised her hands were sweating where she'd had them clasped in front of her. She let them go, sighing with delight. They stood eye to eye, grinning at each other, and Gabby had no idea how much time passed. Then the smiles snapped off their faces at exactly the same moment. The beans had stopped popping. The coloured lines on the computer screen lurched into wild angles and there was the unmistakable smell of scorched beans.

Gabby took Luciano to Kitty Burns cafe in Abbotsford, not far from the river, hoping that if things went well they might extend their date with a walk along the water. The decor of Kitty Burns was inspiring and uplifting, with a glass roof and walls to let the natural light filter down through the blond wooden beams and keep the extensive greenery alive. Bushland surrounded the cafe, providing a glorious, natural setting. All the outdoor tables were filled with people and dogs, taking advantage of the warm sunshine, so they went inside. The floor was a smoky grey and the furniture and fittings the same Scandinavian style, white and iceberg blue. They found an available booth, with the exposed beams of a peaked pergola above their heads giving it an added sense of cosiness and privacy.

Luciano sat down and then sneezed. 'Ah, sorry. I can't get the smell of the burned beans out of my nose.'

'Me too. That smoke got right up into my sinuses.'

'It was busy today,' he said, folding his arms on the table and leaning towards her. 'I'll have to get another batch done this afternoon if we're going to have enough for the rest of the week.'

'I'm thinking we might need another staff member or even two. But I might see if I can recruit Summer or Charlie to help out in the first instance, just in case this upsurge in trade doesn't continue.'

'I'd be happy to teach Charlie how to make coffee.'

She smiled. 'He'd really like that.'

'And Summer too, of course, if she wants to learn. And Celia,' he hurried to add.

'Thank you.' She smiled at him, feeling heat rise up her cheeks just from looking at his lovely warm eyes and thick lashes. 'How were your kids today?' The menus lay untouched on the tabletop between them, neither in a hurry to order.

'Everyone went to school, so that's a start. My mamma's coming over this afternoon after school to teach them how to make ravioli.'

'Nice. Maybe she could teach me one day too.' She said it without thinking, then groaned quietly with self-consciousness. She hadn't meant to make any assumptions about their future. She picked up the menu and hurriedly scanned it.

'I think she'd like you a lot,' Luciano said.

She glanced at him. 'Why do you think that?'

'Because you're brave, you love your kids and you're a smart businesswoman.'

She took a moment to absorb his praise.

'She has an idea for a business she'd like to start. She'd find you an inspiration.'

Gabby put down the menu. 'What sort of idea?'

He inched his hand across the table and hooked his finger under hers. She curled hers around his in response, the feel of his skin ricocheting through her so that she had to concentrate very hard to continue listening to him. 'She wants to start a business called "Rent an Italian Family".'

'Tell me, what is it?' Her voice was husky, betraying her.

'Mamma came from a big family back in Italy, as did Papa. She says Australians miss out on big family at special moments in life. So, when a woman has a baby, she needs the family around to help her care for the baby and the older children, to cook and clean, garden and shop. You can hire individual people to do some of these things but she says what women really need is an extended family, everyone pitching in to support you.'

'I love that idea,' Gabby said, genuinely excited.

'It's probably got merit,' he conceded. 'Same for times of bereavement or sickness.'

'I can testify to that. I couldn't have got through my illness, transplant and recovery without my family there. Everyone I know who had a transplant was entirely reliant on family – older people dependent on their spouses or on going to live with their own grown-up kids, and the younger ones having to move back home with their parents. I've no idea what people without families do in those situations. I'd actually be keen to talk to your mum about that. Maybe I could help her connect with people on the transplant waiting list.'

He stretched out more fingers until their hands were entirely knitted together. 'See, she'll love you.'

A waitress arrived to take their orders. For drinks, Luciano chose the Tasmanian apple cider while Gabby said she couldn't go past the jasmine tea gathered from two-hundred-year-old tea trees, the leaves of which were dried alongside jasmine flowers around the time of the full moon.

'You're a romantic,' he said.

Until very recently, she'd not have thought so, but something in her had started to grow once more.

Luciano ordered the beef burger and Gabby followed suit and ordered the buttermilk chicken burger, before realising that was probably not the best choice for a date – it was difficult to look impressive when you had sauce dripping down your wrists.

They chatted easily, not pausing for breath except to acknowledge the waitress when she returned with their drinks and food.

'Cheers,' Gabby said, lifting her teacup, the delicate aroma of the jasmine flowers wheeling through the steam to her nose.

'Cheers.' He sipped from his cider, but kept his eyes on her.

'Where else have you travelled, other than Italy?' she said.

'Most of Europe,' he said, casually. 'It's easy when you're over there. Everything's so close.'

'I've only been to Ireland,' Gabby said. 'Twice, actually. Mum and Dad took Pippa and me over there when we were in our teens. It felt like an interminable trip on lousy roads past sheep paddocks and rock walls while our parents searched for their ancestors' old houses and churches and so on. We were freezing cold and beside ourselves with boredom. But then Pippa and I decided to go back in our twenties, just the two of us, and we had the most wonderful time together – probably in no small part due to the fact we were of legal drinking age this time and found ourselves in festive bars full of live music every night.'

'Did you go to County Clare?' Luciano said.

'Yes. My great-grandparents came from there. They met on the ship when they emigrated to Australia and married when they got here.'

Luciano's eyes twinkled. 'Did you ever go to that pub, O'Neill's? O'Hara's?'

'Yes! I can't remember the name either but it was an O-something.'

'Did you by any chance cut through the sheep paddock to get there, rather than walking the long way around the road?'

Gabby sat up straighter and put her burger down. 'Yes, we did!'

Luciano also put down his burger, grinning. 'And did the old guy chase you?'

'The one-eyed sheep farmer?' Gabby squealed, laughing. 'It was legendary, a tradition at the hostel. Everyone had to do it or you had to shout a round of beers.'

'"You feckin eejit!"' Luciano mimed, his fist raised in the air. '"I'll cut yer balls off an' feed 'em to da pigs!"'

'Yes!' Gabby giggled, helplessly. 'That's it exactly!'

'I wonder if he's still alive.'

'I bet he is,' Gabby said. 'He was probably only forty but just looked like he was eighty. His face was as cracked and weathered as his rocky field. The poor guy. We were awful to do that to him, really.'

Luciano chuckled and held her gaze, making her skin tingle. He spoke again, gently this time, but still with an Irish accent. 'Aye, but you've amazing Irish eyes when you laugh.'

'Oh, my dad would love you,' she said. Monty had been at work the day Luciano had brought the kids around. 'He is so bloody proud to be from Irish stock.'

'It'd be grand to meet your da,' he said, and reached for his cider.

She put her hands to her cheeks; they were aching from laughter. It was thrilling, this possibility of something new – new beginnings, new life, new relationships, new chapters. It wasn't something she ever took for granted any more.

'Is that your phone?' Luciano asked, nodding to her huge tote beside her on the booth seat.

'What? Oh!' She'd been so swept away in her feelings she hadn't even heard it ringing. 'Sorry, I'll have to get that in case it's one of the schools calling. You know how it is.'

'I do,' he agreed.

But when Gabby pulled out the phone, the name on the screen set her on edge.

'Meri? What's happened?' she asked, holding the phone to her right ear and blocking her other ear with her left hand so she could hear over the background noise. Although she and Meri had occasionally spoken by phone, it was a boundary they tended not to cross. All communication about the kids was to go between her and Cam.

'Have you seen Cam?' Meri asked, anxiety blunting her tone.

'No, should I have?'

'He left for work this morning but didn't show up. The school called me to check if he was okay.'

'Oh, shit.' From across the table, Luciano looked up from his burger, alerted by her tone.

'I don't know what to do.' Meri's voice trembled. 'His phone's turned off.'

'Call the police,' Gabby said. 'Ask them about accidents, alert them to his disappearance.' Now Luciano dropped his food and wiped his hands on a serviette, frowning at her.

'I . . . do you think something might have happened?'

'Clearly, yes, something has happened or he'd be at school. Look, he's probably off smoking somewhere,' Gabby said, as much to calm herself as Meri.

'I don't think that's . . . I haven't seen him . . .'

'He's been on a bender. Haven't you seen the signs?' Her tone was regrettably snippier than she'd have liked, but she couldn't believe that a social worker could be so blind to what was right in front of her.

'I . . .' Meri was lost for words. Mykahla started fussing in the background.

'Look, just start with the police, then call me back, okay?'

Gabby disconnected the call and shook her head in disbelief at Luciano.

'What's happened?'

'It's my ex-husband. He's been falling apart, said he wanted a break from the kids, isn't returning their calls, and now he's gone missing, failed to turn up to work.'

'We should go,' Luciano said, sliding out of the booth.

'Sorry,' Gabby said, following him. There was a low hum of dread gathering force in her veins, and in the back of her mind was a voice reminding her that this was exactly what had happened to Krystal. Evan had left for work and never come home again.

Luciano held out his hand to help Gabby from the booth. She slipped her hand into his and it was like it had always been there. She pulled herself to her feet and they held each other's gaze, her hand still in his.

'I'm coming with you,' he said.

'No, you don't need to.'

'Yes, I do.'

Gabby considered him for a moment, in awe of how he made her feel. Safe and supported. Maybe even cherished.

'It's a bit weird, though, isn't it? You helping me look for my ex-husband?'

'Just because Cam is your ex doesn't make it any less awful. He's your kids' father. He's still an important part of your family.'

Her eyes welled and she bit down on her lip, determined not to cry here in this cafe.

'If he's important to you, then he's important to me,' he finished, putting his other hand on her shoulder.

She nodded her acceptance because she didn't trust herself to speak.

'Come on,' he said, still holding her hand, and they turned to leave together.

28

Krystal arrived at the office to the smell of fresh, warm croissants, and Margie and Janice giggling like teenagers in the kitchenette, steaming mugs of some sort of fancy coffee in their hands, a shiny new glass plunger on the bench with the remains of the grounds in the bottom. 'Morning,' she said, as cheerily as she could, given the weight of all the new information Rebecca had shared with her yesterday. Unfortunately, she had a hangover, and knew her eyes were glassy, her complexion peaky.

'Morning,' Margie said, clearing her throat and suppressing the end of a giggle. Last Wednesday, when Janice had announced the job cut, Margie's hair had miraculously benefited from a timely colour rinse. Today, it had been professionally styled and blow-dried into smooth, glossy chestnut curls. Krystal was resentful that the woman she'd thought was her friend had obviously had a heads-up about the new position and kept it from

Krystal, and she was disgusted that Margie could be so blatant in her intentions to flatter Janice to score points.

'Good morning,' Janice said, unusually cheerful, clearly buoyed by the wooing at hand.

'Would you like a croissant?' Margie asked Krystal, her tone that of a gracious host.

'No, thanks,' Krystal said, the thought of food making her stomach roil. 'I'd love a coffee though, if there's any more.'

'Of course,' Margie said, turning to refill the kettle.

'Well, I'll get to work,' Janice said, placing her coffee mug on the side of the sink. She reached for the tap to start washing up, but Margie stopped her.

'No, leave it. I'll do it after Krystal's had hers,' she said.

Janice beamed. 'Thank you.'

Krystal could barely contain an eye roll as Janice left the kitchenette. 'What are you doing?'

'What do you mean?' Margie said, measuring out gloriously aromatic coffee into the plunger. Krystal practically quivered in anticipation of the beautiful elixir easing her headache and sharpening her focus. 'I'm making you coffee. And you look like you need one. Is everything okay?'

'Fine,' Krystal said, rubbing her forehead.

'Did you have a big night or something?' Margie said, straightening her new, floaty cream blouse. She was trying for amiable, Krystal could tell, but the air of an eager bloodhound wafted around her. She knew she was winning and was looking for the kill.

'Just couldn't sleep, that's all. The boys had bad dreams and kept me up,' she lied.

'Both of them? At the same time?' Margie poured the boiling water into the jug and set the plunger to rest on top while the coffee brewed below. 'That was bad luck.'

'No, not at the same time. One first, then the other.'

Margie pulled a faux sympathetic face. 'Kids. Glad I don't have any. It would make holding down a full-time job terribly tricky, I should imagine.'

Krystal poured milk into an empty mug, then picked up the full plunger and turned to carry them back to her desk. 'Yes, it's tricky. But I manage. Thanks for the coffee.'

Krystal and Margie both kept their heads down, working silently, and Krystal was achingly aware that their friendship – whatever she'd thought it had been – was over. The coffee was good but it didn't stop the throbbing in her head. Her eyes hurt. Looking at the backlit computer screen made her squint against the pain and she considered putting her sunglasses on, but that would surely draw attention. She was slow and making mistakes and acid kept rising up her oesophagus. Her head was woolly and full of images of Evan leading his secret life, of his clandestine trips interstate, of the relationship he'd had with Rebecca. Platonic though it was, it still hurt. He'd trusted Rebecca more than he'd trusted Krystal, hadn't he?

And what was she supposed to do now? Someone out there had been stalking her husband. He was dead now because of them. She thought about him running through those streets in Mosman, just as she and Gabby had done, but Evan had been running for his life.

Her heart rate rose. She could feel her pulse in her ears.

She tried to calm herself by taking deep breaths.

Just breathe, just breathe.

But her breaths couldn't get down deep enough into her body. She was strangling herself from the bottom up. Air was moving in and out but not going to her lungs. Her head spun. Her hands tingled. Was she having a stroke?

'Are you all right?' Margie's voice beside her.

Krystal opened her mouth to speak but she just gulped emptily like a fish flung onto the beach. Suddenly, she could hear herself, hear the rasping, scraping breaths. She stood. She couldn't focus her eyes on anything. All she knew was that she couldn't stop this crazy, rapid breathing.

'What's happening?' Margie turned to Janice.

Janice leapt from her chair and came to Krystal, taking her by the shoulders. 'Krystal, you're hyperventilating. You need to take slow, deep breaths.'

Krystal stared at Janice, her mouth continuing to open, close, open, close. Tears sprang to her eyes. Why couldn't she stop this?

'Come to sick bay,' Janice said, leading Krystal away from her desk. She sat Krystal down on the bed. The room smelled of disinfectant. The fluorescent light shone down harshly from the ceiling.

'Do we need a paper bag?' Margie asked from the door.

'No. That's old school. Can you go and get some water, please?'

'Sure.' Margie left.

Janice sat next to Krystal on the bed and put her arm around her shoulders. 'You just need to focus on finding your normal breathing pattern, Krystal. You can do it.' She spoke gently and calmly, but firmly. Krystal stared at a fixed point on the wall. 'Maybe close your eyes,' Janice continued, her voice soothing. 'Count in your head: in for three breaths, out for four breaths, in for three, out for four.'

Margie returned with the water and Janice thanked her and asked her to close the door on her way out, for which Krystal was deeply grateful. The last thing she needed now was for Margie to gawk at her while she had a breakdown.

'In for three, out for four. Concentrate on slowing the breaths. Make the out-breath longer than the in-breath. That's it, you're doing great.'

Krystal's breathing was changing. Slowly, slowly. She kept her eyes closed, her mind wholly focused on counting the breaths. Finally, fear released its grip on her, and she opened her eyes.

'There you are,' Janice said, smiling. She dropped her arm from around Krystal's shoulder. She passed her the glass of water and Krystal sipped from it with shaky hands.

'What just happened?' Krystal mumbled, tears falling now, to her humiliation.

'Well, you hyperventilated. Normally, that's the result of anxiety or a panic attack,' Janice said, moving away a fraction so she could turn to face Krystal. She reached for a tissue from the box on the shelf and handed it to Krystal. 'Has this happened to you before?'

Krystal shook her head, her bottom lip trembling against the torrent of tears that wanted to tumble out of her.

'I think you should probably take the rest of the day off and maybe go and see your doctor. Is there anyone you'd like me to call for you?'

Krystal was about to wave the offer away, determined not to need anyone's help, but that sudden onset of disabling panic had shaken her badly. There was really only one person she could call on at a time like this.

Roxy picked her up from the sick bay room at school and took her to Staple, a big, cosy cafe on Fitzroy Street known for hearty, honest food. It was like a comforting cave of nourishment. She ordered Krystal a plate of thick sourdough toast, eggs, bacon, potato rosti and sausages.

'Hangover cure,' she said. Roxy also ordered her a pot of tea. 'You need something calming, not coffee,' she said, in full mother-hen mode. Krystal could feel herself relaxing under her friend's care.

'There's a reason you're such a valued carer,' Krystal said. 'You should have been a nurse, really. This calm, caring thing just oozes out of you.'

Roxy fluffed her now-pink hair. 'I've thought about going to uni and doing just that,' she confessed, taking a bite of her fruit toast with rosemary butter dripping from the edges.

'Really?'

'It's never too late, right?'

'You'd be wonderful.' Krystal took a big gulp of her milky tea and leaned back, relishing the act of taking a long, deep breath and letting it go like a normal person.

'So, fess up, love,' Roxy said. 'What was going through your mind when this panic attack happened?'

'I don't even know where to start,' Krystal said, shaking her head.

'Start anywhere. We can circle around if we need to.'

Krystal told her everything and Roxy listened and clucked and gasped in all the right places, and with every word Krystal felt the invisible vice that had worked its way around her chest since Monday night in Sydney loosen.

At the end, Roxy said, 'Two things. Firstly, I love a vodka as much as the next girl but I think you need to take a pause, okay? You've got your mother's genes. I'm sorry to be blunt but I think you've reached the precipice. It's time to take a step back and get your bearings. It's making you fragile and you need to be strong. You have no alternative here but to be strong.'

Krystal swallowed. It hurt to hear but she knew it was true. She'd been in terrible denial. She burned with shame, realising her hangover had probably contributed to the humiliating panic attack this morning. 'You're right. I'll have an extended detox. I'll call it quits today.'

'And because I love you, I will quit with you.'

Krystal snorted. 'You don't have to do that.'

'Yes, I do. We're family. In fact, we're better than family because we actually chose each other.'

'That's true.'

'We'll give up drinking and we'll spend our money on disgusting, healthy green juices or something.'

Krystal shuddered. 'We don't have to do that, do we? Couldn't we spend our money on imported cheese or something?'

'Yes! Even better.'

'All right, done. Cheese it is.'

'Good. Now, secondly, you know you have to go to the police with this, don't you?' Roxy eyed her sternly.

'What?'

'Rebecca was a witness to his murder.'

Krystal was shocked. *Murder?* 'But the way Rebecca described it, it was an accident. She said the driver swerved.'

Roxy counted out points on her fingers. 'They were followed for months. She was scared for her life. They were mounting a huge whistleblowing case against a ginormous, filthy-rich corporation.' She paused for effect. 'Does it sound like an accident?' Roxy threw back the last of her macchiato as though it was a shot of tequila, even licking her hand to get the last drop.

Krystal pushed her now-empty plate away from her as though it was poison. Horror filled her every cell. All this time, she'd assumed it was an accident – that the driver had panicked and fled the scene and it had been a horrible but not unique scenario in which the driver had never been found.

'But what about Rebecca?' Krystal said. 'If I tell the police, what will happen to her?'

'Does it matter?' Roxy folded her arms across her chest. 'She lied. She has knowledge about what happened to Evan and she didn't come forward.'

'That's true. But she was terrified. And if I involve the police, she'll stop talking to me, and I know it sounds crazy, and it probably is, but she has all sorts of information about Evan and memories of time spent with him and I . . . I haven't had anything new about him in so long.' She ached for it, the newness, the freshness of something she'd never heard before, the spark of having her husband close by again. 'I'll think about it, I will. But I need more time. I need to know I've got every last piece of information before I lose her, and him, again.'

Roxy sighed. 'I guess it's already been two years. A bit more time won't matter.'

Krystal thought back to those last hours at his bedside in Sydney. The absolute nightmare of it.

She clapped her hand to her mouth, staring at Roxy.

'What is it?'

Krystal dropped her hand. 'I've just realised something and I can't believe I've never thought of it till now.'

'What?'

'I've got to go.' She leapt from her chair and slung her handbag over her shoulder, leaned down and kissed Roxy on the cheek. 'Thank you so much, Rox. I'll speak to you soon.' Then she dashed away, running for the nearest tram stop.

Krystal arrived, puffing, at the tall silver building near Southbank, a strong breeze blowing off the river, early lunchgoers filling the cafes at ground level. She hurried into the foyer of the Arthur firm's building, past the marble fountain just inside the glass doors, and made straight for the black elevators. She took the moments inside the lift to check her reflection in the mirror, smoothing down her fringe, pulling out her hair tie and redoing her ponytail.

When the lift slid to a smooth halt and let out an understated *ding*, she was ready. A woman in a floral dress sat in the corner of the waiting room, her handbag clutched nervously to her stomach. A huge bouquet of cream-coloured roses sat in a tall crystal vase on the reception desk. Overhead lighting bounced off the shiny black and gold surfaces. Krystal approached the desk.

'Good morning,' the receptionist said. His overly white teeth shone under the lights, and his grey suit fitted him perfectly.

'My name is Krystal Arthur.' She placed considerable emphasis on the surname. 'I am Cordelia-Aurora's sister-in-law and I need to see her, urgently.'

The receptionist's smile wavered. A tiny worry line appeared between his blond eyebrows. He must have had them professionally groomed, she thought. Then he tapped at his computer and stared at the screen as if searching for a solution – or at least pretending to. Krystal waited, resisting the urge to drum her fingers on the glossy surface of the desk.

He picked up his phone and pressed a button. 'I have Krystal Arthur here at reception. She says she needs to see you urgently.'

Krystal braced herself for the dismissal she was certain was coming. She eyed the distance between the desk and the door to the offices beyond – perhaps six metres. She was sure she'd be able to get there before this guy could stop her.

What was taking so long?

The receptionist nodded and murmured, then hung up the phone. 'Ms Arthur is very busy but she has agreed to make time for you.' He stood. 'Follow me.'

Krystal was almost too shocked to speak but managed a 'Thank you' before following him obediently through the door to the office, which, as it turned out, he needed to open with a security card, so she wouldn't have made it through without him anyway. They passed some cubicles with juniors working industriously, and then turned left, where a black wall gave nothing away as to what was on the other side. The receptionist knocked twice, then opened the door to a large office – big enough for Cordelia-Aurora's desk, extensive shelving, a couch, a small table with three cushioned chairs, potted plants and expansive windows overlooking the river.

'Come,' Cordelia-Aurora said, dressed like an undertaker, tapping at her keyboard and not looking up.

'Krystal Arthur is here,' the receptionist said. Cruella de Vil nodded and he left the room, closing the door softly behind him.

'What is it, Krystal? I'm working on a big case.'

Krystal took a deep but shaky breath. 'I appreciate you taking the time to see me, thank you.'

Cordelia-Aurora looked up, stopped typing and shut her laptop. She held her hand out to the small table nearby, indicating that Krystal could pull up a chair, though she remained seated in her executive leather chair behind the desk.

Krystal sat. 'Look, I'm not going to beat around the bush.'

'Glad to hear it.' Cordelia-Aurora regarded her with her chin raised. Krystal could hardly blame her. The last time they'd been in a room together Krystal had been hurling abuse and Cordelia-Aurora threatening lawsuits.

'A couple of days ago I went to Sydney.' Krystal watched her opponent carefully, looking for any sign that Evan's sister knew where this was going. But Cordelia-Aurora was an experienced barrister; she wouldn't be giving away anything she didn't choose to.

'I went to Mosman.'

Cordelia-Aurora's eyelids flickered. 'Why?'

'I wanted to visit the street where Evan was hit.'

'Why?'

'I was looking for closure, I guess.'

'And did you find it?' Cordelia-Aurora sounded exasperated and looked on the verge of sending Krystal away. Her fingers played at the corner of her laptop as though they were just itching to open the lid and start working again.

Krystal nodded slowly. 'Well, I found something else. Some*one* else.'

There! Cordelia-Aurora's face bled of colour, right in front of her. Up until this moment, Krystal had allowed a tiny ember of doubt to burn. A tiny escape hatch through which she could eject all this craziness and suspicion out into space, never to be seen again. But there was substance to what she'd found after all. She was momentarily winded.

'Someone?' Cordelia-Aurora's voice rose just a fraction at the end, betraying a hint of concern.

Krystal looked her straight in the eye. 'Rebecca.'

Cordelia-Aurora threaded her fingers and lifted them to her chin, an unusually vulnerable gesture for her. 'I have no idea who you're talking about.'

'I went to her house on the hill,' Krystal went on, her eyes drilling into Cordelia-Aurora's. 'We had a long chat.' She could feel a torrent of emotion flowing through her but managed to pull herself out of it, as though climbing a tree and sitting up in the boughs and allowing all that choppy, destructive water to pass along beneath her. *You've already been through the worst*, she reminded herself. *You've already survived.*

'When the police called to tell me that Evan was in hospital in Sydney, I got myself and the kids on the first flight out of here. Yet in all that shock and trauma, I never really processed the fact that you were already there at the hospital when I arrived. Your parents and Rupert came the next morning – but you were there. I think I just assumed that the police must have called you too, that they must just do that in those situations, trying to find anyone and everyone who might be next of kin.'

Cordelia-Aurora pushed herself back from her desk and walked to the windows to stare outside, her arms folded across her chest.

'But that wasn't what happened, was it?' Krystal waited, determined not to keep talking, determined to make Cordelia-Aurora explain herself.

Finally, Cordelia-Aurora moved her head at an odd angle, as though stretching her neck. 'I was already in Sydney,' she conceded.

There was a great rushing sound in Krystal's ears. It took her back to the day she and Evan had been walking in the botanic gardens with the kids when they heard a sound, almost as if a fast-flowing creek had suddenly sprung up next to them. They even looked around to find it. It was an overcast day and the noise was getting closer, an invisible force that was about to swallow them up, and there was nothing they could do but look at each other and laugh, knowing that a downpour of rain was moving rapidly through the trees, chasing them, about to drench them. And that was what happened. The kids squealed. Krystal and Evan pulled the boys to them, covering them as best they could while the rain hammered down, smiling at each other in surrender to this unexpected twist in the day. The shower was brief, lasting only a few minutes, and then it was gone, the sound retreating as the heavy cloud above moved on its way.

Now, she blinked at Cordelia-Aurora, the rushing sound subsiding.

'I was in Sydney to . . .' Cordelia-Aurora's voice trailed off. She held her hands to her eyes, waiting for the rare momentary loss of composure to pass. When it did, she folded her arms under her bosom and cleared her throat. She shook her head, obviously deciding not to go on.

'You knew who was in that car,' Krystal said, a statement, not a question.

Cordelia-Aurora turned away from the window to face Krystal, the midday light filtering through the glass and shining on one side of her face.

Krystal stared at her, her mind sifting through memories and conversations until it was all so perfectly clear. '*You* worked on the Farner Seven case,' she said quietly, her insides frozen. 'Evan left the firm after that case ended and you and he never had the same relationship again.' Even as she spoke, a voice inside her was telling her to shut up.

She was afraid.

Cordelia-Aurora was gazing at her steadily, almost vacantly, and it sent chills down her spine. Her sister-in-law had benefited exceptionally well from the result of that case. The Arthur law firm had gained international recognition. There was no way she'd want that case reopened.

Could it be possible that Cordelia-Aurora had played a very real, direct part in Evan's death? But he was her brother! Surely even she wouldn't . . .

Krystal rocketed off the chair to a standing position. The two women stared at each other for several seconds, then Krystal left without another word, her heart hammering in her chest.

29

Gabby watched baby Mykahla attempting to slide along the wooden floor like an uncoordinated caterpillar. Sally gently sniffed Mykahla's fine hair, monitoring her every move.

'You're such a good dog,' Gabby said. 'But you know you don't have to look after her, don't you? The adults are doing that.' The adults in the room – Gabby, Monty, Pippa and Luciano – all nodded. Sally looked up at them briefly, considering the offer, then turned back to the pink Wondersuit-clad, fleshy, powder-scented human on the floor and sat down, on guard. She'd made her decision.

'Doesn't she trust us?' Pippa asked.

'Clearly not,' Gabby said.

To emphasise her point, Sally lay down next to Mykahla, watching her intently, apparently not prepared to leave this creature alone for a second. Mykahla lifted her head up as far as she could to look at her guardian, and broke into a huge, salivary grin. She reached out a chubby hand and touched Sally's golden fur reverently before shrieking in glee.

It was surreal having this gorgeous bundle of baby goodness here in the lounge room while Mykahla's father, and Gabby's children's father, was missing.

'I wish there was something more we could do,' Gabby said, rifling through her brain yet again for any possible places Cam might be hiding out, or old friends he might have turned to. But she realised they were long past that. Meri was his person now and Gabby didn't know those parts of his life any more. 'Maybe I should have offered to go out with Meri, to keep her company at least. She must be going out of her mind with worry.'

'Shall I make us coffee?' Luciano said, getting to his feet.

'Yes, please,' Pippa said, as if she'd collapse if she didn't get some caffeine soon. 'Soy latte, thanks.'

'Monty?' Luciano asked.

Gabby noted how much pleasure it gave her to hear Luciano use her father's name so respectfully.

'Long black, thank you,' Monty said, pausing in *goo*ing and *gaa*ing at Mykahla just long enough to respond. The look on his face was so tender, full of so much delight, that it propelled Gabby back in time to when her kids had been babies. Monty had always been a wonderful grandpa, never afraid to jump in and change nappies, be puked on or peed on, always with a funny face or silly game to make them laugh. Watching him with Mykahla almost made her want another one.

Too late, though. Much too late now.

'Gabby?' Luciano asked, his voice softening to a wavelength just for her. Oh, man . . .

'No, thanks. I think I'm wound a bit too tightly already.'

'Tea, then?' he asked.

Beside her, Pippa was smothering a grin, loving this impromptu version of Gabby bringing home a new boyfriend to meet the family.

Gabby was glad Pippa was here. She'd come over straightaway when Gabby messaged her on the off-chance that she had miraculously seen Cam somewhere. Pippa had busied herself, calling friends and family for Meri while she was driving around in search of her husband.

'Okay, a chai would be great, thanks.' Gabby knew Luciano would brew the chai in milk over the stove, the traditional way. It was really the only way to have it, in her opinion.

They watched him head over to the kitchen.

'Why is he still here?' Pippa whispered, widening her eyes at Gabby. 'Doesn't he have his own kids to go home to?'

'Don't you?' Gabby retorted.

'Harvey's picking them all up this afternoon,' Pippa said. 'It's part of our new arrangement as we work out how to divide their time with each of us.'

'Ouch. Sorry,' Gabby said.

'Have you seen a lawyer yet?' Monty asked. The bruise on his forehead was now a deep indigo. He should still be putting ice on it.

'I'm seeing her tomorrow.' Pippa wrinkled her nose.

'It's not fun, but you have to do it,' Gabby said, getting up to remove a remote control from Mykahla's hand. She handed her a plastic set of keys from the baby bag instead, which she immediately shoved into her gummy mouth. 'It will get easier. This stage is messy and difficult but you'll find your new normal.'

Pippa sighed and adjusted the cowl neck of her sleeveless white shirt. 'I suppose. Anyway, back to your man over there.'

'Shh!' Gabby warned her. 'We were out at lunch when Meri called. I explained and said I had to go but he insisted on coming with me.'

'It's a bit weird, isn't it? Him helping you to find your ex-husband?'

'That's what I said, but he said that if it was important to me then it was important to him.' Gabby glowed just thinking about Luciano's unwavering determination to stay with her to see this through to the end.

Monty nodded in approval.

Pippa cooed. 'Oh, wow. He's a keeper.'

'His mum will look after his kids when they get home from school.' Gabby checked the time. 'Which should be any minute, which means my three will be here any minute too, which means I'll have to explain why Mykahla is here.' She bit her lip. 'What the hell am I going to say?'

They had no time to formulate a plan, because a minute later Celia walked in the door.

'Shit.' Gabby's stomach flipped.

'Hi! Guess what we did at . . . oh! Mykahla!' Celia dropped her schoolbag with a loud thump on the wooden floor and rushed to the baby. Her voice rose an octave. 'Hi, Mykahla. What are you doing here?' She picked up her half-sister and sat cross-legged on the floor with Mykahla in her lap. 'Is Dad here?' she asked, looking around.

Gabby opened her mouth but didn't get a chance to answer because Summer entered the room, dropped her bag next to Celia's and went straight to the baby, smiling at her, Mykahla instantly wrapped her fingers in Summer's long hair and pulled hard.

'Ow, ow, ow,' Summer complained, and carefully prised the vice-like grip off her locks. 'What are you doing here?' she asked the baby. Gabby, Pippa and Monty remained silent, glancing at each other helplessly.

Summer turned to Gabby. 'Where's Dad?'

Luciano arrived with hot drinks on a tray.

'Hi, Luciano,' Summer said.

'Hi,' Celia added.

'Hey, girls. Good to see you,' he said. 'I'm doing the barista thing. Would you like something?' He positioned the drinks in front of the respective parties.

'Hot chocolate, please,' said Celia.

'Latte, please,' said Summer. Then she turned back to Gabby. 'Where's Dad?'

Gabby's heart galloped in her chest. 'Well . . .' She should tell them the truth, she knew that. All the experts said so. If you didn't tell them the truth, your kids wouldn't trust you. And she'd had to do it many times over the years.

Your father and I still love each other but we have decided to live apart.

My heart is sick.

I need a heart transplant.

Yes, it's possible I could die but we're doing everything we can to give me the best chance of life.

Your grandmother died last night.

Children made you say aloud all the things you wished you didn't have to. This time was no different.

'Mum?' Summer prompted.

Monty cleared his throat and put his coffee cup back onto the wooden chest in front of the lounge.

She'd never told the kids about Cam's drug use, though. That was something she didn't feel they would benefit from knowing. If she told them that no one knew where Cam was, they would worry. And everything might still be okay. Then again, it might not be. He could be anywhere and there could be endless explanations for his disappearance. He could have met up with a dealer and gone and got himself so stoned he couldn't find his way home. Or he could have met up with that dealer and something could have gone wrong, like you see on television, and Cam was injured or worse. Maybe he wasn't just using weed any more. Maybe it was harder stuff. Or maybe he'd had an accident. But if he had, surely the police would have contacted them by now. Maybe he'd become one of those statistics about missing people who walked out of their house one day and never came back, the pressures of family life and mortgage stress causing them to run away. Maybe he'd hit his head and had amnesia. Or maybe he'd killed himself. A shiver ran down her spine and she hugged herself.

'Mum!' Summer prompted again, cranky this time.

'Sorry, I was just thinking.' Gabby began to pace. 'We're minding Mykahla for a bit because Meri has some things she has to do.'

Summer frowned, still holding Mykahla's hand. 'But where's Dad?'

'We're not sure, exactly,' Gabby said, casting her eyes at her sister and father. *Is that okay? Is that enough?* Pippa chewed a fingernail nervously and raised one shoulder.

'Okay, look,' Gabby said. 'Everything is probably okay, but your dad left for work this morning and then didn't show up. The school phoned Meri to ask her where he was but she didn't know either, so she's out looking for your dad.'

'What does that mean?' Celia said, putting Mykahla back down onto the floor. Sally immediately sniffed the baby to make sure she was fine and resumed her guarding posture, lying alongside her.

'We don't have all the answers right now,' Gabby said, scrabbling for words. 'Hopefully, your dad just took himself off for a day to have some time out.' She tried to make her tone light.

'Hopefully?' Summer repeated.

'Look, girls,' Monty said, weighing in. 'There's no point getting upset about this right now because we simply don't have enough information. At the moment, all we can do is look after Mykahla and wait for Meri to call us when she's found your father.'

Charlie arrived then, his heavy footsteps clomping down the hall. When he entered the room, he took one look at everyone's miserable faces, eyed the baby and said, 'What's happened?'

'Dad's missing,' Summer said helpfully.

'What?'

Gabby repeated the previous conversation and Charlie shook his head, whether in disgust or despair Gabby wasn't sure, and then he charged upstairs to his room.

Gabby's phone rang and vibrated on the wooden chest. Pippa jumped and leaned forward to read the screen. 'It's Meri,' she said.

'Hello?' Gabby's heart had climbed right up into her throat.

'The police have found his car but not him,' Meri said, her voice hitching.

'Where?'

Around her, everyone clamoured for information.

'What is it?'

'Is he okay?'

'Where is he?'

'What's she saying?'

Gabby waved a hand at them to be quiet. She heard Charlie thunder back down the stairs and into the room.

'The car's at Lillydale Lake,' Meri said. 'I'm going there now.'

'Right. Okay.' All Gabby could think was that stories of abandoned cars found near forests and lakes usually didn't end well. 'Don't worry about Mykahla, she's totally fine. She's playing with Celia and Summer, there's plenty of formula in her bag, we've got it covered.'

'Thanks.' Meri's voice squeaked.

'Call me as soon as you find him,' Gabby said.

She disconnected the call and looked at the waiting faces. Luciano stood behind the lounge, offering his support but keeping a respectful distance from the family in crisis.

'They've found his car at Lillydale Lake, so that's good.' Gabby tried to sound positive but it rang hollow even to her own ears.

Pippa groaned, then caught herself. *Sorry*, she mouthed to Gabby.

'Can we go there now?' Charlie asked.

'Oh, honey, Meri's on her way there and the police are looking for him. I'm sure he's just taken himself for a long walk to clear his head.'

'I want to go now,' Charlie repeated. 'I want to help look for him.'

Monty stood. 'I'll take him.' Then his face dropped. 'Except I don't drive any more. Maybe just this once, as it's an emergency?'

'Emergency?' Celia repeated, her eyes bright with tears.

'No, not an emergency,' Gabby soothed. 'Important, yes, but not an emergency.' She had to admit, though, that she'd feel better if she could help look too. But what if they found Cam and he'd done something awful to himself? That wasn't the last image she wanted her son to have of his father.

'I'm going,' Charlie said, pulling out his phone. 'I'll take an Uber.'

'Wait, Charlie,' Gabby said, realising that her son was now of an age where she could no longer control his choices. 'Just hold on a moment. Dad, why don't you stay here with the kids and look after Mykahla, and I'll take Charlie.'

Monty nodded. 'All right.'

'I'll come too,' Luciano said. 'I'll drive, so you can keep your hands free for phone calls.'

'Let's go,' Charlie said, already heading for the door.

It took them nearly an hour to get to Lillydale Lake, the phone infuriatingly silent in Gabby's hand. When they arrived, they could see the shadows lengthening across the parkland and the lake's surface. Luciano pulled in near the barbecue facilities a few spaces down from a police car, the sight of which made Gabby's legs shake. It was real. This was really happening.

She pulled her denim jacket around her shoulders, the sweet, sickly smell of springtime wattle in the air.

'The lake's huge,' she said, her eyes roaming over the hectares of water in front of them and the forest beyond – an enormous area in which to disappear.

'Where do we start?' Charlie said, standing in front of the visitors' information map.

There were ten kilometres of walking trails, and Cam could be anywhere along them. Two men were out in a small boat, lines in the water. Afternoon walkers powered by while others ambled with dogs on leads. It was idyllic, and yet possibly a nightmare. Tomorrow's papers could be splashed with Cam's photograph.

'Maybe we should split up,' Luciano said. 'We can cover more territory that way.'

'Good idea,' Charlie said, pointing out the paths. 'I'll go towards the rotunda. Mum, you go towards the lookout. Luc, you go towards the dam wall.'

'Okay,' Gabby agreed. 'Everyone got their phones?' Everyone did.

Luciano squeezed her hand and they split up, Charlie moving to the left and Gabby and Luciano to the right, following the same path for a while before they would need to head in different directions.

'It's getting late,' Gabby said, walking past a barbecue, sausages and onion sizzling, the smell drifting happily through the air as though everything in the world was perfectly fine. 'What if we don't find him before dark?'

'We'll deal with it.'

She looked at him while they walked. 'You're pretty great.'

'You're pretty great too.'

'We should do this more often,' she said. 'Not the searching for my lost ex-husband bit. But this bit, you and me walking hand in hand.'

Luciano smiled and rubbed his chin. 'Sounds good to me.'

Gabby felt a tiny spark of joy in the middle of her whirlpool of darker thoughts, and then her phone rang.

'What's happened?'

'We've found him,' Meri said, breathless.

'Is he okay?'

'I wouldn't say that, but he's alive,' she said.

Gabby's hand began to shake with pent-up fear dispersing into the air. 'That's a start.'

Luciano watched her, smiling with relief.

'Where are you?' she asked Meri.

'I don't even know. Somewhere on the trails. I'm with a policeman. We're bringing him back now.'

'I'm here as well. So's Charlie,' Gabby said, omitting Luciano's name for the sake of brevity.

'Are you?'

'We wanted to help look.'

'Thank you.' Meri paused. 'But I don't think Cam will want to see Charlie right now, if that's okay. He's . . .' She searched for a word. '. . . A bit broken, and I know he wouldn't want his son to see him like that.'

Gabby wiped at a tear that had slid down her face. 'Sure, of course. I'll get him and we'll go home and we'll look after Mykahla. Don't worry about her for a second. She'll be totally fine with us overnight. She'll have five people and a dog watching her every move. You just take care of yourself and Cam, okay?'

'Okay. Thank you.'

Gabby clutched the phone to her chest and took a deep breath. 'He's alive,' she said to Luciano. 'I don't have any details but it sounds like he's not in great shape.'

'The important thing is they have him,' Luciano said, reaching for her hands. 'I'm so relieved.'

'Me too,' she said, and without preamble they moved straight into each other's arms, their lips meeting perfectly, the feel of his whiskers igniting her skin. With his hand on her back, he pulled her close until their bodies pressed together. She slid her hands up to his neck, weaving her fingertips through his hair. The setting sun cast them in a rosy glow that permeated her skin and lit up her heart.

She was breathless as they broke apart. 'Wow.'

Luciano rested his forehead on hers. 'Yep,' he whispered. They stayed that way a moment, just easing into each other.

'We should go get Charlie and go home,' she said, gently pulling away. Luciano ran his fingers through her long hair, making her skin break out in goosebumps, and she moaned softly, wanting to stay there under his touch. She held up a finger. 'Just give me one second.'

Luciano grinned and thrust his hands in his pockets, stepping back to allow her to concentrate.

She phoned Charlie. 'They've got him. He's okay. Meet us back at the car as soon as you can.'

30

Krystal lay in bed for as long as possible on Thursday morning, her body aching. It seemed nearly impossible that it was only three days ago that she and Gabby had gone to Sydney and everything had changed.

Jasper was in bed with her and she watched him breathing. He was so cute. He had Evan's lashes and the same smattering of freckles under his eyes. She was supposed to go to work today but there was no way she felt up to facing Janice after yesterday. Then again, she had to get up and get dressed and take the boys to school and day care anyway, so maybe she should just get the humiliation over with. She pushed the decision aside for now, her mind obsessively going over and over everything Rebecca had said and everything Cordelia-Aurora had said, or not said, yesterday.

Was she crazy to think what she was thinking?

Could Cordelia-Aurora really have killed her own brother

to stop him from reopening the case and perhaps ruining the family's reputation? She could well believe Cordelia-Aurora was capable of destroying evidence. But Evan? It was distressing. But it would explain the frosty relationship between him and his sister after that final case, and it *would* explain why he'd felt so compelled to try to make it right.

Jasper rolled over, kicking her in the hip as he did so. She shuffled closer to him, laying her arm like a wing over his body and resting her hand on his tiny shoulder, watching his little chest move up and down with each breath. Paralysing fear gripped her momentarily. She liked to think she'd been through the worst life had to offer; but she hadn't. It could always be worse.

Olly toddled in, carrying his battered Paddington bear, his sleepy face blinking.

'Hey, baby boy.' She smiled at him and opened up the covers so he could climb in too. He lay down next to Jasper and fell back asleep almost immediately. They were so warm, like little heaters, and she had to fling off a corner of the cover. She listened to their snuffling breaths, clinging to the peace and quiet before they awoke and turned into chattering, active, demanding little people who would want food and fun and entertainment, all before they left for school. She'd need a heap of coffee to cope with today, sleep having evaded her most of the night. But for as long as she could, she'd keep them asleep here with her in the big bed, the Mexican donkey looking down at them from the wall. Evan loved that picture. They'd talked about travelling to Mexico together with the kids one day.

Evan, what did you do?

But Evan was silent. Her mind picked over her conversation with Rebecca, again and again.

The scientific evidence had been destroyed during the trial. Burned.

I could recreate it, and I gave it to Evan.

She stilled. Evan had the evidence. Then it must be around somewhere. But where? Her blood thrummed through her veins. She extricated herself from the boys and slid out from under the bedcovers, and began to pace the still dim house. If he'd hidden the evidence in the house, where would it be?

Jasper joined her, flinging his arms around her waist. 'I'm thirsty.'

'Okay,' she said, rubbing his shoulder. 'I'll get you something.' She let her eyes drift around the apartment, wondering. Evan had died trying to make something right. Just maybe, she could finish what he'd started. But it would have to wait until after she got the boys out of the house.

She got the kids off to school, called in sick for work – Janice was hardly surprised, given her panic attack yesterday – resigned herself to the fact that she'd ruined her chances of getting that full-time job, and then rushed home. This was too important.

She tossed her keys onto the kitchen bench and set the kettle to boil, but couldn't wait for it to finish before she began tearing the place apart. So much of Evan's stuff was still here. She'd wanted to keep it for herself and, even more than that, for the boys. That way, as they grew she would be able to pull out something – a jumper, a book, a coffee mug, a cufflink – and know that it would trigger a memory for her, something she could relate to them and in doing so build their bank of memories and knowledge.

She didn't want his collection of things to be a shrine, dusty and abandoned, nothing moved from where it had been when she'd last seen him. She wanted them to be living things, things used around the house, not things the boys were afraid to touch but instead things to love and hold and carry around with them. Olly already slept with Evan's dark red knitted jumper and Jasper liked to look through his father's collection of Lee Child novels, even though he couldn't read them yet. She liked that they would pick up shoes from the closet and carry them to the lounge room and try them on, their small feet inside the big size twelves. It hurt, too, to watch her little men wanting to practise being like their dad, but their smiles always made up for it. Having Evan's stuff moving around the house was like his spirit swirling through the rooms.

There was a hidden closet in the hallway, one that had a manhole in the ceiling and the fuse box on the wall, and in it Evan had stored his paperwork and folders. She pulled out cardboard cartons and carried them to the dining table to rifle through. She searched for anything that might be related to the Farner Seven case, but with no luck. As he'd been part of the Arthur firm back then, everything would have been stored on site, she imagined. All she found were tedious, benign-looking letters or bank statements, law journals, insurance brochures, some media clippings of when either Evan or the Arthur firm had made the news, old telephone books, and disjointed, handwritten notes, the kind he might have made while on the phone to someone, with no connection to anything else.

She went through the back of the linen closet, the top shelf of the wardrobe, and the bottom drawer in the kitchen that was hardly ever opened, pulling things out, spreading them around. The apartment looked like a tip, but she hadn't found a single useful thing. Nothing to do with Farner Seven and nothing that could implicate Cordelia-Aurora in Evan's death. She leaned back in the chair, despairing. She could never succeed against the Arthurs. Never. They were too big, too formidable, too wealthy, too educated, too famous.

She was just too small.

If only she could solve this for the boys' sake.

Then she wiped at her leaky eyes, realising that while she might not be able to solve this on her own, there might still be someone who could help her.

She leapt from her seat and plucked her handbag from the end of the kitchen bench, ferreting around until she found what she was looking for – Trentino Cossa's business card. If she wanted to take on a lawyer she'd need another lawyer to help her do it. Trentino might just be the guy. She fished out her phone and dialled his number. To her happy surprise, he answered.

She told him the story, everything Rebecca had said, her own wild conspiracy theories about Cordelia-Aurora, her search through the house. When she finished, Trentino was silent a moment.

'Krystal, this is big.'

'I know.'

'You have to find that evidence.'

'But where would it be? You're a lawyer, where would you put it?'

'I wouldn't have it inside the house, especially if I was afraid of repercussions for my family. Perhaps with a trusted friend or family member? Or in a safe? A safe deposit box? A long-term airport locker? Maybe even at another law firm or with a solicitor, somewhere no one else would think to go. Hell, I might even bury something like that in a tin in my backyard.'

'We haven't got a backyard,' she said miserably.

'Think hard. You need to find this.'

Krystal ended the call deflated, letting her head drop to her folded forearms on the table.

Where is it, Evan?

She needed to see Gabby. If anyone was going to know what was in Evan's mind, it would be her.

31

Gabby was the only one home when she opened the door to Meri and stepped across the threshold to hug her.

'Come in,' she said, ushering Meri down the hall to the kitchen. 'You look like you could use some coffee.' Meri had dark grey circles under her eyes and wore no make-up. She was dressed in jeans, and a fitted top with a red, Japanese-inspired floral print.

'Trust me, that's an understatement,' Meri said. She spied Mykahla in her bouncer on the kitchen floor and broke into a big grin. 'Hello, baby!' She bent down to unclip the safety belt and pick her up, burying her face into the baby's neck. 'Oh, I missed you.'

Sally followed Meri's moves intently and Gabby couldn't quite tell if the dog was relieved or sad that Mykahla's human had returned. Gabby gave her a reassuring smile and Sally sat down, watching them. -

'She's been fabulous,' Gabby said, turning on the coffee machine to heat the water. 'She slept in bed with me. It was so lovely to have a small, wriggly person with me again.'

'Why are babies so much better behaved for other people than for their own parents?' Meri asked, making funny faces at her daughter, who giggled with delight.

'Frustrating, isn't it?' Gabby laughed. 'Then no one ever believes you when you tell them how difficult they are.' She watched Meri and the baby for a moment, sinking into the warm, fuzzy feelings that it brought. 'How's Cam?'

Meri nodded and shifted Mykahla onto her hip so she could rock her from side to side. 'He's okay. He's still at the hospital but should be coming home later today.'

'Is he . . . have they recommended some sort of rehabilitation program?'

'It's not drugs,' Meri said, sounding snippy, though Gabby could forgive her after what she'd been through in the past twenty-four hours.

'It's not?'

'It's depression. Postnatal depression, specifically.'

'Postnatal depression?'

'Men can get it too,' Meri said, her voice assuming a measured tone now, one Gabby imagined she used often in her line of work. 'It's less common than in women, obviously, but his history predisposes him to it.'

'What history? The drugs?'

Meri took a breath, a defensive one, Gabby thought. 'Yes, his past drug use is a factor. So too is the financial pressure of having to support two families, and a history of stressful relationships.'

Gabby prickled. 'What, with *me*?'

'Any breakdown of a relationship is stressful, divorces especially so, but yours was more complicated because not a lot of time had passed between your divorce and your getting sick. It was an awful time for him.'

Gabby tried to think back to that time. Cam had seemed so calm, so helpful. She remembered being grateful that he'd had his act together so thoroughly. She'd known she could rely on him to be the strong one for them all.

'His kids were under tremendous stress and he had to be there for them,' Meri went on. 'He faced losing you, and while you might have been separated it would still have been a huge loss for him, and he would have had to pick up the pieces for his kids. Everything would have changed. Everyone was on tenterhooks. He had to be ready to drop everything at any time to be there for the kids, to help you, to help your parents. Celia was breaking down at school . . .'

'Yes,' Gabby agreed, feeling a hell of a lot more compassionate towards Cam than she had in the past few weeks. During the years of her illness, it was as though the world had stopped for her. She'd been consumed with worry for herself and her kids; she'd been grateful to Cam, but not particularly concerned for his welfare. At times she'd even been jealous because he'd get to go on living and see their kids grow up and she probably wouldn't.

'So, where do you go from here?' she asked.

'He was in a bad way yesterday,' Meri said, closing her eyes as though trying to block out the memory. 'He didn't try to . . . you know.' She paused. 'But he was so low he couldn't work out how to face anyone, ever again. All he could think to do was hide, disappear.'

'That's awful.'

Mykahla started to fidget so Meri put her down on the floor to squirm around, pulling a rattly toy from her handbag and passing it to her. Sally exhaled happily and lay down, resting her head across her paw to keep one eye on the baby.

'The doctor at the hospital has put him on medication and given him a referral to a psychologist. We've got an appointment next week.'

'That's good.'

Meri crossed her arms over her body. 'I know he's been difficult lately – trust me, I know. But he'll get better. He just needs some help and some time.'

'I hear you. I'm so sorry for what you've been going through.'

Meri shrugged. 'That's life, I suppose.'

Gabby finished making the coffee and Meri swilled it down quickly, anxious to get back to Cam. They hugged goodbye.

'Let me know if I can do anything,' Gabby said.

'Thanks.' Meri waved farewell and Gabby blew a kiss to Mykahla, shut the door and sent a text message to Cam.

I'm here for you, whatever you need.

Not that long ago, it had been her needing help and her parents, Pippa and Cam taking care of her and the kids. Now her mum was gone, her dad needed more help, Pippa was getting divorced, Cam was struggling and she needed to be the one there for the kids. The wheel of fortune had turned one hundred and eighty degrees, upending their positions. Now *she* needed to be the strong one, which was nerve-racking but also rather exciting.

Other than starting a new business last year, she'd still been playing everything very safe. She'd been stagnating, in a way, afraid to live her life in case she did it the wrong way. There was so much pressure to get every day just right in case it was her last.

Now, her fortunes had changed, and so had she. She was ready. She'd just better make sure she didn't die.

After the stress of the past few days – the trip to Sydney, the disturbing visions, the revelation that Krystal had never wanted Gabby to have Evan's heart, the car accident and the crisis with Cam – Gabby was relieved to step back inside her beautiful cafe. She breathed in the rich aromas of coffee and the sweet, rose-scented butterfly cupcakes that had just arrived, so fluffy and soft she could barely restrain herself from devouring a couple right there.

'Gorgeous, aren't they?' Ed said. 'Look at the crystallised rose petals on the tips of the butterfly wings.'

'They're beyond adorable,' Gabby agreed, her mouth watering. 'Oh! And look at these!' In another white box sat a dozen chocolate cupcakes with whipped peaks of Baileys cream frosting, drizzled with dark chocolate. 'Whatever we're paying for these cupcakes, it's not enough. I just need a roaring fire, a Baileys liqueur coffee and one of each of these cupcakes, then I might curl up like a cat and have a wee nap.'

Ed laughed. 'I can help you with the liqueur coffee.'

'Tempting,' Gabby conceded, picking up each cupcake carefully and placing it in the display cabinet. As she was doing so, a customer added one to her order. Gabby was almost sad to see it go. She headed out through the swing doors to find Luciano in the middle of a cupping session. She stopped on the opposite side of the long table, rows of white cups holding dark liquid between them. She grinned at him.

'Hi.'

'Hi.' He put down his cup and came around the bench to stand in front of her. His eyes dropped to her lips, then back to her eyes. Obviously, they couldn't be kissing here, which was a pity. He shoved his hands into the pockets of his jeans. 'How's Cam?'

'He's okay. I saw Meri this morning. He should be out of hospital later today. He needs some help to get back on his feet but he'll get there.'

'That's good news.'

'It is.' She felt ridiculously nervous and wiped her hands down the sides of her skirt. 'What are you cupping?'

'Secret squirrel business. They're competitors' coffees. Just keeping on top of what's going around the city at the moment.'

'Good move.'

The tension between them was thrilling. Gabby hadn't felt this alive since . . . well, she couldn't even remember.

Luciano took his hand from his pocket and ran his knuckles gently down her arm.

'Oh, boy,' she whispered, her whole body vibrating under his touch.

'Have lunch with me today,' he said, quietly, even *lustfully*.

She shivered. 'Yep, okay.'

'Good.' He dropped his hand and smiled, his eyes dark with attraction.

'I'd better . . .' She indicated over her shoulder. 'Back to . . . you know.'

'I'll be here.'

She left the room before she blacked out.

'Here's your coffee,' Ed said, handing her a tall glass with dark coffee smelling of Baileys Irish Cream, a dollop of thickened cream floating on top.

'Thanks. What's that look for?'

Ed smirked at her and flicked her eyes towards the roasting room and back again. Oh, yeah, that wall between them was made of glass.

'I don't know what you're talking about,' Gabby said, and took her coffee. She added one of the Baileys chocolate cupcakes and went to a free table next to the green wall, the same table where she'd first seen Krystal. She stirred her coffee and took a big spoonful of cake into her mouth, and the intense sweetness and flavour distracting her from her feelings of betrayal towards Krystal. Which was just as well, because two mouthfuls later she walked in the door.

32

'Hi,' Krystal said, approaching Gabby's table. 'I'm so glad you're here.' She pulled out the chair opposite and sat, glad there was bustle about them to defuse the intensity of this conversation. Gabby had told her she needed a break, but Krystal couldn't wait until Gabby was ready to come back.

'What are you doing here?' Gabby asked, putting down her spoon as though she had suddenly lost her appetite.

'I need your help.'

Gabby lifted her chin and crossed one leg over the other, bobbing the toe of her boot in an agitated manner. 'I'm not sure I'm in the mood for the paranormal right now. I've had a big few days.'

Krystal's hopes fell. 'I'm sorry to hear that. Is everything okay?'

Gabby folded her arms. 'Not really. I know that you didn't want to donate Evan's organs.'

'What?' Krystal's mind raced to catch up, wondering if she should deny it, wondering who could have told Gabby that, then realising that, of course, Gabby must have seen what Krystal herself had remembered that night in Sydney. And that meant that either the three of them were so enmeshed that Gabby could now pick up on Krystal's memories, or worse yet, that Evan himself had indeed heard every word of that awful discussion with Cordelia-Aurora that night and relayed it to Gabby. Her hands began to shake and she put them under her legs to sit on them.

Gabby told Krystal everything she'd seen and it was all true, and it was utterly terrible to know that she'd witnessed that, to know that Gabby knew Krystal felt forced into signing the papers, to imagine how dreadful Gabby must feel. She waited until Gabby had said all she wanted to say. She was appalled with herself for having been so desperate for Gabby to help her, for rationalising that Gabby owed her, and for not dealing with her own guilt in this matter.

Her moment of reckoning had arrived and she couldn't run from it any longer.

'What you saw is . . . well, it's amazing,' she said. 'That's some connection you've got with my husband there.' The attempt at lightness fell flat. Krystal swallowed, hard. She thought carefully about what she said next, taking her time to try to find the right words. 'It's true, I was resistant to the idea of organ donation.'

'Resistant?' Gabby gave a slight shake of her head.

'We'd never talked about it, Evan and I. It came as a huge, *huge* shock, all of it. The accident, the fact that he'd lied to me and was in Sydney, all the medical explanations, the diagnosis of brain death.' Krystal stopped for a moment, waiting for the hot swelling sensation in her chest to subside. 'It felt monstrous to even consider carving up his body. I'm sorry; I knew people like you were waiting on the other end, living on a knife edge, wanting an organ, wanting to keep living for your own families. But I didn't care about that in that moment. I didn't care about anything other than trying to do what was right for my husband, and trying to not say goodbye. I'd have done anything to not say goodbye.'

Gabby's face softened. 'I can understand that.'

'And yes, the fact that his heart would still be beating when they took it . . . well, it was a deal-breaker.'

'But you let Cordelia-Aurora blackmail you,' Gabby said, and the disgust at this notion was evident in her tone. 'Do you know how that makes me feel? I feel like I have stolen property inside me, dirty goods, a new life founded on deceit and anger and lies.'

Krystal chewed on her thumbnail. 'I'm sorry.'

'What did she have over you that would make you change your mind?'

A jolt of anger spiked Krystal's blood and she welcomed it. Anger was so much easier to deal with than guilt. 'Not long after I moved to Melbourne, I was arrested. It was complete rubbish. I was in the wrong part of town and dressed the wrong way. I made a stupid mistake and chatted up a cop. I didn't know he was a cop. I was riding a high of freedom like I'd never felt before and still finding my feet, still working out who I was. I was talking rubbish. I asked him if I could show him a good time. He got the wrong idea and decided I was propositioning him for money, so he arrested me.'

Gabby's eyes had widened and then narrowed. 'But you weren't . . .'

'Hell, no!' Krystal gave an empty laugh. 'He took me down to the station and we sorted the whole thing out. But that stuff stays on your record. Cordelia-Aurora, that bi–' She stopped herself, looking quickly around to see how close other customers were. 'Well, you know about that night at the hospital; I'm sure you have an idea of what she's like.'

Gabby screwed up her nose in understanding.

'She hated me from the start, so of course she did a background check on me. She told me early on that she was just waiting for the right moment to tell Evan. She held it over me for years.'

'Why didn't you just tell Evan yourself?'

Krystal ran a hand through her unwashed hair, flicking it over her shoulder. 'I should have. But I was stupid and insecure and didn't believe that *he* could truly believe I was the one for him. The longer it went on, the harder it became to tell him the truth, and so I just put it out of my mind. I think I even genuinely forgot about it.'

'I can't believe his sister would use something like that against you at such an awful time,' Gabby said, uncrossing her arms and sipping on her coffee, her hackles lowering. 'So, you signed the papers under duress.'

Krystal's next breath was shaky. 'Yes. But in the end, it wasn't because of Cordelia-Aurora.'

'Go on,' Gabby urged.

'I've never told anyone this,' Krystal said, quietly enough that Gabby automatically leaned forward to hear her better. 'But I think I owe you the truth.' She took a few breaths, steadying herself. She'd been running from this truth for two years, burying it in her subconscious, and lately drowning it with alcohol whenever it came to the surface.

'Cordelia-Aurora didn't scare me. She was venomous and hateful and I wished I could expel her from the hospital, but she didn't scare me. I've survived worse people than her in my life.'

'Then what was it?'

'It was the prospect of turning off the life support that scared me, of it being *me* who did it, and then having to wait for days or even weeks for him to die. The idea of waiting terrified me, having to watch him, the effect it would have on the boys. In that hospital, a minute felt like an hour, an hour a week. I simply couldn't handle it. The boys had nowhere to go. Evan's parents were helping me look after them but they didn't know them all that well, and at any rate, how long can you have a one- and a three-year-old in a hospital for?'

Gabby nodded sympathetically. 'An hour in a hospital with children that young would have been a nightmare, let alone days or weeks.'

'I had no other support I could call on. I was desperate. I wouldn't have been able to stay with him the whole time. I couldn't abandon the kids. But I couldn't abandon Evan either. It was the most awful, torturous decision, choosing between my husband and my children.' Tears rolled down Krystal's face as she looked at Gabby, pleading for understanding. 'I'm so ashamed of this, but the agony just broke me down. I needed it to stop and the only way to do that was to sign the papers for organ donation. Then it would be over.' She looked to the ceiling, where the wooden ladder hung entwined with pretty flowers. 'I told myself I was doing it for the kids, so they didn't have to live through this nightmare that would only end in Evan's death anyway – but it wasn't.' She shook her head, still not able to believe what she'd done. She dropped her eyes back to Gabby. 'I told myself it was for them, but it was for me. I collapsed under the pressure. And so, I sacrificed him. I sent him to the butcher.'

Gabby closed her eyes.

'*I* did that,' Krystal whispered, her fist at her chest. 'Do you know what that feels like? I did the unthinkable. I betrayed him and I sacrificed him to save us, and I'll never forgive myself for that.' She bit her trembling lip. 'And I have no idea if he forgives me or hates me.'

33

Gabby held her forehead in her hands. Krystal's explanation was believable, understandable. She could even forgive her for crumbling under pressure, and she was most definitely still grateful she had Evan's heart, despite how it might have come to her. She straightened. 'Okay, look.' Krystal's face was awash with shame and misery, her cheeks hollow, her jawline sharp. 'Of course I don't love the way the donation came about. I'd always believed it was something more altruistic than that. But you have to forgive yourself.' She reached across the table, put her hand on Krystal's and squeezed it tight. 'No one ever knows how they will react in any situation until they're in it. You were in an impossible position, in shock, traumatised, under time pressure and being blackmailed, with two small children needing your attention. That's a recipe for insanity right there.'

Krystal closed her eyes a moment and sighed.

'I forgive you,' Gabby said.

'Thank you.'

'I can assure you that Evan doesn't hate you. He loves you just as much now as he did then, and it is precisely because of that bond that he's brought us together. I truly think the reason he wanted you to go to Sydney was because *he* wanted *your* forgiveness. He knew lying to you was wrong and that he'd let his children down. He wanted you to be able to rest easy so he could too.'

'How can you know?'

'Because I have his heart.'

Krystal raised her free hand to cover her face for a moment, taking a deep breath to control her emotions. Gabby let go of her hand and pulled a tissue from the pocket of her skirt and handed it to her.

'That's really beautiful,' Krystal said. 'I could put that on a greeting card.'

'Huh?'

'Never mind.' Krystal smiled and waved it away, to explain another time. 'I'm so glad we met.'

'So am I,' Gabby said.

'Do you think you can help me one more time?'

'We've come this far,' Gabby said, shaking her head as if she couldn't believe the wild ride they'd been on together. 'What do you need?'

Krystal was re-energised, filled with purpose. 'After you left Sydney on Tuesday, I went back to see Rebecca, the woman we met at the house.' Krystal filled her in about Farner Seven and the whistleblowing case Evan and Rebecca had been building.

Gabby gasped. 'The burning smell! Remember the second time you came here? I could smell burning. It's . . . oh, I can see it now. A big bonfire and, oh, no, Evan was there, watching.' She shook her head. 'And Cordelia-Aurora too.'

Krystal's mouth turned down with momentary dismay and disappointment. But as Gabby had just said, no one knew how they would respond until they were in a situation. She had no idea what sort of extenuating circumstances might have led to that moment. 'He made a mistake,' she said. 'He wasn't able to stand up to his sister then and he eventually paid with his life.'

'That's a high price,' Gabby said sadly.

'But you were the key to solving the whole thing.'

Gabby shook her head. 'No, we both were. It was you that triggered the visions in the first place. Just being near you woke up something in Evan's heart, something he needed to share. We did this together.'

Krystal paused to allow Gabby's words to sink in. 'I hadn't thought of it like that.'

'You were the one person in Evan's life he'd chosen and committed to forever, even beyond death.'

Krystal felt a tear drop from her eye and wiped it away. 'I'm so grateful to have had this chance to find the missing pieces. Most people don't get that. Thank you.'

'You're welcome, and you've helped me too,' Gabby said. 'Like you, it's been difficult for me, living with a big mystery. Knowing Evan, knowing you, it helps. It really does.'

'I'm glad for you, truly. But there's more. Yesterday, I realised something for the first time. Cordelia-Aurora was already at the hospital when I arrived on the night of the accident. In all the shock and confusion, I assumed the police had informed her too and she'd simply got there first. But something didn't feel right about that. I went to her office yesterday and confronted her about why she was in Sydney that night. She didn't say much, but her *face*!' Krystal leaned very close to Gabby so she could whisper. 'I think she was involved in Evan's death.'

'No!' Reflexively, Gabby's hand went to her chest, covering her heart.

Krystal nodded. Then shrugged. 'I can't be sure, of course. I don't want to believe it. But I have to at least consider it. Rebecca said Evan had the reconstructed evidence, so I went looking for it at home but couldn't find anything. I'd seen a lawyer recently and spoken to him about Evan's family . . . it's a bit of a long story, but I phoned him and told him everything. I want to make this right, for Evan. Trentino – that's the lawyer – says this could be huge.' Her eyes widened. 'But we need to know where Evan put the evidence.' She waited a beat, giving Gabby a chance to catch up.

'So, you need me to try to work it out?'

'You've already done so much, I know,' Krystal said. 'I know you reached your limits in Sydney. But I think this is why Evan wanted to bring us together. He needed us – both of us – to get justice for those sick kids and bring Farner Seven back to court.' She paused. 'And maybe bring Cordelia-Aurora to justice too.'

Gabby took a moment to absorb this. Then she reached both hands across the table and took hold of Krystal's. 'Let's do this.'

'Right now?'

'Yes. This is where you were the first time I had a vision. Let's see if we can conjure him one more time. Close your eyes. Now, think about Evan.'

Krystal did as she was told. 'Come on, Evan. Help us out, hey?' she whispered.

Gabby kept her eyes closed, an image of Evan in her mind. She breathed slowly and deeply, asking him to come to her. Around her, the noise of the cafe – the coffee machine, the cups, the chatter, footsteps on the floorboards, mobile phones – began to fade into the background. Her fingers began to tingle. She felt lightheaded. He must be close.

Come on, Evan.

A moment later, everything spun out of control.

She was dipping and diving, seasick. She let go of Krystal's hands and gripped the table instead.

'What happened?' Krystal asked.

Gabby stared at the tabletop, trying to focus on a single point and stop the motion.

'Are you okay?'

She heard Krystal's voice, but she couldn't bring herself to look at her, fearing the movement of her eyes would make the spinning worse.

'Could you please get me some water?' she said, her lips feeling horribly dry and rough as she spoke.

'Of course.' Krystal sprang from her seat and Gabby continued to breathe, hoping the swaying and spinning would stop. If this was Evan's way of making an entrance, it was too much. Her body felt like it was going to snap in half.

Krystal returned, placing the water on the table.

'Thanks,' Gabby murmured, but when she reached for the water she could see her hand shaking, and pulled it back to grip the table.

'You don't look well. What's happening?' Krystal said. 'Can you talk to me?' Her voice was sharp with concern.

Nausea rose like a tidal wave. 'I . . .' Gabby gasped for breath, waiting for the wave to subside. Her skin burned hot.

'What can I do?'

This was bad. It was very, very bad.

'Hospital,' Gabby said, her voice barely a whisper.

'Shit.' Krystal leapt to her feet to help her up, but the second Gabby was vertical her knees buckled and everything went black.

A siren. A blood pressure cuff on her arm.

. . . dangerously low . . .

Bright lights above her in the back of the ambulance. The awful sway and bump of the vehicle as it lumbered through the streets. Motion sickness from travelling backwards added to her distress. She couldn't speak. All she could do was keep breathing, keep focusing, try to stay here and now and not drift off into blackness and ... and ... death? Was this it? It felt like death. She felt a great tearing inside her, a great separation of her mind and body.

... fever ...

An ambulance officer sitting on a bench next to her, writing in a folder.

... nearly there, love ...

Krystal, somewhere in the van. She could hear her voice now and then, trying to give the ambulance officer as many details as possible.

She thought of her children – her three beautiful, precious, sensitive, creative, dynamic and still-so-young children. They couldn't lose their mother. Not now. Not after all they'd been through already. Not when they still needed her so very, very much. They'd lost their grandmother. Their grandfather was growing frail. Their father was sick and who knew how much longer he'd stay that way. Their aunt was soon to be a single mum. They needed their mother. She needed to be here to guide them, protect them, teach them, love them.

This was *not* the time to die.

But we never get a choice in that. Never, ever. Today could be the day for her, just as it would be for thousands of people around the world, ready or not. No one knew when their time was up. It was never going to be a good time to die. She knew it better than most.

People were always so shocked when they found out they were going to die. Or they were utterly unprepared for their child dying, their sister dying, their dog dying. No one liked to think about it and yet it was the one thing in life that was guaranteed to happen. Any day, any hour, any minute. She thought that if people truly understood that this moment could be their very last moment, they wouldn't be wasting it in road rage, or mindlessly scrolling through social media, or getting drunk. They would be loving their people, giving away all their possessions, imparting wisdom, hugging their kids, taking the dog for a walk, smelling the roses. Once you truly *got* that this day might be the last, you wouldn't be shocked when the moment of death arrived. You would be saying, 'Oh, Death, here you are. I've been expecting you.'

She might have been expecting this moment, but still she begged – *Please not today.*

Her shirt was undone. Her bra loosened. Sticky ECG patches were placed on her chest, her ribs, her lower legs. The printer whirred as it spat out results. The feel of Evan's heart, erratic in her chest, giving its last flutter of life before falling still forever.

The heavy, heavy pull of blackness, sucking her in, pulling her away.

No one knew when their time was up, yet this felt very much like it. Something inside her was dying. She couldn't stop it. No one could.

No! Stay with me, love, stay with me, you hear me?

She rose out of her body.

In the murky space between consciousness and death, Evan came to her.

They sat in a room – dark walls, lanterns glowing golden above their heads, two ornate wooden chairs with velvet seats facing each other. They both wore white shirts, white pants, no shoes. It was warm. Quiet. Gabby felt so light, as if there was nothing to her.

'I needed to see you,' he said, his face so serene, so much younger than she'd seen him before.

She smiled. His voice was like music! It was so warm and calm, so confident and caring. It made her feel joyful, as though a long-lost friend had finally returned home and the piece of her that had been missing them and worrying about them could finally relax.

'It's so good to see you.' She reached for his hands and he took hers. They sat there a moment, relaxing into each other's touch, as though they were twins who only felt whole when they were together.

'Don't be afraid,' he said.

'I'm not.'

She would never be able to say how long they sat there like that – perhaps a minute, perhaps an hour, perhaps a year, perhaps ten. Time had no meaning at all.

But at some point, she became aware of what he'd come to tell her.

'You're leaving me?'

He nodded, gave a small smile. 'Yes.'

The peace she'd felt disappeared and grief leapt to replace it. 'But why?'

'It's time.'

'But what will happen to you? What will happen to me?'

'I'm going to rest, and you're going to live. My heart is yours now. It's yours alone.'

He stood and pulled her to her feet, then wrapped her in his arms. At the same height, their chests met, right where his heart had lived before it became hers. She clung to him tightly.

'Thank you for my life.'

'It's a life worth living.'

All too soon, they broke apart, but when she looked down, he was holding a plain narrow metal box, about the length of a briefcase.

'This is the answer.'

34

Krystal sat beside Gabby's bed, her head in her hands. Gabby was still dozy and weak, an IV line in each arm. She was in a single room on the ward, not far from the nurses' station, and the constant beep of the call bell and chatter from staff, along with the hospital smell and the sound of curtain rings swishing on rails, were giving her nasty flashbacks to her time in the ICU with Evan. She'd managed not to go anywhere near a hospital since then, until the other night with Gabby in Sydney. It was ironic that the next time she found herself here, Evan's heart would again be the focus of attention.

Rejection. Grade four. The worst kind.

'Will this fix it?' Krystal had asked the nurse, indicating the bags of medicine hanging beside Gabby's bed.

'Hopefully,' she'd replied, giving Krystal a reassuring smile but offering no other commitment.

Now, Krystal pulled her mobile phone from her bag and checked again for messages, but there was nothing new. Luciano had rushed to Gabby's side when she'd collapsed at the cafe but he hadn't been able to organise care for his kids so had reluctantly let Krystal go with Gabby in the ambulance. He'd contacted Gabby's father. School was nearly done for the day and Gabby's kids would be coming with Monty. Roxy was picking up Krystal's boys. Krystal was staying here until either Luciano or Gabby's family arrived.

She stood and paced, awash with guilt that she might have caused this by asking Gabby to connect with Evan one more time. There was a panicky flutter in her chest. She longed for Gabby to be okay, and she wanted that even more than she wanted Evan's heart to be okay. She'd loved Evan for his heart, yet, somehow, since meeting Gabby, she'd let go of the idea of its being his heart. It was Gabby's now. Gabby had life because of that heart, but it was still Gabby's life and Krystal wanted very much for her to have a long one yet. A part of her might even love Gabby, maybe because of the connection to Evan's heart, or maybe just because Gabby was a gorgeous soul who was easy to love. Either way, Krystal was sick with worry that she might lose Gabby now when they had only just found each other.

A man with glasses and greying hair walked into the room. A hospital ID swung from his top pocket.

'Hello,' he said, holding out a hand to Krystal.

She took it, feeling out of place given she wasn't Gabby's next of kin. 'Hi.'

'I'm George Thanos, Gabby's surgeon. And you are?' He peered at her down his nose, trying to focus through the bottom of his lenses.

Oh. My. God.

Krystal was lost for words, staring into the eyes of the man who'd held her husband's heart in his hands before sewing it into Gabby's chest.

She shook herself and let go of his hand. 'Um, sorry.' She coughed. 'Krystal. I'm a friend of Gabby's.' She couldn't stop staring at him. He was the person who'd brought Evan's heart back to life. George gave her a quizzical look, then turned to Gabby's bed. He went to her side, placing his hand on her arm with genuine care, a visible connection between them.

'Gabby!' he called. 'Can you hear me? It's Doctor George. Are you awake?'

Gabby murmured and dragged her eyes open, though it was clearly an effort.

'There's my girl,' George said in a comforting fatherly tone. 'How are you feeling?'

'Thirsty,' Gabby whispered.

George nodded. 'I'm not surprised. The medications will make you feel like that, but we've got you on fluids so you will be okay. You know you're having an episode of rejection?'

'Yes,' Gabby said, and swallowed in a way that looked like it must be painful.

'Okay, well, I have some more news. You might need to stay in here for a bit longer than we first thought,' he said. 'The other reason you might be feeling thirsty is that your kidney function test is low. If your levels keep dropping, we'll have to start dialysis. Do me a favour and hang in there, okay?'

'Okay,' Gabby croaked.

He gave her a final pat on the arm, turned to nod at Krystal, and swept out of the room, on to his next patient.

Gabby turned her head very slowly towards Krystal, blinking heavily. 'Hi.'

'Hi,' Krystal said, going to her side. She straightened the sheet around her as she spoke, needing to do something to stop the tremor in her hands, a result of meeting George. 'I'm so glad to see you again.'

'I –'

Just as Gabby started to talk, Krystal's phone rang. 'Hang on, that might be your dad.' Luciano had taken Krystal's number and passed it on to Monty. She hurried around the bed to her bag but the caller identification said it was from Jasper's school. 'Sorry, I better get this. It's the school.

'Hello?'

'Hi, Krystal, it's Janice.'

'Oh, hi.'

'I'm just phoning to remind you that tomorrow is the due date for you to get in your application for the full-time job. I know you've been sick this week, so I just wanted to make sure you remembered.' Janice's tone was caring, something Krystal found surprisingly touching.

'Ah, thank you.'

Janice paused. 'Do you think you'll be putting in an application?'

Krystal was caught off guard. She hadn't even begun to put an application together; right now it all seemed very difficult, and with the amount of campaigning Margie already had under her belt she was pretty sure it wasn't worth it. But perhaps, even more than that, Krystal felt that her time there was done. The job had served its purpose in her life, keeping her from losing her mind and giving her a reason to get up in the morning, but now she wanted something new. Maybe a new job, maybe a stint at university, like Roxy was doing, or travel with the kids, perhaps even overseas to see her sister. Maybe she could start her own business, like Gabby had done. Maybe Gabby would even give her some advice.

She smiled down at Gabby, looking small and fragile there in the bed, fighting with everything she had to stay in this life. If she'd learned anything from Evan and Gabby it was that there was a big world out there and that life was unpredictable and short. It was time to find what she was passionate about and go out and do it.

'Hello? Are you still there?' Janice asked.

'Sorry, yes. Actually, I think I'm going to say no,' Krystal said, smiling with relief, feeling lighter by the second.

'Oh.' Janice sounded surprised.

'It's been a great job for me,' Krystal said. Gabby looked at her quizzically and Krystal gave a small shoulder shimmy out of joy, which made Gabby laugh, and then cough. 'But I think I have to move on and find something that's more *me*, you know?'

Janice paused a moment. 'Yes, I think I know what you mean.'

'But I'll see you on Monday. I'm sure I'll be much better by then.'

'Well, just to let you know, as there will now be only one of you left to apply, we'll open up submissions to the wider community. So if you change your mind, you'll have another two weeks to throw your hat in the ring,' Janice said, sounding decidedly hopeful.

'That's kind of you, thanks. But I won't be changing my mind. Have a good weekend.'

'You too.'

'What just happened?' Gabby asked.

'I just quit my job,' Krystal said, truly happy.

'Congratulations.'

'Thank you.' Krystal sat down on the chair and leaned towards the bed.

'I was just about to say that I have something to tell you,' Gabby said, again swallowing painfully.

'What?'

'Evan came to see me.' She lifted her pointer finger and waved it in a circle. 'You know, out there.'

Krystal's eyes widened in surprise, all thoughts of her job or her future vanishing in an instant. Evan had spoken. 'What did he say?'

Gabby's eyes filled with tears. 'He's moving on. He's not going to be here with us any more.'

Krystal's throat constricted so tightly she thought she'd stop breathing.

'But he had a message for you,' Gabby whispered.

'What was it?'

'He handed me a metal box and said that was the answer.'

'The answer to what?'

'Where to find the evidence, I think.'

Krystal scrambled through her memory of the conversation with Trentino in which he listed all the places he might hide evidence. 'It's a safe deposit box, it has to be. Oh, I have to call Trentino. I have no idea how to find where it might be.' She jumped to her feet. Then sat again. 'But I'll wait, of course, till your family gets here.'

Gabby smiled and shook her head. 'They'll be here any moment. You go. It's too important.' Her voice was raspy.

Krystal groaned and shuffled her feet. 'Are you sure?'

'Absolutely. I'll just go back to sleep anyway.'

Krystal flung herself over Gabby to hug her, and realised her heart was right next to Gabby's – to Evan's – and for the first time in two years, the world almost felt right again. 'Thank you. I'll let you know as soon as I find something.'

35

Gabby awoke as her family arrived.

'Mum!' Celia draped her body across Gabby's, whimpering like a puppy.

'Hi, baby girl,' she said, her voice tremulous.

Summer and Charlie rushed in too, reaching over each other to kiss her and hug her. Monty followed, looking grim. They all wore expressions of expectant dread, and it hurt her to see it.

'What did the doctors say?' Charlie asked, standing up straight. He towered over her bed. Her throat squeezed. The problem with living on the verge of death was that it meant she looked at everything through a lens of impending loss. She wanted to see Charlie as a man, watch him find his way in the world, celebrate his loves and comfort his losses, and snuggle his babies one day too. They all stared at her, waiting.

'Have they given you any answers?' Monty asked, touching her orange plastic identification bracelet.

'It's an episode of rejection, but they've got me on the right medication now so I'll be fine.' She gave Celia an encouraging smile. Her little girl's face had paled. Gabby hoped this wouldn't send her back into an anxiety spiral, especially after what had just happened with Cam. What a terrible thing, for her children to face the prospect of losing both parents within twenty-four hours.

'What grade rejection is it?' Charlie asked, narrowing his eyes so that his ginger eyebrows pulled together with worry. Her children knew too much about this stuff. It was hard to downplay what they knew was so serious. Rejection was to be expected. But once transplant recipients were through the early stages of recovery the fear diminished.

'Grade four,' she said.

'Oh, no!'

'What?'

'The *worst* grade?' This from Summer. She inched back from the bed and Monty placed his hand on her shoulder to steady her.

'It is the *highest* grade, yes. But I just need a few days on the drip and then I'll be good as new. I'm sorry to have given you all a fright, but rejection happens, right? We all knew that.'

'Yes, but you're two years on now,' Charlie said.

'I know.' Gabby held out her hand for him to take and he squeezed it for a moment, the mood in the room sombre. On a physical level, this episode of rejection was her body rejecting the heart. Only she knew it was triggered by the change in Evan's vibration. His withdrawal had created a disturbance, and her body had panicked and did what it thought it should do. But it would settle, it would accept the new normal, and it would be all the stronger for it. This heart was hers now – truly hers – because Evan had given it to her.

'Look, I know this is scary and it's come as a shock to us all. But I have no doubt I'm going to get through this, okay?'

'Of course you will,' Monty said confidently. There were other murmurs of agreement and support, but she had the feeling they were offered because they were expected and not because they were believed. Pippa stormed into the room, interrupting them, her four children trailing behind her, and Gabby was suddenly reminded of mother opossums that amble around with litters of babies clinging to their backs.

'Bloody hell, Gabby!' Pippa said, cranky, as if Gabby had orchestrated this crisis herself. In a completely irrational moment, Gabby laughed.

'Why are you laughing?'

'I was just thinking how lucky I am to have you all,' she said, then burst into tears.

Luciano arrived after dinner, after Gabby's family had gone home and after he'd organised for his mamma to look after his kids. She heard his boots in the hall. He had a strong, even gait she'd come to recognise and it made her smile even before he turned the corner, carrying a cardboard carry tray with four cups of coffee.

'I know it's probably too late for coffee but I couldn't think what else I could do,' he said, placing them on the table next to her bed. She pressed the button on her bed control to raise herself to sitting, simultaneously pleased to see him and mortified that she must look like a wreck and that he was seeing her like this – as a sick person.

'I brought you a long black, a Vienna, a mocha and a flat white.'

She inhaled the beautiful aroma, her mouth watering immediately. 'You're a star. The coffee here isn't worth drinking.'

He murmured sympathetically, then tentatively leaned down to kiss her.

'You taste like *amaretti* biscuits,' she said.

He grinned. 'My mamma baked them today.' Then his face dropped. 'I should have brought you some too.'

'No, I'm not really up to food right now. But thank you.'

He pulled up the visitor's chair and perched awkwardly on the edge. Even in her hazy state, she could see he looked good. His floppy fringe was hanging just the right amount over his forehead, swept to the side with the smallest amount of product. He was in his usual attire of jeans, collared shirt and Blundstones, but this evening he wore a hint of some sort of musky cologne, which she suspected was for her benefit. The idea made her warm.

'Which one would you like?' he asked, gesturing to the coffees.

Gabby swept her hand through her messy hair. At least she had some pyjamas now that her family had brought her some supplies, and was not stuck in a shapeless and revealing hospital gown. Her head spun with the movement. She felt weak as a kitten.

'Maybe the flat white,' she said. 'The Vienna sounds appealing in theory but I don't think I could stomach the cream.'

Luciano's dark eyes crinkled around the edges with concern. He lifted out the flat white and passed it to her.

'Did you go into the cafe to make these on the way over?'

'Of course. I wouldn't trust anyone else to do it for you.'

She tasted it. 'Damn, you do make a fine brew.'

'Thank you,' he said, and reached for the long black. He sipped slowly. 'How are you feeling?'

She raised one shoulder and let it drop. 'Not fabulous, to be honest. My temperature's up, which is giving me aches and shivers on top of the nausea.'

'I think you look beautiful,' he said, huskily.

She looked up at him and smiled, embarrassed. 'That's very kind of you to say.'

'It's not *kind*,' he growled, with a twinkle in his eye. 'It's bold and . . . disarming.'

She snorted with laughter. 'Disarming? Have you been reading romance novels?'

'I'm a complicated man.'

She scoffed. 'I think I might have you beat at that game.' Luciano watched her but didn't say anything, so she ploughed on. 'I think maybe this thing, whatever this is with us, it's got no future, no legs.'

He put down his coffee and folded his arms.

'I'm a bit . . . problematic,' she said, trying to be truthful but not ashamed of her body and the difficulties of living with a heart transplant. She wasn't a catch; she knew that. 'Apparently, even more so than I realised, and that's kind of the point. This journey is so unpredictable – and I know all relationships and all of life are totally, completely, utterly unpredictable,' she said, rushing to halt a protest that Luciano seemed to be about to wedge into her speech, 'but I think that's even more reason why I need to keep some things stable and solid so my life isn't entirely full of moving parts.'

Luciano drummed the fingers of his right hand on his jeans, like a cat swishing its tail in agitation while its face remained impassive. She felt nervous then, worried he might leave his job, which would be awful.

'Please don't leave The Tin Man,' she blurted.

His fingers stopped moving and he shook his head, bemused. 'Why would I do that? I love my job. I love The Tin Man.'

'You do?'

'Yes!' He seemed aghast that she would think otherwise.

'Because I know it's selfish to say I want you in one part of my life but not the other –'

He held up his hand and she fell silent. 'Listen to me. You don't get to claim the top prize for complications. I am still reeling from losing my brother. And the kids?' He shook his head and raised his eyes to the ceiling. 'They're great, don't get me wrong, and I would do anything for them, but I feel like I'm ten years behind where I need to be and they are checkmating me at every turn. They're emotionally volatile, unbelievably hungry *all* the time, and they ask dozens of questions I simply can't answer. Every single day, I'm a drowning man grasping for driftwood to keep myself afloat. I'm relying on my mother to bail me out of trouble every second day.'

'I live with my father,' she countered.

'Cooper sleeps in my bed most nights.'

'The dog sleeps in mine.'

'I'm forty-five and I have a mortgage I can't afford and no savings.'

'I'm forty-one and I'm in debt to a business loan, for which my parents were guarantors.'

'Then between us, we'd better make sure The Tin Man is a raging success,' he said.

Gabby wanted to keep protesting. The prospect of their being together was futile, wasn't it? But a much bigger part of her wanted to take this lifebuoy he was throwing her. 'So, what you're saying is that you're a complete mess too.'

'Mess? I'm a bloody natural disaster! Someone should call the Red Cross to come and oversee the rebuilding of my life.' He reached over and took her hand in between his two big, strong ones. 'So, this is what I think we should do. Ignore it. All of it.'

'Ignore it? That's your plan.'

'I think it's a valid life choice. We'll thoroughly ignore how messy we are and just, you know, jump in.'

'Jump in,' she repeated, feeling the stirrings of a giggle rising in her chest.

'We might need a lifeguard to come and rescue us every now and then, but I think we'll learn to swim eventually.'

She looked at her hand in his, safe and warm, and felt a sense of peace spread through her chest. Maybe all hearts, even the bruised and battered ones, were here simply to be given away to others, because that's when they were the most powerful.

'I'll probably be on dialysis tomorrow,' she said, throwing out her final objection.

'Gabby, you could have one less leg, be wearing a sack and covered in cow manure and I would still want you.' He seemed to genuinely mean it. What an amazing turn her life had taken recently, which just went to show you really could never know what was coming next.

She raised her coffee cup. 'To us and our mess.'

He tapped his cup to hers. 'To our beautiful mess.' Then he kissed her, and it was delightful.

36

It took weeks for Krystal to locate the safe deposit box, which was held at a major bank in the centre of Melbourne. Trentino had advised her to do some forensic accounting, looking for regular automatic withdrawals from one of Evan's accounts or their joint account. When she tracked it down, Trentino filed a motion to the court for Krystal to obtain access to the box.

The woman in the red suit swiped her pass at the door and pressed down the silver handle. Krystal was sweating in her summer dress, despite the air conditioning being a couple of degrees too cool for her liking. The three of them stepped inside.

'Take your time,' the woman said, and left Krystal and Trentino alone. The door latched shut behind them and a *whir* and *clunk* let them know it was locked once more. She stepped further into the room. In front of her were rows of grey metal boxes, each numbered and with key locks, lined up like tombstones.

The lighting was harsh. A small black table and chair sat in one corner.

'I feel like I'm in a movie,' Krystal said, so jittery she thought she might faint.

'This is a first for me, too,' Trentino said, thrusting his hands into the pockets of his cool grey suit pants. He moved to the rows of identical boxes, scanning the numbers. Krystal followed, glad for his company. She was nervous, afraid even, though she couldn't have said why exactly. But it felt spooky in here. Dead silent. Cold.

'Here it is,' Trentino said, his fingers resting on the four-digit number. The door was just above their heads.

Krystal lifted the small key – such a plain, boring-looking key for what might become such an important moment in Australian legal history – and slid it into the lock. It turned. She'd half expected it not to. The door exhaled open, as if it had been holding its breath for too long.

Krystal paused, clutching the key in her hands, studying her wedding ring, the simple gold band Evan had given her when they married.

I give you my heart.

And she had given him hers.

'Would you like me to . . .' Trentino asked, his eyes bright, hungry to get into the box, hungry for answers.

'No, it's okay.' She eased the door back as far as it would go, slid her hand inside, took hold of the metal handle and dragged the security box forward, pulling it all the way out, surprised at its weight as she lifted it down.

They both stared at it.

Trentino reached out a finger and touched the box, as though he couldn't believe it was real. 'Are you ready?' he asked.

Was she ready to uncover her husband's secrets, his final legacy, the thing he died for? Was she ready, perhaps, to discover that the Arthur family had blood on its hands – and therefore that any involvement they might have had in her boys' future would be destroyed? Was she ready to ensure that Cordelia-Aurora was held accountable for taking away Krystal's husband and her children's father, if that was what turned out to have happened?

She was strong enough to face the future, whatever was coming next, she knew that now. She carried it to the table and placed it down.

'I'm ready.'

37

'Test, two, three, four.'

A man's low voice rumbled through the cafe and the patrons turned their heads towards the green wall, where a three-piece jazz band had set up. Gabby had been using her long hours in hospital to think of more creative things she could be doing in The Tin Man – in no small part because Summer had inspired her so much that she felt she needed to keep up – and had made the first Tuesday of the month a live music day between ten and twelve. If it went well, she'd look at expanding it to every Tuesday. This was the first one. Luciano had found the group for her; they were friends of his and only too happy to come along for free food and coffee, and the chance to show off their talents.

Gabby's eyes drifted over to the counter, where Ed and Kyle were whipping through a long chain of orders to supply the packed cafe, along with a host of takeaway orders for patrons milling around.

Pippa arrived, pushing her way through the crowd. 'Sorry I'm late,' she said, kissing Gabby on the cheek, and pulled up a chair beside her sister. 'Have I missed much?'

'Nope, they're just getting organised.'

'Excellent. I lost track of time out in the paddock. Hercules was being so good I just didn't want to get off.'

Gabby reached over and plucked a piece of hay from Pippa's hair. Despite the chaff, she still looked fresh as a daisy in a lovely scoop-neck cotton dress in pale grey splashed with crimson flowers, cinched at the waist with a wide belt, and elegant shoes with a flared heel. Gabby had no idea how she'd managed it while getting dressed in a stable, but that was Pippa to a tee, really.

'Does your horse ever put a foot wrong?'

Pippa grinned. 'Nope. He's the perfect man.' She reached for Gabby's arm. 'Show me your tracks.' Gabby did as instructed and rolled up her floral chiffon bell sleeves. She was back in large, loose, flowing tops and dresses to accommodate the fluid retention from all the medication. 'Ugh.'

Gabby wrinkled her nose. The seeping blue, purple and red bruising definitely wasn't pretty. 'At least I'm still alive,' she said, and meant it. She'd been on dialysis for weeks now. She'd have to go to the hospital three times a week till her kidneys recovered. Hopefully it wouldn't be forever, because she wanted forever to be a long time yet.

'What are your numbers?' Pippa asked.

Gabby gave her all the stats from her tests and Pippa made general murmurs of sadness that things had gone downhill, then relief that it wasn't worse, before a hearty round of spirit-boosting positivity.

'Have you heard from Krystal yet? Wasn't she going to the bank today?' Pippa asked, eager for news.

Gabby felt lightheaded with anxiety. 'Not yet. I'm so nervous.

This has all come about because of the visions. What if they were wrong?'

'Imagine how Krystal feels.' Pippa looked sympathetic.

'I can't even.' They sat in silence for a moment, absorbing the import of the visit to the bank, Gabby imagining Krystal opening the box to find evidence that would help bring the Arthur family to justice, or perhaps something completely boring, like an old will, or perhaps nothing at all.

'Anyway, how are you? How'd things go with Harvey this morning?'

'Good, actually. First mediation session done and we both managed to keep our cool. I'm staying in the house with the kids for now. He's staying with his parents. We'll reassess in six months. But after that, we might have to sell the house, and the kids and I might have to come back and live with Dad too.'

'You're kidding.'

'Yeah.'

'That's a relief,' Gabby said.

'Maybe not actually kidding, though.'

'What?'

'I'm going to be a single mum with four kids,' Pippa said, resignedly. 'Besides, I reckon Dad would love to have us all under the one roof.'

'I don't think there's enough room for us all,' Gabby said, trying to imagine them all packed in like sardines.

Pippa picked up a piece of lavender teacake from Gabby's plate and popped it in her mouth. 'You and I could share your room, couldn't we?'

'We didn't even share a room when we were kids!' Gabby said.

Pippa sighed as if Gabby was being terribly difficult. 'Well, let's not worry about it now. Anyway, you and that hunky man over there might move in together.' She nodded over to the counter, where Luciano had just come through the swing door. He threw a tea towel over his shoulder, smiling at his friends getting ready to play. The bass player caught his eye and they lifted their chins at each other in a manly greeting. He even looked good with a tea towel slung over his shoulder. Gabby tried to imagine them and their kids in the one house, doing the dishes.

'Isn't there some saying about counting eggs before chickens?' Gabby said.

'Not quite.'

'Huh?'

'Chickens before hatching. No eggs.'

'Oh, yeah.'

'But it's only a matter of time,' Pippa said. 'I choose to believe you and your kids are just keeping the beds warm for me and my kids till you move into Luc's place and we move in with Dad.'

Just then Ed brought over a soy chai latte and a piece of pie for Pippa, thankfully, because Gabby was nowhere near ready to wrap her head around plans of the magnitude that Pippa was suggesting. All she wanted to do right now was focus on getting better and enjoying this new feeling of being in love once again, though this time with no sweeping romantic visions of happily-ever-afters. This time everything was different, which wasn't a bad thing, as Luciano had reminded her.

'We're different people now that we've experienced great loss,' he'd said one night, sliding a metal paddle into the woodfired pizza oven in his backyard. Their six kids had been inside his house, watching a movie, while she and Luciano sat in the candlelight, the dancing flames from the oven casting them in a golden glow. 'We know the realities of the world. We know that anything and everything can change in a single moment, because we've seen it firsthand. We know that the only way to live is right here, right now. What other choice is there?'

'None,' she'd agreed. 'Absolutely no other choice.'

He'd bent to kiss her and he tasted of red wine, and the feel of his chest beneath her hands made her murmur with desire.

Luciano must have felt her eyes on him now, as he turned to smile at her, and she almost couldn't believe her good fortune to have found him at this stage of her life.

'You're a treasure!' Pippa said, taking the cup from Ed. She ate a mouthful of vegan key lime pie. 'That's really good,' she said, widening her eyes in surprise.

'I have a new supplier,' Gabby said, proudly. 'Believe it or not, these are just her prototypes.'

'Where'd you find her?'

Gabby laughed. 'Right under my nose. It's Summer! I had no idea she could make something like this, but she came up with it after her school project that looked at ways to make the cafe more environmentally sustainable. This –' she gestured to the green pie with the crumbly toffee-coloured base – 'is the result. She says vegan food will save the world.'

'Winner,' Pippa said, shovelling in another piece.

'Except now she's telling me she's a vegan,' Gabby said, groaning. 'I've no idea what to feed her.'

'She'll tell you, no doubt. She's talented, isn't she? I'm nearly finished the logo for her.'

Gabby nodded proudly. Since Monty had quit his job at the RSL, he and Summer had been working on a line of skincare based on recycled coffee grounds. Just body scrubs so far, but they had big plans. In a few weeks' time when school finished for the year, she and Monty were planning to take their range to markets around the city to conduct customer research.

'Are the kids still going to Cam's over the holidays?' Pippa asked, finishing off her pie in record time.

'Yes, for a few days here and there. He's improved a lot. He sounds a lot better, looks better too. He, Meri and Mykahla came over last weekend for lunch with us all.'

'That's good news,' Pippa said, seriously. 'All our kids need their dads.'

'They do.'

'That's why Harvey and I have to work really hard to keep our egos in check and make this as easy as possible.'

'You'll do it. You already are. I'm very proud of you,' Gabby said. 'And you should be proud of yourself.'

Pippa looked like she was going to scoff at that but then realised it was true. 'Thanks.'

Gabby was looking forward to the holidays, eager to have more time with the kids. Charlie was coming in to do a short roasting apprenticeship with Luciano. She wasn't sure whether she or Charlie was more excited about that. She'd heard Charlie mention a girl a few times now – Mackenzie – and she knew that as he entered these last couple of years of school she would see less and less of him, whether because of a girl or study. She felt like these were the last school holidays she might be able to really enjoy him.

All of her kids would be in the cafe a lot over the break, and Luciano's probably too. Summer would be making vegan pies in The Tin Man's kitchen, Charlie would be learning to be a barista and a roaster, and Celia would probably just be lovely, gentle Celia, skipping about like a sprite, her faithful dog at her side, perhaps practising chalkboard art. She and Antonia and Olivia had become good friends and would no doubt enjoy each other's company. Cooper would be delighted to be anywhere near Sally.

Gabby's phone vibrated with a message.

'Is it her?' Pippa's eyes were huge and she leaned across the table to read as Gabby did.

We got them. Trentino is beside
himself. He says there's more
than enough evidence here
to initiate a case against the
Arthurs. Hold onto your hat,
Gabby. It's going to be a wild
ride! I'll pop in to see you
tomorrow to tell you everything.
Thank you, again. None of
this would have been possible
without you. Kx

'Wow.' Pippa collapsed back into her chair. 'I can't believe it.'

'I'm not sure I can either. But I want to be around to see how this plays out.'

'You will be,' Pippa said, completely confident.

'How do you know?'

'Because it's what Evan would want.'

Tick, tick, tick. The drummer tapped the snare drum to get the band in sync and they launched into a rousing big band swing number. People pulled out their phones and took photos. Others smiled and began to tap feet and sway in their seat. Gabby found herself smiling so widely her cheeks hurt.

A few patrons whistled and cheered as the saxophone whizzed up the scales. Gabby clapped and looked over again at Luciano, giving him two thumbs up. He winked at her, and she grinned like a teenager, feeling young, revitalised, taking it all in, taking in life. *This* life, right here, right now. This amazing gift of life.

Epilogue

Three years later

Gabby stood in Piazza Navona in Rome, licking tiramisu-flavoured gelato in a cone. She listened to the artist as he explained how long it had taken him to paint each of his oil canvases, and watched as each dazzling painting flicked over. Yellow sunflowers. Grey-green olive trees. Blue mountains. Gondolas on the turquoise water in Venice. The partially broken, yet still magnificent, arches of the Colosseum. The Spanish Steps. The Trevi Fountain. The amazing blues and sheer drops of the Amalfi Coast. The ruins of Pompeii. The medieval towns of Tuscany. The statue of David. All sights she had either visited already or was due to see in the coming weeks.

'I can't choose,' she said, shaking her head at the vendor. 'I'll come back later.' The vendor lost interest in her immediately and began hawking to another tourist. The sun shone warmly on the grey slate cobblestones of the square. The Fountain of the Four Rivers splashed nearby and she moved to sit on its smooth edge, resting her feet and relieving herself of her backpack for a few moments.

Pippa would be back soon. She'd gone looking for souvenirs for the kids. Just as her sister had once joked, she had actually moved in to the family home in Camberwell with Monty, Gabby and Gabby's kids. Because Pippa and Harvey shared time with the kids on the same fortnightly arrangement as Gabby and Cam did, the house was a riot for two weeks when all seven kids were there, followed by two weeks of quiet.

Monty had put in a granny flat in the backyard, which the two oldest boys – Charlie and Hunter – shared, and they had all decided it was great preparation for share-house living. Charlie had begun TAFE studies in business and had been working at The Tin Man part-time this year. He had dreams of joining Marco, learning the ropes as a buyer out in the field. Summer would be starting her senior studies next year and had recently been profiled in one of the city's glossy magazines for the fantastic success her skincare line had enjoyed. It had made Gabby rather misty-eyed to read that Summer had credited her business partner – Monty McPhee – for so much of the success so far. Monty's cheeks had gone quite pink when he read that and he had given Summer a big hug, then quickly left the room before his emotions got the better of him. Celia was in high school and showing herself to be a conscientious student, excelling in debating and joining committees of all kinds. So far, she was thinking she might be a psychologist one day, which Gabby thought was a great choice for her.

It was school holidays at present, and Gabby's kids were with Cam and Meri and baby Mykahla, as everyone continued to call her even though she was a walking, talking commander-in-chief in leopard-print leggings and pink boots. Gabby couldn't wait to see what sort of teenager she'd become. Cam was settled and had been nothing but a stellar father for the past two and a half years, though he and Meri had decided not to have any more children. Things were great with just one child and that was good enough for them.

'Look at all the cool stuff I got,' Pippa said, arriving loaded up with bags. She still looked gorgeous and stylish and didn't have any of the over-forty issues that Gabby had experienced, barely even any grey hairs. Gabby wore glasses most of the time now, dyed her hair to cover the greys every four weeks, and had endometriosis to add to her list of ailments, though her kidneys had been working happily for a long time now, which was what had made it possible to travel. Her health was in a good place and Pippa had convinced her it was time they went travelling again while they could.

Pippa pulled out bead necklaces, snow globes, keyrings, decks of cards, model Ferraris and Vespas, and tea towels. She'd even found patches of famous Roman buildings to sew onto Hercules's saddle blanket. 'I'm going to have to either buy a new suitcase or begin posting things home,' she said, though she didn't sound concerned about that dilemma.

'We've only been here a week,' Gabby said, finishing the last of her gelato and licking her finger.

Pippa shrugged. 'We have a lot of children.'

'That we do.'

'Harvey's taking mine camping for a few days.'

'Camping? What's got into him?'

'I know, right? I think he's having a midlife crisis. It's all the young IT kids he has to work with. They're all into rock climbing and hiking. I give it twelve hours before he and our kids are all trying to kill each other, or get dysentery or something, and he pulls the pin.'

Gabby hadn't even started her souvenir shopping yet. She might also have to buy another suitcase. She had her kids and her father to buy for, as well as taking back something great to the cafe and for the staff, and she wanted to get something really wonderful for Krystal and Roxy, who'd both become like extra sisters to her, and something for their boys as well.

Krystal was due for a holiday too. So much of her energy had been invested in starting her handmade greeting card business, which Gabby proudly supported by selling the cards at the cafe, and the case and trial against the Arthur family. Now that the legal processes had wrapped up, and Cordelia-Aurora was awaiting sentencing for a number of crimes, including the destruction of evidence and her involvement in hiring heavies to intimidate witnesses, which had resulted in the accidental death of her own brother, Gabby expected that Krystal might deflate like a popped balloon after running on adrenaline for so long.

The courts had found that Cordelia-Aurora had not attempted to kill her brother, only to scare him into abandoning the thought of reopening the Farner Seven case. Krystal wasn't sure if knowing this made his death any easier to bear. Evan still wouldn't have been running in that street if his sister hadn't been doing everything in her power to terrify him. Wyatt had been cleared of any wrongdoing, something that made Krystal furious because she was convinced he would have known. Rupert had never worked on the case and hadn't been a subject of interest in the investigation, which Krystal was relieved about, as he'd always been the only one who'd even attempted to be kind to her and the boys. The driver of the car, a man well known to the police, was awaiting sentencing for manslaughter.

The legal processes had taken their toll on Krystal. She was even thinner than when she and Gabby had first met. Her face had aged with wrinkles, dark circles had appeared permanently under her eyes and angry eczema flares marked her hands. But she was a strong woman and she would recover, Gabby was certain. It was time for her to relax and finally lay all the ghosts to rest.

Gabby looked out across the square towards the enormous white Baroque church dominating the skyline, the pink and orange rendered walls of apartments, dark green shutters opening onto tiny wrought-iron balconies, potted olive trees and bright red geraniums, and her heart was full of joy. There was music in the air. Pigeons cooed. Happy travellers posed for photos and laughed and kissed. Then she smiled as she caught sight of the greatest view of all.

Luciano.

'Oh, stop,' Pippa said, groaning. 'You two lovebirds make me sick.'

'Don't care,' Gabby said, and got up to meet him, whiskered, his hair longer than when she'd first met him, his smile easier, but still wearing Blundstones. He put his arm around her and kissed her, longingly.

'All right, all right,' Pippa grumped.

'Ah, don't be like that, Pip,' Luciano said. 'We've still got five more weeks to catch you an Italian man.'

Pippa tilted her head. 'How many cousins do you have, exactly?'

'Too many to count. There's got to be at least one good bloke in the lot.'

That seemed to cheer Pippa up and she stood, gathering her many bags of gifts. 'Did you find somewhere for lunch?'

'Of course,' Luciano said, mock arrogantly. 'Here, I am Italian. Everything on the menu is thirty per cent off for us and we got the best table overlooking the square.'

'Skite,' Pippa teased.

Luciano cocked his elbows out to the sides so both Gabby and Pippa could thread their arms through his. 'Ladies, it would be my pleasure to escort you to lunch.' Gabby laughed.

Luciano still lived in his brother's house with his brother's children. The kids didn't feel ready to sell their parents' house and move to another place yet, and Gabby respected that. Cooper, especially, didn't want to move because he still 'spoke' to his parents. Neither Gabby nor Luciano doubted that Cooper had some sort of connection to them. Gabby loved all of Luciano's kids but she did have an extra-soft spot for Cooper, both because of his extrasensory experiences, which she could relate to, and because of his deep love for Sally. She always took Sally with her when she went to stay at Luciano's house and Cooper would barely leave her side the whole time. Sally had even taken to sleeping with Cooper when she was there.

Luciano's house was too small for Gabby and her kids to move in as well, so they'd agreed to keep living as they were. But when Gabby's kids were with Cam she had more freedom to go and stay with Luciano, and she still saw him at work most days, so they both felt they were getting plenty of time with one another.

The waiter, dressed in black and white, with slicked-back hair, spotted Luciano immediately as he returned with his two women and ushered the three of them to the front of the line of waiting patrons, making a show of seating them at a table with views across the whole square. He presented them with menus and flicked out white napkins and laid them on their laps, then rushed off to find them sparkling Italian water. The air was filled with the aroma of garlic and pecorino cheese.

Gabby chose a creamy chicken risotto, served piping hot, which wasn't particularly adventurous but was probably safe as far as food hygiene went. She may have been living life to the full, but it still wasn't worth risking salmonella poisoning. Luciano went for braised pork ragù and Pippa for octopus and potato salad. The waiter returned with their sparkling water and took their orders, and the three of them relaxed into their seats.

'I probably shouldn't have had a gelato before lunch,' Gabby said. But she'd been so hungry, and the rainbow colours of thick, creamy gelato had looked so tantalising.

'Different country, different rules,' Pippa said.

'I agree,' Luciano said. 'Besides, you were making the most of the moment. That's our thing, right?'

'Yes, it is.' Gabby smiled at him, admiring the angle of his jaw and the hint of collarbone peeking out from his shirt. He reached out and entwined his fingers in hers. She took a big breath and let herself soak up the glorious, peaceful vibe in the square, the colours, the sounds, the smells.

Everything here was imprinting upon her memories, her cells.

The longevity of the architecture here blew her mind. Some of it was thousands of years old and still standing. Humans were barely blips on the timeline, comparatively. Life could be hard and cruel but it could also be incredibly generous and beautiful. This moment, right here, would last somewhere in the ether, long after she was gone. She had no idea how much time she had left. But the Italians had a saying that she'd come to love.

Meglio aver poco che niente. Better to have little than nothing.

She had more than a little. So much more.

Acknowledgements

Around twenty years ago, I saw a heart transplant recipient named Claire Sylvia on *The Phil Donahue Show* talking about her unusual experience following her surgery, in which she had a deep connection with her donor. Her testimony affected me so strongly that it sat in my memories until it was triggered again when I watched the first episode of *Pulse* on ABC television, in which a woman contracted a virus and then needed a heart transplant. Instantly, the memory of listening to Claire Sylvia came back and I knew I wanted to write about that, and I went to find her memoir, *A Change of Heart*, to read her story. Claire has now passed away, but I am grateful to her for this inspiration.

I wish to offer my deep gratitude to Jim and Melissa, both heart transplant recipients, for generously sharing your stories with me. You are both so very brave and your stories gave me so much rich imagery to play with. Several people helped me find Jim and

Melissa, through a long chain of phone calls and emails, including people from DonateLife, The Prince Charles Hospital in Brisbane, and the Victor Chang Cardiac Research Institute. All of these are wonderful organisations.

On the coffee side of my research, Marinus Jansen from Padre Coffee in Noosa was exceptionally generous in sharing his knowledge of the coffee trade, roasting practices and cupping, as were Vanesa Joachim and Kayla Byles. And Traecy and Peter Hinner from Noosa Black Coffee gave me a wonderful lunch on their deck and shared their experiences of starting a coffee farm. While I ran out of room to include that aspect of the coffee trade in this book, it gave me a well-rounded appreciation of the 'tree to mouth' cycle and may yet appear in another novel in the future.

Thank you to the team at Penguin Random House for welcoming me into your stable, and to my publisher, Ali Watts, for your structural guidance, humour and tremendous enthusiasm for my writing. To Kathryn Knight for your thoughtful copyediting and filling the gaps in my knowledge of modern technology, and to Clara Finlay for 'top and tailing' the book by being willing to read my first awful mud map of this novel and then for the final proofread. I'm so grateful to you all.

Thank you to Nikki Townsend and Louisa Maggio for their gorgeous design work.

Thank you to Haylee Nash from The Nash Agency for your guidance, faith, passion and commitment. To my husband, Alwyn, for plot-storming with me. To Kate Smibert for always being my cheerleader and willing reader. To my son, Flynn, for being so lovely and funny and for finally learning not to touch Mama's computer (most of the time). And to my animal family for keeping me grounded and making sure I regularly leave my desk to wander in the sunshine.

My beloved golden retriever, Daisy, sat by my side while I wrote this book, almost to the very end of the first draft, before passing away so swiftly, leaving an almost unbearable hole in my heart and life. (And for those who've read my book *Three Gold Coins*, yes, the character of Daisy was named after my dog.) Daisy's personality is firmly embedded in Sally in this book (the way Sally guards Mykahla is exactly the way Daisy guarded Flynn as a baby), though Sally is far cleaner and much better behaved than Daisy ever was.

Finally, and most importantly, I wish to thank all my readers. I write books for you, and without you I wouldn't get to have what is, for me, the greatest job I could find. Thank you for your emails and social media messages of support, which often turn up at exactly the right moment when I need to read them. Thank you for coming to signings and events. You are the ones who make it all worthwhile.

Jo x

Book Club Discussion Notes

1. Discuss the ways in which Gabby's new heart is a blessing and the ways it is a curse.

2. Do you think organ transplant recipients have a 'duty' to live their lives in a particular way?

3. What are your own views on organ transplantation?

4. Did you find it easy to sympathise with Krystal's point of view?

5. What are some of the different forms of family support the characters in this book display?

6. How did you feel about Cam at the end of the book compared to the beginning?

7. Discuss the ways in which animals are therapeutic for various characters in the novel.

8. In what ways are Gabby and Luciano perfect for one another?

9. Josephine Moon's books are often characterised by descriptions of beautiful settings full of colour and sensory detail. In which scenes did you notice this most strongly?

10. Do you believe in life after death?

11. What do you see as being the central themes of the book?

12. Discuss the importance of coffee in this story, and the place of food in general in this novel and others by Josephine Moon.

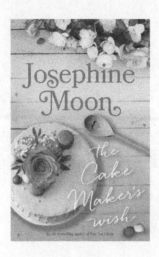

Life in the village isn't always sweet and simple . . .

When single mum Olivia uproots her young son Darcy from their life in Tasmania for a new start in the English Cotswolds, she isn't exactly expecting a bed of roses – but nor is she prepared for the challenges that life in the picturesque village throws her way.

The Renaissance Project hopes to bring the dwindling community back to life – to welcome migrants from around the world and to boost the failing economy – but not everyone is so pleased about the initiative.

For cake-maker Olivia, it's a chance for Darcy to finally meet his Norwegian father, and for her to trace the last blurry lines on what remains of her family tree. It's also an opportunity to move on from the traumatic event that tore her loved ones apart.

After seven years on her own, she has all but given up on romance, until life dishes up some delicious new options she didn't even know she was craving.

An uplifting and heartwarming story about the moments that change your life forever, human kindness, and being true to yourself.

Available June 2020

Discover a
new favourite

Visit **penguin.com.au/readmore**